Here be Witches

THE SNOWDONIA CHRONICLES
BOOK TWO

SARAH MUSSI

Here be Witches

THE SNOWDONIA CHRONICLES
BOOK TWO

shrine
bell

www.shrinebell.com

Here Be Witches
Sarah Mussi

First published in 2017 by Shrine Bell, an imprint of Vertebrate Publishing

Shrine Bell
Crescent House, 228 Psalter Lane, Sheffield, S11 8UT, UK
www.shrinebell.com

Cover design by Nathan Ryder
Cover photo by Keld Bach, www.keldbach.com
Typesetting and production by Jane Beagley
Author photograph © Roger Bool

A CIP catalogue record for this book is available from the British Library.

ISBN 978-1-911342-32-8 (Paperback)
ISBN 978-1-911342-33-5 (ebook)

10 9 8 7 6 5 4 3 2 1

Production by Vertebrate Publishing
www.v-publishing.co.uk

Shrine Bell is committed to printing on paper from sustainable sources.

Printed and bound in Great Britain by
Clays Ltd, St Ives plc

Dedication

To IDRIS GAWR, *Stargazer,* *Overlord and Giant of Cadair Idris*

In the land of Merioneth in the parish of Dolgelley in the commote of Talybont is a mount or peak or large high hill that is called Cadair Idris. And on the highest crown of this mountain is a bed-shaped form, great in length and width, built of slabs with stones fixed thereon. And this is called The Bed of Idris. And it is said that of whoever lies and sleeps upon that bed, from sunset until sunrise, one of two things will happen to him: either he will be a hero or poet or bard of the best kind, or descend from that great mountain entirely demented.

From *The Giants of Wales and Their Dwellings*

Sion Dafydd Rhys, *c.*1600
Peniarth Manuscript

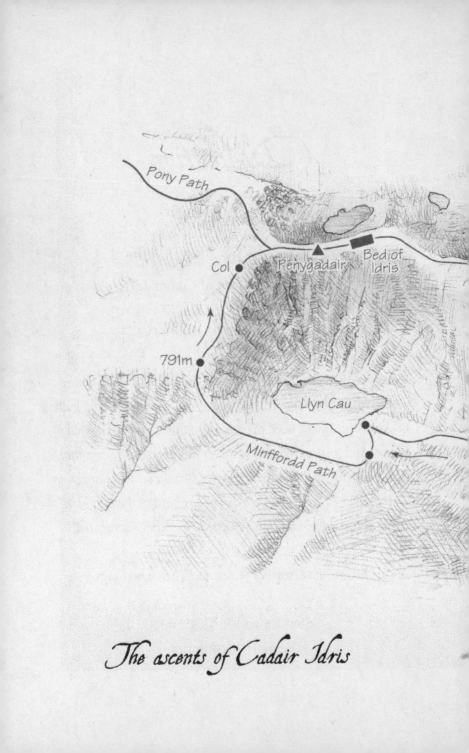

Pony Path

Col

Penygadair

Bed of
Idris

791m

Llyn Cau

Minffordd Path

The ascents of Cadair Idris

Mynydd Moel

N

Minffordd Trail Loop
Cadair Idris
Wales

Road to Dolgellau →

Minffordd

1km

As Above

29 February – Leap Year
At the witching hour upon the eve of St David's Day

The girl turns her masked face to the summit, above her the air shudders. Just seconds left. If only she can time it right. Heart pounding, blood hammering, she poises herself. She pulls out the mirror, angles it, catches the reflection of the dark night and the stars.

I can do this, she tells herself. I am the High Priestess. I am the Supreme One.

Then she recites aloud:

> *'Winds of time meet me here,*
> *Upon the stroke of midnight clear,*
> *Spin a girdle round the heavens,*

When the magick words are spoken,
Let the future rush to meet us,
Let the time between be broken,
Hurry the hours, tear down the clocks,
Speed up the procession of the equinox,
O winds of time, hear me say,
Let tomorrow be today.'

She beckons to the rest of the coven. Twelve girls – faces covered with masks, clad from head to toe in black cloaks, tall hats, dark skirts – all close in. They trace a circle widdershins around a great cauldron set on a smouldering fire. One girl, petite and pretty, chants:

'Oh mighty dragon of the fire,
Grant me the power that I desire,
Power of water and air from the sky,
And earth and fire that let you fly.'

But the Supreme One steadies the mirror, whispers instead:

'Oh mighty dragon of the ice,
Grant me the power in measure twice,
And take thee, thy human sacrifice.'

The girls stop and hold out their left hands. And on each palm is marked a star. They hold them up to the night sky, baring them towards the constellation of Draco, in which the Pole Star – Polaris, the North Star – shines, and they recite:

> 'Air and water, fire and earth,
> In darkest night we wait your birth,
>
> By light of moon, or ray of sun,
> Let Merlin's magick be undone,
>
> The hour has come of this leap year,
> The time is right to reappear,
>
> Forever you were, forever you shall be,
> By Draco's grace we set you free,
>
> Oh mighty dragons whom this spell release,
> Crack open the fortress of Dinas Emrys.'

The moment strikes midnight.

The Supreme One breathes on the mirror, clouds it over with her breath, cries out, 'AS ABOVE – SO BELOW, SO MOTE IT BE!'

The mountain slope shudders. The cauldron boils over. The face of the full moon darkens. There is a roaring and far away the sound of many stones cracking.

Then the mountain splits wide.

An appalling shriek rents the air. Yellow eyes glint through the darkness, teeth crash, talons scrape. A fetid stench slams into the night. And under their feet a ravine opens. A yawning cliff, dropping sheer, smooth, treacherous. And from the lip of this abyss a fearsome creature crawls out.

'Welcome back O White Worm of Wessex,' breathes out the Supreme One.

The dragon blinks at the girls. It unfolds its huge wings and stretches them out, like some nightmarish butterfly emerging from a hideous chrysalis, then it shakes its spiny neck. Its hooded eye settles on the petite, pretty girl.

In an instant she slips. The earth beneath her gives way. A booming, a shrieking tears at her ears. The ground over the old dragons' lair caves in all around her.

The girl skids out of control. She falls. She screams. She stretches out her arms.

'Help!' she cries. 'Somebody help me!' But none dare, as heart bursting, body falling, twisting, turning, she plummets down over the cliff edge.

'SO MOTE IT BE!' roars the dragon.

Down plunges the girl. Down into the dark cavern.

Down on to the sharp crystals.

And as the girl's heart is pierced, the crystals shatter.

At that moment, the whole of the mountain shakes, as if some deep power has been unleashed. There is a rush of heat, a blur of speed. Something passes out of the lair and, like a shooting star, fires up towards the sky. A sudden mist descends; through the darkness the girl-witches see ragged shapes like dark riders galloping away towards the summit of Snowdon.

The air grows cold.

The mountain is still.

The witches blink.

There is no dragon after all. Only their sister-witch impaled upon the rocks below.

The Supreme One hides the mirror under her cloak, takes her birch broom and, wedging it against the rocks, uses it to help her climb down into the roofless cavern. She leaps the last metre to the rocky bottom, but does not check the bleeding body of her friend speared on the broken crystals. Instead she reaches down and picks from the cavern floor a blackened object.

'Yes!' she whispers. The Supreme One slips the charred object beside the mirror, nestles it close to her heart. She mutters to herself, 'So you would challenge me, Ellie Morgan … ' Her voice grows cold, chilling, spiteful: 'We will see about that.'

Then she turns. She reaches the fallen girl.

'Is she OK?' calls a voice from above.

'No,' replies the Supreme One. 'She has passed beyond the veil.'

Then through the dark morning she points a finger at one of the coven. 'Seize her!' she commands. 'Seize Rhiannon!'

Instantly, the witches obey.

'You pushed her,' accuses the Supreme One.

'No!' squeals Rhiannon.

The witches start to chant. One holds Rhiannon. The others circle round her. The Supreme One climbs up out of the cavern. She grabs Rhiannon by the wrist.

'You bring Ellie here,' she says. 'You bring her now! You pin this on her, or I'll pin it on you.'

Then she raises her head to the constellation of Draco shining far above her.

> 'Fair is foul – foul is fair –
> By water, fire, earth and air,
> Fair is foul – foul is fair –
> Let those who challenge me, BEWARE –
> Fair is foul – foul is fair –
> FOR I HAVE DESTROYED THE DRAGONS' LAIR!'

So Below

Act One

Here be witches, so they say
Two from the hill and nine from the plain
One for her blood shed all in pain
Summoned by She, from over the sea
Here be witches
Here they be.

From the Coven Song of Dinas Emrys
Anonymous

Day One: 1 March – St David's Day
Wing a Pathway to the Stars

One

This is where it starts.

Sweat streaming down my forehead, my hands clenched tight. Deep inside me, screaming that never ceases. For a split second, I can't remember what I'm screaming about. Then it all comes flooding back: *the dark hillside, the storm, the wind howling off white-topped rocks, bracken tossing.*

The riders in the mist.

Dark shapes, cloaks tight around them, the screech of a landslide, rocks cracking open, sheer drops.

I blink.

I drag my sleeve across my forehead. I glance at the clock. Midnight. Did I actually drop off watching telly?

OMG! I am now officially old aged!

But I saw him. For one second I looked into Henry's eyes. I know I did. (I'd have gone through a hundred nightmares for that alone.)

I saw him.

I try to hang on to the moment. Our eyes met. He said something. Snatches of words play in my mind, like cloud wisps drifting across mountaintops. I try to remember.

Then my phone pings.

Great.

His face fades.

The words evaporate.

I reach across the sofa, scrabble about to find my phone. Just my luck. It's bound to be George. *Meeting eyes with Henry, after so long* ... and then George spoils it. Typical. He *would* ring me in the middle of the night, right when I'm having some kind of weird déjà vu, true love, visiony thing. Sometimes I think George has got a sixth sense; it's called: Something Is Going On With Ellie Let Me Check Wot And Be A Pest.

So I ignore it. But when it doesn't stop, I reach over and press the Shove-Flipping-Off button.

I glance at the clock again. I really should go to bed. It's 00.10 and cold. The heating's gone off.

And then the phone pings *again*.

Really, what kind of nutter never gives up pinging you? I'm not even going to bother acknowledging it.

<u>Inside George's head</u> (I'm sure he thinks in **bold**):

Oh it was 29 FEBRUARY three seconds ago, when I know she was thinking of Henry and Not Me – why don't I keep on pinging her just in case there is the remotest chance she wanted to ask me to marry her and forgot?

I chuck my phone across the room on to the armchair. Then I drag a paper and pencil across the coffee table and try to draw a sketch of the dream. *Those riders, like they were made of mist … Bit of shading, smudge it with fingers … And Henry. The way his face … his eyes … his thick wavy hair …*

The phone pings again.

Whoever wants my attention isn't giving up, are they?

I slam the pencil down, get up to retrieve the phone from the chair. I shiver. It actually is very *very* cold.

I pick up my phone, swipe it open.

And while I'm doing that, it rings too.

So I give in, press the green thing and scream, 'WHAT THE HELL DO YOU WANT? THIS IS SO NOT FUNNY!'

A faint, worried, female voice on the end says, through

a zillion crackles, 'Am I through to a Llanberis mountain-rescue volunteer?'

Oops.

Kick self in bum. I sit down on the sofa again, flick off the telly and angle myself under some cushions.

Awwww-kward.

'Yes,' I say.

Em-barr-ass-ing.

'Sorry. I thought you were ~~my friend who is a dope~~, um, somebody else.'

'I know it's late but there's been a landslide over by Dinas Emrys, and at least one casualty. I can't seem to contact other members of the rescue team.'

'Oh,' I say. *A casualty?* 'No, of course. I mean, *yes*, you can't get them, because they're going to a mountain-rescue conference over in Leeds.'

At least one casualty …

'I mean, some have gone already, and my mum is going really early tomorrow – I mean today – it's part of her certificate. She can't go out now though, alone, she's off rota … ' My voice peters out.

A landslide at Dinas Emrys?

I don't add: *nobody thought there'd be an emergency, not tonight, not in the middle of winter, after midnight, on St*

David's Day. It's traditional not to go on the mountain … not this side of it anyway.

Dinas Emrys? Henry?

The line crackles. 'I see.'

'So there's only me and my friend ~~the one who is a dope~~ on our side of the mountain … you'll have to phone the emergency services – the police,' I say.

What if it's Henry?

I continue, 'Or there's the Caernarfon team … on second thoughts, it might be best to call them … Dinas Emrys is right by the main road just up from Beddgelert.'

I'm not thinking straight.

'OK, thanks. Sorry to ring your number. I'll get on to Caernarfon right now,' she says.

'OK,' I say. I don't add – *but how did you get my number?* Because the words 'Dinas Emrys' are sending shock waves right through me.

Dinas Emrys, you see, is an old fortress on the far side of Snowdon, which also happens to house a dragons' cave. And also happens to be where Henry, *my* Henry, the boy I've promised to love forever, is lying entombed.

Don't ask. I will explain.

Then I noticed the other twenty-two missed calls.

And pings.

Rhiannon

Ellie. OMG. Someone's died. I don't know who else to message. You've got to come and help me. I'm up at Dinas Emrys. I CAN'T TELL MY DAD. EVA. There's been a DISASTER. This is V V V urgent and V V V V V V V terrible. Hire a cab – I'll pay. Anything. JUST GET ME AWAY FROM HERE. I'm so scared. Please come ELLIE.

More calls …
   More pings …
   And …

Rhiannon

Ellie? I'm SO not joking. IS YOUR PHONE ON SILENT OR WOT? I've called and called you. YOU HAVE TO COME. Don't tell anyone esp. George. There are these shapes in the mist. Delete these messages. And HURRY.

More calls …
   And …

Rhiannon

My battery is dying. I'm scared. I'm waiting for you. ELLIEEEEEEEEEEEEEEEEEEEEEEEEEE?

I read the pings.

My mobile buzzes half-heartedly with an alert: Low Battery.

I ping her back.

Ellie

Hang on Rhi I'm coming – can I call anyone? What should I tell them? How bad is it? Do you need police? Be as quick as I can – but need to charge battery/do stuff to be safe ... it's a long way – but I'll hurry xxx

But really, don't you think we should call your dad?

I reread the pings.

An electric shock jolts across my chest. I try to breathe. A landslide. *Dinas Emrys*. Shapes in the mist. Someone dead?

Henry?

My déjà vu just goes mental.

I must get there. I must check the cave. And what does Rhi mean 'V V V urgent and V V V V V V V V terrible'?

My heart pounds. Even though I'm shivering, another sweat breaks out across my back – it turns icy. Then I shiver some more. And because it's so cold I pull the knitted patchwork blanket over me and don't do anything at all except shiver. Because you know how it is, when you get that sudden fear on you – you hardly know what to do.

Grab things. Keep on shivering? Go and *do* something? Think first? Everything gets in the way.

If I'm going to get over to Dinas Emrys, I'm going to have to take my bike. I mean, hire a cab? At this hour? Is Rhi out of her mind? Everything in Llanberis will be closed. I'd have difficulty even getting a taxi from Caernarfon in the middle of the night. No, I'm going to have to cycle all the way up through the pass, up to the top and then down the other side towards Beddgelert. So I better get going.

Slight problem: phone has low battery.

Emergency Rescue Rule Book (LMS&R Hand Book. Section 33): 'Emergency rescue recovery missions in serious weather: NEVER set out without a fully charged battery on a minimum of two mobiles or handheld devices.'

OK, I only have one and it is flat.

Stay calm and charge your phone, Ellie. Rhiannon is such a drama queen: Miss V V V Urgent and V V V V V V V V Terrible. She'll just have to wait. I mean. The landslide hasn't toppled on her, has it? Why isn't she calling Caernarfon? (Perhaps she has …) I totally understand why she can't tell her dad. What the hell is she doing over at Dinas Emrys anyway?

With *my* Henry.

Perhaps it really is awful.

Arrgh! I need to hurry.

Think it through, Ellie, I tell myself. This isn't going to be a walk in the park. It will take you at least three quarters of an hour, maybe longer, to bike it. It's all the way up past Nant Peris. (It will take definitely longer.) It will be dark. It will be cold. Grab something to eat. Carbohydrate load. Poor Rhiannon, she must be terrified. Take your daysack. Think it through. No good setting off before you've *thought it through*. Rhi is going to have to wait. The emergency services will get there soon. They can take her home. (But I'm still going, you know. What about Henry?) If the emergency services can't take her, she can ride pillion over the back wheel. We can freewheel into Beddgelert, ditch the bike … wait for a bus … are there night buses? Take extra bike lights.

Charge. Your. Phone.

Take money. Oh, and your bus pass.

I go into the hall. I look in the big mirror. Yuck. I drag a brush through my hair, pull some extra socks out of the tops of my wellies, put them on, take two huge fleecy hoodies off the pegs and pull one on top of the other.

It really is brutally cold. I go to the kitchen. I stand hopping from one foot to the other on the freezing flagstone floor. Wow, it's totally below zero. I grab my walking boots from the back porch, pull them on. Outside it looks like it's actually trying to snow. Winter is *supposed* to over by now; you know – snowdrops and daffs and crocuses and things are supposed to be coming out. There's mist everywhere – really tight up against the farmhouse. Ragged lines of cloud strain through the grey night, just like the Brenin Llwyd.[1] I remember the riders, the shadows in the mist.

The Riders!

That dream I just had.

The dark hillside, the storm, the wind howling off white-topped rocks, bracken tossing.

Dark shapes, cloaks tight around them, the screech of a landslide, rock cracking open, quartz splitting through crystal down to sheer drops.

And the body of the girl screaming, falling.

The Brenin Llwyd. Working his evil visions.

He's out there in the cold and dark.

Waiting for me.

---

1. The Brenin Llwyd, in Welsh folklore, is the most powerful and perhaps the oldest Lord of the Grey Dark. He is said to haunt Snowdonia, hiding in the mists of the mountaintops. His breath, a thick fog, descends in the space of a few heartbeats; it drives unwary travellers to their deaths by hiding the edges of precipices and icy llyns. He is a brooding, silent, evil figure, who lies in wait for those who venture up into his mountains. Those who are never seen again are said to have been taken by the Brenin Llwyd and his grey riders.

Two

I grab water and chocolate. Should I wake Mum? She needs to sleep. Hell, I'm tired too. We got totally exhausted yesterday rescuing newborn lambs up on the high pastures. It took hours. Getting them back down to the farmhouse and safely into the barn was no joke. Tomorrow morning – *this* morning, Mum is heading all the way to Leeds, too. She can't do anything about Dinas Emrys, anyway. It's way too early. Imagine it:

ME: Hey Mum. Wake up.

MUM: Huh?

ME: Someone rang looking for mountain rescue, but that's sorted. Anyway, I had this thing while I was watching *Horror Her*, I've decided to go out in the middle of the night for a bike ride to meet the Brenin Llwyd.

MUM: Huh?

  ME: I can't tell you exactly what's happened – something about a landslide – but I thought I'd wake you up anyway. Oh, and Rhiannon's pinging me.

MUM: Huh?

  ME: OK, now you can go back to sleep.

MUM: Ellie?

  ME: It's fine. Night night. Have a nice time in Leeds.

Amazingly stupid idea. But I ought to at least say goodbye – she actually *is* leaving at the crack of dawn, and I might not be back. On the other hand, I ought not to wake her up … dilemma.

So decide, I tell myself.

So I do: I am not going to wake her. After all, I'm practically grown up now, sixteen going on seventeen (pretty soon). I Do Not Need To Inform My Mum Every Time I Leave The House.

So instead, while I wait for my phone to charge, I'll write her a note. She's going to be confused and do her puzzled face. It's not something a normal teenager thinks of doing. Oh yes, I think I'll just go for a lengthy bike ride, at half past midnight just because … well, it seems like a good idea.

So I start writing:

Dear Mum,

Then I realised this is the moment when: I Have To Tell Her About Henry. Ha. Ha. Biggest Awwwwww-kward Ever.

What to say? I glance at my phone battery icon. Green bar only a third up. *Come on green bar – hurry up!* I glance out of the kitchen window again. No answers out there. The mist is tighter against the house than before. I can hardly see a thing. I strain through the glass hoping to catch a glimpse of the moon; after all it should be full, shouldn't it?

An evil shiver suddenly shoots down my spine. Was that something moving?

Grey shapes, dark against dark. All the tiny hairs on the back of my neck go prickly. *What if there really are grey riders. What if the Brenin Llwyd actually exists?*

Stop it. Focus on what to tell Mum. Currently, she doesn't know anything at all about Henry.

Hmmm.

·But how to tell?

I continue the wake-up scene in my head:

    ME: OK, (clears imaginary throat) I'm going out,
             mostly because of something that started

around Christmas and Rhiannon's texts.
And the two are connected.

MUM: Huh?

ME: You see, I met this boy, but I never told you about him.

MUM: Huh?

ME: And it's a long story, but the short version is: he is a dragon.

MUM: Ellie, if he's not very nice, are you sure you should keep on seeing him?

ME: I'm not 'seeing him', and he is very nice.
I mean he really *is* a dragon – you know fire and wings – not bad tempered or whatever.

MUM: OOooooh-kaaay.

ME: So I have to go out to check he's locked up in his cave.

MUM: All right darling. That's just fine. A pitch-dark freezing night is a fabulous time to go on a date/visit an inmate/check your pet monster is under control. Off you go. By the way, *my* first boyfriend was a three-headed griffin with bad breath. Have fun!

Right. There is probably no way to tell The Person Who Loves You Most In The World just exactly why you were/ are ready to risk your life on a relationship that has only lasted a week (ish) and involves a dragon in a cave. I mean, that's what happened, at Christmas.

Risk my life. And leave her all alone. Forever.

But I will have to try. Because I've got a V V V bad feeling about tonight.

Green bar is up to halfway. Can I risk it?

Only yesterday, I saw a figure standing up on the mountain above the pass, opposite Clogwyn on the great knife-edge that Mum and I call the Devil's Bridge.

I saw him standing there, when we were working so hard to save those newborn lambs. I tried to dismiss it; told myself. It Couldn't Possibly Be Henry. But now, all this … oh, be still my beating heart.

Whatever. It was definitely a sign. So I'm going to have to let Mum know. Everything this time.

Including what happened at Christmas, just in case …

Green bar is up to two thirds. Yay! Just another five minutes and I can go.

I sit down with a pen and a piece of paper and I start again:

Dear Mum,

I have to tell you about Henry. I don't know how to start, because you're probably going to think your teenage daughter has gone loopy. I should start at the most important point and come straight out and tell you that Henry is a dragon and I am in love with him. (Not some cuddly toy for sale in the Llanberis railway station souvenir shop. NOT one of those huge, great, big, ugly, red dragon things. PUH-LEEESE.) No, Henry Is Not A Cuddly Toy. He is a boy (though very cuddly. In fact, he's cuddly, gorgeous, fit, lush, tall, kind, special: OK get out the thesaurus and add in all your fave synonyms for AWESOME.), and he's also a dragon/boy. OK?

Not OK.

She'll think I've been reading too many paranormal romances and am certifiably bonkers. Or am trying to cook up some sort of lame drama-thing, because I'm a teenager and obviously I don't have a boyfriend because I live halfway up the largest mountain in Wales. The days in which boys would climb towers (or mountains) to see the girls they love are over. Or never were.

Nowadays boys would never even consider doing all

that romantic stuff (except for George and he lives up here anyway, so that doesn't count). Sigh.

I put down the pen. Maybe Mum will think Henry is someone I've met on World of Myth/War/Mountain/Craft and is a gamer, who has an avatar who happens to be a red dragon.

So I add the following:

It all started long ago with the Mabinogion and Merlin and Y Ddraig Goch, and I can't go into all of that, because I've got to go off and see what's happened asap, so you'll just have to believe me when I say that's the way it is. I'm in love with Henry, and I have promised to dedicate my entire life to try and free him from this curse that's hanging over him, which also involves his worst enemy: Oswald, the White Dragon of Wessex, who happens to be his uncle btw.

I know it sounds odd. Try to get over that bit. Anyway, I would like to have told you all this properly but Rhi's waiting for me, so that's all I can say for now.

Love you very much.
Ellie.

I put the letter into an envelope. I don't read it through, because I know if I do, I will start ~~to cry~~ to imagine how (when she comes back from Leeds) I'll have to sit across the breakfast table from her and tell her the whole story. And I really don't want to.

Green bar is over three quarters now. Yippee!

So I put the envelope behind the clock on the mantelpiece in the front room, because I know she won't look there, until she needs postage stamps. And who the heck ever needs postage stamps these days, what with direct debits and the internet? So that means the letter will stay there. Unread. For. A. Very. Long. Time.

Phew.

But if the stuff at Dinas Emrys is really V V V urgent and V x woteva terrible and I have to go off and do other V urgent and V terrible things and I never return, it will still be there. And she will find it eventually, and she will know what has happened to me, and then George will have to tell her the rest.

I grab my mobile. Three-quarters charged is good enough.

I go into the front room and put the letter behind the clock. Ceri, our sheepdog, whines and raises one ear quizzically. I shush her. Then I leave Mum a temporary, stand-in note scrawled on the fridge in whiteboard marker:

GONE OUT TO SEE RHIANNON. HAVE A NICE
TRIP XXX

Then I put on my waterproofs, pick up my gear and sneak
out the front door.

Three

Outside it's even colder. A mean wind blows, and the mist whips past in thin serrated shapes. I think about the grey riders. I think about the Brenin Llwyd. Stay calm, I tell myself. Even if the grey riders are real, even if what they say about the Brenin Llwyd is true, you have to get safely to Dinas Emrys. Keep your head. So I send another ping to Rhiannon:

ELLIE'S PHONE

Setting out now. Be there soon. Hang on. UPDATE ME PLEASE.

XXX E

I pull the farmhouse door shut behind me, as softly as I can. The latch clicks to, sharply jolting the silence. Cripes, I must be mad! It's the middle of the flipping night.

I hear the sheep, little bleatings, followed by deep husky snorts. I think of those tiny, cute newborns, cuddling into their mothers. I go across to the barn. I put my head in and check they're all fine. Inside the barn smells lovely, all warm and woolly, and filled with that sweet scent only newborns have. 'Sleep tight little babies,' I whisper, and secure the latch on the barn door behind me.

Then I drag my mountain bike out of the side shed and take a deep breath. You can do this, Ellie, I tell myself. You have to. You must find out what's happened at the cavern. Rhiannon is waiting. Henry may need you. Then I pull my gloves off and test the tyres on the bike. They seem OK. I adjust my daysack on my back, put my gloves back on and push the bike across the drive.

I wheel it up to the gate, unclasp the latch and pull the gate open. Once through, I close the gate behind me, and jump on. Sheets of thin mist lash across the pastures. They seem to condense into terrifying shapes. I turn my thoughts away from them. It's *not* the Brenin Llwyd, obviously. I pedal my way through the darkness down towards Llanberis, down the long track that winds through the foothills of the mountain.

Icy sleet stings my cheeks. My fingers, already numb, ache. I try to take them off the handlebars and shake them out, but that just makes them hurt more. Unable to see further than a few metres ahead, I turn on to the track that stretches alongside the slope under Moel Cynghorion.

I cycle past the turning where it branches off to George's place, and onwards downhill.

The great silence of Snowdon hangs in the air, broken only by the crunch of my wheels on the track, the swish of my waterproofs, and the faint roar of Ceunant Mawr waterfall in the distance, as it thunders down into Llanberis.

It's kind of awful and awesome all at once.

After about five minutes, I make it to the tarmac section of our lane. The wheels whisper on the fractured asphalt and it's much easier going. This is the good bit I remind myself: freewheeling down into Llanberis. After this, it's uphill all the way to Pen-y-Pass.

Not a shop is open. Not even Spar. No, really! The modern world has not hit Llanberis. A luminous yellow light shines out apologetically, from under its closed-up doorway. Brilliant. The only convenience store in the whole of Llanberis is inconveniently shut. All the B&B signs read 'CLOSED'. Llanberis is The City of the Dead.

Actually Llanberis is really just one long, main street that runs straight from the train station down towards Caernarfon. So it's more like The Street of the Dead.

Along one side cluster all the guesthouses, interspersed with the outdoor-mountaineering-type shops and a few restaurants, all of them for the tourists who swamp the place in the summer. Parallel to the main street runs another road, down alongside the lake. And across the waters of Llyn Padarn, on its far side, the slate quarry glowers, like some half-carved monstrous sculpture.

I know it's there, glowering away, through the mist, even though I can't see it. I shiver and turn the bike uphill towards the pass. I start to hammer down on the pedals. Snowdon lurks invisible to my right. Only the gradient of the road confirms it's still there. Icy rain lashes my face. This Is Not Terrifying. Not one bit. It's just an invigorating midnight bike ride in the hills. What could be nicer?

I realise when I've been going for about ten minutes that I've forgotten to attach a flashing LED light behind me. That is worrying. I am totally out of breath, plus I seem to be hitting pockets of zero visibility. What if some boy racer, on his way back from town, comes charging up the road? In this mist, I might get smacked off my bike. Delightful thought.

I scramble around to see if I can attach one of the LED blinkers I've clipped on the front of the bike to my daysack – or hang it around my neck backwards. That makes me even more out of breath, plus the bike wobbles under me.

Maybe one bike blinker won't be enough anyway? Better to keep as close to the verge as I can.

A sweat breaks out across my face. I hope my eyebrows don't dissolve. (Yes, I admit, I did put some make-up on, just in case.) The sweat kind of goes icy. I hope my eyebrow pencil stick is waterproof. Driving sleet half blinds me. The sweat spreads. My clothes start to stick. I start to shiver and the bike wobbles even more. Note to all: Don't try biking up a mountain in the middle of the night for fun.

I twist about trying to fix the light. I refuse to stop and get off. If I do, all those things in the dark might catch up.

And now I'm imagining the Brenin Llwyd.

And I'm all by myself, under the huge escarpment of the mountain.

I can actually feel the massive slopes of the pass, rising on either side.

Holy cripes – this must be the most stupidest thing ever!

And I hate Glyder Fawr. I hate it. It's a huge, creepy upheaval of bare rock. And it's lurking over me, RIGHT NOW.

Climbers find it awesome, apparently. Although what they discover on the top, aside from those naked rock fingers, I don't know. Glyder Fawr's a half-formed, monster, alien thing – a kind of afterthought. A mutant relative of Snowdon.

The feeling of it there, waiting … UGHH.

It's a long haul going up Llanberis Pass on a pushbike, I can tell you. And if you've never ever done it before, don't be too upset. Much better to stay indoors and snuggle up under your duvet. I tell myself exactly that, as I'm pummelling down on those pedals.

Much. Better. To. Be. Under. A. Duvet.

Why. Are. You. Not?

The further I get up the pass, the more ragged the mist becomes. Plus there are some horrible howling noises going on. I am trying hard not to be afraid. My heart is beating really fast. But I tell myself that's just from pedalling. I am absolutely sure there *are* dark riders, just alongside me. They seemed to say: *Go on! Go faster!* And the howling sort of underlines it. Like, if you do not speed up some werewolf is going to catch you.

Weirdly, there's something about that which pees me off. I just hate being 'managed'. So instead of going faster, I go slower. The gradient plays a part admittedly. What the heck – if those grey riders are going to catch me and take me to the Brenin Llwyd, so be it.

And with that thought and being very pig-headed (George's assessment of me because I won't fall in love with him), I r-e-a-l-l-y s-l-o—o—o—w right down.

And suddenly it all comes together: *the Pass, Glyder Fawr, Snowdon, the mist ...*

And I remember the dream:

The dark hillside, the storm, the wind howling off white-topped rocks, bracken tossing. I am standing right on the summit of Snowdon. There below me is the cafe. I'm leaning on the circular stone tower at the very peak. And Henry is with me. I lean against him. He puts his arm around me. I turn in the haze. The wind is rushing up into our faces, driving sleet into our eyes, below us a rumble of thunder.

We cling together. There by the pinnacle of rock, the clouds at our feet, the icy mist swirling up until I can hardly even see the cafe.

And we're flying out over a sea of whiteness way above the world. It's almost déjà vu. A memory. It's like the time we first kissed, so long ago on the Devil's Bridge.

'Look,' Henry points at something in the distance.

As far as the eye can see continents of clouds are swirling, seething in smoky plumes, twisting towards us.

'It's coming,' he says. 'You must be prepared.'

A column of white sweeps up at us. I sway, scarcely balancing. He slips his arms around my waist and pulls me close against him. He says, his voice tight and hard, 'Be brave, beautiful Ellie. I should never have involved

28

you in the way of dragons ... May the stars forgive me.'
He holds me even tighter.

He presses my head into his chest. I can hear the hammering
of his heart. I cry out suddenly afraid.

'Draco, forgive me,' he says. Then he bends his head and
kisses me.

I sink into the darkness. Nothing but weaving shapes around
us. Then I see he is pointing at something.

Figures in the mist.

Dark ragged shapes, cloaks tight around them.

A flash of lightning, the screech of a landslide, rocks cracking
open, sheer drops.

Henry's grip around me tightens. He looks into my eyes.

'Be brave, Ellie.'

It's a warning. I stop pedalling. Pull over. Try to figure out
exactly what I've got to be brave about, apart from cycling
over Snowdon in the dead of night, obvs.

I try to remember the sweetness of Henry's kiss ...

Ahhhhh ... sooooo ... niiiiice ...

Suddenly there's a blasting and a shrieking; a roar, like a
plane crashing. The ground seems to shake. For a second
the road actually buckles under my bike.

It's like Glyder Fawr has reached out and, furious at being labelled a half-formed-monster-mutant, is shaking the pass all around me.

THE PASS IS SHAKING!

Thank God I stopped.

My ears!!

The whole north side of the gorge seems to shift. *Holy crap!* I can feel it in my teeth! *Landslide! Earthquake!* With a crashing loud enough to wake all of Nant Peris, rocks start tumbling. Bouncing.

Rocks!

Avalanche!

How close? Darkness. Mist. I can't see a thing. Unsure whether to turn and belt back downhill, or crouch, or scream, I freeze.

The mountains close in. The sound thunders in my ears. I bend my head, clasp my hands over my ears. *Don't move. Don't go on. The Brenin Llwyd: this is what he does!*

He sends his riders to hurry you over a cliff.

To hound you into a lake.

To force you into the path of an avalanche.

This is it.

This really is it.

Four

Long after the rumbling stops, I stay there crouched down by my bike, hands over ears, trembling. When at last I dare to move, I unclip my bike light and walk a little way up the road, shining the light from left to right.

Woah!

Massive rockfall.

Shedloads of it. Nearly blocking all of one side of the road. If I hadn't deliberately gone slower, if I'd hurried in the slightest … I shudder. I'd be there, right under all that tonnage.

I am not allowed to swear at home. My mum doesn't even like it if I say 'hell' and 'cripes' and 'crap' and all those other pseudo swear words either. (She hates things like 'Oh sugar' too.) But right then I swear. (I was not at home, obvs, but still, gotta respect my mum, so I swear in code.)

'Oh coded words!' I say.

Coded fog and coded pitch dark.

If anything comes up here and runs into that rockfall, it'll be fatal. I should call the police or somebody.

I pull out my phone. Thank goodness I charged it. I wipe it against the front of my jacket and swipe it open. But it's no good. No flipping signal.

Unsteadily, I attach one of my bike blinkers to the rocks as a kind of warning. Hope it works. Then I push my bike round the rockfall, and head on up the pass. Maybe up there I'll get coverage. Shaking, I get back on my bike.

By the start of the Pyg Track, at the top car park, I'm puffed out and I stop. I get off the bike again and crouch down by the side of the road, squinting through the darkness, until I swipe my phone.

Still no signal.

I try holding it out at all sorts of odd angles. I cross the road and climb up on a low wall. A single bar shows. The phone buzzes. Two new pings.

George.

George

Can't sleep. Lying in my bed and thinking about you on this auspicious night. Please imagine all my thoughts and add some.

32

The second is from some random number.

> **+44 7654 111156**
>
> So where is your BF then? I told you Hands Off or it was WAR.
>
> Well, eat your heart out GF cos his <3 belongs to me now.

Whaaat?

Who sent that?

My first thought is Sheila, but it isn't her number. And it's been sent earlier than George's, in fact at exactly 00.10.

Why would Sheila send me a text like that in middle of the night? Because Sheila ~~is a cow~~ has been after Henry from the very first. That's why.

Why would Sheila *not* send me a text like that in middle of the night, though? Because she is lazy, and wouldn't bother waking up to text anyone.

Sigh. Sheila is my friend who sometimes doesn't act like one.

And anyway, why has it only just come through now?

But what a nerve!

I pull off my glove and message right back.

> **Ellie**
>
> Go suck bananas.

And one to Sheila – just to double check.

> **Ellie**
>
> Did you just text me?

Then I ping Rhiannon as well.

> **Ellie**
>
> You OK Rhi? I'm on my way – already up at Pen-y-Pass. Miracle I got a signal up here. Just letting you know. Did you want me to call anyone? XXX

I press send.

I wait for a reply, but none comes. I call the police about the landslide, but only just manage to shout out: 'ROCKFALL ON LLANBERIS PASS!' before the signal goes down again. I really should tell them about Dinas Emrys, despite what Rhi says. Perhaps they already know. I wave the phone in the air, turn it off, turn it on again, climb down from the wall and try the other side of the road.

Zilch.

It's like that on Snowdon. Coverage comes. Coverage goes. It's almost as if Snowdon itself decides which messages it will carry and which it won't. I know from experience, I could muck about up here until tomorrow, hoping for a signal and might never get one. So, praying the police have got the message, I stuff my phone down the top of my parka, underneath my hoodie, close against my skin, so if coverage does come back on, I will feel it vibrate.

As I turn to go, the clouds clear for an instant. The moon shines through. I look back down the road. I see the mountains unfolding below me. It's a crazy sight. Like I'm standing on the top of the world as it ripples and falls away in huge chunks. A haze of low-lying mist seamlessly merges dark land into dark sky until the mountains look like waves rising and falling on a mysterious midnight sea.

Then it blinks out.

That text really was ~~foul~~ not very nice, was it? 'Eat your heart out GF … ' I bite my lip. Not that many people know about Henry and me – even fewer know the curse about giving his heart. Which makes the bit, 'his <3 belongs to me now … ' so much more than just five words. (~~I bet it was Sheila, the cowbag.~~)

I really need to get to Dinas Emrys. Nobody can have his heart, can they? It's mine. He's My Henry. I try to reassure myself but an imaginary text thread burrows its way into my mind:

ME: His heart is encased in crystal in a cavern.
     It'd take an earthquake off the Richter scale
     to shatter the cavern, and the Hadron Collider
     to break through the crystal. You're worrying
     for nothing.
RANDOM TEXTER: You are thinking in terms of pure
     physics.
ME: Huh?
RANDOM TEXTER: It was the magick of Merlin that
     encased his heart and the power of Draco that
     holds the key. I am more powerful than Draco
     and possess older magick than Merlin.
ME: Who are you?
RANDOM TEXTER: Your worst nightmare.

I jump on my bike and take the last little bit of rise.
I pound the pedals like I'm in the Tour de France. I hit the
downhill slope.

   Going downhill on Snowdon is scary. The road falls away
in front of you; it curves out into a bed of mist. You know
that a huge cliff lies on one side and at any minute there
might be a hairpin bend. Then you hit cloud. It clings on
around you. You can hardly see the road as it drops and
drops away. You get a wave of vertigo, as if you're flying off

into nothingness. And you hold your breath, as you tear through cold air.

I hold tight on to the handlebars, hardly touching the brakes. I freewheel, all the way down to the junction on to the Beddgelert road. I race through the misty darkness like the wind. The bike flies beneath me. To distract myself from what I'll find at Dinas Emrys, I wonder why Rhi didn't want George to know.

Rhiannon and George have got this thing going, you see. Or rather *not* going. In fact it has been *not going* for so long, it feels like it *is* going. Everybody knows about it. Rhiannon is totally nuts about George. George is *not* totally nuts about Rhiannon. George is totally nuts about me (though I am *not* nuts about him). Anyway, I have to pretend I don't know anything about all the totally nuts stuff that is *not* going on between them.

It's sort of like *A Midsummer's Night Dream* without Shakespeare.

Anyway, it was weird of Rhi to say, 'Don't tell George', because Rhiannon likes to see George under any circumstances. Even when she might not have done her hair/ fake eyelashes/eyebrows/lip gloss – you know – to look her prettiest best. Not that George notices that kind of thing. But anyway, under ordinary circumstances, she'd totally like to see him in the dead of night, when he could rescue her from some lonely location, and the darkness would hide any lack of blusher.

So why text me?

I've never quite got that – I mean the girly rescue thing. I'm pretty much a mountain boots, mountain girl. I'm best off in a waterproof jacket and a pair of jeans with a daysack on my back, rescuing myself.

Not true.

I can do pretty, really well in fact – especially if there was any hope Henry might be around ☺. And actually, I *would* like a free voucher for Make-up Unlimited just as much as Rhi. If I had the offer of one.

But Henry isn't going to be around, is he? He's entombed under Dinas Emrys.

With his heart sealed in crystal.

Imprisoned.

With the White Dragon.

His mortal enemy

And without me.

Or at least that's where he should be …

Five

ELLIE'S PHONE

No coverage. No coverage. No coverage.

I hit the Beddgelert Road at speed. Freezing air whips my hair back, stings my eyes. The clouds lift a little. The mist rolls back. Moonshine glimmers through. This side of the mountain lies covered in a fine, icy frost. It glitters, ghostly.

I twist my head to see if the shapes are still chasing me, but they're gone. I crouch back over the bike and make as much headway as I can.

Head down, pulverising the pedals, my hands literally frozen in place, I race downhill all the way to Llyn Gwynant.

And I wonder what the heck I'm doing.

The water on the lake stretches out smooth and black. Spectral slopes rise from its shores. The road lies totally deserted; the mountain is all mine. Sometimes I like it best that way. Just Snowdon and me. Pals. Sort of.

I race past Llyn Gwynant scrooched down low. No sign of human life. No telephone pole. No cottage. Just the grey road winding on down alongside the Afon Glaslyn, down to Llyn Dinas.

I sit back on the bike seat and squint into the distance. My heartbeat jumps about. The fortress of Dinas Emrys lies smack ahead. What will I find there? Rhiannon's words send shivers through me. What did she mean: 'Someone died'?

The moon goes behind a cloud. Darkness closes in. Rhiannon must be mental coming out here at midnight. What the flip was she doing? I bet it was something to do with her new obsession with witches. Only last week I sat through a whole evening of tarot readings with her, trying to figure out meanings (it was actually quite a lot of fun). What had my cards said? Something about the Lightning-Struck Tower and the Ace of Swords?

I think of Henry lying curled tight in the cavern, so near. He'll still be there, won't he? A bad, bad, bad feeling ripples through me, like something has crawled over my grave. *What about the White Dragon?* Everything about tonight is really bad, bad, bad.

Tonight? Suddenly, I have a light-bulb moment!

What did George write?

'*Auspicious.*' That's it! It's a leap year! That's why Rhi went out. She'll be doing all that witchy stuff with her 'coven', and trying to come up with the ultimate love potion; the Make-Me-Irresistible-To-George Charm. You know: look into the mirror and see your intended (George) appear over your left shoulder. Yeah. Right.

Being a witch is actually quite cool. Although those bunch of loonies from Betws-y-Coed are well known to be evil ones who turn into cats, which is not so good.

And why up here on Dinas Emrys? I bite my lip.

An image of Sir Oswald flashes across my mind. He'll be under the mountain too. Nobody would want to see his face in the mirror. I shiver at the thought.

A light flashes. Away down the road, somewhere near the National Trust car park, more lights. As I draw nearer, a glow of flickering orange. A siren wails, screeching into the night. It's serious then. Has to be. Emergency services don't come out for nothing. Yikes. Someone *must* have died. How the hell did that happen?

Instinctively I slow down. Lights and sirens mean police everywhere. And that means a police cordon. How will I be able to get to Rhi or check the cavern for Henry, if I can't get access? And then I think – what if Henry is still there and the police find him? I mean, he's in his dragon form and has to stay that way for the next seventy-two years under the Merlin curse rules.

I imagine the *Snowdonia Chronicle* headline:

Mabinogion Legends True After All:
Landslide Reveals Sleeping Dragons

I mean, it could happen – think of the Titanosaurus find ...

Best to avoid the police.

I swing off the road and cycle up towards a farm, avoiding the car park and the lights and all that police stuff.

I take a shortcut I discovered on one of my treks to Henry's cavern. I do that sometimes, you know, visit the place where he lies, pray to Merlin, beseech the Constellation of Draco, beg Snowdon to show me the way to find him again. Sit there with my heart breaking. Sometimes I think I hear him – just a rumble from the depths of the mountain – as if he knows I'm there. (Don't say anything. Keeping lonely vigils over your buried beloved is too depressing to think about.)

Anyway, there's this turning to a farm, and from there, to a lane and a row of mobile holiday homes. Behind them you can scramble up a steep slope between trees, all covered in moss and get to the fortress from the back. The bracken is tight and scratchy, but it's really not too far and saves a good three-mile trek.

Anyway, I pedal very carefully once I've got up through the gates to the farm, as it's private property. Once through them, I take a sharp left along a dirt track towards the mobile homes. Frozen grass pokes white through the middle of the road. It really is bitter. My fingers are totally numb. I dodge the potholes. As I near the chalets, I get down and tiptoe.

I am very wary creeping through the holiday homes. They're supposed to be empty at this time of year, but actually everyone knows they're pretty much lived in for the entire winter. They're rented out in the high season for silly prices to silly tourists who have more money than us locals, but at the first sign of frost, the owners come sneaking back in, after they've probably been sofa surfing at their auntie's all summer. Then they live in the chalets for the rest of the year.

It drives the local council nuts, trying to get them to stick to the rules of holiday home ownership. And that makes me even more super-quiet. These guys are really jumpy and ready to shout at anyone. They'll think I'm here to spy on them.

So, very carefully, I hide the bike behind the first chalet, where I see a pair of muddy wellies shoved against an upturned bucket (what did I tell you), then I sidle round it and head for the first row of homes. I slip down between them. I don't want some bloke with his stripy pyjamas and a big attitude to come busting out of a caravan and start yelling at me. I don't want to have to cycle down to the National Trust car park either and get stopped by the police, or walk three miles back across country. I'd get to Rhi by the end of next week.

It kind of goes OK, 'til I see a light go on in the first chalet. I swear I never made any noise. These guys must have trip wires or something. Then the light snaps off and I hear the caravan door open. I freeze.

A definite pyjama-shaped shadow falls across the gravel. *Oh no.*

I don't move. The shadow goes the opposite way, checks the front. I slip into the woodland at the back. Phew.

In front of me rises a steep bank, covered with spindly trees. Thick green moss coats every patch of bark, and the roots are tangled knots of black. In parts, the rocky hillside is almost sheer. Still need to be totally quiet.

I hoist myself up from trunk to trunk. Yuck, slimy cold moss. I try not to go all urrrgh; to stay strong. I've been pretty scared of Dinas Emrys ever since I was first brought here by the White Dragon. I tell myself: Sir Oswald can't get you any more. I hold my breath. He's like my worst-ever nightmare. Totally evil. But he's shut up under the fortress, isn't he? I briefly cross my fingers. Then I carry on struggling up the dark slope.

Halfway up, I check my phone to see if there are any new pings. Actually, I stop to get my breath back.

The bars on the phone are down. No coverage. Snowdon has shut down. Locked us all in.

I puff a bit (OK, a lot). It's very steep, and I'm out of breath. I get going again; have to crawl on hands and knees in places, up towards a pile of stones – all that's left of the ruined ramparts of the old castle.

Legend has it that the fort of Dinas Emrys was the ancient stronghold of Vortigern, the king who disturbed the lair of the dragons. He was the ~~pillock~~ guy who started the problem to begin with. I seriously blame him for that. If he hadn't decided to build his stupid castle up here, Merlin would never have got involved. And the curse that took Henry away from me would never have been cast. It is all Vortigern's fault. Though I guess I should thank him too, because if he hadn't dug up the dragons and Merlin hadn't offered them the chance to become human, I'd never have met Henry.

That's history for you. Perverse.

I mean, why would you want to build a castle up here? In the most inaccessible spot ever? I seriously pity his workers. If my mum even tried to ask a builder to do a job on the top pastures he'd tell her where to go. And just because they didn't have human rights in the Dark Ages, that was no excuse. They were still humans. Except for Henry, obvs.

I try not to think about Henry, down under the mountain.

At last I get up off all fours, dust bits of random moss and lichen from my knees, round the top of the escarpment and start to descend on the other side.

And then I blink.

My heartbeat shoots up, way over healthy.

WHAAAAAT?

Six

Holy heck.

Half of the north face of Dinas Emrys has split open.

Trees uprooted, boulders cracked *right through*. Great half-broken trunks stuck up in the air. It looks like a train crash. There's an overpowering smell of crushed foliage and damp earth; a thick, sickly smell. I try to stay sane, breathe in great gulps after the long bike ride, the scramble up the hill …

Someone's screaming.

The mist about the ramparts of Dinas Emrys suddenly closes in. It feels like nothing else in the world exists apart from that great scar, that huge open crack. *Half of the*

47

flipping fortress is gone!

I close my eyes. Reopen them. It's all still here. The hill, the landslide, the police, the lights, the diggers, ropes, torches, sirens ...

I hear another scream. I wheel round to my left, standing in the mist; way up ahead on the lip of the crack is Rhiannon.

'ELLIE!' she shrieks. 'ELLIE, THANK GOD YOU'VE COME!'

She's pale, distraught, wearing some kind of funny outfit. I make my way over the top towards her. She scrambles over the rocks and throws herself at me.

She latches on to me with fierce frenzy.

'THEY'VE GONE! THEY LEFT ME!'

'What *have* you got on?' I say. She's all dressed up in some shapeless black (lacy!) cloak thing with a fish-tail, plus an extra-wide, fur-trimmed hood, totally covered in sequins, pulled over a pointy hat! A mask hangs from elastic around her neck.

'It's all gone wrong!'

'What?' I say.

'She's dead!' shouts Rhiannon. 'She's DEAD!' Rhi points into the crevasse right behind her.

I try to get my head round that. Has the earth shifted,

opened up right down to the cave? What does she mean? My heart jumps around in my chest. 'Who's dead?' I ask.

'Fiona.'

'Well shove over then,' I say, 'so I can see.'

Rhiannon lets go of me, clutches her head, screams, 'She's dead. They left me. With someone *dead*! DON'T TELL MY DAD.'

I try to squeeze past her but get a blast of vertigo. I realise she's standing on the edge of some huge drop.

Don't tell my dad? Where did that come from? 'Tell him what?'

'There was no phone signal,' she cries. 'I didn't even know if my messages got through.'

I look up towards the peak of Snowdon. *You knew though, didn't you?* I think. *You know which messages you let through and which you don't.*

'Snowdon's funny like that,' I say. 'Go on.'

'Nothing's funny,' Rhiannon screeches at me. 'It was TERRIBLE.'

'OK, stay calm. Breathe out through your mouth. That's it. You'll be fine ... ' All my mountain-rescue training kicks in. 'But I need to know everything.' I try to untangle myself from Rhi, so I can look over the edge of the crater.

'It was the Supreme One's idea,' she said. 'We were just

doing girl power thingies.'

The Supreme One?

'I didn't know what would … I thought it was going to be different.' Rhiannon sounds aggrieved.

'What did you do?'

'We were going to wake up these dragons and ask them to tell us the future.'

My heart misses a beat.

'It wasn't supposed to be *real* witchcraft,' she says, 'just pretend. We had to have clothes and hats and brooms and be all dressed up, which was *fun*. I thought we'd look all sexy-Wiccan princess. And, you know … do *love* spells …'

'What?'

'You know – LOVE SPELLS.'

'How can that be OK?' I say. 'I mean, *making* someone love you. Seriously Rhi?'

Rhiannon shrugs. 'Not everyone can be as fussy as you.'

'Then what happened?' I try again to get free, but Rhi's got some kind of death grip going on around my neck.

'Well, The Supreme One – that's the High Priestess – it was all her idea.'

'Can you let go?' I say.

'Someone's boyfriend brought us in a van. I don't know

whose – one of those other girls.' I don't really know them anyway. Meryl refused to join and nobody bothered asking you … ' She stops.

'Why don't you sit down?' I say. 'And let me look at what's happened.'

Rhiannon starts shrieking. 'NO, DON'T! DON'T! SHE'S DEAD!'

I really need to see if Henry's OK …

'OK – just sit. Try to breathe evenly.' I pull her down beside me, put my arm round her. 'It's not safe anyway standing on these rocks.' Maybe if she sits down I can get her a bit calmer and then I can try and find out what's happened. Rhiannon tightens her grip.

'We had to walk all the way up the slope, chanting. Once we got up here, we formed a circle and said the magic words. And you know, called the dragons.'

I go cold all over.

'Then this huge crack opened up, something white and, like, *weird* rushed out. Honestly, I swear it looked like some kind of dinosaur or something, and I thought maybe it *was* a dragon. I thought maybe it was just all of us standing in the wrong place and it'd rained a lot and that's why … '

Oh God, I think. Oh My God. I hold my breath. I can't

believe it. But what else could be that huge and white and … weird?

'OK, describe it.'

I just want to see for myself.

'It was like a sinkhole opening up.'

'No, the dragon thing.'

'Like some kind of … breath of death flying out of the mountain.'

Breath of death?

'And that's when this girl, Fiona, just screamed and toppled in. She wasn't even standing at the edge. It was as if when that white thing came out, it kind of sucked her in.'

I've heard enough. I pull her arms off me, a bit roughly. She'll be OK. She's calmer. 'Stay there.' I clamber up over the last heap of stones and lean over the lip of the crevasse. I look down.

There are the ruins of the cavern. There, impaled on crystals, lies a girl. A policeman in a white spacesuit thing is moving around. The girl looks like a broken doll. One of the crystals has pierced right through her. I can see the dark spread of blood seeping around. I think I gasp or mumble or moan. I'm not sure.

A policeman looks up, angrily waves me back, turns

to someone and points up at us. I inch my way back to Rhiannon.

'Didn't anyone go down there, check she was still alive?' I ask.

'The Supreme One went down, but she said there was nothing we could do,' wails Rhiannon. 'She went with the rest of the girls to go and fetch someone. They left me here to tell the police … and … '

Well, that's weird, isn't it? Leaving Rhi here all alone.

I clamber back from the lip of the crater. I sit shaking on the rocks. Apart from the girl down there and the two crystals and the blood there is nothing.

Nothing!!!!!!

Except a feeling; an eerie fear, like a curse has been fulfilled. No White Dragon. No Red Dragon. *No Henry*.

And – come to think of it – it's pretty weird of Rhi to agree to stay.

A policeman appears, climbs over the rocks towards us. Rhiannon grabs my arm, whispers, 'I'm so sorry. Please forgive me, Ellie, I love you really.' Then she stands up, hurries forward.

'Steady there,' says the police officer.

'HELP!' screams Rhiannon. And she flings her arm out, points straight at me. 'IT WAS HER!' she yells.

'SHE PUSHED FIONA IN!'

'Whaaat?' I say, for the third time tonight.

'YOU DID! YOU DID!' screeches Rhiannon.

'Hang on,' I start.

'You pushed her! You threatened me and you've been standing here ever since forcing me to send you fake texts, because you know on Snowdon the coverage is unreliable – so that you can pretend you didn't do it!'

'*Rhiannon!*'

I'm totally shocked.

Totally.

Totally.

'HELP ME!' weeps Rhiannon. 'SHE DID IT! SHE DID IT! I'm so scared. She's gonna push *me* in.'

I feel all the blood draining out of me.

'I –'

'Please don't move, Miss.' The policeman steps towards me.

'But I've only just arrived.'

I can't believe this.

'Well, we didn't see you,' says the policeman.

'I scrambled up at the back way,' I say.

'Did any of the residents there see you?'

I can't believe this.

'I think we better go down to the station, Miss.'

'But … '

'You have the right to remain silent, but anything you do say will be taken down in evidence and may be used against you.'

Ohmygod.

I didn't wake Mum. OMG. Nobody in Llanberis saw me. I don't know if I got through to the police when I was on the pass. OMG. I didn't text George back. *Nobody will be able to vouch for me.*

Oh My God.

It's my word against Rhi's.

I don't believe this.

But surely the Supreme One and the rest of the coven … they know I wasn't here.

OHMYGOD.

'Please come quietly.'

He removes the handcuffs from his belt.

'OK, Officer,' I say. 'I'll come.'

Seven

I pull out my phone. I've got to let someone know.

ELLIE'S PHONE

Status: ... *no signal*

Recent updates:

Sheila

Why did you ping me? Is this about a boy? If it is, I bags him first.

YES! Even your PRECIOUS Henry! Mwahaha.

I close my phone.

Great.

A team from Caernarfon comes. They remove Fiona. *How horrible.* I feel ill. It takes a long time. I don't see any of it. I sit in a police van, and watch the dawn not happening. Horrible. Horrible. Horrible. Cold mist rolls down off the slopes, hits the blue-flashing police lights in weird puffs, like the breath of the Brenin Llwyd for real. My phone has no bars showing. *Poor Fiona.* I wonder if Mum has woken up and is freaking out that I'm not back, or thinks I'm staying over with Rhi.

Rhi?

What the heck is going on with her?

I actually still can't believe it. I try, but my brain gets stuck. I sit there. I watch as they remove a lumpy black shape into an ambulance parked across the road. So Fiona's really dead? Somehow I was hoping …

God, it's just so awful. Impaled on the heart crystals? I shudder. I don't even know where Rhiannon is. They led her off, sobbing. Her face was puffy and her eyes couldn't meet mine. 'Rhi?' I shouted at her, but she ducked her head low and leaned on the policeman supporting her, as if I was like: Evil Incarnate.

And no Henry.

Where is he?

I scanned every corner of that ruined cavern. I even saw the pool where George poured the potion. I saw the alcove at the back, where we'd hidden. I couldn't possibly have missed two huge dragons, could I?

I start thinking this is a nightmare. *This is a total nightmare.*

I must have fallen asleep on the sofa, or I'm having more *Horror Her* visiony things.

But you don't really have visions about sitting in the back of a police car. Do you?

Eventually another policeman arrives. There's a quick conversation, then the policeman who arrested me starts the engine. He doesn't say anything. He doesn't even glance at me. We drive off down the mountain, through Beddgelert, towards Caernarfon. At least he doesn't put on his stupid siren, as if I'm a mass murderer. Maybe he believes everything Rhiannon said. Maybe he's so used to arresting teenagers in the middle of the night, he doesn't think anything. I can't think anything either. I can't get over the fact that this is happening.

I keep expecting to wake up.

But I don't.

I stare out of the window at the mist and rain. Henry can't have just disappeared.

I have to say something in my own defence, so I mention my bike, and how that might prove I really did come through the chalets at the back.

But then again it might not.

Inside those chalets might be whole gangs of stripy-pyjamaed bike thieves: who will obviously nick my bike and pretend they aren't in their mobile homes at all; even if the whole of North Wales Police pounds, all night, on every door.

The policeman calls someone, asks them to check.

I don't hold my breath.

After dark, mountain roads in Wales are quite scary, even in police cars. In thick mist they're even worse. At one point I almost wish he *had* put on the siren, just to warn anyone coming the other way. I realise, I'm probably freaking out about the twisty roads to stop myself freaking out about Henry not being there – and that poor, poor dead girl …

And Rhiannon.

Rhiannon!

I just don't get it.

I can't think about it, either. It's actually unthinkable.

So I'm officially not thinking.

At the police station, the officer parks the car round the back. I'm still not thinking. I'm taken into the charge office. It's very humiliating. But I'm not thinking about that either. I have to empty everything out of my pockets including my ratty old bits of tissue. They take everything.

When it comes to the interview statement, I have to start thinking.

And the first thing I think is: they are not going to believe anything about dragons. If I mention Henry, they will freak out and get a psychiatrist in.

Not going there.

They get someone in anyway. I think she is called an Appropriate Other.

APPROPRIATE OTHER: We are going to have to
     interview you about what happened.
  ME: I wasn't there. I swear. I keep telling them.
POLICE OFFICER: We are recording this interview
     at 5.30 a.m.
  ME: Cripes, is it 5.30 already?
 THEM: Please confirm these belongings are yours.
     They are being sealed in a plastic envelope.
  ME: OK.
 THEM: Sign.
 THEM: Your full name?
  ME: Arabella Bronwyn Lily Morgan.
 THEM: Age?
  ME: Sixteen, nearly seventeen.
 THEM: Address?
  ME: Uchaf Cwm Brwynog Farm, Llanberis.
 THEM: Next of kin?

ME: My mum, Mrs Gwen Morgan.

THEM: Please tell us exactly what happened.

ME: OK, but first of all, I want you to know that it's not true. I didn't push anyone into that crevasse. I didn't try to kill anyone.

THEM: Please relate everything as it happened.

I stare at them. I sigh.

'Can you write it yourself,' the policeman says, 'or would you like to dictate it to me?'

'I'll write it myself,' I say. I don't want him putting my words into his words. I take the pen from him. He pushes a sheet of paper towards me across the table.

'I want you to tell me absolutely everything that happened from 11 p.m. last night, through to this morning,' he repeats. 'You need to write it down and sign each part of the statement.'

So I do.

I only miss out the weird Brenin Llwyd and dragony bits. He tells me that they have made enquiries, and no, they have not 'found' my bike – that the chalets are in fact *all* empty and there is no sign of me having hidden a bike behind any of them.

What did I tell you?

He reminds me that knowingly giving a false statement is a criminal offence.

~

After all that, I wait for a long time in the charge office. They take away my stuff. They put it in plastic bags. Then they show me into some other room. I notice when they go out that the door won't open from the inside. I'm basically locked up. I knock politely at the door. Nothing happens. I push the door.

I am locked up!

I pound at it and shout. 'HEY!' Someone yells back at me. 'BE PATIENT!'

Be patient?

I need to get out of here.

How could Rhiannon do this? After everything I've done to help her!

And where's Henry?

And where's Oswald?

I need a cup of tea.

After what seems like ages – at least three or four hours – a policewoman comes back and says they've tried ringing my house repeatedly and there's no reply. Is there somebody else they can contact?

I sigh. 'I've told you already, my mum's gone off to a conference.'

'What about her mobile?' she asks.

'I don't know her mobile phone number off by heart.'

And I can't look it up, because it's on my phone and *you've* taken my phone and put it in a sealed plastic bag, ~~you idiot~~ officer.

'It's on my phone, which you have.'

'Oh. Well then, we'll have to wait for the arresting officer to get the details.'

Grrrrr.

Imagine if I was a *real* criminal, and I needed to try and sort out my defence.

Anyway, now I come to think of it, it's probably a good job that Mum is away. I don't think it would be very nice for her to get a call at the conference, saying that her daughter's in a police cell. Besides, she won't even have got there yet. And it would take a while for her to get back. So, great, I might be locked up here until tonight, by which time the station will be closed, and who knows what will happen then.

Then I get a brainwave.

Gran.

That's Granny Jones. George's gran, actually. They're

our neighbours. She's an Appropriate Other too, isn't she? She could come for me.

And what's great is, I know *her* phone number off by heart. That's the thing about landlines – people have had them for so long – and when their area code is exactly the same as yours, you kind of learn them without trying. Mobile numbers you don't – even your own.

I tell the female officer that I want her to ring Mrs Jones of Cwm Brwynog Bwthyn. 'She's my gran,' I lie, 'and I want to speak to her myself.' I seem to remember you get allowed one phone call. It was on *Real Police Chases* or something on TV.

At last, she lets me out of the cell and takes me back into the charge office to use the phone. 'I'm going to call your grandmother first,' she says, 'and then you will have the chance to explain yourself.'

'OK,' I say.

So she dials the number and after it rings a few times, I hear George pick up.

'This is Caernarfon Police Station. We need to speak to Mrs Jones,' says the charge officer.

I hear George say, 'Yeah, yeah, and this is The Vatican and I'm the Pope'.

There's the sound of a scuffle. Gran must've grabbed

the phone. 'Hello,' she crackles.

'We've got a young Miss Arabella Morgan in the charge office here,' says the police officer. 'She'd like to have a few words with you. She has named you as someone she'd like to contact.'

'Yes,' says Gran, impatiently. 'Put her on immediately,' almost as if she was expecting the call.

The police officer hands me the phone. 'Gran,' I say, 'I don't know what's going on, but I'm here in the police station, please can you come? You can borrow Mum's Land Rover. There's been an accident and – '

'ARE YOU HURT?' bawls out George in the background.

I hear a scuffle for the phone again. Gran wins.

'Well, what are you being charged with?' she asks. Just like Gran. Straight to the point.

'Nothing yet,' I say, 'but, well, there's been an accident at Dinas Emrys, and – '

'ACCIDENT?' I hear George yell.

'Shush!' says Gran fiercely.

'DINAS EMRYS!' hollers George.

'Don't mind, Sior,' says Gran. I hear a hand go over the mouthpiece. 'Go and sit down, Sior,' Gran orders crossly, 'before the mountain cuts us off.' The hand comes off the mouthpiece.

'Continue.'

I take a deep breath. 'I'm being interviewed about pushing a girl into the cavern.'

'Are the police completely insane?' enquires Gran. And then, cryptically, 'Well, I'm not surprised'.

'The girl died,' I whisper. 'I wasn't there and I didn't do it, and I don't know what to do.'

'Of course you didn't do it. This is the work of something much more powerful than you.' Gran Jones is far too sensible to ask how I managed to end up in the police cells.

'That's what they've wanted all along: blood and sacrifice. Poor girl. I'm coming there, right now. We'll borrow your mother's Land Rover. Yes? I know where the keys are,' she says. 'George will drive.'

'If you can get hold of Mum – ' I say.

Perhaps I *should* interrupt her conference.

'I'm not going to bother your mother,' says Gran. 'She knows nothing about High Magick and will just get in the way.'

'BLOOD AND SACRIFICE?' screams George.

'OK,' I say.

'WHERE'S ELLIE?' George wails in the background.

George probably thinks it's Henry who's putting me in danger, again. Not that he'll say as much. He never does.

He won't even roll his eyes. Not at me anyway. He'll just be even sweeter than ever and offer me the last few crisps left in his bag. And I hate roast chicken flavoured crisps. Or his last piece of gum. I like gum, but how can you take someone's last bit? So I'll refuse, and then he'll look sad.

I hate it when he looks all sad.

Either way, I'm going to end up feeling really horrible.

'OK,' I say again.

Everything is already horrible anyway.

I hand the phone back to the police officer who has been standing there waiting and listening. 'Thanks,' I say.

I overhear Granny Jones say in her sharpest voice ever, 'You can expect me there within the next hour'.

'Please bring identification with you,' the police officer replies. And with that she puts the phone down.

I'm offered a cup of coffee. The policewoman seems kind.

'What's going to happen now?' I ask.

'I don't know, love,' she says.

'Please?'

'I don't know what kind of a scrape you've got yourself into. I can't discuss the details.'

'I know,' I say, 'but what's the normal procedure, then? What happens in general?'

'Well, if your grandmother comes,' says the police officer.

(I don't confess she's not actually my grandmother.) '*If* there is an option to have you bailed, we can sort that out at this police station. But it depends on the charge, love – if it's very serious it will have to go before the magistrate, if there is one; it's a holiday you see, here in Caernarfon – St David's Day. Sometimes they can get an on-call, but if it's beyond the magistrate's remit, it has to go to the High Court.'

'When … where?' I ask.

'And that's really a custody matter.'

A custody matter!

'Well, the magistrate can set bail. So best to be ready,' she says. 'Either way, it will definitely be sometime this morning that you'll find out. Your grandmother does need to get here quickly though.'

Her police radio beeps. A tinny voice crackles out: 'Defendants to court three.'

'Right, where were we? It appears they've got an on-call magistrate. That was a call to get the lads from last night into the vans.'

Cripes! I'm going to be in 'the vans' with a lot of hungover boy racers from Bangor!

'If your grandmother gets here in time, maybe we can sort this out and/or get you down to the courts before midday.'

It's all very confusing. And I don't really understand. I try asking her more questions, but I don't get very far.

'I can't really discuss your case with you now,' she says. 'If you like, we can contact a welfare officer to visit? You could talk to her.'

'No need,' I say. As if a welfare officer is going to believe in dragons and magic and witches.

I'm shown back into my cell. The minutes drag by. No mobile to play on. I sit staring at the white wall. Why did Rhi say I'd pushed Fiona? And that breath of death thing she described. Was that Oswald? Is the White Dragon on the loose again?

And will he come after me?

And that's when I see it.

I mean *it*!

The figure of *a nun* – I swear it – a nun – and I am not even joking. *I am not making this up.* She walks right through the wall across the room and straight towards me, swerves, then passes out through the wall behind me. As I watch her go, she turns her head and fixes me with a look.

Immediately I feel a pressure around my neck. I start to choke. *I can't breathe.* My hands fly to my throat.

I struggle, try to gasp in air. My fingers brush against the charm that was my real grandmother's, a silver moon with a constellation of tiny stars set in diamonds. The pressure eases. I am able to suck a few sips of air into my lungs.

I know what you're going to say. Go on, say it.

That did not just happen.

Ghosts do not exist, and if they did, they wouldn't haunt a police cell.

You were not suddenly, psychically, attacked by a dead nun.

That's stress.

Overtiredness.

Mental derangement.

A dead girl, nun or otherwise, cannot strangle a living one.

I sit down on the bench thing. I breathe slowly. I blink. My heartbeat shoots way up.

Just stay calm.

There must be an explanation.

None of this is happening.

You just saw a ghost.

In broad daylight.

Get. A. Grip.

I get up and cross over to the wall. I run my hand over it. Maybe it's some kind of trick; a stray beam of light. I check the window.

It doesn't happen again, but I don't let go of the silver charm. My heart rate gradually gets back to normal.

At last they call me back into one of the offices. The policeman who interviewed me to begin with is sitting there with Granny Jones and George. I never knew how pleased I'd be to see them. My heart jumps, but this time in a good way and my eyes tear up.

'Well now,' the policeman begins. 'Isabella (I don't correct him), your grandmother here (I don't correct him again) is ready to stand bail and offer an address to bail you to, but the charge is very serious. You've been accused by a number of witnesses of reckless premeditated behaviour, which brought about the death of a young lady. This is possibly a manslaughter or *even* a murder charge. At the very least, we cannot actually process your grandmother's application at the moment. So we are going to take you down to the local magistrates' court now and arraign you. Your grandmother and your brother, George (I am never, ever going to correct him about anything), are welcome to follow us there.'

George shakes his head. Sends me an unhappy smile.

'Murder?' I whisper.

Gran reaches out her hand, lays it on mine. 'Steady child,' she warns.

'Once there, the magistrate will hear the indictment against you,' continues the officer, 'and then we can proceed with bail, on the terms decided by the court, and after that, if everything goes well for you, we will be able to allow you to go home, pending our further enquiries and investigations as to what actually went on last night up at Dinas Emrys.'

George grabs my hand, squeezes it.

The policeman mutters something about needing to arraign me quickly, as it's St David's Day and we'll be lucky if the magistrate does more than one sitting.

I hang my head. I don't know why I feel so guilty. I am totally *not* guilty. I don't know why I don't feel angry, why I'm not shouting and cursing Rhiannon, but I'm not.

'We'll get you out of here,' whispers George. 'Trust me.'

I just don't understand it. I don't understand any of it, and my head hurts, and I'm tired, and I haven't slept the entire night, and now I'm being haunted too. And I'm so worried about everything. I can't think straight, even when I try.

And where is Henry?

After the officer has shown Gran and George out, I'm taken back downstairs and into an underground car park. I'm put in the back of the police van with half a dozen twenty-something lads and one older man who smells a bit ripe. They all look like they've got hangovers.

Today has to be officially the worst day of my entire life.

Eight

OK, so here's what happened: we got to the magistrates' court, and we were led to some cells at the back, downstairs. That is the only way I can describe them. They were definitely cells. And someone had definitely been in them before. Possibly very many people, because there were a lot of scratches and swear words all over the walls.

Like I said, I am not going to put swear words in my story. So I'm going to code them here. The code I'll use is ✺.

I can tell you, on those walls there were words like ✺, and ✺ the ✺ and ✺. Those last two are *extreme* coded words. I will leave you to imagine the rest.

Anyway, I was the only girl in the cells, which is presumably why I was put in a cell all by myself. I don't think it was because they suddenly decided I was a mass murderer, and must be kept away from others. Or at least I hope not.

When I am taken upstairs, I'm led straight into court. I have to go and sit on a bench and wait my turn. In front of me are two others. One of them has been accused of smashing a shop window and inciting racism by shouting revolting words at the place, which happened to be owned by an Indian family. The judge is not very sympathetic when the guy says he was drunk. He gets remanded over, and put back in the cells, because apparently he has done this before. A lot.

He doesn't look very sorry, when he tries to say sorry, either. I don't think he convinces anyone, not even his legal counsel, who keeps frowning at him, plus he didn't even stand up promptly when the magistrate needed him to.

Mental note to self: Stand Up Quickly And Properly And Look Suitably Humble And Sorry When Addressing The Magistrate.

The second person – the older man – has been caught in possession of some drug or other. Apparently he has a long string of offences for carrying drugs. The magistrate is a little more sympathetic with him. She asks his counsel why they have not yet set up the intervention that apparently was agreed upon the last time he appeared before her.

The person defending him launches into some long-winded bureaucratic story. Even the magistrate taps her fingers. She seems to be more lenient towards this man, though. She extends his bail and reminds him that he must live at the address he has given the court. He looks grateful. And then it's my turn.

It is all over very quickly. She hears the police indictment. She is given some papers. She takes a cursory glance at them. She asks the police when they think a plea can be entered. The officer reminds her that it's a local holiday today, and he can't get the necessary people in to see to the necessary things that need necessarily seeing to.

Then she turns and addresses me directly. She says, 'We will give you a date when you can enter a plea. Do you understand?'

I nod my head. I say, 'Yes, your honour'.

She says, 'This court does not look lightly on matters of the occult, particularly when they result in loss of life. You are not to leave the area, and you will need to report to the police station to help them with their enquiries if necessary. Do you understand?'

I nod my head. I say, 'Yes, your honour'.

The magistrate turns to my counsel. 'Meanwhile is there anyone who can provide bail for her? Is there an address that can satisfy this court – that she can be bailed to?'

Somebody who has been appointed to speak on my behalf says, 'Yes,' and reads out Granny Jones's address and gives her name.

The magistrate says, 'That's all then'. She turns back to me. 'You must live at this address and you must not commit any further offence if you do not want to appear before me again. We will see you in roughly three weeks' time.'

She nods to the clerk. He looks in a ledger, whispers something back to her.

'We will see you on 20 March to hear your plea.'

They give me back my stuff and that's it. Suddenly I can just walk away, walk outside and I do – out through the glass doors and into the waiting area.

And there's Granny Jones and George. Gran takes me by one arm, George takes me by the other, and then we are outside the building and there's Mum's Land Rover parked on the street, and I'm getting into it, and I don't know why, but suddenly I'm crying and saying, 'thank you, thank you, thank you!' And my breath is coming all rushy, and George has put his arm around me, and I'm burying my head in his shoulder, and Gran is tutting and saying, 'You can't drive *and* cuddle her, Sior. We *need* to get her home.'

'Hey, Elles,' says George. 'It can't be as bad as you think; we've been in worse places.' (Hugs, squeezes.) 'Come on, give us a smile.'

I pull myself together and bite my lip and nod my head, but I do not trust myself to speak.

Instead I pull out my phone.

ELLIE'S PHONE 1 March 12.30

Status: Unavailable Foreva (well, seventy-two years)

Recent updates:

Rhiannon

I'm sorry. I really am.

Mum

Bye darling, have fun with Rhiannon, and I'll call when I have a chance, but don't worry if I don't, it's going to be an intense three days. Love you. Kisses. Mum. XXX

Sheila

Where are you – you old hag-bag?

Meryl

Hon, what's happening? You aren't picking up.

Meryl

You OK?

Meryl

Shall I come over?

Meryl

I'm coming over.

Rhiannon

I'm sorry. I REALLY am. *If you get this: Please DON'T tell George.*

If I get this?

Is she for real?

I text Meryl back:

Ellie

Thanks Meryl, you r my best friend. Cos you really care, but I'm
OK. I'm going to George's.

George starts the Land Rover up. And we head through
Caernarfon towards the mountains.

And Gran starts.

N.B. she is wearing a wildly colourful yellow shawl with
pink and orange swirls. Underneath is a throwback item
to her youth: a purple velvet waistcoat. But her words are
a stark contrast to her get-up.

'Wales is in great danger,' she says. 'If I am not mistaken,
today is the first day of the end of the world.'

Nine

'Yesterday at midnight, the high magick was broken,' says Granny Jones.

George turns the car radio off, so we can hear.

'There are now no constraints holding back the Olde Deepe Magicke.' She nods gravely. 'It's going to be bedlam.'

'How? I don't get it,' says George.

'The Olde Deepe Magicke is a system of enchantments that little is known about, other than by those who seek it; those who travel west, with the words of power – but there are some things commonly known.' Gran leans forward to address me from the back seat.

'What?'

'It is wild and powerful and must be brought under control.'

'Right,' says George. 'Bit like me then.'

That actually makes me smile.

'You'll need to tell me everything that's happened, Ellie, as soon as you can.'

I nod. I still don't really trust myself to speak.

'When you're ready,' says Gran.

I gaze out of the Land Rover window. The mist closes in tightly around us. My breath steams up the glass. A white haze appears on the pane. I inhale, swallow the lump in my throat and tell myself self-pity is a character flaw.

I love Meryl. I hate Rhiannon.

'OK,' I say. My voice wobbles a bit but I tell them everything: from staying up late last night watching *Horror Her*, to George's text, the pings I got from Rhiannon, the bike ride up the mountain, how the Brenin Llwyd chased me into the dark – almost into the path of the rockfall – how I got to Dinas Emrys, what I saw and learnt there, and how Rhiannon accused me. I tell them about the police cell, and the ghostly nun.

All the time I'm talking, Gran does not say a word. I keep glancing at her, but she stares fixedly ahead out of the car window. By the time we reach our turning, up towards Snowdon and the dirt track that takes us along the side of Moel Cynghorion, to her little cottage, I'm just about through. My voice is steadier. I've stopped apologising every three minutes for the random, weird, bonkers nature of it all.

George flashes me a smile and nods his head, as if I've been talking about a shopping trip, and am explaining the ins and outs of a new laptop I just bought.

'I see,' says Gran at last.

I wait for more, but she says nothing. I glance back at her. Her mouth is a tight straight line.

I start to get worried.

Something inside me is saying: this is serious. This is so flipping serious, you don't even know how serious it is. This is more than just me and Henry and true love. This is … but I can't think what it is, and nothing feels more serious than the way I feel about Henry.

We come to a halt on the slope outside her cottage. I go to get down from the Land Rover. But Gran stops me. 'Wait child,' she says. 'It's not safe for you at the moment. Now we are on the mountain, the Coraniaid will be listening.'[1]

'The Coraniaid?'

Gran lays a thin finger over her lips.

A light dusting of snow has coated the yard. Snowdon looms hazily above us. A chill wind blows. The daffodils

1. The Coraniaid are a race of beings from Welsh mythology. (*Coraniaid* appears to be related to the Welsh word *corrach* translated as 'dwarf'.) They appear in the *Mabinogion*. They are characterised by a sense of hearing so acute that they can hear any word the wind touches, making action against them impossible.

that looked so spring-like yesterday have bent stalks; their heads hang. Some are flattened. I look around; other things are flattened too. And in the light dusting of snow, I see great swirls like wide white footprints.

'The Coraniaid, AKA dwarf-goblins,' says George, winking at me.

Gran gets down from the Land Rover and traces a circle three times around it. As she does, she chants in Welsh.

Fel hyn y mae awr y gormesoedd yn dychwelyd

A drechwyd gan Feibion Beli Mawr

Yn yr hen flynyddoedd drwy rym hud …

Since the events of last New Year, I try all the time with my Welsh, and I think she's saying something like this. (But maybe it scans and sounds a bit better in Welsh, and is sort of more spooky, but here's the full English translation.)

So does the hour of the gormesoedd, return,

Laid low by the Sons of Beli Mawr.

In olden years through the magick's power,

And can we the cures of yesteryear relearn?

Of Lludd helped by his brother Llefelys,

Like Nuada Silver-Hand and Lugh and thus,

Vanquish the dwarf and dragon white,

Strike hard against the giant's might,

Win against three magical trials,

To save again our homeland Wales,
Give me heroic valour and witches' spell,
To cure the ill and makes things well.

Gran turns towards Snowdon. She holds up her hand in the kind of gesture I've seen her do before when she was trying to protect me from the curse of the dragons. Then she goes into her garden and plucks some herbs from her little border. I sit in the car. George mumbles, 'You know … you *should* know by now … totally batty … but you gotta let her …'

I shush him. I trust Gran. I watch.

After a bit, she appears back at the Land Rover. She comes up to my side and opens the door. She gives me the herbs. She says, 'It is now safe to get down. Come – we'll have something to eat and I'll explain everything I can. But do not say any word further – on any matter – until I say so.'

~

I drink huge cups of tea and eat a massive wedge of cake; George goes out and brings in fresh logs for the fire. We bank it up and soon have a roaring blaze going. Gran pulls up the sofa and pats it, encourages me to lie down. And I do.

She covers me over with a knitted blanket. 'Rest,' she says. 'I don't suppose you got much in that cell ... you've a long journey ahead ... you must take heart, stay strong ... '

George hangs over the arm of the sofa, really near my face, and every now and then I have to shove his elbow off when it catches a strand of my hair.

'Ouch!'

George backs off a bit, pulling a sorry-but-how-can-I-not-lurk-over-you-when-you-are-lying-down-in-front-of-me look.

And Gran does one of her usual nutjob things. She passes a piece of copper pipe to me and one to George. I think they are short bits left over from some kitchen plumbing. I raise one eyebrow at George. Definitely weird.

'This is very important,' she says. 'Because of the Coraniaid, we must only talk to each other through copper.'

'Ohhh-kay,' says George and rolls his eyes at me.

I put the piece of pipe to my lips and find it's pretty difficult to speak through it. I have to kind of purse my lips and hiss.

'Good,' hums Gran through her piece of piping. She settles herself down in her rocking chair. 'Now you are a little stronger and we are protected with some temporary charms, I'm going to tell you something.' Her hissy voice through the copper sends shivers down my spine.

'Why have we got to talk through leftover kitchen waste?' sounds George back.

'Sior, stop it. I want you to listen, very carefully.'

George waves an imaginary wand over himself and mouths, abracadabra. I. Am. Listening. Then he mimes being all ears.

I shoot him a get-serious-Sior look, and nod my head. I've learnt from experience that when Gran has something important to say, it's best to get serious. (I wrote down everything that happened around Christmas which made me arrive at this conclusion. You can read it if you want. It's in a manuscript called *Here Be Dragons*. Send me a note and I'll get you a copy.)

'We are caught in the middle of an age-old battle,' Gran hisses very dramatically through her piece of copper piping. 'A war as old as Snowdon itself, from a time when great creatures walked the earth, and the Olde Deepe Magicke was abroad.'

'Please Nan, not "Ye Olde Deepe Magicke",' says George trying to aim his words into his pipe. 'Let's think practically first: we need to get Ellie a lawyer or something, and plan what we're going to say to Rhiannon.'

Gran ignores him. 'What you need to understand is that these mountains hold great power,' she pauses, then hisses very dramatically, 'and there are those that would like to steal that power and harness it for their own evil ends.'

I put the copper pipe to my lips. 'What's happened to Henry?' I ask.

'The ancient battle between the Red and White Dragons is being played out, right now, and we are part of it ... '

George stands up, shoves his chest out and says, 'Fe fi fo fum'.

'Sior!' shushes Grannny. 'If you climb to the top of Yr Wyddfa and look out over the mountains can you doubt Snowdonia is a stronghold of power?'

George raises one shoulder, lets it drop, rolls his eyes and sits down.

'But why? That is the question you must ask. Why must these two dragons continually be at war?'

I know he feels embarrassed. I do too. I mean, even if she's right, she doesn't have to go all Gandalf on us.

'It is because the evil White Dragon of Wessex wishes to dominate the world, but until he can subdue Wales and break the High Magick of Merlin and take the Golden Throne of Arthur, he is trapped and cursed and doomed to fail.'

I nod my head. Maybe she is a kind of Gandalf.

'But our mountains are not undefended.' Gran pulls her shawl closer. 'They have heroes who have sworn to protect them, to protect the powers that lie beneath them. We have Henry, the Red Dragon, and Owain Glyndwr and Saint David – but how far we can count on their aid I do not know, so you must understand the stakes, the danger – and the fact that our chances of success are very slim – before we decide what to do.'

Gran stops and even though it's broad daylight, she goes across and closes the curtains. I look up at George. He looks down at me. A mission? He raises his eyebrows in quick succession. We nod and silently agree to let her talk.

BTW: George has uberly lush eyebrows.

'On this *mission*,' breathes George enthusiastically, possibly to make up for being so sceptical, 'do I get to use my new axe?'

Gran holds up her hand and silences him. She seems to be listening intently.

'OK, then just remind me why we've got to talk through these pipes again?' whispers George.

'I've told you already – the Coraniaid,' hisses Gran.

'Ooh-kaay,' says George.

'The Coraniaid have hearing powers that are magical.

If they overhear us, they will know our plans and tell our enemies. Only the element of copper is alien to them, so we are safe if we speak through it.'

'We have a plan?' I raise my eyebrows.

'Ahhh,' says George. Like, what a dummy I am. That was so *totally* obvious. 'So right now you think the Coraniaid – little dwarfs, possibly with long beards – are listening to us?'

'Obviously,' hisses Gran back. 'Do you think I whisper through bits of old plumbing for fun?'

'But,' I say through my copper pipe, 'I don't understand what's happened? Why, since this morning, has everything gone weird.'

'I will try to explain,' she says. 'First of all, you realise that yesterday, being the 29th of February, was an auspicious day – it marks a leap year. And a leap year is one of the years that counts in the precession of the equinoxes – it shifts the constellation of Draco around the Pole Star.'

'Ah, the constellation of Draco,' I murmur. The great God of Dragons.

'It is through eighteen leap years that the Red Dragon must wait under the mountain, before he is allowed to walk abroad as a man.'

Yes, she's right. I learned that at Christmas. Henry must

lie for seventy-two years under Snowdon before he can come back as a man – a boy really – because he can only ever be eighteen years old.

Which is a painful point, because, if I live long enough to see him again, I'll be like, old. Eighty-eight in fact.

'And then he only has eighteen days, between the feast of St Lucy on the 13th of December – once the feast day of the winter solstice – until New Year's Eve. Eighteen days when he can walk abroad, free from the curse of Merlin – as a man – or fly to the stars as a dragon.'

I'm not sure why Gran is reminding me of all this. She knows it's a sore (heart-breaking) point. Sometimes I think she is cunningly trying to get in a plug for George, who obvs is her grandson and somebody she might prefer me to fancy. I try to send her a shush-now-this-is-all-very-upsetting look. And she fails to read it.

'Eighteen days only, to do what he can to try to defend Wales. After that the Red Dragon must return to the cave under Dinas Emrys.' She sends me back a wake-up-to-the-truth-because-there-are-more-boys-than-one-on-this-planet look.

But I notice she's missed out the key bit of info, like during those eighteen days he is also supposed to be looking for his true love: moi.

Don't get me wrong. George is well fit and everyone fancies him. It's just that I don't.

So I sigh, and remember instead that evening, high up on the mountain at Halfway House, when Henry told me all this and far more. My breath catches; will I ever see him again?

George intuitively reaches out, strokes my hand.

'And it was on that *very* night, *yester-eve*, when the witches came *upon the witching hour* to Dinas Emrys.' Gran gets into full poetic-Wicca mode. 'The Supreme One came and using her *evil art* and *black magick* – tricked time itself – sped up the leap years, into a mere eighteen seconds, then froze time itself and opened up the cavern!'

We watch as Gran dramatically throws one hand in the air. Both George and I jerk backwards and are suitably awed.

'Knowingly, she released the Olde Deepe Magicke,' repeats Gran fixing us with shining melodramatic eyes.

'Then she must have released Oswald the White Dragon as well?' I say.

Gran nods, darts her eyes around the room, points emphatically to the pieces of copper piping. 'With a sacrifice, just as the words of Draco's spell demanded,' she hisses.

I think of Fiona's broken body, twisted over the crystals. I remember the words of the spell that binds Oswald:

'Give a woman to your heart and live as a man,

Or to the cave under Snowdon as fast as you can.'

And I shudder.

'Henry too?' I stare into Gran Jones's keen blue eyes.

Gran screws up her forehead.

'Then where is he?' My heartbeat quickens.

'The Supreme One released all of the magic stored inside the mountains,' says Gran. 'So Henry too has been released, though in what form and under what enchantments, I don't know.'

George's hand on mine tightens.

'Yes,' says Gran, 'once the High Magick of Merlin is broken – the Olde Deepe Magicke is released – that is what Oswald desired more than anything – and it must be so, otherwise how can the Brenin Llwyd rise up so easily against a mountain girl and go down on to the high road by Nant Peris?'

The temperature in the room seems to drops a few degrees.

'How can a childhood friend turn against another, and accuse her of murder?'

Gran fixes me with a meaningful stare.

'How can the nun of The Black Boy Inn walk abroad through Caernarfon to strangle an innocent?'[2]

An icy chill descends on the room.

'And how can the Coraniaid have left their mark on my front garden? How can they?'

The fire seems to splutter, punctuating a weird silence. And I imagine the Coraniaid all over the mountain, listening. Ugh. Creepy. Horrible.

'And there are other things awake now,' whispers Gran. 'Things that know no allegiance to either dark or light.'

'You better stick with me at all times,' George hisses at me. '*And* hold my hand and snog me constantly.' He raises his eyebrows in quick succession again.

Not Funny George.

'Yes,' says Gran, 'the White Dragon of Wessex, Oswald, walks abroad and is planning your downfall, Ellie. Of that we must be very sure.'

'He better not cross me,' threatens George.

'But why me?' I whisper very quietly into my pipe.

'Because, Ellie, you have crossed him and got the better of him once already, and *that* he does not forgive.'

I think of that last fight in the cave, how the flowers

---

2. There have been many stories of ghosts at the sixteenth-century Black Boy Inn in Caernarfon. One of the spirits is known as 'the strangler'; it is said to manifest itself with a feeling of hands being placed around the throat. Some claim to have seen a nun walking through walls. While others say ghosts sit at the bar to drink and eat ghostly victuals.

of Blodeuwedd spoiled his aim, how Gran's potion overcame him, how George's axe wounded him. 'We've all crossed him,' I whisper. 'He will not forgive any of us.'

George eyes his new axe, lying against a pile of hewn logs by the fire. '*I* don't forgive *him* either,' he says.

'And you should know by now, the world of magic is not new to you,' adds Gran through her copper piece. 'You, Ellie, with your love for Henry, are the one weak link in Oswald's plan. True love is always their weakest link. It is as wild as the deepest magic and, some believe, more powerful.'

'I wish,' sighs George.

I know better than to doubt her words.

'They will try at every turn to eradicate you, already they have tried thrice today.'

I gulp. A shadow seems to fall across the room. The fire splutters again. George bends down and picks up his new Husqvarna Forest, hickory, long-handled, steel, hand-forged axe. (I know those details are accurate. Believe me, I had to listen to its comparative virtues against the Estwing E24A Sportsman's Axe with leather grip, which, btw, he *also* insisted on having.)

Gran looks at him. 'Yes, Sior,' she says, 'you will need your axe before we see the end of three days.'

Ten

'Three days?' I say. I don't get it.

'Three is a very magical number. If you can't get a full coven, three witches can cause a lot of trouble.' Gran starts counting on her fingers, a perplexed frown drawn tight across her brow.

'Like in Macbeth?' says George.

'But you said three *days*, not three witches?' I say.

'Well, it's twenty-one days, including yesterday, from when they cast the spell – until the 20th of March and the vernal equinox. You must be always sure to count in that magical Leap Year day, the 29th of February, for without that day they could not have struck at all,' Gran nods her head to herself. 'And remember a witches' day is not the same as ours for it only gets going at sunset and will not end 'til sunrise.'

'But twenty-one days is three *weeks*, Gran, still not three days.'

'Ah ha – but the witches have sped up time! They use magical numerology to do it. They take the number 21 and weave a spell around it. They slice and boil the numerical values down; compress them, they convert the 21 to 2+1 which equals 3. It's their dark formula to condense time; three weeks thus becomes three days.'

I stare at her, trying to see the logic in that.

'That's how it works,' says Gran in a matter-of-fact way. 'Well, usually. It could be three hours, or three seconds, magic has its own symmetry, but if it were three seconds, we'd already know. Besides, they too need a little time to plan their work.'

'But what are they planning?' asks George. He's got his bit of copper piping angled like it's a cigarette. He raises one eyebrow as he catches me watching, whispers, 'I know: *debonair.*'

Gran gets down a calendar from the wall and starts doing little sums in pencil on the edges of it.

I start to panic. *Only three days?* That can't be right. We'll never work out a way to find Henry and defeat Oswald in three days. We don't even know what breaking the High Magick means.

'Can you explain again about why we've only got three days?' I say. My head is suddenly pounding. I feel sick.

'In the everyday world, free of witches' curses, the days will flow as usual, twenty-one of them, one after the other – but for us, those of us caught up in the witches' spell, we'll only get three true calendar days, I'm sure of it. I think they will probably appoint the first and the tenth and the nineteenth as the days of the calendar, they intend to make count – that's if I know my magical numerology ... ' muses Gran. '1+10+19 adds up to 30 – see! And 3+0 = 3.' She waves the calendar at us and points to her scrawled sums.

Look on the bright side, I tell myself, swallowing down my panic. Though things are really bad: HENRY IS FREE.

'With a gap of nine unmagical days in-between each of the chosen days that they will designate to be enchanted ... ' Gran scribbles some more figures down. 'Nine, I see it now! 9 = 3x3. Oh, yes, very, *very* cunning. They've thought this through, you know. They've woven everything very tightly around that number 3. There is no way we can undo it, time will be sped up and we must therefore act immediately.'

'I have to find Henry.' I say. Then I really panic. If Henry *were* free he would have found *me* by now, wouldn't he? That means something is *definitely* wrong.

'Don't worry if you don't understand it,' Gran consoles us, putting the calendar down. 'That's the thing with magick, it follows laws of it's own. They hardly ever correspond to the logic of our world. Just remember: three days – that's all we've got.'

'I'm not trying to understand it,' says George. 'I'm trying to get Ellie to pay me some attention.'

Lots of things are wrong. Obviously. There's a dead girl stuck right over Henry's heart crystal, for a start. How has that affected him?

Gran sighs. 'Try to contain yourself, child,' she says. 'Henry is not dead, you cannot kill dragons easily.'

I look into the flames. I look at their blue centres, at the flickering yellow and orange. He hasn't found me, though. And he could be hurt, or trapped – and I may never know, may never see him again … and dragons *can* die … And Oswald is out there, trying to kill him.

Gran smiles kindly at me. 'Hold yourself strong,' she says. 'We have other work to do. With Henry's fate unknown, we must assume that Oswald will be hard at work. We can guess what it is that he is after, and if I am right, then we are all in serious danger.'

George leaves the arm of the sofa, comes round next to me, pushes my knees up, sits down beside me and says,

'I give up. If you won't notice me, Ellie, I shall have to be more noticeable.'

I try to give him a little smile. It seems to do the trick.

He leans forward. 'So give us the worst, Nan,' he whispers through his pipe. 'Don't pull your punches. We can take it.' He raises his eyebrows at me in quick succession and flexes his biceps.

'I do not know exactly what happened when they opened up the chamber at Dinas Emrys, destroyed the spell and went against the will of Merlin, but I can see that one thing *has* happened – they have unleashed the forces of magic under the mountains, that is why Glyder Fawr can shake his crown of rocks and cause landslides, and all the other things that we have already seen.'

Gran pauses and gives a nearly spent log a poke. Embers fly. A blue flame sprouts out the side of the piece of wood.

'And with the Olde Deepe Magicke on the loose, we can be certain Oswald is fast at work securing allegiances from all the monstrous creatures who are now waking up.' Gran places a fresh log on the blue flame. 'He will be directing them, if he can, to destroy Ellie and to take over Snowdonia.'

'So what are we to do?' I say. 'What *can* be done? If there is anything to do, I'll do it.'

'Not without me,' says George, grabbing his axe. 'If anyone tries anything with you again, they're going to have to get through me first.'

'We will need your courage, Sior,' whispers Gran, 'but put away your axe, and give me your teacup.'

'Teacup?' I say.

'Keep calm and drink tea,' whispers George.

'The teacup is mightier than the axe,' I whisper back.

'Both teacups,' says Gran, irritated. 'And hurry up.'

'Just give them to her.' George takes my cup from me and passes it to Gran with his own.

'We need to read the leaves and plan what to do next,' says Granny Jones.

'Go for it, Nan,' says George. 'Tell us what they're after.'

'Shush!' she says, holding the teacups up. 'I'm thinking of the critical question.'

'Like will Ellie ever love George?' asks George, making puppy eyes at me.

Gran tips the remains of the two cups into one. She swishes the cup to the left three times, holds it in her left hand. (It's one of those huge cups.) She holds the saucer firmly in her right. (It's one of those huge saucers.) She turns the cup upside down on the saucer. She tilts the saucer slightly over the hearth and allows the liquid to drain out into the grate. She rights the teacup, mumbles a few words, clears her throat. Then with her left hand, she turns the cup three times to the left.

The curtains shiver, as if the wild wind racing around the cottage can blow straight through walls.

The fire suddenly rages. A single yellow flame surges up the chimney.

Gran holds her hand on the cup in that position, seems deep in thought, then slowly counts to nine.

She turns the handle of the cup to point at me.

She lifts the cup free of the saucer.

My heartbeat shoots up.

It's just tealeaves on a saucer, I remind myself.

'Tell us what they mean,' says George.

Gran straightens herself in her seat, lifts the saucer towards her. 'Well, here,' Gran points at the area between the centre of the saucer and the rim. 'These zones represent either the distance or the weight of the omens. Images nearer the centre will come sooner, while the images nearer the rim come later. In addition to that, images at the centre represent heavier omens – nearer the rim they are lighter or more joyful.'

I peer closely at the dark spread of tealeaves.

'This big clump here augurs trouble on its way. These

drops of liquid tea that didn't come off with the draining represent tears. They indicates future sadness, great sadness.'

Gran stares into the fire deep in thought.

'Just tell us, Nan,' says George. 'How bad can it be?'

'Well,' says Gran, 'there are some things I don't understand, but I will tell you, because later on, it may be of use.'

'OK,' I say.

Gran peers at the saucer and says, 'I will tell you of the images I see. Remember them well and let them advise you.'

My heart starts thudding. I bite my lip, hold my breath.

'This *anchor*, at the rim, means stability, constancy in love.'

'That's me,' whispers George. 'I'm your anchor.'

I breathe out.

'Maybe,' says Gran, 'as here is an *axe* – which means you have the power to overcome difficulties.'

'Definitely,' says George.

'Here's a *bag* – a trap; if open – as it is here – it means a trap from which you can escape, *if* you think clearly. The *bat* here is a situation calling for alertness and caution.

'This *crow* or *raven* is an ill omen, a warning, or an ambush. And this *cat* – an untrustworthy friend.'

'Ha!' I say. 'I know who that is.'

'But look another *cat* sits over here,' warns Gran. 'These *dashes* and *dots* indicate many setbacks, which may cause wasted time. This *exclamation mark* means pay attention; beware of impulsive actions. These *lines* mean a journey and as they are wavy, the path is uncertain. And this *snake* – someone who does not deserve your trust.'

'You can always trust me though,' says George blowing me a kiss through the piping, which actually sounds like he's blowing off. ☹

'This *triangle* shows you are involved in a three-way relationship; and this *wolf* means you will be challenged or betrayed by someone. While these very small tealeaves and this huge one tell me that you can trust the tiny and the very big ... '

'And this – ' Gran stops, blinks rapidly.

'Yes?' says George.

Gran sighs. 'This tangle of *dragon* and *crown* and *throne* and *wand* below these *stars* under this *mountain*,' Gran points at a pile of leaves near the centre that are curiously mountain shaped, 'can only mean one thing,' she says.

'*What?*' I catch Gran's worry. A cold sweat breaks out down my back.

'It means a dragon – Oswald, of course – seeks ultimate power. This *crown* with the *throne* means it must be the Golden Throne of Arthur that he seeks, long hidden by Merlin under Snowdon.'

The Golden Throne? I try to rack my brains, to see if I can remember anything about Arthur's Golden Throne. Nothing jumps to mind. 'What if he does?' I ask.

'Whoever sits upon Arthur's Throne will be all powerful,' announces Gran.

'And?' says George. 'You mean like in real life – or is this just in a myth?'

Gran runs a hand across her face. 'It is said that the Hours of the Golden Throne will bring about a time when myth and magic meet with mankind,' she says. 'For so it was when the Throne was wrought in the olden days when Arthur ruled the land – and so it will be again when the hours of his kingdom shall come to pass.'

I try to take that in. Like *real* magic, in *real* time – the second coming of King Arthur – and all that.

'But Oswald knows, only too well, that he cannot find the Throne or sit upon it, unless he defeats those who protect it from falling into the hands of such a one as he.'

Oh crikey – rewind – strike through ~~the second coming of King Arthur~~ and read the first coming of King Oswald!

'And the Throne's greatest defender is the Red Dragon. For he has sworn to fight Oswald in his dragon form, to match dragon fire against dragon ice, to strike claw for claw, tooth for tooth for all eternity.'

But where is Henry?

'Though, I see no sign of the Red Dragon in these leaves,' says Gran, as if reading my thoughts.

On no … Henry isn't there!

Eleven

Gran lifts her piping to her lips, 'Take courage,' she reminds me. 'Though we know not the fate of Y Ddraig Goch, there are other defenders of Wales and the Throne too; there is St David and Owain, and most important of all, the Cave of the Sleeping Knights.'

'The Cave of the Sleeping Knights,' I say, careful to use my piping too. 'But surely that's just a King Arthur fairy story?'

'This very mountain, Snowdon, is the place where Arthur died,' Gran says. 'He was shot down in Bwlch y Saethau above Cribau – you know that.'

Actually I didn't, or if I did, I'd forgotten it.

George kindly strokes my arm. 'It's because you didn't go to junior school here.' He's practising a new technique of speaking into the pipe sideways. 'We had to do it in

Class Three: *Le Morte d'Arthur*, shortened edition. We all got a trip to Crib Goch and ate Marmite sandwiches.'

'Everybody ate Marmite sandwiches?'

'Everybody who mattered,' whispers George.

'What's the story then?' I ask.

'Arthur's final battle is said to have taken place on Snowdon.' George angles his piping so that I can feel his breath on my cheek. 'One story says that he died at Tregalan, where he was brought down by a hail of enemy arrows at a pass. Oww, ouch and all that.' His breath tickles so I push the piping aside.

'To this day that valley is called Bwlch y Saethau, or Pass of the Arrows. Anyway Arthur's knights covered his body with a cairn of stones. It used to be known as Carnedd Arthur or Arthur's Cairn. Are you getting the picture?'

Like, obviously. I know this mountain, every inch of it. I know Bwlch y Saethau even better than George does. I just never knew the full Arthur bit, and anyway, Carnedd Arthur – the cairn – isn't there anymore. So ner.

'After his death,' continues George, now deliberately blowing through the pipe all over my face in swirly patterns, 'all Arthur's knights, who were pure in heart, sealed themselves in a cave below the summit of Y Lliwedd, where to this day they slumber, fully armoured, ready to fight

106

at their king's side when he awakens to save Wales in her hour of greatest need.'

'OMG!' I hiss. 'A whole cave full of fit, pure, lovely, lush, strong, brave, sexy men ... cripes! Does Sheila know?'

Sheila's my friend who is not my friend. Remember? She is a cow not at all considerate when it comes to boys. She thinks every male from Llanberis to London belongs to her.

'I don't know what this thing is between you and Sheila,' says George, 'she seems like a very nice girl.'

I know George is trying to wind me up. He knows very well how Sheila tried to stitch me up (however much she protests her innocence). Plus he knows she's always had the hots for Henry. And come to think of it: *any* boy I've ever looked at. Which obvs is V annoying.

George looks at me, all sugar-sweet and wide-eyed.

Why she has never made a play for George, I'm not sure. Maybe because she knows she'd fail. Sheila doesn't like to fail.

'Well,' says Gran, really softly into her plumbing, 'the Sleeping Knights will never let Oswald take the Golden Throne from their cave.'

So, it'll all be OK?' I ask.

'Only if we act,' hisses Gran. 'For we are part of the great puzzle of the future. I have consulted the tealeaves and I trust them more than anything. I could consult the Oracle – the Menhir of Mawr, but it will only show me visions of what might be, *if* we don't take any action.'[1]

Gran pulls her shawl closer around her. 'But one thing we must face is that it's possible the Sleeping Knights will *never* be able to defend the Throne, because Oswald plans to kill them while they sleep.'

George exhales loudly. 'News, bad news and more bad news, and you haven't finished yet, have you, Nan?'

Gran sighs. She goes across and checks the windows yet again.

'I think,' she whispers slowly, so that her breath coming out of the piping sounds like the wind sighing, 'that now Oswald knows about Ellie, he fears the power of her love. He fears that she will find a way to rescue Henry, and he is determined to act before that happens.'

And Gran is *so* right.

'But he has acted, hasn't he?' blows George. 'He's got the help of some pretty powerful witches to break Merlin's spell on Dinas Emrys.'

'So,' Gran ignores George. Instead she continues through

---

1. Of the cairn known as Carnedd Arthur, only a single stone now remains, known as the Menhir of Mawr. Legend has it that this stone shows the way to the Cave of the Sleeping Knights and has great powers including that of telling the future.

her pipe, 'he has planned well.' She yanks the curtains even tighter against the cold outside. She flicks on her old record player and the strains of her fave, Rod Stewart, croon out. 'It'll help to cover our conversation. More things might be listening than just the Coraniaid,' she says mysteriously as she draws back to the fire.

Good thinking Gran. Any self-respecting troll or goblin would have to be mental to want to listen to Rod's warbling for long.

'On 20 March it will be the vernal equinox – the first day of spring and a day of great power,' continues Gran. 'It's the time when things can renew themselves; grow strong after a winter of dying back. And this is a leap year, as well. If Oswald can raise an army, he will attack the Cave of the Sleeping Knights at the first ray of sunlight on 20 March – at the very moment darkness gives way to light.'

'How do you know that?' I ask.

'Because that day there will be equal darkness to equal light, and such balances are important in magic. It will be then, that Oswald will act. He will have the power of the witches with him, for their day doesn't end until sunrise, and he will have the influence of Draco behind him, for at that hour Polaris must shift. Oswald will use these advantages to strike and slay all the knights, then he will be able to seize the Golden Throne.'

'But Nan,' George starts tickling my feet for some reason. 'Apparently the Golden Throne isn't in the cave. That's what we learned in school. Merlin took it and hid it among the cliffs north of Crib-y-Ddysgl, under Garnedd Ugain, just in case.'

Gran nods. 'That may be true, but it may not be. Though, with Merlin's High Magick broken, no hiding place is safe. In any case, first Oswald must get rid of his enemies.' Gran stares thoughtfully at the saucer again. 'He has somehow disposed of Henry, so his next plan will be to defeat the knights, by any means he can.

My heart skips a beat. *Disposed of Henry.*

'But,' argues George, skilfully tilting his piping so that it looks as if he is blowing a flute. 'The Sleepers in the cave are … well … asleep, so they're not much of a threat, are they?'

'But Sior,' reminds Gran, 'they can be woken up.'

I breathe in deeply, remind myself to be strong: nobody can dispose of Henry for very long.

'Yeah,' I say poking George with my piping, 'nobody is going to carry on having a nap when the Golden Throne is under attack, are they?'

'Ellie, use the copper piping properly,' reminds Gran. 'The Coraniaid are always listening.'

'OK, fair point,' says George, pointedly hissing through his piping.

'There's a bell in the cave, and anyone who enters knocks against it. That wakes the knights up, and as they sleep standing up, leaning on their shields, they are all ready to go,' adds Gran.

'WOW!' blows George. 'All up-an-at-it! All Bam! Boom! Kazap!'

Gran sighs. 'Oswald would have no chance of success if the High Magick was still in place, for none can enter that cave without ringing that bell. But now, if he can raise his army, why, he could send in the Brenin Llwyd; he could summon the ghostly nuns of the Black Boy Inn to strangle the Sleepers; he could send in the Cŵn Annwn to rip out their throats.'[2]

'The Cŵn Annwn?' asks George.

Phew, at least there are some legends that I know and he doesn't.

'The hellhounds – the white wolves of Snowdonia. Mostly they hunt on Cadair Idris. They are evil creatures that serve Gwyn ap Nudd,' I say, raising one finger up and stroking the air in victory.

'But those that belong to the Olde Deepe Magicke are

---

2. In Welsh mythology, the Cŵn Annwn are the white spectral hounds of Gwyn ap Nudd, the King of the Otherworld. The white wolves hunt on specific nights such as those of St John, All Saints, Christmas, New Year, St Agnes, St David … in the winter … chasing the souls of their unfortunate victims in the after life …

not always willing to serve,' muses Gran. 'He will need the witches to weave very powerful spells … '

'That is *so* not one up to you,' retorts George mimicking me. 'I'm like a billion ahead, already.'

'But,' I stop. I think of the howling noises last night; that eerie baying before the rocks fell. The Cwn Annwn might hunt *mostly* on Cadair Idris, but with the High Magick broken, the whole of Snowdonia must be their hunting ground by now.

'It is no use saying "but",' sighs Gran. 'If we cannot alert the defenders of Wales and rally them to the standing stone, the Menhir of Mawr, to guard the Cave of the Sleeping Knights by dawn on 20 March, and there undo the spell cast by the witches, Oswald will win.'

The defenders of Wales. 'We need you, Henry,' I whisper.

'Yes, we need him,' snaps Gran so her piping positively rings. 'And if you are going to insist on bringing him into every conversation, I wish sometimes you'd call him by his Welsh name.'

'His Welsh name?' I say. 'Y Ddraig Goch?'

'No. *Hendre.* In Welsh it means "the home in times of winter". Winter is when we need defending against many evils. *Hendre* is the name we give to those who defend the home.'

'Oh,' I blink. 'I never knew.'

I'm not sure I can get used to it either. I prefer Henry.

'Gran,' hisses George, 'there's still something you're leaving out, isn't there?'

Gran nods, stares again at the tealeaves. 'The last bit is very hard news,' she whispers.

'Just say it,' breathes George.

'Ellie is in mortal danger.'

George goes very very still.

'And you are too, Sior.'

Outside the wind howls down from the mountain.

'Oswald fears her love will triumph even over the Olde Deepe Magicke.'

'Gran,' warns George, 'we need to know everything.'

Grans sighs, adjusts her piping. 'The leaves say blood will be spilt, and if Ellie loses faith, for even a fraction of a second, she and all those around her will die.'

The flames in the fireplace gutter as if the *breath of death* has suddenly shot down the chimney. Gran starts, the saucer crashes to the floor, shatters. The tealeaves splatter on the hearthrug.

Gran looks away. I think she's biting her lip. 'You only have three days,' she finishes.

Three days to find Henry.

Three days to rally the forces of good.

Three days to undo the witches' spell.

'Oh, no!' I wail. 'The 20th is the day I have to go back to court!'

Twelve

ELLIE'S PHONE 1 March 14.17

Status: Unavailable Foreva (well, seventy-two years or possibly less if H is around and still <3 s me)

Recent updates:

Rhiannon

I'm sorry. I really am.

Sheila

Where are you – you old hag-bag – don't make me have to ask you twice!!!!!!!!!!?

Meryl

Glad yr OK – got revision to do ☹

'There is nothing for it Elles,' says George. 'We'll have to go down and confront Rhiannon.'

'Ugh,' I groan.

'We need answers. It's the only way we can start to figure out what's happened to ol' Hen.'

'Don't call him "Hen".'

'Why not? He's pretty foul,' grins George.

That is so *not* funny. I am not going to acknowledge it. George may be jealous. He may even love me the way I love Henry. (And I love him too; just not like that.) But there are limits.

'Plus he can flap his wings,' continues George.

Now I am officially annoyed.

'Take your copper piping and be back before dark,' says Granny Jones. 'I'll see what charms I can make, and what help can be summoned to keep you both safe.'

I don't need to ask why.

'If we've only got three days and today is one of them,' says George, 'we'd better get going.'

'Right,' I say. I am usually a pretty big coward when it comes to confrontations. But Rhiannon has got this coming. *How could she do that to me?* The thought of driving up to her dad's hotel, getting out and giving the Land Rover door a good hefty slam and stamping into the foyer, suddenly gives me one hell of a rush. Plus I am annoyed.

Serve her right. How *could* she? Me – her bestie! The one

who was willing to leave her lovely, warm, comfy, remote, wonderful family home in the middle of the night – and not *any* old night, mind you – but a rotten, cold, creepy night, and get on a freezing, nasty old mountain bike, which by the way, I have not forgotten, is now gone forever and wasn't all that nasty anyway – and like I said, cycle over treacherous, icy, haunted, spooky, scary mountains, chased by weird things, avoiding rockfalls, only to be falsely accused of something hideous!

Oh yes, I *definitely* have a few things to say to Rhiannon.

'Go easy on her, old girl,' says George.

I flash him a look. The look says: *Don't* tell *me* what to do. And then I flash him another look, which says: You Had Better Choose Whose Side You Are On, George.

And I know there's no contest anyway. But you see George is always Mr Nice Guy – and because he knows that Rhiannon is totally bonkers about him, he's always trying to defend her, which is weird logic, but I think it's really a guilt complex. Sort of: I feel so totally bad that I am *not* in love with you, that I want to make everything else very *easy* for you, including making excuses to the girl who I really do *love* and thereby making her mad at me, which is very upsetting.

Mr Nice Guy with an Uneasy Conscience.

George pulls a smirky kind of slightly sorry grin. 'I better take my axe, then,' he says, 'in case things get unpleasant.'

'Feel free,' I say. 'I'm going to be slicing someone's head off, myself.'

Gran leaves us at the door. 'Be very careful,' she says. 'If I'm not here when you get back, the key will be in the usual place. I am going up on to the mountain later to look for insects.'

As you do.

When the whole of Britain is under threat.

I catch George's eye, as he sticks a finger out of either side of his forehead. He waggles them, as if he is waving around insect antenna, and I get the giggles. I do not know why George always has to be so immature. Or why it has the ability to reduce me to childish giggling.

'WOW, that is sooo fascinating, Nan,' says George. 'What sort of insects? Bugs? Beetles? Or are you after a few ants?'

Gran sighs, and says, 'If only you had read the *Mabinogion*, Sior, it would be a lot easier, but as you haven't, and I don't have time to instruct you, I will have to go and look for the insects myself.'

As she turns around and closes the front door behind her, George calls out, 'Ellie prefers worms. If you see the flying variety ... '

We climb into the Land Rover. George starts it up. I look out across the hills, deep shadows are creeping into the valleys. A chill wind drills through the fleece of my jacket. It's only three weeks (days for me, thanks to that *fabulous* witches spell) 'til 20 March and the first day of spring. And right now it feels like we are in the middle of the deepest, coldest winter ever.

Thirteen

It only takes us half an hour to get down off the mountain and through Llanberis. Soon we are on to the main approach to the Pen-y-Mynydd-Gwryd Hotel. That's Welsh for the head of the mountain bottom or fathom-deep hotel, which is a stupid name, but differentiates it from the Pen-y-Mynydd Hotel, which is at the top of the mountain, obviously.

George glances at me out of the corner of his eyes. 'What's the plan?' he asks.

'I don't know about your plan,' I say. 'My plan is pretty simple – it involves one hefty punch on one pretty little nose.'

'You can't mean that,' says George.

'Try me,' I return.

'Aw, don't tell me we drove all the way down here, just to

spoil Rhiannon's good looks now, did we?' says George.

'First things first,' I respond, throwing him a mean-ass look.

But really, I suppose not. Because if she's got a broken nose, she won't be able to speak properly, and we need her to explain herself, plus tell us what happened. *Everything* this time. I mean, *all of it*.

'OK,' I say, 'I'll behave myself.'

'That's my Elles,' says George. 'Just let me do the talking.'

He's probably right. I'm sure he can get a lot more out of Rhiannon just by smiling at her than I could with all the nose punches imaginable, even chucking a few broken teeth into the bargain.

'In fact,' says George, 'I've got a good idea. Why don't you just stay in the Land Rover and let me handle it?'

'Think again,' I say. 'There is *no way* that I am not going to be there. If she's got news about Henry, I'm going to hear it.'

George sighs. 'Come on then. Let's get this over with.'

We get down from the Land Rover. I give the door a big slam. It feels very satisfying. I could have slammed it a lot harder, but it is Mum's after all, and it's not in the best shape. So too much slamming might finish it off. And that would be another problem we don't need.

We walk up the main steps of the Pen-y-Mynydd-Gwryd Hotel. I look at the place where the two stone dragons used to stand. I remember how they cracked last New Year's Eve. There are two large urns there now, filled with frozen flowers. I think of Henry. I stick my chin up, put my shoulders back. If Rhiannon thinks she can shop me to the police and then come back and have an easy time of it, she's got another think coming.

Inside the Pen-y-Mynydd-Gwryd Hotel, a thick Persian-style carpet covers the floor of the main foyer. Stags' heads with their tangle of antlers sit high on the walls of the great staircase. Through an arched doorway, I can see the conservatory. The tables and chairs are all laid out in cosy clusters.

The lady at the reception desk looks across at us, enquiringly. She knows us by sight and picks up the phone. 'Friends here to see you, Miss Rhiannon,' she says into the receiver.

I hear Rhiannon's voice, on the other end of the phone. 'What friends?' She sounds cross.

I grab the phone off the receptionist. 'It's me, vomit-face,' I say, 'and if you don't want a big scene, you'll come down and talk to us right now.'

I hear a distinct wail down the line, then Rhiannon's

voice very clearly: 'Is George with you?'

'Yes.'

'*What have you told him?*' I smile as I hear a satisfying note of panic in her voice.

'What do you think, dummy?'

I hear more wailing and Rhiannon saying, 'OK. OKAAAY. I'll come. Go into the conservatory. Find a table. Don't cause a fuss, *Ellie???* Pleeeeeeease. This is my dad's business, right?'

'You started it,' I snap.

'OK. Just wait. I'm coming.'

The truth is, I would actually quite like to cause a very *big* fuss, and I am not entirely sure that I *won't* cause one. So I hand the receiver back to the receptionist, grab George by the arm, and give him a look: You Will Be There. On My Side. Whatever Happens.

Together we go through the grand hall and into the conservatory. We pick the far end of it, by the doors that lead to the path that runs to the ornamental lake. We choose the table furthest away from everywhere and sit to wait for Rhiannon.

We don't have to wait very long. Rhiannon joins us in less than five minutes. That must be a record even for her. I can see she's been crying.

But, like, so *what*?

She hasn't got her eyelashes on. She hasn't bothered with lipstick. Her hair is all stretched back into a ponytail. I do notice she's managed to put a cunning bit of sparkly blusher on though.

Ah! So she's playing: Poor, Poor Me I Am Too Distressed To Put On My Make-up.

Puke.

She plonks herself down on the seat beside us, waves to the waiter and orders us all Coca-Cola and a large plate of munchies. Then she turns to George and fixes him with limpid eyes. I just watch.

'You don't believe *everything* you've heard, George,' she says, 'do you? You know *every* story has two sides.'

I nearly choke on my soda.

'You're so lovely, I know you won't believe *anything* thing bad of *anyone. Please* don't believe bad things about me George.' Limpid eyes and a limpet hand on his arm.

I ~~retch~~ snort.

'Hey Rhi,' he says, 'did I say I believed anything bad about you?'

'OMG!' I say. 'George, how can you say that? One look from Rhiannon's big brown mollusc eyes and you forget everything we talked about.'

'No, I haven't,' he says. 'That's not fair, Ellie. You know I'm totally on your team; it's just that we really should give Rhiannon a hearing. A girl has died and that is really serious. And we need to understand how and why. We need to know Rhiannon's side of the story, don't we?'

I definitely Do Not Need To Know Rhiannon's Side Of The Story. Please don't forget I was the one who was there on the mountain when she pointed her finger at me. Oh and *accused me of murder*. I do not need to hear anything from Rhiannon, except where to find Henry and what's happened to him.

Rhiannon turns her tearful gastropods on me. 'Please, don't believe bad things about me,' she says.

Sea slime.

'Please Ellie, I did say "sorry" before I had to tell the police it was you.'

'Like that makes it OK?'

'But I *had* to.' Rhiannon's eyes are welling up. Her voice escalates several octaves.

'No, you didn't,' I say. 'You didn't *have* to do anything mean and horrible like that. Do you know what kind of a day I've had?'

Rhiannon bursts into full-blown tears. 'Do you know what kind of day, *I've* had?' she wails.

'This is not a competition on who's had the worst day,' says George. 'Let's stay focused. Fiona died. You were both on the mountain …'

'SHUT UP George!' I'm shrieking now.

'Don't start on George,' says Rhiannon, all protective and revolting. 'It's not *his* fault.'

'No, it is not *his* fault,' I say. 'It's YOURS, Rhiannon. I get up in the middle of the night. I get on my bike. I go out on my bike. I cycle at GREAT RISK to myself, all the way over to help YOU because you've got yourself into a massive problem on the other side of the mountain. And *then* when I get there, all the thanks I get is *you* telling the police that I did something that YOU KNOW I DIDN'T!'

I am officially shouting now.

Rhiannon is officially crying.

George is officially shushing.

I am officially NOT going to stop.

'I don't even know why I'm sitting here. YOU ARE TOTALLY NOT MY FRIEND ANY MORE!' I shout. 'You are TOTALLY TOTALLY TOTALLY NEVER going to be my friend again!'

I can feel that spring inside me getting more and more wound up.

'Plus, I lost my bike because that creepy man in stripy

pyjamas nicked it.'

'Now, let's take this calmly,' says George.

'Take this CALMLY?' I screech back at him.

'Don't start on George,' says Rhiannon again. 'And I'll buy you a new bike.'

'Don't tell me what to do!' I say. 'And STUFF your new bike.'

I mean. Does she think she can buy me off? I don't need her to buy me a stupid new bike, just because she has money. (I do actually. But that's not the point.)

'A GIRL DIED!' I yell. 'And do you know I've got to go back to court on 20 March to tell the world why I *didn't* kill somebody that, hang on, *I Didn't Kill!*'

'I know you didn't kill her,' says Rhiannon.

Hallelujah!

'Quick George, get out your phone. My battery is flat – guess why. I want that on tape. Say that again,' I say.

George pulls out his phone. 'This is important evidence, really Rhi,' he says.

Rhiannon looks at George. Her chin quivers. Her throat is doing all sorts of sad swallowing stuff. Tears are welling up and wobbling in her eyes. Do I Care?

'I know you didn't kill Fiona,' says Rhiannon quite clearly into the phone.

I am flabbergasted. I didn't expect us to actually get that on record quite so quickly. A surge of relief swells through me. Well, that will deal with one of the witness statements. Only another eleven to go ...

'Now,' says George, 'I know everybody is upset, and actually to tell you the truth, I'm quite upset too – but we've got into something, *way* bigger than whether or not Ellie's going to get a bike back. Even bigger than being arrested.'

'Yes,' I say to Rhiannon. 'Bigger – much bigger. Do you know anything about these mountains? No, you do not. But you think it's OK to go tramping over them and casting spells and waving wands, as if you are in some stupid primary-school play.'

'Elles,' says George, 'blaming Rhi right now, isn't going to help. It's wasting time.'

Time. Yeah, he's right. We've only got three days and today is nearly over. Hastily I glance out of the conservatory. It seems to be getting dark already.

'Where is Henry?' I force Rhiannon to look at me. 'What did you do with him?'

'What do you mean?' says Rhiannon 'What's Henry got to do with this?'

I remember that Rhiannon actually doesn't know much

about what happened at Christmas. For starters she doesn't know that Henry is – in point of fact –a dragon. So I try a different tack. 'OK,' I say, 'tell me, exactly, in complete detail, everything about last night. Go over and over it, as if I am brain dead, again and again. Let me help you. Start here: you went up to the mountain. You chanted magical spells. You sped up time. The mountain cracked open and then what?'

'It was just awful,' wails Rhiannon. 'Fiona slipped and fell.'

'And? Yes?' I say, 'Then what happened?' I shudder. *That poor poor girl.*

'The S.O. – that's the Supreme One, went down into the crevasse and … '

Rhiannon pauses.

'Yesss?' I add.

'I'm trying to remember,' wails Rhiannon. 'It was soooo *awful.* She seemed to be looking for something … '

'Yesss?' I continue.

'Well, I think she found it, because she held something up.'

'Can you describe it?' I say.

'It was sort of a lumpy and black and … nothing really. I thought it was a rock. That's all.'

'Did you see any … ' I hesitate, but Henry is more

important than whether Rhiannon thinks I'm mental, so I continue. 'Did you see any dragons by any chance? A red one perhaps?'

Rhiannon looks at me. Her eyes go wide and weird. She pulls a random expression with her mouth. She rolls her eyes. She looks at George for help.

God bless George. He just nods his head, like it's a perfectly sensible question.

Rhi shakes her head. 'No dragons.'

'So what did you see?' I ask.

'Well, first of all, I heard a shriek. It was horrible. Then I thought I saw yellow eyes. And I thought I heard giant teeth or claws scraping. And then there was a horrible smell. And it looked like – from the lip of the abyss – some foul creature was crawling out. It had huge wings and a spiny neck and hideous eyes.'

'Like a dragon?'

Rhiannon twists up her mouth. 'Sort of, but it wasn't cute and cuddly and red and like the Welsh Dragon. It was like a worm, but like obviously way bigger. But … '

'Yes?'

'But then Fiona fell in, or maybe she had already fallen – it's like it all happened at once, like time had somehow come to a full stop. There was crashing and screaming and a kind of earth tremor – I think I imagined all that, because you know, I was in *shock* and we'd all drunk some potion. And I don't actually think the worm thing did crawl out of anywhere – in fact the Supreme One said it didn't, and we were to forget any visiony thingies because that was just the potion.'

'Ha!' I say. 'Your Supreme One is trying to brainwash you. Something crawled out of that den all right.'

Rhiannon lifts one shoulder, then lets it fall.

'Was there anything else, Rhi?' says George. 'Try to remember.'

'There was a rush of heat, like something shooting past towards the sky. Then it got all misty.'

'But no Red Dragon?' I insist.

I can't believe it. *Henry was in the lair.* If Oswald the White Dragon was there and crawled out, what happened to Henry?

For one dreadful second I imagine he died and Oswald ate him, but the thought is so foul, it makes me want to vomit.

'But that wasn't actually all,' says Rhiannon, very quietly.

'OK,' I say patiently, 'tell me the rest.'

'Do you promise to keep it a secret?' asks Rhiannon.

'*What?*' I ask, less patiently.

'You see, if the Supreme One finds out that I told you …'

Rhiannon's voice trails off. Her eyes dart around the room. She makes the sign of the cross over her heart, which is weird, because she is not religious, although apparently she *is* a witch.

'We promise,' says George.

'I don't know if *I* do,' I say. 'If it affects Henry, *I'm* not promising anything.'

'Please?' Rhiannon looks so pitiful, like she's truly afraid of something.

If I don't promise, she might not tell me.

'OK,' I say. I have my fingers cunningly crossed behind my back.

'Well, after the police took you, and I'd finished making my statement, we – I mean the whole coven – all had to meet up again.'

'Again?'

'Today, up on the mountain – behind your place.'

'Behind *my* place?' I say? 'Why?'

'We all had to go out to this rock thing and bury some-thing.'

'*Bury* something?' I realise I'm parroting everything Rhi says.

'Yes,' she says, 'we had to go and bury that black thing.'

'Go on,' I say.

'We had to put everything else on hold, and I was really *tired*.' Rhiannon's voice develops a slight whinge.

'Where exactly?' I say.

'Do you know the place you went to?' says George.

'Of course I do,' says Rhiannon.

'Right,' says George, 'we're going to dig it up. Get your hat and coat and gloves, because it's cold out there. You're coming with us to show us the place, right now.'

'RIGHT NOW?' screeches Rhiannon.

'Yes,' I say. 'Right. Now.'

It's obvious Rhiannon doesn't have a clue how serious this is. She doesn't have a clue what they buried either.

Neither do I for that matter, though I'm beginning to work it out.

'Apart from burying the black thing, did you cast a spell or anything again?' I ask. I figure if they did, it'd be better if we knew about it.

'Yes,' mumbles Rhiannon.

'Can you remember it?'

'Mostly,' says Rhiannon.

'So?'

'We had to chant –

"Round and round and round we go

To bury our secret down below

At the Black Stone, where legends start

We inter the dragon's heart."

'Or something like that, but better.'

The dragon's heart?

A cold shiver goes through me.

'You went to bury a dragon's heart under the Black Stone?'
I ask.

I don't know what I'm thinking. I don't understand
anything. I don't want to think that a blackish lump was
the shining heart I remember.

Henry's heart?

Surely not.

But then, I remember that anonymous text I got up on
the pass.

So where is your BF then? I told you Hands Off or it was WAR.

Well, eat your heart out GF cos his <3 belongs to me now.

A shiver runs down my spine: *'his <3 belongs to me now'*.

And the Maen Du'r Arddu. The Black Stone of the Darkness.[1]

No Henry. A blackish lump. Broken crystals. Evil Sir Oswald.

---

1. There is a Black Lake, a Black Precipice and a Black Stone of the Swarthy – *Llyn Pur, Clogwyn Du'r Arddu* and *Maen Du'r Arddu* near Lower Llanberis. In ancient times, some used to worship at the Black Stone and it is sometimes called 'Black Pete' or 'Pierre du Diable' – The Devil's Stone.

Blood of a sacrifice. An interment. At the creepy Black Stone. A heart that was mine.

Was meant to be mine.

What does it all mean?

'Pull your boots on, Rhiannon.' I say. 'You're taking us to exactly the place where you buried that dragon's heart, and you've got a decision to make: either you're on our side, with George and me, or you're the enemy.'

Fourteen

It's absolutely dreadful in the Land Rover.

Rhiannon is sitting in the back, looking even more puffy-eyed and tearful than ever. Every few metres, she makes a low little moan and whimpers out, 'I am so sorry'.

Like that fools anyone.

'It wasn't my fault,' she blubs.

Puke.

'The Supreme One threatened me.'

Zillion eye-rolls.

'What was I *supposed* to do? I was scared she'd push me in the hole.'

Bored now.

'And I didn't mean it. I was always going to take my statement back.'

Whatevs.

'Please don't tell the Supreme One.'

Yawn.

To which George, being the darling he is, tries to cheer her up by saying, '*Nobody* is going to push you in a hole or bully you, Rhi. Not with me around. But you shouldn't have done it. Firstly, because that poor girl's family won't know what to believe. Secondly, it really is very serious. Thirdly, it's going to look bad – you withdrawing your statement when eleven others haven't. Also, it's really upset Ellie.'

Yes. It. Has.

I am sitting in the front and not listening to all her moaning. I am not feeling sorry for her. That is because I have not forgiven her. Not yet. Especially when she says: 'Do you think the police will charge me for wasting police time, then?'

It is so obvious she is still worrying about *herself* and not worrying about Fiona – or Fiona's family, or me, and how all her stupid witchy stuff has led to this. So therefore she's not really sorry at all. Plus she just doesn't want George to think badly of her. Plus she probably won't change her statement if the Supreme One has another go at her. That is the entire sum of how much I matter to her. Full stop.

'Who is the Supreme One anyway?' I say.

'I don't know,' moans Rhiannon. 'She always had a mask on and spoke in a weird voice.'

'But surely you noticed something?' asks George.

Rhiannon starts weeping again and complains that he's sounding 'cross'.

I do not sigh. I do not roll my eyes. I do not forget that this is not about Rhiannon or me.

'So how did this Supreme One persuade you and the others to join this coven?' I say.

'She contacted me online,' whispers Rhi.

'So?'

'That's it.'

'What, and told you to go up to Dinas Emrys in the middle of the night?'

Rhiannon sends me an evil look. Then rolls her eyes in the direction of the back of George's head.

Ah, I get it.

A love spell.

Oblivious, George carries on driving. He tries to keep everybody cheerful. He starts saying, 'Oh well, at least we are all together'. And then, 'At least we've started to put the problem right'.

Until I have to mutter, 'Oh for Christ's sake, shut up!'

Rhiannon shakes her head at me and makes Please Don't Tell George eyes.

I just want answers: 'Well, what *do* you know about the Supreme One, then?' I ask. 'Who is this person who can destroy a dragons' den?'

'I don't know,' sobs Rhiannon. 'I told you, she always wore a mask.'

'Well, try and tell me what you can,' I say.

'Her mask was all lacy and it had like raven wings, like a carnival sort of type-thing. We all wore masks too,' wails Rhiannon.

'Yes, but was she tall, small, fat, thin … ' I am not being facetious. I really want to know.

Rhiannon suddenly yanks at George's arm, as if she's had a eureka moment. The car swerves. 'WE ALL WORE MASKS! Do you think she knows who I *really* am? Like my address and everything? She only knew my username, so maybe she doesn't!'

'Hardly,' I say. 'If she can destroy half of Snowdon, and awake all the Olde Deepe Magicke, I think she can work out who *you* are.'

'What was your username?' asks George more kindly.

'Rhiannon,' says Rhiannon.

'I rest my case,' I say.

Rhiannon slumps back, starts sniffing again.

We leave Llanberis and head up towards our farm. Around us, the mountains close in. Clouds settle on the peaks. I don't like the way they are gathering over the summit of Snowdon. Even the nearby slopes seem to be rapidly disappearing into sheets of rolling white mist.

'Will you know the way?' I ask Rhi. 'Cos, it's gonna be very misty.'

Before she can answer, George butts in: 'What about her voice?' he asks. 'Did she have an accent? Or a lisp ... '

'No, she spoke through an interpreter,' moans Rhiannon.

'An interpreter?' I say (tbh, quite snappily – I know – please don't judge. I can only say in my defence that I'd had a bad day).

'Not a person,' says Rhiannon. 'A sort of pipe thing. It looked like a long piece of brass, or some kind of copper horn. It changed her voice.'

'So,' responds George, 'she's not the only one who wants

to stop the Coraniaid from hearing her plans, then.'

Cripes. *We've not been using the copper piping!* Gran is going to be sooo mad with us.

'The *what*?' says Rhiannon.

I don't bother explaining. It's all too much. Plus I'm not sure I can get Rhiannon up to speed, the mood she's in. 'So whose side is this Supreme One on?' I say, mostly to George.

I thought there were only two sides. Henry's and mine: with Granny Jones and George and everyone good and lovely. And then Oswald's side: with everyone revolting and evil.

But suddenly I think of the Brenin Llwydd and his grey riders. Whose side are *they* on? And are they gathering, watching our Land Rover right now, deciding where and how and when they will swoop down on us?

'How long have we got until dark?' George asks in a worried voice, as we pull off the main road and on to our side of Snowdon. 'How far exactly, up the mountain, did you bury this thing, Rhiannon?'

He seems to be calculating whether to drive on past my place and head for Gran's.

I, for one, am totally sure that we should not stay out after dark. I am sure Gran would say COME HOME

RIGHT NOW. In caps. But if a coven of hateful witches has buried my Henry's heart out on the mountainside, I am not going to leave it there for one second longer than I have to.

And after all, I reason to myself, I went out last night, I biked all the way up through the pass, and I survived.

Didn't I?

I force myself to forget about the terrible howling, forget about rockfall. If I can get on my bike at midnight on 29 February and brave all those scary things to save Rhiannon, what more can't I do to save Henry?

'I don't like this place,' says Rhiannon suddenly. 'It's like we're being watched.'

I don't contradict her. I too have the same weird oppressive feeling, like something really is watching us.

I shiver.

The mists close in. The bracken, dark red against the snow, looks like dried blood.

George doesn't laugh, either. He frowns and draws his eyebrows together. Have I told you before that George has the most amazingly fantastic eyebrows? Well, he has (though I still don't fancy him – obvs). Right now, they look like a kid's drawing of a seagull; all meeting in the middle, in one, long, dark, expressive line.

Anyway, all of a sudden, as he frowns, he pushes his shoulder blades back against the car seat and rubs them, as if they're sore. I know that movement. It's one I make sometimes, when I get the feeling that something is running its fingers down my spine.

I peer out of the car window, trying not to let my imagination run wild. It would be only too easy to think something is moving among the rocks outside; something that is managing to keep just out of sight.

We've barely moved a few more yards up the track, when George points to his right. 'Look! Something is watching us!'

I swing round and look out. Perched on a big rock is a bird. Its head is thrust to one side and it's staring straight at us. Its eye is round and dark and does not blink.

'It's a carrion crow,' mutters George.

I shudder. I hate crows. I hate the way they tear out the eyes of newborn lambs. I hate that.

As we pass the rock, the crow doesn't move. Not one of its feathers stirs. It doesn't blink its eye even. But after we pass, it makes one elated hop and lets out a shrill caw. A horrid feeling curls itself into my stomach. That shrill caw feels like an announcement, an update for other things, hidden in the mist, waiting for us up on the mountain.

I remember Gran's reading: 'This *crow* or *raven* is an ill omen, a warning, or an ambush.'

'Let's stay on our guard,' I whisper to George.

'It took us about an hour to walk there.' Rhiannon says bravely. I can see that she's trying very hard not to let that crow frighten her too. Something inside me starts to relent. After all, she was my very best bestie.

'An hour?' I say.

'About that, I think,' says Rhiannon. 'Maybe more.'

I smile. Rhiannon's not a mountain girl, like me. She doesn't know every rock and tussock. Plus she doesn't know all the shortcuts either. The whole coven must have taken the long way round to reach the Maen Du'r Arddu – the Black Stone. The idea of a bunch of girls all dressed up as witches, traipsing through heather and bracken, getting stuck in bog, going cross-country from the Llanberis path, makes me smile.

But I don't indulge myself. I don't turn to Rhiannon and say, 'Cripes! That must have made you all very muddy and cross. Why didn't you use your broomsticks?' You see, I haven't totally forgiven her yet. Although I think I might be softening a little.

'I know a shortcut,' I say. 'We'll park the car at my place, and take the path through the upper pasture, it'll save a load of time.'

George looks doubtful. He pulls a face. He steers the Land Rover along the twisting track.

'I'm not really sure, Ellie,' he says. 'That may not be such a good idea. Why don't we wait and go tomorrow morning, at first light?'

Tomorrow? At first light?

Is he loony?

I am sooooo not going to agree to that. But I take a moment to think of the best way to convince him.

'Let's figure out how far we'll have to go,' I say.

'We've got about an hour,' says George. 'After that the sun will go down behind the mountain and it'll get very dark.'

'Try to describe exactly where you went,' I say to Rhiannon. I'm buying a bit of time. Trying to think of a way to convince George.

'Well, we just kept on going past your place up as far as the track would go,' Rhiannon pauses. 'And then we kept on going towards that dark brackish sort of lake – under that black cliff. You know *that* place,' says Rhiannon.

I know that place very well. Clogwyn Du'r Arddu, the Black Cliff of the Darkness; one of the most frightening places on Snowdon.

'The Supreme One said it was a magical spot, that the stone had ancient properties, and if we buried the dragon's heart there, it would stay protected by the darkness of that cliff and some old witchy stuff … ' Rhiannon's voice trails off.

I know exactly where she means.

'That's the Maen Du'r Arddu. The Black Stone of the Darkness. And the witch associated with it was called Canrig Bwt. Anyway it's way before you get to the Black Cliff. It's not far up past my place,' I say to George. I look at him. I place my hand on his shoulder, 'I think we can make it within the hour.'

Crikey. I am such a liar. There is no way we can get up to the Black Stone and back before it's pitch dark.

'Please, let's go there straightaway,' I say.

I think George hears the desperation in my voice. I think Rhiannon hears it too. She stops sniffling and says, 'OK' in a sad, surprised sort of way.

'Righty-ho, then,' says George.

That's the thing I love about George. He is always ready for anything, even if he doesn't think it's a good idea.

'We'll need to leave the Land Rover a bit nearer than your place, and cut across country,' he says.

Over the ridge, where the bracken grows really thick

in a red-brown carpet, I catch a glimpse of my place. Mist clings to the lawn around the house. The air lies still and heavy over the buildings, as if a thunderstorm is waiting to explode. Only the whine of the windscreen wipers punctuates the silence, as they clear the sleet settling on the windscreen.

It is only as we go past the end of the long drive up to the farmhouse that I remember.

'Wait!' I shout.

'What?' says George.

'The newborns!' I say. 'We brought them in because of the cold.'

'When? Where?' asks George.

'The lambs,' I say. 'I was supposed to feed them. They'll be thirsty, hungry. We must go up to my place right now.'

'OK,' says George, 'I'll give you a hand.'

See what I mean?

Mr Totally Lovely Nice Guy.

'We're not going to be able to get to the stone anyway,' says Rhiannon from the back of the Land Rover.

'Why?' I ask.

'Because the Supreme One laid charms all around it. And she wrote words in the air, which will protect it 'til she comes back. And she said she'd put the watchers on it too.'

Rhiannon's voice shakes a little.

'Well, we'll just have to try,' I say.

We start the long drive up towards our farm. Grey stone walls blend into grey mist. I fret about the lambs; remember how this morning they were all so warm and cuddly.

As soon as we get into the yard, I know something is wrong.

Firstly there is a thick, sweet smell of something earthy, like the scent of fox. And secondly, the shed to the newborns is unlatched. I know I didn't leave it that way.

And then I notice tracks in the snow.

The tracks of dogs, many dogs – and we only have one dog, Ceri, and she should be in the farmhouse.

My heart beats faster. A horrible cold shiver goes down my back; all those tiny, little, snuggling, sweet-smelling lambs.

And Ceri?

It's absolutely quiet.

Not a sound.

Only the distant call of that crow again. And it should *not* be silent. The whole yard should be filled with the sound of bleating: the soft snuffly snorts of the mother ewes, the tiny mewings of newborn lambs.

Only silence.

I race to the sheds.

'Wait! Hang on Ellie!' calls George. 'Don't go in!'

Rhiannon screams.

I wheel around. There, to one side of the shed, is the carcass of a ewe, ripped open from her neck right down to her belly. Blood smears the snow. Her throat has been chewed out.

'No!' I cry. 'NOOOO!'

My heart. I can't think. Breathe. *I can't breathe.* Not my lambs. I can't stop myself. I race to the sheds, yank at the door. It's already flapping on its hinges.

Inside I smell it: blood and death.

The smell of suffering.

I flick on the shed light.

It's the worst mess I've ever seen: every single one of our ewes, mauled to pieces. Every single one of our new lambs …

My babies.

My sweet cuddly little newborn babies.

My hands start shaking, my knees dissolve, can't seem to hold me.

I can't believe what I'm seeing.

All my little ones.

My heart pounds.

I can't believe it.

'Steady,' says George. He places a hand on my shoulder. 'We need to get out of here fast,' he says.

'NO! *My little lambs*,' I cry. 'Maybe one's left. Please, let me look. Maybe one's survived.'

'Ellie,' says George, 'this wasn't done by any stray dog. Look at the way they've been savaged. Even an Alsatian couldn't rip their heads off like that. And can't you smell it? Whatever creature did this, is still around.'

I don't listen. I struggle through the mess. Lift limp, still-warm carcasses — *Oh still so warm.*

Maybe cuddled beneath one is a tiny, surviving baby lamb?

'Let's get out of here. Please Ellie.'

But I shake George's arm off. I pull and tear and sob and there's sheep's blood on my hands and fleece stuck to my fingers and there's nothing. *Nothing.* I hear the Land Rover door slam. I hear Rhiannon screaming. And I can't stop searching. I look again and again among the strewn bodies. I kick the straw aside. I pull at bloody carcasses hoping for a live, nestling newborn ...

Nothing.

Not one.

All slain. All throats ripped out. All bloodstained coats.

'We must get out. Now,' insists George. 'Stop, Ellie. Listen!' George grabs hold of my arm.

And I do stop. I lift up my head and I hear it. A long, drawn-out, eerie howling.

And I remember Ceri.

Ceri, our dog, stuck in the farmhouse.

'Ellie, I'm telling you,' George drags me. 'We need to *leave*, get back into the Land Rover.' He opens his backpack, removes his axe.

'I'm going to get Ceri.'

I don't wait for an answer. I race to the farmhouse. Out of the corner of my eye, I see something glinting through the mist. I scrabble for the key above the lintel and open the front door.

Thank God! Thank God!

Ceri jumps up at me, licks my face, wags her tail, winds around my legs, barks, turns round in circles and throws herself repeatedly at my chest. I have never seen her so pleased to see me. She's shivering all over, looks in a terrible state.

'Come on,' I say, 'I'm not leaving you here.'

I grab her lead. I grab her. I don't stop for anything else. I slam the door behind me. George and Rhiannon are there. We turn; get past the barn and the race for the Land Rover.

But it is too late.

The whole yard field is filled with them.

Cadaverous. Deadly.

I've never seen anything like these things before.

Huge wolf-like creatures.

'Stand back,' says George. He brandishes his axe above his head.

But the wolves glide eerily towards us.

Fifteen

There are more than half a dozen of them, thin, ragged. They creep towards us. The lead wolf is huge. His coat is flecked in silver, his muzzle dark, jaws open. He snarls, flashing huge incisors. Flecks of spittle hang on his coat.

All of them have wiry bodies; their heads long, pointed; ears flattened against bony skulls; mean white eyes; gaping mouths reveal rows of sharp teeth, drooling tongues. Their fish-white chests are stained wet with lambs' blood.

'Stay back.' George pushes me behind him. Ceri whimpers, hides between my legs, nearly trips me up. Rhiannon screams.

Heart racing, suddenly dizzy, I clutch at the farmhouse wall. George brandishes his axe. I stare at the creatures.

Are they wolves? *But we don't have wolves on Snowdon.*

We don't have wolves *anywhere* in Britain.

And they don't seem to care about the axe.

They don't seem to care about anything in fact.

The smell of death is everywhere. Rhiannon shrieks in impossibly high-pitched bursts. The lead creature doesn't stop, doesn't even waver. He just lets out a series of snarls, darts his eyes around and howls, hackles raised.

His fangs shine in the gloom.

George can't fight them all.

One of the creatures lunges. For a second we're rooted to the spot, but only for a second. Instinct kicks in. We race across the lawn towards the Land Rover.

'Stop!' yells George, he swings his axe low and wide around him, the creatures back off a little, crouch down and wait. He points.

I understand.

Rhiannon seems to be hyperventilating.

We've been cut off. There is no way we can make it to the Land Rover, or back to the safety of the farmhouse.

'Take the upper path!' screams George. 'Get away from the buildings!'

The path that leads to the mountain.

But I see what he means. Barns, high walls, no escape routes.

But surely they'll outrun us?

I spin around, looking for some place, somewhere safe to get to. There's nothing, just open farmyard, dead ends and hillside, beyond the dark sweep of the mountain.

Uphill and not down.

'Make for the top pasture!' I yell. I'm going to try and trap them in the lambing pen.

I edge to one side, press my back against the gate catch, make sure it's open.

'I'm going to sprint across the pen,' I hiss at George. 'Hold Ceri back. When they follow, dart out from the cover of this barn and slam the gate shut. Then head up on to the mountain.'

'No way Ellie,' says George.

'Don't worry – I'm on home territory,' I say. 'I can do this.'

I don't wait. I don't need George's permission. Gently, I push open the pen gate. I flex my legs slightly. George throws another axe slash at the wolves. I turn then I'm through the gate, and sprinting across the lambing pen.

I know they want me; I know wild animals.

And I know dogs. They have some kind of hardwired instinct, which tells them 'chase' when they see something run. These wolves are no different. Sure enough, they chase, howling into the wind, like banshees.

Into the lambing pen.

And I run like I've never run before.

The pen is not too wide; perhaps only twelve metres across, but it feels like the longest twelve metres I've ever run. At every stride I expect to feel fangs sink into my legs, feel the weight of some huge wolfish thing bring me down. My breath comes in gasps. My chest burns.

I … make … it … to the other side.

Hallelujah!

I put one hand on the top rail, and the other on the side paling. I gate-vault over the far fence and I'm amazed at my own agility.

Number one: after the stress I've gone through, I didn't think I had the energy left.

Number two: I have never been able to gate-vault over a fence successfully. (Although I've always wanted to.)

I don't even experience landing on the far side. I hear the gate click to. George did it. *We* did it, bought ourselves a few minutes.

George yells, 'Run for the hills!'

I wish I'd said, 'Run for the hills'. It's one of those lines that afterwards you'd laugh about. A long time afterwards.

If there ever was going to be an afterwards.

We run.

We fling ourselves through a gap into the top pasture, and we're bursting up the slope in a flurry of frosty dead red bracken.

How long will the lambing pen hold them?

I'm almost at the last fence. Almost. George isn't far behind. I look back at him. I'm thinking: *Run. Hide. Run. Hide. Run! Hide!* Don't let them break out.

Suddenly he is right beside me. 'Keep going, Ellie,' he hisses. 'I'll help Rhiannon.'

I leap from a drystone wall, I burst through the heather, don't bother with anything else. Ceri is beside me, yelping, her tail flat against her back legs. I'm halfway through the top pasture. I pull at sedge and leap stones. I tear into undergrowth, swerve sround boulders, rip through air like a lightning flash.

Footsteps crash behind me. *Them? Rhiannon? Is she OK?* Must be George. Brave George.

I can hear ragged breath right at my back. Something's howling. Up ahead is just mountain. I weave between boulders, zigzag, leap, twist. Once they're out, how fast can those creatures run? The ground's covered with trailers, dead, twisted stems. *Treacherous.* If I slip, I'll fall down. A wailing, shrieking tears past me. *Christ they're out!* They're coming.

Holy hell!

Our only chance is to get across the slope. Make it to the Black Stone. Keep going. I topple a pile of rocks, kick on turf. My lungs can't take it. One chance. Gasping, coughing. My chest. *My chest*. On the other side of this slope is the Black Stone: down, round a corner, past boggy streams.

One chance.

Get there.

Just run.

Just pray.

Just make it to the stone.

Rhiannon needs help. Stop? Help her? I know she's been horrible, but she is my friend.

Where is George?

Stop then. Check.

There's a deafening howl behind me. I look back. They've broken a gap in the pen. The wolves are through into the upper pasture.

The last farmyard fence may delay them for a bit.

Rhi and George are only ten metres behind me.

'There!' I point at the bank ahead. 'Get to the Black Stone. Climb it.'

I run. Take the slope. Jump over boulders. I'm in the air. I scream. My arms are outstretched in front of me. I hit the mountainside still running and tumble forward.

Get up. Keep running.

Through white icy mist, I see it. About thirty metres above us, and to our right – a high, black-topped, flat-shaped boulder standing out against the sky: the Black Stone – the stone where the witches buried Henry's heart.

Make for that! Climb on top. We'll hold them off. Beat them back.

I'm splashing through icy swamp: *Oh My God. So cold.* Stumble. Freezing water over the tops of my shoes.

I flounder up the hill. Head diagonally across the mountain slope; make for the bottom of the stone. 'George,' I yell. *'C'mon!'*

Behind him the wolves are streaming out of the farmyard. Some are trying to leap the last fence.

Finally, George, half dragging, half carrying Rhiannon, catches up.

The stone is huge and hard to climb. I lace my hands together and yell, 'You first, George. You're stronger. I'll give you a leg up, then haul us up?' George steps on my makeshift step-up. I hold hard, push.

And push.

I can feel veins popping; I'm trying so hard. George gasps as he struggles up on to the stone's level top.

At last, he's there.

Rhiannon screams, 'Now ME!' She scrabbles at the rock front. '*ME!*'

George reaches down, grabs her hand, hauls. I push her from below.

More veins pop. I'm sweating. I swear Rhi weighs a ton! She slips. Hits my shoulder. Ouch! That hurt. I shove harder.

At last.

George and Rhiannon are safe above me. I glance behind into the gloom. White shapes race up the mountainside. They're through the last fence, over the stone wall. A few more seconds and they'll be here.

Groping for a firm hold with hands, and bracing my feet beneath a sea of bracken, I too look for a way to climb up.

'Grab my hand!' yells George. He leans over, reaches out.

In reply I pick Ceri up and throw her into George's outstretched arms. She scrambles to safety on the rock.

Now me.

The wolves come, skimming up towards the bog, flattening the sedge grass. They find it difficult to check their speed, when they see that beneath the bog is a mountain stream. One spins out of control on a patch of iced-over swamp; it somersaults. The rest change tack, splash and skid through then race across to intercept me.

'ELLIE!' yells George.

Quickly I bend down, fingers fumbling beneath the heather. I scoop up rocks, pull up something out of the bracken – a length of stunted hawthorn. I yank it free and swing it straight at the lead wolf.

It gives me a second.

In that one split moment gained, George lowers half his body down, stretches out his arms. I jump and hang on. George yanks me towards him. I drag his arms, pull on him. I can feel the breath of wolf warm against my leg. Teeth snap shut.

Missed. Thank God.

My face scrapes stone. My feet scrabble at the rock surface. *Please let me make it to the top.* George pulls. The sinews in my shoulder stretch. Owwwww.

I'm on the top of the boulder, weeping and panting with George beside me. He bends over me, whispers, '*Thank God!* For a minute there I thought you were going to have to miss your court appointment.'

Above us a bird cries harshly three times – sour, angry. The wolves circle the stone with vicious yelps. I lie there, face pressed against stone, gasping.

'Sucks to be them,' says George.

'I can't get a signal on my phone!' shrieks Rhiannon.

'They'll wait us out,' I wheeze.

'I'm *cold*, George,' whispers Rhiannon.

George puts his arm round her. Rhiannon smiles.

I straighten up, pull myself into a sitting position. Ceri whimpers and inches across the rock. She lays her head on my lap. We made it. We're safe.

For now.

Safely marooned on an island of rock.

Suddenly the slopes ring with the distant sound of bells. Llanberis church maybe? Sound travels in the mountains. Bells, sweet and lovely on the cold evening air.

Of course! It's still the 1st of March – St David's Day. People in the village will be heading down to chapel, wearing their leeks, giving thanks, going to dinners, parties, eisteddfodau … [1]

Rhiannon starts sobbing. 'I'm gonna miss all the fun at the hotel!'

The wolves whimper. Something about the bells seems to spook them. A weird light spreads down the mountain. I look up towards the summit. The sun is setting fast. A curious rosy glow fills the air over the Devil's Bridge. My breath is all white clouds. The air smells sharp, of frost

---

1. An eisteddfod is a Welsh festival of literature, music and performance. The tradition of such a meeting of Welsh artists dates back to at least the twelfth century. Smaller-scale local eisteddfodau are held throughout Wales. A popular time for this is on Saint David's Day.

and cold mountain.

And there on the bridge: dark against the mist; tiny, yet surrounded by a halo of light, a figure stands. My heart misses a beat. *Henry?* I remember how yesterday I looked up and was sure I saw a figure there on the Devil's Bridge too.

Whoever it is, the wolves don't like it.

As if to drown out the bells or discourage the figure, they point their muzzles at the mountaintop and set up a continuous howling. Then they circle the stone and leap up at it, howling all the while.

One of them tries to jump high; its claws scratch on the stone as it slithers back. I cross my fingers and send up a silent prayer: 'O great Snowdon (*let it be Henry*). Please don't let these things get me. Take care of your friends, Ellie and George and Rhi. *Please*, don't let any of the wolves jump high enough to land up here.'

I look out, over the heads of the creatures. *What if it's not Henry?* We're miles away from anywhere. And the High Magick is broken. *God knows what things will stir and walk abroad tonight.*

I shiver. The sun is nearly gone. A rosy glow spreads out across the sky, like the glowing coals in Gran's hearth. All that running has made me sweat, and now the sweat is icing up. The rosy sky actually looks a lot more like the open mouth of hell than any fireside.

We can't last out here all night. We'll freeze to death.

Ceri whimpers. I cuddle her close. I squint up at the glowing figure.

I nudge George. 'Look,' I point at the Devil's Bridge. *Please let it be Henry.*

The figure moves closer. Seems to be almost floating. Not clambering over rock and heather. The wolves howl louder. What dreadful thing can spook the Cŵn Annwn?

What if it's not Henry?

Wildly I look around. Gone is any last hope of reaching safety; all about us are only mountains.

Soon it will be pitch dark.

And at our feet, are wolves.

Sixteen

All around the great rock, the wolves circle. Their baying echoes from the mountainside, drowning out the bells, drowning out even Rhiannon's sobbing. Their howls, spooky, malevolent even, seem like they're planning some unholy fate for each of us. Their wailing bores in to my bones and makes my teeth ache. Rhiannon is trembling all over. I put my arm around her too. She snuggles down between George and me. 'Hang on Rhi,' I say.

I don't bother to try and explain anything. I just say: 'This is what happens when you do stupid witchy stuff.'

I know. It's a bit finger wagging, but hey, she asked for it.

Then I feel that she needs a bit of encouragement,

so I add, 'Don't give up hope. Hope is what keeps us going, yeah?' And I squeeze her, and add, 'And don't dangle your legs over the edge like that.' She doesn't answer, just presses her trembling shoulders closer to me and pulls her feet in a few inches. I tighten my hug around her.

I look up towards the Devil's Bridge again. I don't know what I'm hoping for, what I'm not hoping for.

The fiery light still hangs around the figure. It looks like it's moving closer. Could be a trick of the light. I really hope it's not Y Cythraul (the Devil). Maybe it *could* just be a red dragon?

My heart pounds, doing some mad, fluttering dance. Against all reason, I'm still hoping to see him.

I know, don't say it: How can it be Henry?

But love makes you hope, whispers crazy stuff in your ear. It's nuts of course. And if I really did see him there yesterday does that mean he's been standing there on the Devil's Bridge during the whole of the night and all of today? Waiting for me?

Where there's love, there's hope, right? It *could* be him. The witches have messed time up. And the Devil's Bridge was our special meeting place.

I remember how I first saw him, in the mist, up there on the Devil's Bridge on Christmas Day ...

It's kind of like déjà vu. So it kind of could be true?

I squint into the gathering gloom right at the glowing spot.

'George,' I grab his shoulder. 'It's moving towards us, isn't it?'

George looks at it, then back at me, his eyes wide, like, 'now what?' But all he says is, 'We didn't use the copper piping'. He shifts slightly on the cold stone. 'It's my fault. The whole of Snowdonia must know absolutely everything about everything by now.'

Of course! Of course!

Smack self on head!

That's why the wolves were waiting for us at the farmhouse. That's why that crow was perched in the field, waiting to tip them off as soon as it saw us pass.

A new ominous growling comes from the wolves. They seem uneasy about the glowing figure.

NOTE TO SELF (in caps & underlined): Always Pay Attention To Gran And Do As She Says.

'They *can't* climb up here, can they?' shrieks Rhiannon.

I look back down to the base of the rock. The wolves are gathering at the side furthest away from the light. As they pass the lowest edge of the rock, they rise up, stand straight on their back legs. Stiff claws scratch stone. Their eyes are weirdly pale, polar blue; the insides of their ears, blood red. There's something about them that's revoltingly creepy. A prickly feeling shoots up my spine. The wolves run their muzzles over the stone, sniffing the surface and then give forth long, drawn-out howls. They raise their snouts and nose the air, breathing up at us. They *stink*!

One of them – foul, horrible, disgusting, jaws slick with spit – takes a running start and leaps up. Its back legs are so majorly powerful, the stone actually shakes. It lands only a metre below us. Its pale lips pulled back in a snarl.

For a moment it hangs there, and in that moment I see its pale eyes seem totally blind. *They have no centre. Nothing is looking out.*

A shriek escapes my lips.

I hear Rhi cry out.

I feel a yank on her body, the heavy weight of human and wolf half pulls me over.

It's got hold of her leg!

Frantically, I grip at her arm. It slithers through my hold.

'*HELP!*' she screams.

'Pull!' yells George. I grab her jacket. The material starts to rip.

I can't hang on. I can't balance on the top of the stone. More wolves come. *I'm being pulled off.* They jump, tug, snarl.

I hear the swish of George's axe. I hear the crunch of

steel on bone. A fiendish yelp. These nightmarish things, can they feel pain? The thing slides backward, its paws unable to find any hold on the smooth rock surface. I hear the slow screeching of claws, like nails on glass. Its body twitches. It flops to the ground with a thud.

'*George!*' I can't see what's happening. He must have hacked the thing in half. The pull on Rhi stops so abruptly, I almost catapult back over the other side of the stone.

'*Oh my God, oh my God,*' sobs Rhiannon.

We haul Rhi back on to the top. She's as white as a ghost. One of her boots has disappeared completely. *Thank heavens she's OK.*

We drag ourselves right to the very top and huddle together.

I turn my head towards the summit again. 'O Snowdon, greatest of mountains,' I pray. 'Please make this stop.'

We can't last the night. Sooner or later one of these creatures is going to scramble up and overpower us. I look up towards the Devil's Bridge again. *If only.*

That figure is definitely closer.

'O Snowdon,' I groan. 'Pleeeease?'

'I'm sorry, Ellie,' George says. 'I should've known better. Gran always drilled it into me that when she gives advice, I Must Follow It.'

'Forget it,' I say. 'It's not your fault.'

'Oh my God. Oh my God. Oh my God,' whimpers Rhiannon.

The glowing shape on the mountain glides down the hillside towards us. It's obvious now it's not Henry. My stomach knots up. Who is it?

Things can't get much worse though, can they? Stranded on a rock, saturated in witches' curses, surrounded by hell-hounds; a ghostly apparition bearing down on us; Sir Oswald somewhere up there, beating his skeletal wings, spying with his dragon's eyes; and the Coraniaid listening, snitching and smiling.

'Come on,' says George, 'don't give up.'

I shiver.

He slips his arms out from his jacket. He puts it round my shoulders.

'Thanks,' I say, 'but I think Rhiannon needs it more.' I remove it from my shoulders and place it around hers. She's trembling so hard I can feel her heart pounding against me.

'Try to rub your hands to warm them, Rhi,' I say.

The figure glides relentlessly towards us. The light around it starts to dim. The wolves begin to slink back from the rock. They form a semicircle on the far side. Their bellies press close against the turf. Their tongues loll out. Specks of spittle tinged with lambs' blood fleck their muzzles. It creates a revolting, thick, pink cream, which dribbles on to the bracken.

They press their tails against their haunches. One of them starts a wailing noise – not the shrill bark of the chase – it's more like a summoning cry, calling other hideous things out of the shadows.

Rhiannon moans in a distressing, broken way.

George tries to send me a hopeful smile through the darkness. He doesn't say, *This is all your fault, Ellie. I told you, we should've gone back to Gran's.*

He just puts his arms around us both, and says, 'Hey girls, I've got to be the luckiest guy ever, marooned out here with the two most beautiful girls from Llanberis and a whole night ahead of me!'

Oh George.

Seventeen

The figure moves forward. It glows. It seems to emit a small, high-pitched noise.

I peer into the darkness and listen. It's just under the shadow of the mountain.

The moon rolls in the mist above us, luminous, powder blue. I imagine the stars shining behind the clouds right up to the Pole Star.

For the first time ever, I send up a prayer to the Great Draco, 'Mighty dragon who lives in the sky, just take care of Henry,' I say, 'and please spare us'.

The figure increases in brilliance. The wolves stop their wailing. They back away, silent. They huddle on the dark side of the stone, their pale polar eyes reflecting back the moonshine.

A pillar of fire rises above the approaching figure.

A pillar of fire?

Hang on, perhaps I'm wrong! Not a pillar of fire, but the mouth of hell? Perhaps that figure really is the Devil fresh off his bridge! After all this is the Black Stone, the Maen Du'r Arrdu, where all evil things are bound to gather.

And then everything becomes odd.

It's like I hear singing. The church bells start pealing again. It's like a bird swoops down from the sky and aims straight at the figure.

But it's not a dragon. And it's not a crow – it's too small and light. It sort of … hovers. *The beauty of a dove descending.*

Why do I think of that?

A bird, white like a lamb, but with a golden beak.

I look again. It's just a bird. Duh. And it's not a pillar of fire glowing around him either, only the last rays of the setting sun bouncing off the clouds.

And then everything seems to slow down.

Like in a trance he comes, like in a dream of stardust, dressed in a robe of pure white, his light playing over the darkness.

Where the heck are these thoughts coming from?

Get a grip, Ellie, I tell myself.

Don't let any creature take over your mind.

I swallow. It definitely isn't Henry. But it isn't the Devil either.

The figure hovers slowly towards us. I narrow my eyes and try to make it out. Reality check one: it's a he and he's not gliding at all; he's clambering laboriously over frozen clumps of sedge. Two: he's not mystical or shining white either; it's just a trick of the light.

A lost hiker perhaps? But what the hell is someone doing out, after dark, off the path, walking straight towards us. *He's lost. That's why. He's looking for help.* I panic.

He doesn't know about the wolves.

'Hey!' I yell. 'GO BACK!'

He hesitates.

'Wild dogs!' I yell. 'GO BACK! CALL FOR HELP – WE'RE STUCK.'

The wolves sound out a queer yelping. The three of us start yelling and waving from the top of the Black Stone of the Darkness.

'Whaaaat?' he calls. And carries on coming.

'STAY. AWAY!' I holler, my throat suddenly hoarse.

'GO BACK!' shouts George.

'GET HELP!' squeals Rhiannon.

NOOOO! – He's going to get mauled right in front of us.

'Wait,' whispers George, suddenly tightening his grip around me. 'He could be anyone, could be anything … *He could be some kind of ghoul.* With the High Magick broken and the gateway to the Olde Deep Magicke thrown wide, anything can come through, *anything* can manifest out of the dark and totally be here ... '

He doesn't look like a ghoul. Actually he looks a bit like a teenage Jesus, with hair down to his shoulders, a bit of a beard and, perhaps a scattering of acne.

Jesus with pimples?

I stand up. I balance on the rock, straining to make him out.

'Don't look into his eyes,' warns George. 'Gran says never accept food from supernatural beings – *or* look into their eyes.'

Rhiannon whimpers. Ceri starts thumping her tail feverishly against the rock.

The person reaches the stone. And from the darkness, his voice rings out. 'Since when have the wolves of Cŵn Annwn chased youngsters across the slopes to the Black Stone?'

The wolves, already silent, now draw back, blink and slowly snarl. One tries to growl, but its bark is too high and it sounds more like a whine. The rest cringe even further away. Then they waver, turn tail and flee.

Just like that.

Soon there's only the rattle of stones from the opposite

slope of the mountain. Then nothing.

The glow around the rock and around the hiker, if that's what he is, seems to shimmer and die.

The hiker comes right up to us, places his hand on the stone. Looks up at us.

'No closer,' warns George, axe in hand.

I can't help it, but I look into his eyes.

Deep, serious, serene, like looking into ...

George shakes me. '*Ellie*,' he warns, 'STOP!'

I shake my head, try to clear my mind. I find myself looking down on to a dark sea of frosty bracken, and at this weird young man. I tremble oddly. I lean down, put out my hands to him. I send up a silent prayer to the mountain and say, 'Would you please help me down?'

He stretches up and places his palms on my palms.

A sensation, like a surge of electricity, jolts through me.

George tugs me back.

But I'm mesmerised. He's sort of strangely beautiful. I just can't explain. And he's wearing something very odd: a sort of robe, all loose fitting, brilliant. It flutters behind him, giving the appearance of wings.

The clouds roll back, the moon shines through, I blink.

The trance ends.

He's not emitting any kind of light, stupid! It was just

moonbeams in the mist. He's not wearing a flowing robe either; he's just wrapped a space blanket around himself that's reflecting light back.

And he's *not* weirdly beautiful. OMG. He's really *hairy*. I am such a loony. And, yep, he definitely has pimples.

Phew. I breathe a sigh of relief. Thought I was going a bit bonkers there!

Shock. Must be.

Being chased by wolves and all that.

'Where did you come from?' I ask, hoping he can't read my mind.

'I don't really know,' he says. 'I think I must've fallen and bumped my head, because the first thing I remember was standing on the hillside. It felt like I'd been standing there a very long time, too.'

Since yesterday? No. Not possible.

Can't possibly be the same figure I saw when Mum and me were getting in the newborns.

'What's your name?' I say. I look at him closely. He is V strange. A fresh crop of down blooms on his upper lip. And he's got a fair-haired, wispy beard thing going on. Very wispy. Loads of straggly hair at the front, frames his face, right down to his shoulders, and at the back, it looks like he's tied it in a long ponytail. But on top he's going a bit bald. He's got the look of some sort of Indian monk or Guru about him. But with a space blanket, obvs.

'Davey,' he says. 'My name is Davey.'

'Can't you remember *anything*?' asks Rhiannon.

'Well that's the spookiest thing – I don't know why I'm here. I don't know what happened. I don't even know where I am. All I know is that I'm Davey and I'm extremely cold.'

'OK,' I say. I look at him. Suddenly, I remember all my mountain search and rescue volunteer support member training … *hypothermia, a fall, sudden trauma* … I switch into reassuring mode.

'You're going to be just fine,' I say.

He's obviously in some kind of shock. But he has a space blanket … I squint, trying to get a good look at him, to see if perhaps he's already going a bit blue.

'How come those wolves were scared of you?' asks George.

I notice George's still got his hand on his axe.

Rhiannon struggles down off the stone. 'Let's go,' she wails. 'Let's get back to yours, Ellie, before those *things* come back.' She hops up and down, trying not to let her one bootless foot touch anything.

'How did you know they were the hounds of Cŵn

Annwn?' asks George.

I refocus. Yes, how did he?

'C'mon! C'mon!' insists Rhiannon. 'Who cares whose dogs they are? They've gone right now – but they might come back.'

'Not before we've retrieved the heart,' I say.

'Oh My God! Hurry, then!' screeches Rhiannon.

Davey mutters something about some last memory that he's held on to, before the Great Blank happened, and he found himself up on the Devil's Bridge. 'I was on some sort of a mission … ' he says. 'I definitely had to do something … '

'Can't we just get it and *go*?' wails Rhiannon.

The silhouette of Yr Wyddfa looms darkly against a blue-black sky. A chill wind blasts down the slopes, scuffing the snow and whirling it up at us. I shiver and flap my arms around, stamp my feet. I try not to think of all the spells and curses laid around the stone. 'Obviously,' I say. 'Pass Ceri down.'

'OK, OK,' says George. He chucks Ceri down and jumps off the stone himself.

Ceri wags her tail like crazy and seems dead pleased to meet Davey. She runs circles round his legs, pressing herself against him, and she lets out happy little yelps.

Davey smiles and stretches out his hands and pats her. I guess if Ceri likes him, he can't really be from The Dark Side, can he?

We stand there shivering in spite of our jackets.

'*C'mon*,' says Rhiannon.

'Do you know the way to an inn, or somewhere I can lodge for the night?' asks Davey.

An *inn*? Which century does he come from?

I grab George before he gets right into helpful mode. 'The heart?' I remind him.

'We need to get out of here,' wails Rhiannon.

'It's just,' says Davey, 'I seem to have forgotten where I came from … '

'*You've* got a hotel,' I say to Rhiannon. 'You can take him there after.'

Rhiannon rolls her eyes at me through the gloom, mouths out, 'Thh-anks'. Like she is thinking: great, Ellie, why not saddle me with every random who can't remember where he's from and obviously won't be able to afford an en suite.

I ignore her. Now the danger of the wolves is past, I haven't forgotten that she stitched me up.

'What is it that you seek here?' Davey asks.

I was right. He *has* come straight out of the Dark Ages. I mean, 'What is it that you *seek* here?' Lol.

'At this old cromlech?' continues Davey.[1]

I suddenly realise that's what the Black Stone is: a crom-lech! I'm a bit shocked. I never guessed *that* before. The Black Stone of the Darkness must be the capstone of a burial chamber.

How did Davey know? The guy who doesn't seem to know what day it is?

I kick at some disturbed ground around the base. The soil seems to fall away. 'Is this where you dug?' I ask Rhiannon.

She nods and pulls her jacket tighter around her. The earth at the base of the Maen Stone opens up a crack.

'Back off a bit,' says George. We stand aside as he swings his axe. The turf splits. After a few more super-George swipes, the ground crumbles. Underneath the stone seems to be a space. Bits of grass and sedge fall away. George swings again.

There it is: the entrance to a burial chamber.

~~~~

George makes a hole big enough for us all to squeeze through. One by one we pass down between two damp, half-buried rocks, through the centre of the dolmen, down

---

1. Cromlech (from Welsh *crom*, 'bent, curved' and *llech* 'slab, flagstone') is a term used to describe prehistoric megalithic structures. The term is now virtually obsolete in archaeology, but remains in use as a colloquial term for two different types of megalithic monument. In English it usually refers to dolmens, the remains of prehistoric stone chamber tombs.

underneath the great Black Stone of the Darkness.

In the darkness we huddle together. The stench of damp stone, peat and something putrid, chokes me.

George flicks his torch app on. The tomb glows in eerie light.

'This is where we buried the heart,' says Rhiannon. 'Right here, right in the middle.'

'Then it's here that we must dig,' says the stranger. (I wonder if he is usually a bit weird or if the bump on the head has made him talk all 'olde worlde'.) Davey picks up a piece of stone shaped like slate and hands it to George.

'Great,' says George, 'do I look like a grave digger?'

'Oh. Sorry,' says Davey.

George smiles. 'Don't worry,' he says. 'But if I have to be the one who does all the work, then I'll use my axe.'

Eighteen

Status: Worried sick

Recent updates:

Sheila

Ha ha ha! Heard you got into a spot of bovver. Lol.

Meryl

Now I am worried. Sheila says that her friend from the rugby club saw you in the POLICE CELLS? Hon, are you OK? What happened? Can I help?

Sheila

If you accept that Henry is mine, I'll give you an alibi. Member: I DID BAGS HIM FIRST.

Inside the burial chamber it smells.

And it's not nice.

A bit like Sheila's texts.

Why, I ask, do I get coverage under a rock, when I don't get any on top of it? And secondly, why do I not block Sheila? She is a cow A COW.

I am trying not to let her text upset me.

And the smell is really disgusting. Really foul. It's not like the normal kind of earthy smell. Normal soil smells nice and loamy and fresh.

This doesn't.

It's kind of creepy and evil.

Just like Sheila's texts.

(OK, maybe the text wasn't exactly creepy and evil, but *she did not bag him first.*)

Rhiannon feels it as well. 'I hate this place,' she moans. 'I wish I'd never come here. I don't want to be a witch any more.'

'Bit late for that now, isn't it?' I hiss. (I know that's mean, but sometimes I just *am.*)

I take a few deep breaths (poo!) then I relent and give Rhi's arm a little reassuring thump. She's way out of her depth. We all are. I hate Sheila.

George digs. A bead of sweat rolls down the side of his face.

Davey stands there looking serene. I am ~~never going to go out of my way to be nice to Sheila ever again~~ not going to let Sheila upset me.

We clear the foul-smelling soil from inside the centre of the cavern. I get out my mobile, and shine the torch down. It's so cold down here my fingers are going numb. George finally makes headway. His axe hits metal. We hear a sharp clang as steel bounces off something.

'Tis no doubt the iron box,' says Davey. Like he knows all about this thing.

I force myself to stop thinking about how hateful Sheila is, because now I am officially wary. Who is this guy? He knew the Black Stone was a dolmen. He knows there's an iron box ... he uses words like 'seek' and 'tis' ... the wolves were frightened of him ...

Perhaps we should be too.

'How do you know?' I challenge. I swing the torch up at him and shine it in his face.

'Tis often told,' he says, 'that the Coraniaid cannot touch iron. No fairy folk can. They cannot hear through copper and they detest metal. But iron especially burns them.'

Ooooh kay. Right. But like, what kind of an answer is that?

I give him a really, really weird look. *Now*, he knows all about the Coraniaid. What a little mine of information he's turning out to be.

Rhiannon moans. 'I hate it here, I want to go home … '

'Did you *actually* come here willingly and do all this, or did the Supreme One have to drag you here in chains?' ~~I am getting fed up with her now~~. I should be a bit more understanding. But right now I'm finding it pretty hard to understand how Rhiannon got into all this stuff.

I mean, number one: she's a big wuss.

Number two: she cares more about cute outfits than shapeless robes.

And why would she want to be a witch in the first place? Plus the 'Supreme One' is a really annoying name.

'*Just hurry*,' she says.

Like we're not.

OK, more deep breaths. Now, I *really really really* am *not* going to let Sheila's texts get to me.

I exhale.

George clears the earth from around the top of a shape. It's about the size of a lunchbox. He drags it out of the ground and brushes dirt off it with his sleeve, then fumbles at the catch. I shine my torch on it, trying to get a better look.

Davey's right: it's an iron box. Spidery engravings glint in the mobile's light.

My hand trembles. The beam wavers. *Henry's heart may*

be in that box.

I wonder if it will look anything like the heart I remember; that beautiful, sparkling heart caught in the crystal – held there by the High Magick of Merlin.

'George,' I say, my voice shaking. 'Can *I* open the box?' I try to keep the torchlight steady. I hold out my hand to take the small metal container off George. 'Please?'

'Whatever you want, Elles,' says George. 'Just be careful. It's really heavy and really cold.'

He hands me the box and it is heavy. I squat down, knees weak. I put the box on the floor. Something dark and sticky is wrapped around it. Where George's axe hit home, the sticky layer is torn, showing the metal beneath. It feels like black silk soaked in something like engine oil. It's revolting and smells totally rank.

I don't care. With trembling fingers I tear off the oily cloth. I unwrap every shred of the foul stuff that I can and rip the rest away.

I ease the catches of the container back and flick open the case.

George takes my phone off me and shines the light into the box.

Rhiannon moans, *'Pleeeease hurry'*.

There, balanced on something reflective, is a dark object.

187

Tentatively I touch it. It's hard and smooth, like a piece of obsidian, about the size of my fist.

'That's it!' cries Rhiannon. 'That's the dragon's heart!'

I stretch out my hand and put it firmly around the heart; that poor, hard, blackened thing. I'm certain that Henry's heart can never hurt me, whatever potion has been poured over it or magic cast around it.

I clutch it tightly. My fingers tingle. For a second I feel an icy numbing touch, and then I lift it up.

It is much *much* heavier than it looks. Much heavier than it should be. My whole arm suddenly aches with the weight of it.

It's Henry's heart, I tell myself. You can bear the weight of it. *He told you to be strong.*

I breathe out: *I am strong.*

Something shines at the bottom of the box.

What looks like a hand mirror with an ebony handle, and an oval, silvered front glints up from the darkness. It looks like one of those mirrors that Edwardian ladies used, or mermaids maybe.

I put the stone heart in my inside jacket pocket, next to *my* heart. Strangely the cloth of my jacket does not sag. I weigh the heart in my hand again: heavy. I let it lie in the pocket: virtually weightless. I don't understand. It is as if touching it somehow creates its weight. Vaguely I wonder what that means, and then I pick up the mirror.

Big mistake.

I hold it up and look into it.

Even bigger mistake.

It shines, as if it reflects the distant light from unseen stars, galaxies hidden way above us. I don't see my face at all. It's actually quite shocking to be so suddenly and completely erased. I look into the mirror, hardly believing that I am *not* there. With some relief, I see that it isn't entirely full of that shining dark. A huge shadowy range of mountains zooms in at me. They're covered in mist and snow, above them moonlit skies.

And it's as if I'm on a plane, flying through time zones. In the distance there are tiny pinpricks of light; far away, dawn is breaking on some distant horizon.

The little lights pull at me, tug at my eyes.

George shouts. He sounds very faint. I can't quite hear him.

I should have known better. Especially when I didn't see my own reflection.

Like, if you find a mirror that has been buried under an ancient, evil tombstone by witches on 29 February, and if you look into it, well, you really *should* expect anything, shouldn't you?

I try to warn myself.

But it's too late.

The heart lodged inside my breast pocket suddenly drags against me, pulls me down – and quite abruptly I'm being sucked towards the centre of those pinpricks of light.

Dizzy.

'Hey!' I cry.

And I fall forward. The mirror seems to widen. Somewhere in the periphery of my vision, I see Rhiannon. Her hands are flung over her face. She's screaming. I see George standing there with his axe raised as if he is about to smash the mirror.

I see Davey. He is smiling.

And then the darkness closes over me.

Nineteen

ELLIE'S PHONE 1 March 19.16

Status: ....

Recent updates:

... pending ...

Sheila ....

No reply, eh? So you're ignoring me now ...

I don't know where I am. I look around. It's a hot sunny afternoon. I am lying on springy grass high up on the mountain, somewhere near the Devil's Bridge. Above me, I can see the peak, smoking pink in the hot afternoon sun; the call of birds sounds high overhead; a fresh breeze cools my face.

'Isn't it fabulous here?' says a voice I know and love.

I turn my head. 'Henry?'

There, right beside me, lying on the heather, with his arms thrown out is Henry. He looks as impossibly beautiful as ever. His thick chestnut hair has got bits of bracken stuck in it, and he's smiling.

I fling myself at him – give him a massive hug. 'Is this some kind of dream?' I ask, my face buried in his neck.

'Yeah,' he laughs. 'And no.'

Typical.

'OK,' I say. 'Is this a game?' I flop back beside him.

If he's not bothered by the fact that even though it's only just March, we are lying on the grass on a hot afternoon, high on the mountainside, why should I be? Why should I wonder that in the brilliant blue sky overhead pipits and meadowlarks are singing?

'I can't believe it!' I say.

'I know,' he says. He reaches out a hand and grabs mine. And we just lie there with our backs on the turf, staring at the clouds, twining our fingers together. So close together.

OK, I decide. I'm not even going to try and understand what's going on. I am going to forget about wolves and tomb-stones and blackened hearts and witches. It's all absolute rubbish and nonsense anyway. I've probably been listening to Granny Jones for far too long. And now I'm where I've always wanted to be: out on the mountain with Henry.

As we lie there, staring up into the blue yonder, behind us, over the peak of the mountain, a dark cloud starts to form. I look at it puzzled. In its centre something dark and massive is swelling.

'Do you think it's going to rain?' I ask.

'That's not a raincloud,' he says.

'It doesn't look very friendly,' I say.

'It isn't.'

I just lie there. I'm not going to think about it. I'm not going to leave this place. I'm going to stay here forever, in this long sunny afternoon, holding hands with Henry and lying on the heather. I don't care about dark clouds glowering over the summit of Mount Snowdon. I don't care what they mean. I don't care that I should not be here.

I just don't care.

I don't care about anything right now; my heart is bursting with happiness.

And I realise how much it has been aching. Just to be here. Just to be alive. Just to know Henry is close by.

'You know, of course, we can't stay,' says Henry.

I didn't suppose that we could. But I didn't suppose anything. I don't want to think about anything. In fact, I say as much.

'This is the place in-between,' says Henry.

I sigh. 'OK,' I say. 'The place in-between what?'

'Well,' says Henry, 'I can't actually say what is outside or surrounding this place, I only know that this is the place in-between.'

I don't care where it is. I'm here with Henry. I raise up his hand and kiss the back of his fingers.

'Perhaps in-between Now and Then, in-between What Is and What Is Not, in-between what Might Be and What Might Not Be. It's hard to say.'

'Can't we stay here?' I ask.

'No,' says Henry.

'Why not? What happens if we do?'

'Bad things.'

'Like?' I say.

'You can't just ignore the rest of the world. If you do, anything can happen to all the people you care about back there.'

I sigh.

'Am I their shepherd, then?'

Henry squeezes my hand. 'Look how you felt about your lambs,' he says. 'You have to be the shepherd.'

I sigh again. It hurts. I don't want to think about the lambs. I don't want to be a shepherd. I don't want to have to take care of anything right now. I want to lie here on the heather with the sweet smell of the mountain, and the sun warm above me. I want to lie next to Henry and listen to the songbirds, why should I have to do anything else?

'And because everything is wrong,' says Henry. 'And not how it should be.'

'Why not?' I ask.

'You ask too many questions,' smiles Henry and suddenly he puts his arm around me and pulls me close and squeezes me.

He kisses me.

I kiss him back. With all the longing and the wanting and the waiting that's been bottled up inside me.

My heart pounds.

His heart pounds.

I take a deep breath, bite my lip.

'OK,' I say. 'What have I got to go and do?'

'Right now,' says Henry, 'you are in the most dangerous place you can possibly be. It is evening on the first day of March and you are under the Black Stone looking into a witch's mirror. You have to go back and get out of there.'

A shiver runs through me. 'OK,' I say. 'And where are you right now?'

'I am flying through the heavens,' says Henry, his voice fading a little. 'I am winging my way towards the great constellation of Draco.'

'What the heck are you doing that for?' I say. 'I need you here. We all need you. Something has gone wrong. Did you know the witches broke open your cave at Dinas Emrys – and laid a spell on Snowdonia?'

'I know,' he says. 'It was they who cursed me.'

'Cursed you?' I ask.

'Yes,' he says. 'When one of their number died upon the crystals, it broke the High Magick of Merlin. Oswald meant that to happen, so he could return as a man, or as a dragon whenever he wished. He sent his thoughts out from under the mountain and made his followers prepare the spell. I couldn't stop him. The thoughts of dragons are their own, though I knew what he was up to. He twisted the magic of Draco, so that when a girl was sacrificed to his heart, he had power. I have never twisted the magic, but the sacrifice landed on *my* heart too.'

He pauses, draws in his breath, seems to grit his teeth.

'My crystal killed the girl as well, and now my heart is forever tainted.'

Oh my God.

Of course.

Poor, poor Henry.

That's it.

That's why his heart is blackened and shrivelled.

He inhales sharply. 'My heart is now turned to stone, I am cast out from Earth and must go to the great afterlife of dragons in the sky, where I will join my maker, the great dragon Draco, and start my penance – as a single pinprick of light in his constellation.'

He pulls me closer, wraps me in his arms. 'I'm so sorry,' he whispers.

I don't understand. I *won't* understand. And I don't answer. I don't let it sink in *at all*. I don't want to feel what this means. I don't want to ask any more questions. I don't want to say, 'But how can there be a Wales without the Red Dragon?'

Or:

'Who will save us from Oswald?

Or:

'How can I live without even the hope of seeing you again? Even if I am like, old?'

I look up at the blue sky. I'm going to stay here. I'm not going to accept what he's told me.

'All this is true Ellie,' he sighs, 'even if you do not want to hear it.'

Up overhead, the huge grey cloud is rolling in.

Oh my soul.

'OK,' I say. 'But I've retrieved your heart. I got it out from under the Black Stone. Just tell me what to do and I will restore it. If one girl's blood can taint it, then perhaps another girl's blood can purify it?'

'Would you really do that for me?' he asks quickly.

I give him a good punch in his ribs. Stupid question.

The cloud has completely covered the summit now. It's reaching out, casting its shadow down over the slopes towards us.

'We haven't got much longer,' says Henry.

'What do I have to do?' I ask.

'You will have to talk to Draco.'

Talk to Draco? How? Um, considering he is a constellation of stars like, one billion zillion miles away.

The grey cloud reaches us. Its shadows, dark like a raven's wing, start to swallow the heather around us. Henry's hand on mine grows tight.

'You can help, Ellie,' he calls. 'If only you are brave enough ... '

Stupid him. Of *course* I'm brave enough.

'If you are brave and true in heart, nothing will hurt you ... '

His voice suddenly sounds faint. The shadow floods nearer.

'Henry!' I scream.

He's fading.

'Find the Stargazer,' he calls. His voice, fainter: 'And then ... we need to talk about us ... sooner rather than later ... '

Talk about us? My hearts beats unevenly.

'Find the one who can talk to the stars ... ask him to beg Draco to release me ... so I can help repair the damage the witches have caused.'

I try and think: *talk about us in a good way?*

The cloud sends tentacles out across the grass. I sit up abruptly.

Or talk about us in a bad way?

Like, no us.

Henry?

Henry is fading so rapidly there is only the sensation of his hand in mine.

And all around me is just the night-time, the icy cold, and a feeling like my insides have been sucked out.

'*Henry?*' I cry.

I feel a strong grip on my arm. I feel my hand being opened, as if somebody is prising that last sensation of Henry away from me.

And I hear a voice.

'**Ellie**,' it says. '**Let go of the mirror.**'

My fingers are bent open and Henry's hand is wrenched from mine.

And suddenly I am back under the tombstone with George.

George has torn the mirror from my grasp.

'Nooooooo!' I scream.

Twenty

ELLIE'S PHONE 1 March 19.16

Status: ......

... no signal ... no signal ... no signal ...

Recent updates:

Pending...

...

Sheila

It's WAR then TOTAL OUTRIGHT WAR!!!!!!!!

SO PREPARE YOURSELF YOU MINGER.

MWAHAHAHA

George holds the mirror out of my reach.

'We need to hurry,' Davey says. 'The wolves may return.'

'Please,' I say, reaching for the mirror. '*Please* George.

You don't understand. We need to find the Stargazer and ...'

But George just holds it way out of my grasp. 'Come on,' he says, 'all we need to do is get out of here. You just went really weird, for your information.'

'Once they have spoken with their master, they will no longer fear me,' says Davey.

'I don't get it,' says Rhi.

'What master?' says George.

'I don't know ... I can't remember ... ' says Davey obscurely, 'but they have a master ... they must have a master.'

'They're wolves,' says George, 'not hounds.'

I want to scream. I don't care if the wolves have a master or not. I want the mirror. I want to get back to that hillside. I want to be once again in the endless sunshine of that long afternoon. Forever with Henry on the heather ...

But it's gone.

And I can't get back.

I remember the cloud reaching out, covering us. I shudder. 'I'm so cold,' I say.

'There is something I'm supposed to remember,' says Davey. He strokes at his beard in a worried way. 'Something I'm supposed to do ... '

'We need to get out from under this stone,' yells George.

He literally grabs my arm and hauls me out on to the freezing mountainside.

We walk a few yards downhill. Rhiannon crawls out and hops on her one booted foot. Davey follows. He catches her elbow. She leans on him. I think she's worried about the wolves. I hear her say, 'But why? *Why* won't they be afraid of you?' I can't catch what he says.

'I'm so cold,' I say again, shivering.

'Well,' says George, 'just say the word and I'll warm you up. You won't need a coat either.'

Rhiannon overhears. 'And me *too*, George,' she wails. And with a few determined hops she catches us up. For a girl with one boot, she can't half move fast when she wants to.

In answer, George links one arm through mine and one through Rhiannon's. 'Lean on me, Rhi,' he says. He yells at Davey: 'C'mon, give us a hand!'

And we all march down the hillside, as quickly as we can, half carrying Rhiannon, over the frozen heather, away from the Black Stone, and back towards the farmhouse.

Ceri races ahead, her tail tucked firmly between her legs. Henry was right. This must be just about the most dangerous and stupidest place to be.

'I'm seriously and majorly going to need cuddles when we get to the Land Rover,' Rhiannon reminds George.

He glances back up the mountain. 'Right now, an invigorating hop is the best way to warm you up,' says George. He hauls Rhi half up on to his shoulder and quickens the pace.

And for once he's not laughing, or flirting or trying to make anyone feel better.

'Until we are all safe at Gran's, this is the closest you're gonna get to any cuddles, Rhi.' And with that, George tightens his grip around Rhiannon and urges everyone on downhill.

Twenty-One

Status: Cold

Recent updates between Ellie and Sheila:

Ellie

Hi – I wasn't ignoring you – just everything got a bit manic, and I was up on the mountain.

Sheila

Doing what?

Ellie

Oh you know. Just the usual. A spot of magic. Digging around under old dolmens and breaking witches' curses. That sort of thing.

Sheila

LOL ☻ you are so funny.

See what I mean about Sheila. Even when you try to be nice, she ~~is a cow~~ can't help herself.

Holy smoke, but it was soooo good to be back in the Land Rover.

And even better when we got to Granny Jones's place.

Everywhere was so neat and warm and lovely. And ooooh the smell of food. All delicious and scrummy and wafting everywhere in her tiny cottage.

I'd forgotten how hungry I was. Crispy bacon, sizzling sausages, bread toasting: breakfast at supper time, with slices of ham and endless pickles and potatoes and veggies and thick wedges of cheese. Gran calls it 'high tea' and it's totally yumptious!

'Hungry, I expect,' she calls out from the kitchen, as we take off our coats. 'I'm so relieved you're here. Just going to top up the kettle.'

Welsh cakes, flat, brilliant with little currants in them, beam up at us; plates sport eggs – hard boiled and fried sunny side up. Mushrooms, so fresh, as if she'd just

205

picked them – juicy and tender. And in the centre of the table a humongous Victoria sponge cake. Oh My God, I just *love* Gran's high tea!

Gran comes through from the kitchen with the tea tray in her hands. She's wearing an outlandish tasselled shawl and a long Indian cotton skirt.

And then she sees Davey.

I'm not quite sure exactly what happens. Maybe she trips over the tassels on her shawl, or the fringed hem of the skirt – but – yikes and – C-R-A-S-H. The tea tray drops, smashes on to the flagstones. And hot tea sprays *everywhere*.

'OH MY LORD!' Gran cries in a squeaky voice. Her hands fly to her face. Splashes of tea dribble down the wall. Gran drops to her knees. 'Oh forgive me!' she says. She bends her head and seems to be groping around for broken china. Then she clasps her hands together in a really bonkers way, as if she isn't kneeling on the floor to pick up shattered crockery at all, but as if (improbably) she's actually in chapel, kneeling before God.

'Oh my Lord!' she says again, as she struggles up. Then she bolts to the kitchen.

George grabs tea towels, kitchen roll and some pyjama bottoms (which are handily drying by the fire). He hastily soaks up the liquid mess of cooling tea, scones and soggy toast. He calls out, 'Don't worry Nan! It's only a bit of tea. It'll really improve the flavour of the scones. Tea on toast – smashing!'

Steam rises from the flagstones. Davey stands there with a puzzled look on his face. He takes a step forward and calls out, 'We must find the Stargazer, Mother Jones, can you help us?'

Like, *ran*-dom.

'Yes! Find the Stargazer,' Gran repeats in a majorly mental way from the depths of the larder.

Then I remember where I heard those words last. '*Find the Stargazer.*'

And I am back on an impossibly beautiful mountainside, lying in the sun of an afternoon that never ends …

'*Find the one who can talk to the stars … ask him to beg Draco to release me … so I can help repair the damage the witches have done.*'

'George,' I say, '*please* can I have the mirror.' If there's any way I can get back to that in-between place, I'm going to find it.

Surprisingly, George just hands it over.

Gran comes back from the kitchen. She carries a B&Q bag from which bits of DIY stuff protrude. She composes herself, sweeps strands of grey hair from her face, breathes out a long rush of air and says, 'Oh dear, what a waste of Earl Grey. Now, tell me everything. And where did *he* come from?' she waves a hand in an embarrassed flutter in Davey's direction.

'The Devil's Bridge,' says George. 'Actually, the Black Stone. That's where we found him. Or rather he found us.'

'And what brings you to Snowdon, young man?' she enquires.

'He's lost his memory,' says George. 'I said he'd be OK to stay with us. Rhi too. It's not safe for them to go out there again, Nan. It is OK, isn't it?'

'I'm not sure why I'm here,' says Davey, 'but I definitely had a mission ... '

'Yes, of course you must stay,' says Gran directly to Davey. ''Tis a blessing unlooked for. You can help to break this cursed spell.' Gran looks relieved. 'It's the first piece of good luck we've had. Meeting someone called Davey on St David's Day. The Lord's blessing.'

'So I should stay and assist you in your undertaking?' asks Davey. 'Though I cannot remember a lot, I feel I have much knowledge about the sacred myths of Wales, which may be of use.'

'Could be,' I say, daring myself to look into the mirror.

'And I've nowhere else to go,' he adds rather sadly.

'But shouldn't you see a doctor?' says Rhiannon. 'Maybe you've got concussion.'

'Rhiannon,' says Gran quite sharply, 'have you looked out of the window? Do you know where we are? Can you imagine how long it will take us to get into Caernarfon?'

'Well, we could ring 111?' Rhiannon suggests.

'Go ahead,' says Gran. 'They will tell you, that for concussion, you need to apply cold compresses, reduce the swelling, check for bleeding and then rest with paracetamol. We don't need to drive to Caernarfon to be told that.'

'Did you bump your head badly?' asks George, full of concern.

'No,' says Davey. 'I've no head injury, no swelling and no bleeding.'

'Exactly as I thought,' says Gran. 'These are not normal times. You are here for a reason and, when the time comes, you will remember what that reason is.'

'Well, I was just *trying* to be helpful,' says Rhi a bit huffily.

Gran sits down in her rocking chair. 'Now.' She folds her hands on her lap. 'I want to know everything.' She rummages in the B&Q bag then passes lengths of copper piping round to everyone. 'First things first, and *please* use the piping at all times.'

'Oh crikey,' says George, 'not *more* enchanted plumbing.'

Rhiannon holds her bit of piping suspiciously, as if it's still attached to a toilet cistern and has somebody's you-know-what running through it.

Gran smiles. 'It's been washed, Rhiannon,' she says. 'Now, as you're telling me, eat your supper while it's hot.' And, 'there's juice on the table'. She fixes George with a steely look. 'Whatever's wrong with you, Sior? Go and make some more tea.'

George rolls his have-pity-on-me eyes and makes what looks like a witch's hat over his head with both hands before disappearing to put the kettle on.

We sit at the table and eat while Gran commands us through her piping. 'Start at the beginning, and don't stop until I know every last detail.'

So we use the piping and tell her everything: right from meeting Rhi at the hotel, to the lambs and the wolves, to digging up the heart and my trance. Davey listens intently as well. From time to time, he asks questions about Oswald and the history of the dragons, but mostly he just strokes his wispy beard and listens.

I don't say anything about meeting Henry though. Gran gives me an odd look. It's almost impossible to put anything past her. But I simply shrug. I don't know why

I don't tell them. I'm just not ready to discuss Henry in front of everyone (i.e. George) yet.

At first, Gran doesn't say anything. She just nods. Then she asks to see the mirror. I pass it to her, a bit worried that she'll do what I did, and end up in the in-between world with Henry.

She looks *at* it.

She runs her fingers *over* it.

She looks *into* it. I gulp.

Nothing happens.

And then she looks at me. Pointedly. And I can tell from some expression deep in her eyes that she *knows* I've been through the mirror.

'Ellie,' she says (through her bit of piping), 'that was very reckless of you. You must not go there again.'

Davey seems thoughtful. (He hasn't touched a bite.) Perhaps he's trying really hard to remember what *his* mission is. (I'm on my third crumpet.) At Gran's words, his trance breaks. He gently squeezes my arm (rather too long) and says, 'You'll be all right, I'll take care of you until Henry needs you back. You stay with me – you'll be fine.'

Which is weird, because I didn't tell *him* about Henry either, plus the squeezing.

'Hmmf,' snorts George. '*We* will take care of Ellie, you mean.'

211

He narrows his eyes at Davey.

'Who's gonna take care of *me*?' wails Rhiannon.

'Now, Rhiannon,' says Gran, 'you're going to have to start taking care of yourself, and make an effort to help undo the problem your foolish spell created.'

Which shuts Rhiannon up.

Davey mumbles, 'I will help you too, Rhiannon. I am ready to dedicate my life to taking care of you.' Davey starts squeezing her arm now.

Rhi looks at him in horror and mumbles, 'S'ok. Don't worry.'

The rest of us top up our plates a second time with waffles, beans, tomatoes and slices of a Spanish omelette that has miraculously been discovered under the bacon and ham platter. Davey still hasn't touched a thing.

'It's the little things in life that matter to me,' adds Davey, 'and you were so worried about the possibility of concussion, Rhiannon. I can never repay you for that kind thought.'

'Eat up,' says George, through a large mouthful of bacon. (Yuck, see what I mean about boys?) He pushes eggs and chipped-up potatoes in Davey's direction.

'It's not high tea the boy needs,' says Gran. 'It'll be salt and bread; that'll be it. I'll get it for you.' Gran dives back into the kitchen and produces a small brown loaf. 'Here you are. The salt is on the lazy Susan,' she adds.

Ah, I get it! Lightbulb moment. Davey is one of these new-age hippies who only eat raw food (or bread and salt). And are always wandering around on auspicious dates, checking out standing stones and researching ley-lines and being experts on all that random woo-woo stuff.

Davey helps himself to a thick crust of Gran's best homemade. 'Thank you so much Mother Jones,' he says, being very careful to use his piping. 'You are so thoughtful. It's the little things that count.' He pauses, as if once again, he's searching his memory. 'I'm sorry, I can't introduce myself. It's very kind of you to trust me to help you with your quest … I know I have some mission to accomplish … perhaps this is it … ' his voice trails off.

'Yes, yes,' says Gran. 'Try not to worry about it.'

And try not to keep repeating it, I think.

'And I have a feeling too, that something bad is going to happen … ' says Davey. 'If I could only remember … '

Gran sighs. 'You just eat. I need a bit of peace and quiet to think things through.'

I look at Davey. I too know that foreboding feeling. I tell myself, there's something about this person; it's the second time he's triggered your memory.

And I remember the dream: the dark cloud over the mountain.

I remember Henry's warning.

'It's coming ... you must be prepared.'

And I know Davey's right.

Something bad *is* going to happen.

Twenty-Two

We all fall silent. Despite the fire, the air in the cottage grows colder. Gran puts a fresh log on the embers and sinks back in her rocking chair. She glances towards the window, and for one ghastly minute, I think she's about to make us listen to Rod Stewart again.

'Can you imagine?' says George hissing quietly through his piping, right into my ear. 'If it never stops snowing, you will *so* need taking care of – you'll need skin-to-skin contact to keep you warm.'

'Stop it,' I bat his pipe away. I swear a bit of chewed bacon rind shot right through it and hit my cheek! Honestly! Gross or *what*?

But it *is* getting colder. And it's a kind of unhealthy chill, like however much you try to stay warm, it gets inside – into your bones – and makes your teeth rattle. How can it be so totally sub zero, and getting colder, on the first day of March?

Davey whispers, 'Tis the Fimbulvetr'. Like he can read my mind. 'Tis all part of the bad things I feel coming … during the Fimbulvetr, there will be no let-up in the cold.'

Is it me, or is Davey just a teensy bit gloomy?

Rhi rolls her eyes. 'Le Fimbulvetr … what the heck's that?'[1]

'What he means is,' says Gran, 'without the fire of the Red Dragon to battle the White Dragon, ice and snow will triumph – unless Oswald is defeated, it will be winter forever.'

Davey looks up at Gran. He nods his balding head. 'You understand,' he says.

I make evil eyes at Rhiannon: *All your fault.*

Rhiannon shoots back aggrieved innocence: *I've said sorry.*

But I understand too. When that girl fell on to the crystals, she fulfilled the magic of Draco. And now Oswald's back for another seventy-two years. Another seventy-two years of winter. Maybe more.

Without Merlin's Magick, maybe forever.

---

1. Fimbulvetr is the harsh winter that precedes the end of the world and puts an end to all life on Earth. Fimbulwinter (this is the English word for it) lasts for three successive winters where snow comes in from all directions, without any intervening summer. During this time, there will be innumerable wars and ties of blood will no longer be respected: brothers will kill brothers, friends will betray friends.

Maybe the next ice age!

'Yes,' says Gran. 'Oswald's back and he'll have his day, until things are put right in Snowdonia. And I think, Davey, this is part of your mission.'

I look at Rhiannon again with: *So you'd better help too.*

Rhiannon looks back at me with: *Watch this then.*

'Put right?' says George. 'How?'

'Use your piping,' scolds Gran.

Rhiannon turns to Davey. 'I'll try to help you remember stuff,' she says, doing an excellent version of: *I Am Now Being Uber Helpful.* 'How. Old. Are. You. Davey?'

Davey looks at her, puzzled.

Gran turns to me. 'Now, what news of Henry?'

'Not really much,' I lie. I'm sooooo determined to help Henry, but what if it doesn't fit with the plan to stop Oswald? If I tell her everything ... well, I remember how last Christmas she actually tried to stop me being with Henry ...

Rhiannon gives up trying to 'help' Davey and puts her piping down and her headphones on.

'*Ellie* ... ' warns Gran.

'OK. He said when the crystals were broken ... ' I pause. George is glowering at me.

I look at Gran. (I just hate it when George is mad at me about Henry.)

'Continue,' says Gran.

I look at George again. (I let one shoulder rise and fall. Like, what's the big deal – *you know* I love him?)

Davey smiles like an encouraging guru.

I take a deep breath. 'He said his heart was tainted, and he's got to rejoin Draco.'

Gran frowns.

George smiles. (How could you George?)

Rhiannon sings out loud, '*All of me oooo – ooo-ooo – loves you …* ' She points playfully at George and bobs along to her headphones.

I look at her too with: *Why are you flirting with George when we've all got to go on a desperate mission and I have got to appear before a magistrate due to your stupid love spell and now the rest of mankind is probably doomed?*

She pretends not to understand.

Davey nods his head again, 'Yes, it surely *is* the Fimbulvetr'.

'No,' I say. 'I won't believe it's the Fimbulvetr yet. And anyway, Henry can put a stop to it. We – I mean *I* – can save Henry too. Probably. Definitely. All we have to do is find the Stargazer, who can talk to Draco and get him to persuade Draco to send Henry back.'

'Is that *all*?' smirks George.

'Yes.' I narrow my eyes at him.

'Aw, so sorry to say "bye-bye" to ol' Hen, then,' teases George.

'You must save him, Ellie,' says Davey, carefully using his copper piping. 'And we will help you; for only dragons can fight dragons. Only fire can fight ice. Only … '

Fight Fire with Fire. Henry told me to remember that too.

'Oh yes, we must rescue Henry,' agrees Gran.

Phew. I breathe out. I didn't realise how tense I was about telling them.

George shakes his head in mock dismay, and does throwing-himself-off-a-train-in-despair gestures.

Rhiannon stands up and wraps her arms around George's neck in a throttle hold, singing (she has a nice voice actually) '*Loves you so much ooo – oooo – oooo … *'

'The Stargazer,' hisses Gran, so that her piping positively whistles, 'is Idris Gawr.'[2]

I start to smile. *There is a way to save Henry. Get Stargazer. Beg Draco.* So I take a big breath and add the difficult bit: 'Henry said to cure his heart, it'd take one girl's blood to purify another's … '

---

2. Idris Gawr in English means: Idris the giant. He lives on Cadair Idris, a Welsh mountain, which literally means 'The Chair of Idris'. He was said to have studied the stars from the top of it and it was later reputed to bestow either madness or poetic inspiration on anyone who spent a night at its summit with him.

He didn't actually say that, I did. But it's the same difference.

'*And I will make you mine* … ' trills Rhiannon, draping herself over George.

She is being *majorly* annoying. Though George seems to enjoy it.

Gran goes rather pale. I watch her closely. I cross my fingers. *Please don't let Gran change her mind about helping Henry.*

George leans over to me and says, 'I won't allow it. I will not allow you to shed one drop of blood. Not to purify anything.'

'It's not up to you, to "allow" it or not,' I say.

'Then I won't come. I won't help you find this Idris Gawr.'

'Yes, you will,' I say.

'Oh, OK,' says George.

How easy was that?

'But only because you'll go anyway,' says George. 'And you can't blame me for trying.'

Gran, still very pale, leans over and pokes George with her piping. 'This is no time to be difficult, Sior. Of course you must go. You must find out from Idris Gawr what can be done.'

Davey carefully puts his pipe to his lips, 'We must speak

with Idris Gawr before the vernal equinox, before Draco turns in his precession, before Oswald has a chance to freeze springtime.'

Then he just sits there munching on his dry bread. Every now and then, he dips it into the salt pig. As you do. If you are some kind of religious, hippy person with a memory-loss problem. He's probably forgotten how good bacon tastes.

'Will you come with us to see Idris Gawr?' I ask Davey. 'Gran seems to think you're part of this.'

He looks up at me, his eyes very pale and far away. 'I think I may be of use … I've followed everything that you and Mother Jones have said: until the heart is purified, the dragon cannot return … the witches' spell must be broken … it will be winter forever … all of Wales will suffer unless the Red Dragon returns … Oswald wants to control the Golden Throne … that's all I think. I'm trying to figure everything out … put it all in order, you see?'

'But who is Idris Gawr?' I ask.

Davey ignores my question: 'All I need to know now is, should we leave before daybreak?'

'I'm ready to,' I say, a sudden urgency catching me.

'What, before I've had a rest?' complains George. 'Being with the two most beautiful girls in Conwy, Gwynedd and *possibly* Dyffd – is extremely tiring work ... '

Rhiannon seems to hear that. She pulls out one of her earphones and yells: '*Take all of me oooo – ooo – oooo.*'

George relents and puts an arm around her.

Sometimes Rhi can be so puke-in-a-bucket.

(I am obviously not jealous.)

'Yes, you must leave to see Idris as soon as you are able,' says Gran. 'Remember, the witches have sped up time; it is nearly the end of the first day. You only have tonight and two more full days.'

I bite my lip.

Only two more days.

Then Henry will be lost forever.

Twenty-Three

Recent updates:

Meryl

Night hon. See you tomoz?

Sheila

So what does that update mean?

Sheila

I hope you are not getting up to any little tricks without your Frenemy!

Sheila

NB – Don't forget Henry belongs TO ME.

NBB – Who's this Draco anyways? Draco Malfoy? Harry Potter?

I don't even bother responding to Sheila. I wouldn't know where to start. I know I shouldn't let it get to me. It's just her weird sense of humour. Ha ha. Puke.

I'm tempted to send a snippy message back, but there's no point. I've been 'friends' with Sheila, like, forever, and she's always been a nightmare. (This is one of the upsides to having The Street of the Dead as our go-to hang-out place. Obvs. Lol.)

However, I ask myself: is 'having been friends forever' really a good enough reason for carrying *on* being friends forever?

But right now isn't the time to start sorting all that out.

Friends. They're complicated.

Speaking of which, Rhiannon is making huge puppy eyes at George. 'I'm *soooo* coming with you to find the Stargazer too, aren't I?' she says.

'No,' I say. 'And if you're going to talk about our plans, Use. The. Piping.'

I can't imagine Rhi being anything other than a total liability, what with all that draping herself over George.

'Pleeeeease,' she says through her plumbing. 'I want to be there for George.' (See!) 'And after it's all over, we can

224

have an Easter party. I could invite Darren down, and we could have a treasure hunt thingy with eggs and things.' She looks up hopefully at George.

What a really good idea. Not.

Granny Jones brushes her shawl down. The fine lines around her eyes crease up. She sighs. She raises her piping to her lips. 'Ellie, so much of all this is about you. I don't know why or what role in the great mythologies of Wales you must play, but I will try to give you the best odds I can.'

'I don't know either, Gran,' I say. 'It's not something I've chosen – I don't want to make life harder for you all. It's sort of chosen me … '

'I know,' she says. 'Now you, George and Davey must set out immediately.'

'Where to?' I ask. I mean, it'd be nice to know.

'NOOOO! Not without me,' shrieks Rhiannon. 'I'm *not* staying behind. I *daren't* go home. What if the Supreme One finds out I showed you where the heart was?'

~~Ha! That's her problem.~~ Oh dear that would be dreadful.

'No one is going to do anything to you – not while I'm around,' says George.

'But you won't *be* around if you go off with Ellie!' shrieks Rhiannon.

'It's not going to be much fun, Rhi,' I say. 'Besides,

225

you haven't even got any winter gear.' I cast a critical eye over her bizarre outfit. 'Oh, and you've only got one boot. Stay by Gran's fire if you can't go home yet.'

'I can borrow Gran's wellies,' whines Rhi. 'Wellies fit everyone.'

'Mother Jones is right.' Davey says carefully through his copper piping. 'We must leave as soon as we are able; every minute strengthens the arm of the White One. Soon there will be no way that we will be able to get through to Cadair Idris. When Oswald realises that is where we are bound, he will try to cut off all roads, all highways.'

'And without the Land Rover, they know there'll be no way through the mountains on foot,' says George.

'*Cadair Idris?*' I say.

'Yes,' says Gran. 'Did I forget to mention that? Cadair Idris is one of the last great mountains in the south of Snowdonia.'

Huh?

'It's where you'll find Idris Gawr,' she says.

'Oh, I see.' I reply, not seeing anything.

George turns on the telly, tunes it to the news. 'Better get the weather forecast then.'

The TV local news headlines blare out:

'**Mysterious weather conditions attack North Wales.**

Temperature in Blaenau Ffestiniog lower than in the Arctic Circle.

The spring holiday season badly affected.'

'Idris Gawr is the giant who sits on the top of Cadair,' explains Gran.

Oh. OK. Giant. Mountain. Miles away. Fantastic. Marvellous. Hang on. *Giant*?

The urgent headlines banner scrolls across the bottom of the TV screen: **TRAFFIC ALERT: BREAKING NEWS! ALL ROADS OUT OF LLANBERIS PASS CLOSED. RESIDENTS ADVISED TO STAY INDOORS**.

'Oh Hell!' says George.

'Sior!' exclaims Gran.

'So can I come?' says Rhi.

'Absolutely not,' I say. 'It's *miles* away and you'll have to climb a mountain Rhi. Snow. Cold. Icy slopes. On foot. Think about it.'

'This is the work of Oswald,' says Davey mournfully. 'Nobody but Y Ddraig Goch can unfreeze his grip now.'

Y Ddraig Goch.

Henry.

My Henry.

Davey drones on: 'The whole mountain range will be a death trap. There will be accidents – terrible accidents, hikers slipping on treacherous cliffs ... '

My hand tightens on the mirror. I just want to be with you.

'People freezing to death on camping trips, Arctic winds that no sheep can survive ... ' adds George with a grin.

Oh great Snowdon, show me the way to help Henry.

Gran grows quite pale and sits down. Her rocking chair squeaks on the flagged floor. 'The beginning of the end,' she whispers.

'What do you mean?' I say.

'There is an old prophecy,' she says, 'that when the spring brings winter, when friend turns on friend, when the son of prophecy is no more, the world shall come to end.'

Fabulous. Wonderful. Cheerful even.

George makes a X-finger sign in Gran's direction, says, 'Step away from the prophecy, folks'. Then he goes out and returns with coats, daypacks and an assortment of extras. 'Never give up hope. We have Land Rover plus LURVE! And besides, they'll probably get the snowploughs out soon.'

'Not up here,' I say, catching some of Davey and Gran's gloom.

Rhiannon grabs a daysack. 'I. Am. So. Going. Too.'

'Sior is right. All is not lost,' Gran announces suddenly, almost shouting down her piping. 'I have an idea. I'll get to work on it straight away.'

'But I still don't understand about Idris Gawr?' I say. 'Do you mean like a *real* giant?'

'Obviously,' says George. 'That is the meaning of the word giant. You know – *big*. But don't worry, he'll be no match for me.'

'I may need a little time, so you rest while I prepare,' Gran instructs.

Rhiannon starts choosing the prettiest outfit from the assortment of snow gear.

George stands on a chair beating his chest going, 'Fee Fi Fo Fum, Idris Gawr can kiss my bum'.

Honestly. Sometimes George is so V V V immature; I am even beginning to think Rhiannon might be suitable for him, after all.

Davey starts praying. Fervently. 'Into your hands we commend ourselves and those we love. Be with us still, and when we take our rest, renew us for thy service … '

He is *definitely* a v v v pessimistic person.

I try not to worry. As I feed Ceri all the leftover sausages, I tell her, 'You had better eat as much as you can, because it's going to be a long walkies'.

It turns out Gran's 'preparations' take a little longer that expected. After about an hour she informs us we can't leave until first light.

Then she is adamant that no one can take care of Davey, except her. On strict instructions, he is put in the tiny loft above the spare room, where he seems to want to lie on a mat. Frankly, I think that's taking the whole hippy thing too far. But Gran doesn't even try to get him to sleep on the bed. Instead she sends me and George up with hot-water bottles and extra duvets.

Anyone would think he actually *was* a monk or guru.

Rhiannon predictably insists she *has* to sleep 'somewhere very comfortable, like George's bed,' and that she 'can't possibly share it with Ellie'.

So George ends up on the sofa, and I end up on a put-you-up on the landing.

But I don't mind. At all.

Because when I'm sure everyone is asleep, when all the lights have gone out, when I'm hidden from the entire world, with Gran's old blankets pulled over my head, I slide the mirror out from under my pillow.

This is the moment I've been waiting for.

I dare myself.

I flick my phone on and shine its torch on the mirror.

I take a deep breath.

And then I look into it.

My heart pumps. A strange, half-excited, half-terrified butterfly flutters around my stomach. I watch my breath steam up the mirror's glass. As it fades, I feel it pulling me in. I close my eyes, trembling with excitement. I say to myself: *let Henry be here. Let Henry be here. Let Henry be here.* I squeeze my eyes tight, and then I flick them open.

I am once again on a mountainside …

Twenty-Four

I am standing on a rocky incline. I look around. I can't quite place where I am. I know Snowdon like I know my mother's face. And yet I have never seen a peak like this before. It sweeps down to the shores of a lake. It's not Llyn Ffynnon-y-gwas, nor any llyn I know.

I squint up towards where the summit should be. But there's no summit there, only a long saddleback range. I look back at the lake; it's deep turquoise blue. Its aquamarine colours shine up at me. This is not a lake I've ever seen before either.

'That's because this is not a lake on Snowdon,' says Henry.

My heart leaps.

It's him!

I know it's him. It's his voice. I tremble all over with excitement. I'd know his voice even in my dreams! It's seared into my very soul.

He *is* my dreams.

My pulse starts dancing.

I wheel around, 'You're here!' I shout, looking wildly around for him.

'Yes, I'm here,' he says. 'You know, I will wait for you – through eternity – wherever you go.'

And suddenly here he is. *Right beside me!*

I throw my arms around him. He pulls me close.

He kisses me.

I kiss him.

A lovely shiver runs right through me. Electric. Awesome. This is just where I want to be. Here with Henry, just kissing.

'But where is *here*?' I ask at last.

'This is Llyn Cau on Cadair Idris.'

'Cadair Idris?' I say. 'That's weird, that's the mountain of Idris the Stargazer.'

'Yes, I know.'

'You know everything, of course!' I say.

I don't ask him whether he knows when I go to the bathroom, or if he watches me. For obvious reasons.

'Yes. I see everything,' he says. 'Dragons have excellent eyesight.'

I blush.

That means He. Must. Have. Seen. Me. In. The. Bathroom.

Aww-kward.

'Dragons can see into the past and into the future,' explains Henry, 'but that does not mean what we see will necessarily come to pass.'

I don't even bother to try to understand. If dragons have such amazing, wondrous eyesight, good for them. As for me, I can't really see past tomorrow, and how I'm going to manage spending multiple hours in the freezing cold with Rhiannon and George and Davey – on any kind of road trip – without going bananas.

'But why are we here?' I ask.

'It's the mirror,' says Henry. 'The mirror you found with the heart is a very powerful witch's mirror.' He kisses the top of my head and snuggles me tight up next to him.

I shiver with delight.

'It belonged to Nimue, the Lady of the Lake. You can see many things in it, including me.'

'I only want to see you,' I say. 'But it seems to be showing me a very nice turquoise lake on Cadair Idris as well.' I put my arms round him. I kiss him back, on the cheek. (!!☺ ☺ <3 <3 <3!!) I'm so happy.

'And that is no accident either,' says Henry. 'It means there is something about this lake that we ought to understand.'

'Well, come on, Mr Dragon Eyesight Foresight Know-all,'

I say, 'tell us.'

'Ah,' says Henry, 'seeing into the future is not as easy as you might imagine. It is like a mountain walk. If you take this track, you see one view; if you take another, an entirely different vista opens up. And it is uncertain and dangerous to trek unknown paths. If you act on such visions you may change the future for the worse. What you fear may become real, and what you hope for may be lost.'

I think I understand.

'And anyway, I only have eyes for you. Which colours everything. And all prophecy is veiled from me.'

'Oh Henry,' I say, 'then, why don't we climb up on that rock over there, and just sit and be together?'

'Ellie, you think of the most delightful things.'

Why bother about anything else if we can just be together?

'But don't underestimate your witch's mirror,' says Henry. 'It will have powers even I can't see. We should at least try to understand why it has placed us here below the Bed of Idris.'

I wave the mirror in front of his face. He smiles and shrugs. I laugh. He grabs hold of my hand, and together we walk along the shore of the lake, leaving footprints behind in the damp sand.

Everything is so perfect.

We reach the bow of the llyn, where it curves around under

the mountainside. We climb up on to a great boulder that's rolled right to the water's edge. The boulder has a conveniently flat surface, with just the right amount of space for two people to sit closely cuddled up.

Everything is just how it should be.

The stone ledge has even been warmed by the afternoon sun.

And we kiss and hold each other.

And we laugh and look into each other's eyes.

And we skim pebbles out over the lake.

Little ripples swell back at us.

Henry has his arm around me. I have my head on his shoulder. And we gaze out into blue sky. And the sun shines down. And a gentle, warm breeze caresses the skin of my face. And the water gently laps the shore. And Henry turns his face towards me. He raises my chin up and our lips meet.

And we kiss again.

And this one is the best kiss ever.

It is sweeter than any kiss I've ever had.

And Henry smells of honeysuckle and warm sunshine and all the perfumes of the mountain. And I want to be with him, kissing forever.

Suddenly he draws back.

His grip on my shoulder tightens. 'Look,' he hisses.

I turn my face away from him and look down over the lake. There in its centre, I see a slow whirlpool is forming.

'*There!*' points Henry. '*There, Ellie!*' The ripples on the whirlpool spread outwards. They gain speed and smack at the base of the boulder.

I feel his grip upon my shoulder weakening. I whip my head around.

HENRY!

He's fading.

And all the fiery loveliness of him is evaporating. *I'm sitting next to a ghost.*

He struggles to speak ...

'This is what the mirror is trying to show you ... ' shouts Henry. His voice is weak, hardly there.

I stare at the centre of the lake and right in the bullseye of the whirlpool something is bubbling.

Something huge and angry is making the turquoise llyn boil.

And rise up in a terrifying fountain.

A wave of frothing, angry liquid.

And I am alone on a boulder, over unknown waters.

Act Two

Double, double toil and trouble;
Fire burn and caldron bubble.
Fillet of a fenny snake,
In the caldron boil and bake;
Eye of newt and toe of frog,
Wool of bat and tongue of dog,
Adder's fork and blind-worm's sting,
Lizard's leg and howlet's wing,
For a charm of powerful trouble,
Like a hell-broth boil and bubble.

Double, double toil and trouble;
Fire burn and caldron bubble.
Cool it with a baboon's blood,
Then the charm is firm and good.

Song of the Witches: 'Double, double toil and trouble'
by William Shakespeare (from *Macbeth*)

Day Two: 10 March
Out of the Darkness

Twenty-Five

Recent updates between Ellie and Sheila:

Ellie

Look – I know it's a kind of running joke all this *Henry is mine* thing, but I'm starting not to, like, LOVE it. I don't find it very funny any more. I'm going through a bit of a rough time – which you've probs heard about – AND I've got a court case hanging over my head. It's really distressing. Henry is his own person and doesn't belong to either of us. Sorry to sound boring. I'll try

241

to lighten up, I promise. Got to get through the next couple of days and then maybe we can meet up? Love U, Obvs. ☺

Sheila

It's not a joke.

Ellie

?

Sheila

Henry can either *choose* to be with me or flap his little wings and buzz off. Mwahaha!

Ellie

I don't know why you're being like this.

Sheila

I DID tell you it was WAR ages ago, you nitwit.

Ellie

OK, look I gotta run, like I said I've lost my sense of humour.

Sheila

Soz – just winding you up – not. Where the heck are you anyway? And when shall we meet again? When the hurly-burly's done?

Ellie

When the battle's lost ☹ and won ☺ by end of 20 March (hopefully if I'm not in jail).

I tuck my phone away with the mirror and the heart. Sometimes I just don't get Sheila. Why carry on teasing me, when she knows it's upsetting?

Is she that insecure? Does every new boy on the block *have* to have gone through her hands first, before anyone else gets a look in?

Why doesn't she target George and start peeing off Rhiannon, then?

Sigh.

I end up waking George up, when he should be all tucked up and warm and fast asleep. If it's possible to be all of those things on a two-seater sofa.

'Has Sheila ever come on to you?' I ask.

I hear the wind battering the cottage, rattling the windows.

'Not my type,' he says rolling over, stretching and throwing out his arms to me.

'Why not?'

'My type is smart and kind and totally gorgeous-looking and brave and funny and her name starts with an E.'

'Oh, shut up.'

'Are you feeling cold? Wanna climb in?' George winks at me. 'Get one up on Sheila?'

'I had a nightmare,' I say, folding my arms and frowning at him.

He shakes his head at me and says, 'Don't. Use. The. Mirror. I know it's hard, but don't trust it.'

I don't try to explain. I don't understand it myself, so I say, 'Let's get up – get ready'.

George smiles, ruffles my hair and doesn't say anything snarky or rude. George is so totally like that. All he says is 'Ellie … ' Then, to make things easier: 'Gosh this must be my lucky middle-of-the-night – to be woken by the loveliest girl in Snowdonia. What did I do to deserve such a treat? Tell me immediately and I'll do it again and again and again and again … '

'Shut up,' I repeat, 'and get up.'

'I'm up already,' says George, brightly. 'Sometimes I sleep in my clothes.'

YUCK. Boys.

'I'm worried,' I say. 'We have so little time – it's nearly dawn already and we're into the second day. We need to get the Land Rover packed and started. Maybe we should do it before Rhi wakes up and starts whinging. And before Gran starts taking more precautions.'

Gran's preparations could easily involve more plumbing, tealeaves and Tolkien mumblings. Perhaps some dried fruit and a sleeping potion – who knows?

'OK,' he says. He frowns at me a bit.

'Sorry,' I say, 'I don't mean to be nasty about Rhi, but I'm still mad at her, and really I *am* just thinking of Gran.'

George smiles and throws back his covers. 'Under-standably,' he says.

And that's how day two starts.

~

Outside, a gale is definitely howling. It's like that up in the mountains. I personally think Snowdon has a thing about being the second highest peak in Britain – so it's continually trying to prove a point, like staying forever icy and living up to its English name with overkill.[1] And that's before Oswald gets going.

The gale is thick with driven snow; it's nearly a total white-out. I struggle to stay on my feet. Can't even see the Land Rover. It's not funny! The icy air actually makes it hard to breathe.

I'm out and into the snowstorm before George though, and I find the Land Rover half buried in a drift. I manage to get the door open and climb in. I turn on the engine, fingers crossed, praying the weather won't have drained the battery or frozen any vital bits.

Like a trusty friend the vehicle responds and coughs into life after a few tries. Then I start revving it up.

I'm not allowed to drive the Land Rover. I'm still waiting

---

1. Snowdon in English is 'Snow Hill'. In Welsh, Yr Wyddfa, meaning: The Burial Den.

for my licence (as soon as I'm seventeen – yay – here I come!) but Mum's taught me anyway, just in case, seeing as we live in the back of beyond, and you never know when you might need to go for help.

But I've only ever driven during good weather. I wouldn't dare try and take it out during a storm like this. I peer anxiously back at the cottage, to see if I can make out anything through the snow. I turn on the headlights. They bounce back at me from the white-out. I put the car heater on and sit and shiver while the engine turns over. I double check that we've got the first aid stuff and emergency kit and additional coats and thermal blankets – I think about hot coffee in a flask … that'd be nice … At last the shadowy form of George staggers out through the snow and bashes on the door of the Land Rover. Behind him I see Gran, wrapped in her shawl, battling through the storm towards the wood shed.

'Cripes!' he says, as he climbs in. 'It's rough out here and getting worse by the minute.'

I slide across to the passenger side. He shoves the Land Rover into gear.

'Gran getting logs in?' I ask.

'Getting the hens in from in the henhouse. She's scared they'll freeze if they stay out any longer.'

I think of my poor lambs. Yes, best to get the hens inside.

'Told your mum we took her Land Rover?' he asks.

I shake my head. No point now. She'll already have noticed I suppose, plus right now she'll be fast asleep, and what good would waking her up do?

'You sure it'll be OK?'

'Course,' I say. Mum won't mind – though she might demand a full explanation later, which could be awkward.

George releases the handbrake. Snowflakes whirl down in mesmerising patterns. The engine pulls. The wheels spin.

I bite down on my lip and start restlessly kicking my heel in the front footwell.

'Just a bit of wheelspin,' George reassures.

'OK,' I say tightly.

He revs the engine again. The clutch whines. The wheel spins faster, and the back of the vehicle slews round.

'Don't stress,' he says. 'It's just a bit of ice – I might need to tighten the snow chains.' He saws the wheel slightly from left to right, tries a higher gear, lowers the throttle.

Question: how can you stop being stressed, when you are stressed?

'Don't s'pose this Land Rover comes equipped with sand ladders or anything useful like that?' he asks.

I shake my head. It's not going to move, is it? We're

snowed in. We have only two days left to save Henry/Wales/the universe and the freaking Land Rover won't move.

'Cheer up,' says George. 'I'm making up a silly limerick to take your mind off things.'

A limerick? Is the boy normal?

He tries again, but the wheels just dig more firmly into the snowdrift.

Of course. Oswald wasn't going to let us go for help was he? No. He wants the heart back. And he wants me dead. Instinctively, I clutch at my breast pocket. What if he's around planning an attack? Beneath its wrapped layers, my fingers close around Henry's heart.

'Here's what I've got so far: *there was a young Ellie, called Madam.*'

'You mean there was a young madam called Ellie,' I say.

What if Oswald is up there right now, hiding behind the clouds?

'Yeah, but it doesn't rhyme like that.'

Suddenly I get a horrible feeling. It crawls down my spine and into the pit of my stomach.

George yanks the wheels left and right again. '*There was a young Ellie called Madam.*'

'But –'

'Just listen.'

'OK.'

He slams the gears into four-wheel drive. '*Who fell in love with a dragon.*'

'Oh God,' I say. 'That's ghastly!'

'Wait – listen to the rest.' Gently, he releases the clutch.

The back wheels engage, gain traction. I try to swallow. I cross my fingers. The feeling of impending catastrophe grows stronger.

'*There was a young Ellie called Madam,*

Who fell in love with a dragon,

But he was stuck in a cave,

And couldn't be saved … '

The Land Rover starts to pull forward.

I've left my silver charm in the house … If Oswald strikes now …

'That doesn't rhyme, either,' I snap at George.

'Does nearly.' George eases out the throttle.

I hold my breath, cross my fingers. *Let the car work.* The wheels drag. *Please.* The engine races. *And no Oswald.*

'Anyway I couldn't think of a last line. Luckily for you.' The back wheels stick, spin again, keep spinning.

'Plus it's not funny. It is *so* not funny IT. IS. NOT. FUNNY.'

The Land Rover slides sideways.

'Just off to check,' says George. He jumps out. I watch him through the frosty glass. I realise I'm gritting my teeth far too tightly.

George checks the wheels. I hear him pulling on the chains.

'Oh God,' I say.

I'm sure I can hear the flap of skeletal wings.

George pulls open the door. A blast of polar strength chills my face. George sticks his head back in, shakes the snow off himself. 'This car isn't going anywhere, Elles,' he says sadly.

Biting my lip, I get down from the car. If we can't use the Land Rover, how the heck are we going to get anywhere?

From inside the cottage, Ceri starts making desperate high-pitched yelps.

The sky above us seems to darken.

Why is Ceri making such a noise?

A smell, putrid, nauseous, abruptly wafts over us.

The air crackles.

A tonne of snow suddenly gusts upwards.

And George, with the speed of a skydiver, rugby tackles me.

A flurry of snow. White everywhere. Ceri barking. And I'm rolling over and over, winded, gagging.

'What the … ?'

A huge shape swoops down.

I knock my head on something. I think it's George.

The snow swirls.

Snow in my mouth. Snow in my eyes. Snow up my nose. I gasp, splutter. Cold. Wet. A hand drags me sideways. I blink. I drag my sleeve across my eyes. Blink again.

Oswald.

'DOWN!' yells George.

A huge staring dragon eye.

An arctic blast.

'NO!' Someone is screaming.

Vaguely I hear Ceri barking louder. The door of the cottage slamming against the wooden trellis of the porch.

A jet of ice hits the Land Rover.

For a moment it glitters, as if all its metalwork has been caught in the silver light of a disco ball. Then there's a cracking and a crackling. The windscreen crumbles into ice cubes of glass. The metal of the door shrieks and splits. The wing panels buckle. The front bumper curls, twists and falls off. A curious knocking starts – which I realise is the whole chassis of the car shattering to bits.

A moment ago, I was sitting in that car.

I twist my face upwards. There he is! Oswald. His glittering eye, his spiny neck. He's drawing his head back ready to strike again.

I'm not wearing my charm!

George drags me towards the cottage but I spot Gran;

she's trudging through the snow trailing her hens after her.

'GRAN!' George yells.

In a split second she looks up, raises her hand, makes a sign in the air and screams 'SARFF FELLTIGEDIG, EWCH I FFWRDD!'[2]

And Oswald strikes.

Down tunnels a tornado of twisting ice. It seems to hit some invisible barrier. It deflects, spins to the side, strikes wide of the mark.

Hits the little clutch of hens scrambling through the snow.

All of them.

Icy feathers flutter in the gale.

Torn little bodies.

A frozen spray of red blood.

'INSIDE, BOTH OF YOU!' yells Gran.

I scramble to my feet, still gasping, still half blinded by snow, and stumble through the front door of the cottage.

George follows and doubles up, breathless.

Gran is right behind him and intoning (shrilly): 'Yn enw'r Ddaear, Gwynt, Awyr a Thân. Yn enw perlysiau Blodeuwedd a sêr Draco. Am dri diwrnod a nos, ni allwch gyffwrdd yr hyn sy'n perthyn i mi.'[3]

---

2. 'AVAUNT THEE CURSED SERPENT!'
3. 'By Earth, by Wind, By Air, by Fire. By the herbs of Blodeuwedd and the Stars of Draco. For three days and nights, you cannot touch my domain.'

For a minute we remain half doubled up, sucking air into our lungs.

Those poor hens.

'That was close,' says George.

'You saved my life,' I say.

Poor Gran. She loved her hens.

'I guess we won't be getting to Cadair on wheels then,' murmurs George.

Poor Mum. Her poor Land Rover.

That was terrifyingly close.

My heart starts thudding all over again at how v v v v v close that really was.

'But at least I've cracked it!' George grins a bit hopelessly at me.

'Cracked what?' *We're trapped. We're stuck here. Unless you've cracked that, we'll never save Henry.*

'*There was a young Ellie called Madam,*

Who fell in love with a dragon,

But he was stuck in a cave,

And couldn't be saved,

And then it all went Armageddon.'

Oh boy.

Oh no.

And such lousy rhyming.

Trust George.

Armageddon.

The end of the flipping world.

Twenty - Six

For the next ten minutes Gran scolds us about going outside: Without Telling Her and Without ADEQUATE PROTECTION.

With no mention of the fact she saw us.

And followed us.

And didn't say a word.

I think she is very upset about the hens.

After blasting us thoroughly, she rushes off to the kitchen. George and I just look at each other. Try not to think about another encounter with Oswald. Try not to think about those poor Rhode Island Reds.

George opens his mouth, has that look in his eye –

I'm sure he's about to say something about 'frozen chicken legs'.

Which would NOT be funny. Gran reappears, potion in hand, marches to the front door, flings it open, and whistles at us to follow.

I mean it. She actually whistles.

She then proceeds to sprinkle the potion in little dribbles all around her house and garden.

We stand there shivering, trying not to look at the wreck of the Land Rover (now almost completely covered in snow) or the little snowy graves of the hens.

'I've prepared a solution,' she calls, as she splatters a bit more of the brew over the path to the wood shed.

'No escaping Plan B then,' whispers George.

'Last night I went up on to the mountain and whispered our needs through my piping into the wind,' says Gran.

As you do.

Gran tightens her shawl around her. 'And now, we will see whether the mountain's been listening.' She lifts up her head and calls out in Welsh: 'Merlod mynydd. Mae arnom angen eich cymorth. Rydych wedi addo dod yn ein hawr o angen.'

'Oh crikey,' says George, going a bit yellow.

'What?' I say. My Welsh is definitely not as good as his.

'Merlods,' says George. 'All the way on merlods.'

'What are merlods?' I say.

'Just wait.'

The snow lets up a little. There's a break in its swirling. Far away in the distance I hear the sound of something drumming on frozen ground.

'Oh no,' I groan. What has Gran gone and done now?

The drumming gets louder. It sounds like the footfall of something familiar. Then I hear the high call of a pony. And down the mountain, out of the mist, race a herd of fleet-footed, sleek-backed Welsh mountain ponies, with manes flying and nostrils flaring.

Through the garden at the back of the cottage they pour. They stamp and steam to a halt at Gran's front door.

Fearfully I glance up at the sky. Gran rests a hand on my arm. 'T'will be all right. He cannot come here again.'

The lead pony, a bright chestnut, whinnies, tosses his head and pounds at the frozen soil.

A window from the cottage is flung open. 'Oh My God!' yells Rhiannon at the top of her voice. 'We're not going to have to ride *all the way* on horseback, are we?'

I look up at her. She's such a drama queen.

'Yes,' I say. 'If you're still determined to come, you better cowgirl-up!'

With a bit of luck she'll decide not to.

'On *those*?' Rhi points very rudely at the little ponies, stamping their hooves and shaking out the cold in front of Gran's cottage.

'Rhiannon!' Gran's voice is sharp. 'You need to be appreciative of what Snowdon has provided for you. In the days to come, any small offer of help should be treasured.'

'Plus, you can always go *home*,' I say. Tee hee.

My phone pings. I pull it out hoping for some good news. Pleeease. After all, I think I deserve a break. Something good, like the police have dropped the charges, or Llanberis Council has decided to send a snowplough up the mountain.

Instead I read:

Random texter +44 7654 111156
I told you Hands Off or it was WAR. So don't be surprised.

My heart sinks. It has to be Sheila. I'm not taking that. I start pinging.

Recent updates between Ellie and Sheila:
Ellie
Sheila? Please stop mucking around. You're freaking me out.

Sheila

Whaaat?

Ellie

I just got a weird message. I thought it was you. Was it?

Sheila

Are you saying I'm a weirdo and I get my kicks trolling you?

Ellie

No. I'm not. I'm sorry. I'm just a bit stressed with all that court case and things. Anyone can get it wrong.

Sheila

Some friend.

Now I feel bad. That wasn't fair of me. Just because Sheila made a mistake last new year (albeit a rather huge mistake; one which nearly ended up with me dead in a cave), I'm being unforgiving. And with Rhi too.

I will try to be nicer.

If I can.

But I am stressed. About Henry mostly.

I text the number back. I probably shouldn't. It's probably best to ignore texts like that.

But I am a flawed character, obvs.

Recent updates between Ellie and +44 7654 111156:

Ellie

Look, I don't know who you are, but just back off.

Random Texter

You don't know who I am?

Ellie

No, and I don't want to.

Random Texter

Oh you'll want to know all right. I am your worst nightmare.

You can call me the SUPREME ONE.

I brush the snowflakes off my phone and put it away. The Supreme One. What a *stupid* name. Worst nightmare, my *foot*. Pathetic little witch.

I check I have the heart and the mirror safely in my pocket.

Davey joins us. He's pulled a thick jacket over his hippy outfit and looks, if anything, even weirder than ever. He smiles and nods his *hello*.

I smile *hello* back to Davey, then look up at Rhi again. 'Yes, you can go home,' I mouth. Instantly forgetting about being much nicer.

Rhiannon mouths back: 'Oh shut up', from the cottage window.

Gran beckons me over.

'Let Rhiannon go with you,' she says. 'One of the ponies has volunteered to carry her, and there must be a reason for that, even if we do not see it straight away.'

'OK,' I sigh, ignoring her claim that a pony has 'volunteered' something.

'You take the chestnut,' Gran continues. 'He is called Keincaled.'

The pony rolls a wild eye at me, then plunges nearer. He tosses his silky mane. Little flakes of snow caught in the strands of his hair sparkle like diamonds.

'Davey, take the bay – there – the one with the star on his forehead. His name is Bayard and he is willing to carry you.'

And George?

Already I have caught sight of a slightly taller than average pony, more like a cob, sparkling white, bold.

It pushes forward, nudges others aside and comes to a standstill in front of George. George smiles. The cob stretches his head, and lets out a long happy snort.

'Ah, it looks like Sior has been chosen,' says Gran, 'by Graine, the best of horses.'

'Hey George,' calls Rhiannon, 'now you've got a shining white charger, you are most welcome to carry me off.'

She leans out of the cottage window, showing far too much cleavage.

I think of a snappy retort, but I don't say it. I am practising being much nicer. George grins at Rhi and shouts back, 'Aw, Rhi, you are too kind'.

Two more ponies – one, a grey mare with dappled markings, the other black as coal tar – trot out of the small herd. The black pony pounds the ground beside Keincaled, the chestnut, he snorts and puffs. Great clouds of white steam mushroom out into the snowy air.

One is for Rhiannon, I guess, but the other? Is Gran coming too?

Gran lifts up her copper piping. 'Diolch, fy rhai annwyl,' she croons towards the band of ponies.[1] 'We will look after your dear ones and return them to you. And forever it will be sung upon our side of the mountain that the Welsh ponies of Snowdonia came to the rescue of Y Ddraig Goch in his hour of need.'

The ponies lift up their heads and whinny and neigh, as if they have understood her every word.

'Now,' she turns back to us and waves her piping in the air. 'Come on, look lively. You must trust these ponies. They have come of their own free will and are ready to

---

1. 'Thank you, my beloved ones.'

carry you to the summit of Cadair Idris. But they will not suffer you to harness them; and they will not be spurred or whipped. And should any of them decide that they no longer wish to carry you, you must accept their decision, for they are friends and not servants.'

The front door opens, Ceri rushes out, bounding through the snow like crazy. She jumps up and around in front of the ponies, all tail-wagging and doggy-dancing and yip-yapping.

Rhiannon comes out too, dressed in the most fetching of snow-suits. It's bright pink with snazzy bits. It would definitely have looked truly bizarre on Gran, but Rhi somehow makes everything look glam.

'Ta-dah!' She waves her arms about and pirouettes.

Well Oswald won't have any trouble locating us wherever we go then, will he? She's probably visible from outer space.

I shudder. I open my mouth to say something. I close it again. I. Am. Going. To. Be. Nicer. Besides, Oswald has dragon vision; he can probably see the rings round Jupiter with his eyes shut anyway.

George helps Rhiannon on to the dapple-grey pony. Gran stands upright in the porch, looking for all the world like a small female Gandalf in a velvet skirt and paisley shawl.

'Is the black pony for you, Gran?' I say. I'm really hoping

she'll come with us. I know George is strong and all that, but Gran knows so much more – I'd feel a zillion times safer.

Gran shakes her head. She stretches out her hand. The black pony, moves closer, nuzzles it like an old friend.

'I am not going with you,' she says. 'I am too old to ride ponies over mountains. I would only slow you down.'

'Then the black pony?' I say.

'Don't ask,' advises Gran. 'These ponies know what they are about. And by the way his name is Widow-maker.'

'Widow-maker?' says Rhi.

'Yes,' says Gran. 'On account of those who have tried to catch and ride him.'

I blink. Wow.

'But though I am not coming, I have been thinking of your safety,' she says, 'and I have a gift for both of you girls – should you need it.'

'Typical,' sighs George, as he springs on to the back of the white cob. 'The only thing I ever get is orders.'

Gran ignores him, rather superbly. 'For you Ellie,' she says, 'I have prepared this. It's a powder made of the insects I spoke of.'

I stretch my hand out rather gingerly. I am not sure I want insect powder.

'Do not fear,' says Gran through her piping. 'I have made a dust from their shells; they cannot harm you. The Coraniaid hate these creatures and the time may come when you will need to throw this dust in their eyes.' She nods wisely and hands me an old plastic-topped yogurt pot, full of something brown and icky looking. 'And on that note, don't forget your piping.' She hands each of us a fresh length of copper piping, as if the bits we'd been using were past their sell-by date. 'Never discuss anything of importance except through these. As you have seen, your lives may depend on it.'

The extra bits of plumbing are duly handed round. It occurs to me that we've probably enough between us to plumb a small cottage, if we fancied it.

'Now, for you Rhiannon,' she says kindly, 'I've suspected from the start, that you had a role to play in this quest, so I've searched the hills and found you an adder stone. You must wear it around your neck and use it when the time comes.'

'A what?' shrieks Rhiannon. 'An adder stone?'[2] She flaps

---

2. An adder stone is a small rock or pebble with a naturally created hole running through it. Usually found on beaches, they were thought to possess magical properties. They were used as a cure for certain illnesses and ailments such as whooping cough, and were often worn as a charm to protect against witchcraft or evil. They were also thought to prevent nightmares.

The name 'adder stone' is derived from the story of their origins: according to legend, the stones were formed from hardened snakes' saliva, occurring as a result of a strange and rare phenomenon where a cluster of snakes would wind themselves together to form a living ball or 'egg'. The resulting stone could be used to draw venom from a snakebite wound.

her hands about. 'But how will I know when the time comes?' Rhiannon looks over at George, her eyes ~~turned up to full volume of pukey manipulative patheticness~~ wide and beautiful.

'Now Rhiannon,' says Gran sharply, all her gentleness gone. 'Do not play games. You willingly joined a witches' circle. You know they will find a way to use you, to control you, to force you to betray the mission – if they can. You are already familiar with the Dark Arts, and have used them to bring about much harm. You are known by those who would practise Black Magicke and they have put their mark upon you. The adder stone, sometimes known as a hag stone or witch's stone will protect you and, trust me, you will *definitely* know when it is time to use it.'

I *love* it!

I mean: Oh dear, poor Rhiannon. A hag stone.

LOL.

I put my hand out to the chestnut stallion. He obligingly steps forward, nuzzles my palm and then headbutts me gently with his broad, intelligent forehead. He tosses his head as if to say, 'get on already!'

George comes closer. He puts his hands around my waist and lifts. It seems like the chestnut bends down a little, and there I am sitting on its back.

George is very slow to remove his hands. Suddenly he says, 'Oh Ellie, I think you left something inside'.

'Huh?' I look at him puzzled.

'Do you want to jump down again and get it before we go?'

'Or you could get it for me,' I say.

'Aw shucks!' says George. 'Rumbled.'

I've got to say one thing about George: he certainly never stops trying.

'You should have pity on me,' he whispers. 'It's not fair; the lies a guy has to tell to get his arms around you.'

I aim a kick at him but he's too fast and jumps back, laughing.

I can't say I am an expert at bareback riding. I can't say I'm an expert at riding at all. In fact I've only ever ridden a few times – and that was when Rhiannon's dad decided tourists might like to have a go at pony trekking up Snowdon, about three summers ago. It was a great idea that never caught on.

And I never got further than the bumping up and down stage of trotting.

The chestnut lets out a little sympathetic whinny. He's only a foot or so bigger than a sheepdog, but he carries himself with dignity. I'm sure he must feel eighteen hands high in his own heart. Well, at least it's not far to fall.

'Do not be fooled by looks,' says Davey as if he knows exactly what I'm thinking. 'Welsh mountain ponies, though they are small, are strong and can withstand a level of cold and hardship that would stop any thoroughbred in its tracks.'

They'll need to. It's biting cold and hasn't stopped snowing. I lean down and pat Keincaled's neck. 'I trust you,' I say.

'Take the old Druids Way, Sior, to Blaenau Ffestiniog and on to Cadair,' interrupts Gran. 'I have used what arts I possess to shield you on this first leg of the journey, but you must hurry, for my charms are weak and will barely last the day. Sior, you *do know* the Druids Way, don't you?'

'I haven't been your grandson for the last seventeen years and forgotten the old ways across the mountains, Gran,' he says.

'Well, if in the snow, you lose sight of landmarks, trust the ponies, for they have come from far to answer our call – some even from as far as Carneddau – and they use the Way of the Blessed often.'

'Don't worry, I'll find it.'

'Make sure you do. None from the Olde Deepe Magicke can attack you on that path,' says Gran. Even Oswald cannot, though he may send others to confuse and trick you, to try to chase you off it.'

'Right,' says George.

I bite my lip. I notice he has packed both his axes.

'On the way, look for unexpected help. The Olde Deepe Magicke will have woken up all kinds of things, and not all of them are evil. And finally … ' Gran counts things off on her fingers. 'Trust nothing, trust nobody and never eat fairy food. That's all.'

'OK. All understood and copied,' says George.

I nod my head too.

'Then the hour has come for you to leave,' Gran says.

First she crosses over to Davey. She places her hand on his pony and mumbles something through her piping. Then weirdly, she bows down before him on her old arthritic knees and says, 'Lord be praised, that I have lived to see you. May your shadow forever bless the beautiful land of Wales.'

Davey looks a bit puzzled, but takes her hand and says, 'When the hope of Wales is held in such a heart as yours, there is no fear for the future.' He kisses her hand.

I gawp. Then panic. This is way too *Lord of the Rings* for me.

Gran comes next to me and mumbles again over Keincaled. I bend to kiss her goodbye. She whispers into my hair: 'Expect trouble, but have courage. You must follow the path your heart dictates. It is your destiny. Seek by any means to get Idris's help. Only he can get Draco to free Henry. But never forget the White One will hunt you to the bitter end. You have crossed him already and dashed his dearest desires – and you carry the heart of his enemy – both in its form in this world, and in its true form, for Henry loves you. Oswald would take great joy, for that reason alone, in destroying you – he has set his purpose upon it – but be brave, for those that have Y Ddraig Goch's blessing will be blessed. You have seen how you bear a charmed life already. Now, to business, I have sought out the herbs of Blodeuwedd to protect you.' Swiftly she ties a bunch of dried flowers into Keincaled's mane. 'Make sure they stay there until you are safely on the Druids Way.'

For some silly reason, I feel my eyes tearing up. I love her so much. 'Take care of Ceri,' I gulp. 'Tell Mum whatever you think best.' Then I bury my face in the side of her cheek.

Next she whispers her instructions to Rhiannon. Lastly, she turns to George. 'Do not try to use rangers' paths, Sior,' Gran warns. 'They are too dangerous; there is far too much chance that Oswald will find a way to attack you.

Those routes offer no protection. Stick to the Druids Way and Sarn Helen – the old Roman road, they're your best chance.'

'Yes Nan, no Nan, three bags full Nan,' says George. But I notice he is nodding his head.

Gran merely smiles. Dear old Gran. 'God bless you then,' she says. 'And if in danger, remember what I have said.'

I am the last to leave. I ride the chestnut pony out after the others. I turn behind me to raise one hand in farewell to Gran. But the cottage is gone, quite gone, hidden by snow and out of sight.

Twenty – Seven

ELLIE'S PHONE Second Day of the Magic – 10 March 08.30

Status: Scared and worried. Probably going to turn this phone off to save the battery.

George takes the lead and heads his cob, Graine, out over our side of the mountain, towards the old Druids Way. The Way follows a ley line that runs across country, over wild peaks, from Yr Wyddfa to Blaenau Ffestiniog. After Ffestiniog it joins the route of Sarn Helen – an ancient Roman road which runs straight (ish) to Dolgellau and on to Cadair.

On our side of the mountain, the Druids Way is not a clearly marked track, and though I have heard of it, I hardly know which way it goes. Many of the old ley lines – lines of power, along which legendary heroes once walked

– cross and criss-cross the UK.

I do not feel much like a legendary hero.

A howling gale blows in from the north, straight off the peaks. 'Which way do we go?' I shout through it.

'Down … this side … centre of Snowdon,' George yells. 'Across … marked by cairns … worry. Davey and me … here … protection.'

I look at Davey who btw is v v v thin and weedy. I have my doubts.

'Not loving this,' complains Rhiannon loudly. She is right in front of me. 'You could at least have asked me to wrap up warm when we went up to the Black Stone, Ellie. You knew it was going to be practically sub-zero. And this pink is so … *pink*. And as for my make-up … ' Her tone is accusing.

I remind myself to be patient. I do not make a remark about her face matching the snowsuit.

You see. I am being much nicer.

'Don't you think George looks lush on a horse?' she sighs, when she sees I'm not taking the bait.

'Pony,' I correct.

'Stallion,' she whispers breathily and titters. I'm not sure if she's referring to the pony or George.

We skirt the top pastures and climb the ridge that

runs behind the cottage. On the far side of Moel Cynghorion we descend. The snow is deeper than ever here. The ponies have to high-step, like they are doing some dressage routine with elevated goose-steps to make headway. Their tails swish on the snow, their hooves crunch into drifts.

The wind drops. We struggle on. From time to time, something breaks with a snap, like the sound of ice cracking; Rhiannon's grey mare snorts, or Keincaled breathes out in a rushy blowing of air.

A shadow falls over the mountain. I look up; grey sky. I listen intently. Yes. There! I'm sure of it; something beating the air.

Despite my extreme-arctic-weather, Canada-goose-down-filled parka, a shiver runs through me. I reach out and touch the herbs that Gran has tied into Keincaled's mane. *Please let them work.*

Even the ponies feel it. There's an urgency in their movement; despite deep drifts, they don't ease up.

Just let the charms hold him off 'til we reach the Druids Way.

Oh, please let us reach it.

We keep heading south.

We leave Snowdon behind us.

I'm not sure how long we can keep this speed up.

Hour after hour.

After hour.

~

Around midday, George says, 'Let's make for that stone wall. *There.*' He points at a distant place, a long way away.

I squint my eyes up until I can see a low, crumbling, snow-capped stone wall. It's bounding a belt of woodland following the contour of a far hill.

'How much further is *that*?' complains Rhiannon. 'And btw, have we actually got to ride *all* the way?'

I want to say, 'No, you can walk,' but I don't.

'We could stop there,' says George uncertainly. 'Have a little rest – if you're tired?'

George is so lovely. He's trying so hard to make the journey easier for her.

Unlike me who's thinking: if you hate riding so much, why the heck did you insist on coming?

I think I say something to that effect out loud. Oops.

Bad Ellie.

'You sound all cross and horrid,' Rhiannon sulks. 'And you don't tell me anything. You've known for *ages* all about these dragony, magical things and you *know* I love all that stuff. And I wanted a pet unicorn, but you never tell me anything.'

I snap back, 'Sometimes it's better not to know anything, that way you can't *tell* anyone'.

'Oh thanks!' Her voice is laced with hurt.

I ignore her.

'At least George's gran believes in me. She gave me an adder stone for a reason.' Rhiannon sniffs loudly.

'Be on your guard,' says George. 'Between us and the wall is open ground. It gives me a creepy feeling: it's way too exposed.'

Actually everywhere is creepy. There is no traffic on the road below, no planes overhead, no baa of sheep – only the howling wind off the mountaintops.

'George is right,' says Davey. 'If we carry on over these slopes, we're bound to be seen.' He looks up. 'I wish those birds weren't flying so near either. It'd be much better if we could get down there by that woodland – get into a bit of cover.'

I look up. He's right. A small flock of birds is wheeling in a tight circle right above us. They're jet black. A *murder* of carrion crows.

George and Davey move off at a swift pace. Rhi and I follow.

As we move, they move.

Every now and then one of them lets out a deep,

hoarse cawing.

I shiver. I remember my tiny slaughtered newborn lambs. *The birds and the wolves hunt together, don't they?*

A sixth sense flares up in me. 'We should hurry,' I call. Something suddenly screams out in my head: DANGER! DANGER!

'*George!*' I shout.

Keincaled feels it too. He needs no encouragement to race forward.

The wind whips at my face, carrying the sound of distant howling. My heart pounds. An icy sweat breaks out across my forehead.

'*GEORGE!*'

'Don't leave me at the back!' wails Rhiannon.

Above us, the birds form a bullet-shaped cloud.

The black pony, Widow-maker, starts rearing and snorting.

My throat goes all dry. '*George?*' I try to croak out.

I'm sure that's not just the wind howling.

Davey and George are going so fast and the path is so narrow, I can't draw level with them. The wind blows my words away.

At last I reach them. '*Please,*' I yell. '*Something's up …* '

'Got … mirror?' Davey turns and yells.

'Yes,' I say. Like, random question! I'm trying to tell them:

Those Crows Are Seriously Bad News, and Widow-maker is not happy, and Rhiannon is scared and I know Oswald must have seen where we are and *something is going to happen.*

And Davey is asking me about the mirror!

George waves me closer, yells, '*Keep up – hurry*'.

Davey with his head still turned, nods vigorously. 'It has powers – the time may come – may save or slay us.'

I strain to hear him, plus, you know, we're going at full gallop.

'Explore its wonders – carefully at first – of course – '

And wish I hadn't. OMG he's got such a ~~patronising~~ formal way of talking. Plus if he doesn't listen to what I'm trying to say, I might just whack him with it!

'*DAVEY!*' I holler. I put my hand inside my jacket and pull the mirror out. '*Not the best time!*'

He turns his head, slows Bayard and carefully enunciates: 'We must be very careful, admittedly. Such a powerful magical object could possibly undo us.'

'Undo us?' I stare at him. *Is he totally unhinged?*

'Listen,' I call. '*Behind. The. Wind.* Can you hear it?'

'I have already heard it,' he says with a weird wrinkle of his nose (like I'm a favourite but really slow child). 'I do not think the wolves will attack us in the open.'

'You don't?' Maybe he knows something. I send him a questioning look.

'No,' he returns.

'But you could be wrong?'

Davey slows until he is quite level with me. 'Yes.'

'But if they *do*, you've got some super-duper powers to protect us right?'

'No.'

'But they ran away from you yesterday.'

'I don't know why.'

Great.

We come to the downhill stretch nearer to the broken stone wall.

'OK,' says George. He looks around. 'I need to halt – just for a second – got to check the map – I can't do that when we're moving.' He smiles at me. 'Maybe eat something?' He looks hopefully at the bag, packed on the black pony.

'George,' I start again, 'I don't think we should stop. Listen.'

There below the wail of the wind is the baying of wild creatures.

'Hey Elles,' George's face is sad and lined. 'I know. But I've really got to make sure of the route. I promised Gran to stay on the path. Here where our backs are protected is as good a place as any to do that.'

I look carefully at the spot. George has chosen well. The broken wall behind us skirts a sheer drop into a disused quarry. An attack from behind would be impossible.

Rhiannon dismounts and says, 'Gosh, you must be like, starving, George – I'll go and get you something'.

If I am going to die, I have one last request: please let Rhi stop doing all that gushing-over-George stuff. It's utterly puke-in-a-paper-bag.

'Aw, thanks, Rhi,' says George, with a smile.

And he totally encourages her. Makes her do it all the more. And if I say anything, he'll just ask me if I'm jealous.

I am totally absolutely not jealous.

Obviously.

George unfolds the map from its bag and, sheltering it from the wind, peers over it.

The ponies huddle together, try and knock the snow from tufts of grass to munch at frosty mouthfuls. Davey smiles at me and nods his head.

Perhaps he's right after all – perhaps while George is checking the route, I should explore the mirror. I get it out and hold it up in front of me. If it has other powers, I obviously need to master them.

Plus I might just get a glimpse of Henry.

'Do you really think that's a good idea, Elles?' says George, looking up from the map and munching a fistful of cake and a chicken drumstick simultaneously.

'Yes,' I say. Looking into the mirror is the best idea I've had all day.

'Oh, c'mon,' says George.

'Davey thinks it has powers that may destroy us,' I say. 'He suggested that I find out what. If there're other dangers out there, I want to be prepared.'

'Let her try and master the mirror,' says Davey mystically.

Over the mountainside the wind whistles. Below its piercing scream, the baying seems a little louder.

'I'll come and help you map-read, Georgie, if Ellie just wants to admire herself in that creepy mirror,' says Rhiannon, sweeter than the sweetest saccharine. She waves a huge bacon sarnie and a slice of leftover Spanish omelette in front of him.

I sigh. And look into the mirror.

At first I see only my face, my worry and my eyes looking back. Then a mist seems to form quickly across the glass.

I am not looking for Henry, I remind myself. *I am not looking for Henry.* I am looking to see what dangers and deadly perils lie in wait for us.

The mist clears a little. In the mirror, shadows move.

281

Through the dimness, I see the way we've come, the path that winds along beside the crest of the hill. I'm sure I can even make out Gran's cottage – just a faint smudge of grey, far in the distance.

And I see other things.

They creep over the trampled miles of footprints, nose at the snow, yet on they come; across the slopes, following the scuffed trail. I peer closer. The shadows stop. They sniff at the air, as if for the first time they've caught scent of their quarry, and then they begin to lope. Faster and faster.

I see what I already fear: the Cŵn Annwn – the loathsome creatures of the night.

The white wolves of Snowdonia.

Twenty-Eight

'We've gotta go!' I say. 'They're coming! I've seen them!' Frantically I urge Keincaled forward.

'COME ON ALREADY!' I yell.

Davey looks worried. 'We must be careful not to jump too hastily to any course of action. We do not know the *intent* of the mirror. We must consider,' he says, 'just as you can see them, maybe they too can see us? Maybe by looking at them, they learn of our whereabouts. Or maybe the mirror sets us a trap, tricks us into running thoughtlessly forward, into certain danger ahead.'

A lethal feeling, all cold and prickly, shoots down my spine. He could be right. Oswald's flying somewhere near for sure, listening, watching, waiting for a chance to break through Gran's protection. I check the little bunch of flowers is still tied to Keincaled's mane. I remember the words: *Blodau'r derw, banadl ac erwain a greodd Blodeuwedd; ni allwch hela unrhyw forwyn sy'n dal y blodau hyn*.'[1] I cross my fingers, send up a prayer to the mountains: *let the charms hold*.

'But,' I say, 'the mirror showed me. The wolves are on our trail.'

Widow-maker pricks up his ears. He sends out a sudden frenzied whinny.

Rhiannon begins to cry. 'Ohmygod, OhMyGod, OHMY-GOD.' She gets shriller.

The ponies abruptly become restless, stamp their hooves, toss their heads.

'Keep faith in the Lord,' says Davey.

Bayard starts neighing in a wild fashion.

'You see,' I say. 'You *see*! The ponies know the wolves are coming. C'mon. Let's go. *Please*.'

This time Davey doesn't argue. George checks the map again, peers across the mountainside. 'Maybe, if we hurry … all this snow – it's confusing … Gran marked the Druids Way as running here … if only we could reach it … '

---

1. *Oakblossom, broom, and meadowsweet; created Blodeuwedd, you cannot hunt any maiden who carries these flowers.*

Rhiannon struggles back on to her dapple-grey pony.

'OK,' says George, 'let's go. I'm pretty sure that's the way.'

We set off at a canter, down by the wall, through the snow. I twist a lock of Keincaled's mane through my gloved fingers, grip hard with my knees, keep my eyes squinted to try and avoid the flurry of snow from Bayard's hooves.

Ahead of us, the trail opens up on to a track. A few trees line it, stunted, heavy with frozen moss. Further to our left, the waters of a llyn shine, weirdly glassy.

My nose goes cold. I catch faint howling. It reverberates in waves of sound. The ponies snort, agitated, clouds of steamy breath fill the air, wild manes billow. The small black one, Widow-maker, drops to the rear again, lays his ears flat against his skull and swishes his tail.

At the front, Graine breaks into a gallop.

'We must get there,' shouts George over the wind. 'Down past Beddgelert. We'll be safe there ... they can't attack us on it ... '

Davey shouts a reply: 'It's true ... the Way of the Blessed is hallowed ... '

I totally hope so. The ponies are utterly spooked out. And I'm crap at riding. I've never galloped. Not like this. I bend as low as I can, ducking under branches. And hang on.

'We must slow down … we can't risk a fall.' George waves an arm up and down to slow us.

'Bayard, Bayard!' Davey yells. The bay pony tosses its head, as if it hears.

'S-l-o-w the pace.' George is hollering now.

Bayard whinnies, seems to be talking to the other ponies, and the mad pace slackens. The frenzied gallop slows. We settle to a fast trot.

God, I hate trotting.

I hold on to Keincaled's mane. I bump along. 'I'm so sorry,' I whisper into his chestnut neck. 'Don't mean to jolt you.'

Keincaled seems to understand. He rolls his eyes, but his pace stays steady. His hooves crunch snow, hit frozen soil in a bone-shaking, regular, drumming rhythm. God, even my teeth rattle.

I'm sure you're supposed to 'rise' to a trot or something, aren't you?

Rhiannon's dapple mare flares her nostrils; she snorts out steamy air in an effort to control her panic. I see George talking to Graine, asking for his help to calm the others. Graine swishes his tail, whinnies.

Then suddenly, through the mist on the far slopes, we see them.

Wolves.

White streaks – flowing in a white wave – tails stretched – hundreds of them.

Racing towards us.

And it's too late. The grey mare is spooked. She breaks into a sudden wild gallop.

Then the rest follow.

And like racehorses we flee down the valley, along the side of the llyn.

The stones on the track are slippery with ice. The dapple mare stumbles. Rhiannon cries out.

They both go down.

Down.

For one terrible moment I see Rhi, a blur of pink, and white flying snow.

There is whinnying and one long scream.

And then a rolling blur of hooves and pony and girl.

Oh no! Rhi?

George jumps free of Graine and races to Rhiannon. Graine pounds to a snorting stop and trots after George, neighing at the dappled mare to calm down.

The grey mare struggles to her feet. Her flank is bleeding. George picks Rhiannon up. Her face is as white as the snow all around her.

'You *Ooh-kaay*?' I call.

'I can't do this,' she whimpers.

'Yes, you can,' reassures George. 'Your pony broke your fall, even though she went down. You're shaken, but trust her. Look – she's bleeding, she saved you.'

Rhiannon looks at her little grey mare and throws her arms around the pony's neck. 'Thank you,' she whispers.

'C'mon,' urges George. I see him looking out over the lake.

I focus on the long stretch of bank on the far side of the water. More of them. Shapes racing through the mist. Glint of eye. Shine of teeth. Pale tongues. Bone-white fur.

I lean forward and whisper into Keincaled's mane, 'I think we should get going'.

At once Keincaled understands. He lifts his head, rolls his eye back at me and breaks into a canter. He takes the lead while George stays near Rhi. Davey drops back to bring up the rear with Widow-maker.

Down the track towards the main road, into another field, the path is narrow alongside a stream, hard to follow. Twigs and frozen moss tear at me. The clouds clear, just a bit. A very little bit. The snow stops falling. The moon shines out in the afternoon sky. Weird. Scarily bright.

How far 'til we hit the Druids Way? As if in answer, a howling breaks out. A great din of barking and wailing.

And it's so much closer.

They must have caught our scent.

But as I lean forward and whisper to Keincaled, *'faster, faster,'* to my horror, an answering howl shatters the air.

A god-awful, monstrous yowling coming from *in front of us!*

They are up ahead too?

'Follow the track, 'til you come to the road – turn right,' George's voice hollers above the howling.

Icy air whips down at me. I grip with my knees and twist a knot of Keincaled's mane into my fist. I hang on as he shoots into a furious gallop.

'Go right,' I call to Keincaled, hoping he can hear.

What's in front of us?

In my mind, I imagine *'a great creature with a blood-smeared mouth'* – some story Dad used to tell me. *Waiting on the road.* I don't know why I think of that … I don't want to think of that …

There's a tearing noise. Something crashes through undergrowth just behind us. *So close.* I twist my head round, strain into the whiteness. And then I see the wolves, not far behind Davey, George and Rhiannon – there – streaming out of the mist. Light shining off their coats. Glittering on their yellow teeth. Catching the fire in their eyes.

They're here. They've reached us.

I whip round, steady myself on Keincaled and peer forward. We're going so fast. The wind stings my face, blinds me. It's so cold even my teeth are frozen. I've never been this fast on a horse before. God, don't let me fall.

'*Trust Keincaled*,' I hear Granny Jones's reassuring tone. '*He is handsome and hardy and will let none he chooses to carry slip from his back.*'

I flipping hope not.

Towards the road, right towards the village of Beddgelert.

But that howling. Oh God, don't let them be in front too.

We burst through the hedge on the mountainside, barely noticing the thorns or the sharp gnarled twigs.

Only to be greeted by another long drawn-out howl.

I was right. It is coming from in front. An eerie wailing that pierces the air like *The Hound of the Baskervilles* meets *The Hour of the Werewolves.*

Oh Henry, let us survive.

We're on to the road, racing like a bullet. No phantom hound just yet. Maybe I was wrong. Keincaled leaps the ruts on the verge, gallops down the centre of the road. *Oh God, I hope he knows what he's doing.* He tears through the snowdrifts, swerves ice patches, rips through air like lightning.

There's a thudding crash behind us.

I daren't turn round. I'll lose balance. The wind whips past. *My ears. They hurt.* My heart drums. My legs shake with the gripping. I screw up my eyes. *My eyes.* I can't see. Up ahead is something. Buildings? *Reach them.* The wolves won't risk going near people, will they?

Weave in-between potholes, duck, twist. *How close are they?* Don't look back. *Ground's covered with ice. Can't slip. Can't fall.*

The long drawn-out howling from ahead starts up again. Holy smoke, they're behind us *and* in front!

Please dear Snowdon. Please …

A pounding shakes the road. *Christ we're trapped*, I lift my head. Snatch a glimpse of something large, as it bursts into view.

Larger than large.

Howling and howling.

A *huge* hound.

I knew it. Another demon from the world of nightmares. Some kind of Gwyllgi; some monstrous dog of darkness.

Holy Heck! Its teeth are bared. *Holy holy heck.* I bend low against Keincaled's neck. Our only chance is to get off the road. I look for a way, a gap in the high bank. Nothing.

No way to get to the village.

Pray for a miracle.

Keincaled drives forward. *Brave pony.* We race down the road, pound across treacherous tarmac. Ice chunks skitter, a spray of crumbling road flies out behind us.

No time to look back. No time to think. Just pray. The gigantic beast up ahead yowls. Hooves race. It's no use; the hound from hell is blocking the way. *Where did it come from?* No need to answer. Just hold on. Just breathe. And pray.

And as we race towards certain death, I think of Henry. And I think of George.

Henry. I'm so sorry.

Rescue me, George, please save me.

Maybe the wolves have already caught him.

I can't bear it.

No George.

No Henry.

The monstrous thing ahead howls again.

Blocks our path.

Keincaled yields up one, long, screaming neigh and we skid to a halt.

Twenty-Nine

I nearly shoot straight over Keincaled's head.

He twists under me, stops me from falling.

There is no escape. The side of the valley to our right is blocked by a two-metre-high snowdrift. To our left: a fence.

Through the mist, the howling wolves sound out their call into the wind.

Within a split second, Davey, George and Rhiannon arrive. The ponies strike the frozen road, turn around and strike again, trapped between the huge hound and the wolves.

The smell of dog, wet, pungent; I suck in air. Stay focused Ellie.

'Form a circle.' George reaches for his axe. 'Stay together. I'll face the wolves. You – Ellie – get behind me with Rhi. Davey?'

George drags his axe free. The ponies whinny and stamp,

but they do not run. Instead they form a rough circle. One of them rears up and smashes his hooves down as if to show us that they too can fight.

But hardly has George drawn his axe, when the black pony – Widow-maker – races into the path of the oncoming wolves. He rears up, lays his ears flat against his skull, his nostrils flare, blood red. He watches the lead wolf, rolls his eye, and – quick as a flash – smashes his hooves down, crashing into its head, crushing it into a pulp of bone and blood and tissue.

I can actually feel my eyes widen. Wow, so that's why he came along.

George pounds forward on trusty Graine and lands his (relatively) new Husqvarna Forest, hickory, long-handled, steel, hand-forged axe right in the next wolf's head. The axe lives up to its reputation and splits its skull in two.

Ugh. Yuck. Stuff sprays across the white snow. Blood and bone. Foul. I close my eyes, just briefly, press my tongue against my teeth, fight back the urge to be sick.

'Davey?' calls George.

I don't somehow think Davey is going to be any good at fighting. But he moves bravely forward to George's side. Yesterday, the wolves seemed afraid of him; today they show no fear. Too bad. I was hoping.

Widow-maker rears and strikes again in a fury of hoof and teeth and crushing kicks.

Davey seems to be praying. Rhiannon is screaming. Keincaled lets out a whinny of surprise. I feel myself jolted forward, as Keincaled bounds towards the hellhound.

I really wish he were wearing a bridle. If he were, I would tug down on the reins, *very* hard.

But there's no bridle. Not even a bit of string. And even more worryingly, Keincaled seems to show no fear at all.

I grip with my knees, hang on to his mane. '*Keincaled!*' I shriek, '*Nooo!*'

Keincaled takes no notice.

At the back of my mind, I hear Gran whisper. '*Trust your steed, my dear.*'

I cast one hopeful glance at George, but he's enmeshed with three huge wolves, swinging his axe wildly, as Graine and Widow-maker slash and kick about them.

So I turn to face the hellhound.

Looks like I'm going to have to fight it all by myself. I yank out the mirror. 'If you've got powers, you better show them,' I hiss. I pray to the heart. '*Henry, protect me.*'

And I turn, prepared to smash the mirror over the head of the hound, if I possibly can. *Oh God, it's so enormous.*

Grey, ragged, more like a wolfhound than a wolf.

So scary.

It bounds forward. I time what may be my one and only blow, grip Keincaled's mane with one hand, raise the mirror.

But amazingly.

Totally gobsmackingly.

When my arm is raised, the great hound lets out a bark of recognition, lopes forward and briefly *nuzzles* the face of my pony!

OMG.

What is going on?

For one horrible minute, I think I'm deceived, Keincaled has betrayed me, and then I hear Davey shout, '*Lord be praised!*'

My heart misses a beat. I don't get it.

'*Tis Gelert, the faithful hound, risen from his bed to come to our defence!*' yells Davey, filling in the gaps for me.

I drop my arm. I peer forward, squint at the hellhound again, and see that it is not a hideous monster at all, but a true wolfhound, dark in colour, though majorly huge. And I remember the story ... [1]

Keincaled wheels back, and with Gelert at our side (tbh

---

1. Gelert is the legendary dog associated with the village of Beddgelert. The dog is alleged to have belonged to Llywelyn the Great, who returned from hunting to find his baby missing, the cradle overturned, and the dog with a blood-smeared mouth. Believing the dog savaged the child, Llywelyn drew his sword and killed it. After the dog's dying yelp, Llywelyn heard the cries of the baby, unharmed under the cradle, along with a huge dead wolf. From that day on, Llywelyn never smiled again.

Gelert is practically as big as Keincaled) we charge back.

Widow-maker and George stand together in a mess of hair and blood. The snow on the road is pulped to a pink mess. Widow-maker has a long gash along his flank and George's axe is down, embedded fast into the neck of a dying wolf.

The sight of Gelert sends hideous snarling along the ranks of the white creatures.

The wolves cower back. One, a thin, evil-eyed creature slinks to the side, springs forward at Rhiannon on the tiny dapple-grey pony. Gelert strikes faster than an arrow; like a bolt of lightning, he has the creature by the throat. One twist of his mighty jaws and the thin wolf's neck breaks with a revolting crack. There's a crunch and blood from the jugular vein shoots out in an arc of crimson.

'Ooohhh!' shrieks Rhi.

'Be not afraid,' consoles Davey. 'We are saved, for the wolves hate and fear Gelert.' He moves closer to Rhi and explains: 'He slew their ancestor, their wolf king, and paid for it with his life. He is a saint among dogs and a demon among wolves.'

'Oh Davey,' sobs Rhi, 'are we really saved?'

George springs down from Graine and retrieves his axe. Widow-maker goes to his side and bares his teeth.

And Gelert howls out his hunting cry.

Thirty

The wind whips down, cold from the mountain. Gelert howls and howls. The howling echoes from valley to valley.

The wolves hesitate, then turn and slope away. George wipes his bloodstained hands down his jacket.

Yuck. Boys.

Don't they ever think of how clothes get washed?

He turns to me and says, 'Thank God, you're all right'.

'What about me?' cries Rhiannon. 'Aren't you going to say: thank God, *I'm* all right?'

George looks at her and smiles. 'Of course I am,' he says.

'Well, then *say it*,' she insists.

'Thank God you're all right, Rhi,' says George with one of his huge, sunny smiles. It lights up his handsome face. Have I told you before how handsome he is? Well, right now he looks amazing: big smile, even his fair hair in a dishevelled Viking plait looks awesome.

I sniff. Why does she get the sunny smile? Like, was Rhiannon the one charging off to meet a hellhound straight from the Devil?

No. She was not. She was sitting behind George and Widow-maker, protected on the other side by Davey and me. But I don't say anything. I'm actually, really, totally glad all of us are OK. Even Widow-maker's wound is not as bad as it first looked, and he was right in the thick of it. Plus George does not belong to me.

Do you think I actually might be jealous?

Honestly, I am not.

I have never fancied George. There is *no* spark. He is just a friend. He has never fancied Rhi. And anyway, I am in love with Henry.

With one short triumphant round of barking, Gelert summons the ponies and leads the way back down the road towards Beddgelert.

George nudges Graine across, so that he is trotting flank by flank with Keincaled. He reaches out a hand and grabs hold of mine. He squeezes it. 'That was very brave of you,' he says.

I blush. I melt. He does care. And it would be nice to take the credit, to let him carry on squeezing my hand

and praising me. But it's not the truth. So I say, 'Thing is, George, I wasn't being brave at all. It was Keincaled. He charged at the hound – I mean, before we knew it was Gelert. I didn't have much choice.'

'Aw, don't run yourself down for me,' says George. 'I was impressed.'

'Shut up,' I say.

'But there's nothing new in that,' says George. 'I'm totally impressed with you all the time.' He squeezes the fingers of my hand tightly.

'Stop it.'

I glance behind at Rhiannon. She's noticed George whispering to me. Ner to her. Serves her right.

Perhaps I *am* just a teeny weeny bit possessive about George.

At a turn in the road, where a cliff face rises sheer overhead, Gelert comes to a standstill. He fixes Davey with his eye, like Davey can read his mind.

Who knows? Perhaps he can. He seems to be able to read mine.

Davey turns to us and says, 'Gelert's bed is just beyond that pasture there, after the river – the Afon Glaslyn.

He cannot stray too far from it, and now the immediate danger is past, he is going to return there to sleep again.'

My heart sinks a little. It felt so safe having Gelert with us.

'It won't be sensible for us to remain upon the road after he is gone. We must move on quickly towards Blaenau Ffestiniog, join the Druids Way while the Cŵn Annwn lick their wounds. They won't have gone far. Once they know that Gelert is asleep again, they may seek to ambush us up ahead,' concludes Davey.

Vaguely I wonder how come he has suddenly become such an expert on the Cŵn Annwn. And how come they aren't afraid of *him* any more.

Davey nods at me. 'You are right,' he says, like he really is Mr Mind Reader. 'I have realised that they are growing in strength. Yesterday they feared me, today they fear Gelert, tomorrow they will fear no one.'

Davey is always so delightfully encouraging.

'But why?' whines Rhiannon. 'Why are they getting more fearless?'

'It is the work of the Olde Deepe Magicke, it grows in power towards the equinox.'

Something clicks in my brain. 'You're not really a hiker, are you?' I say. 'You're something else.' Davey just smiles at me. 'You're something the Olde Deepe Magicke awoke as well. That's why you were on the hillside. That's why you don't remember anything ... '

'And who knows what else walks abroad this day?' he adds, skilfully dodging my question.

Or flies abroad, I think, racking my brains.

'Then why don't *you* grow in strength too?' asks Rhiannon.

'Perhaps my strength is for a different purpose,' muses Davey.

Instinctively I look up into the grey clouds. Like, what's up *there*: Oswald? Witches on their broomsticks? Another murder of crows?

'You're right,' I say. 'I don't know how you know all these things, but I'd feel a lot safer off this road and on the Druids Way.'

'May the Lord protect us,' he says, still smiling.

And I smile back, but inside I'm thinking: *so who the heck are you, Davey*?

———

At the next gate, we leave the road. A narrow path winds down the side of one field. In the distance lies the village of Beddgelert. Already the streetlights are glowing in the mist about half a mile away. It looks marooned, isolated, deep in snow. A lone blackbird sings its evening note.

The air, scented with nightfall, pine and frost, makes my face tingle. We follow the path as it curves through a patch of woodland and joins another track, snaking from the left.

'At last, the Druids Way,' announces George.

'Praise be!' says Davey. 'For though they knew not the glory of our Lord, the Druids had many skills. They marked out the ley lines, put charms along the sides of their ways and none that belong to the Olde Deepe Magicke like to cross such lines of power.'

OK ... so Davey is *not* a creature of the Olde Deepe Magicke then?

I look at the track. It's very narrow. In places it seems to disappear entirely in a tangle of snow-covered bushy weeds and long tussocky grass. The sky overhead lowers oppressively. And up ahead are huge mountains. Dusk seems to be setting in at speed. The blackbird still calls. Maybe it's my imagination, but I'm sure I can still hear the faint baleful howl of a wolf.

But nothing else, except the slight smell of woodsmoke. None of the ponies seem alarmed.

We trudge on. Uphill. Along twisting, winding, stony hill paths.

As we head for Blaenau Ffestiniog, along the long-forgotten Druids Way, across the mountaintops, even

Keincaled becomes weary.

Twilight turns into hazy dusk.

Night falls. Still up and up we go. Miles and miles. At least eight, but uphill, so feeling more like twenty. Over mountain. Through snow. Across icy streams. Frozen moss on stunted trees. Wide stretches of shadowy slopes. A biting wind always at our backs. Dark skies. Huge mountains. Slippery pathways.

So tired. So desperately tired.

And cold.

And the second day is ending.

And we are still nowhere near shelter.

Or Cadair Idris.

Thirty-One

They find us of course.

They trail us. Just on the other side of the mists. As we are coming down from the mountain pass, I see them in the mirror. I sneak it out and look. There they are; white shadows on the far side of the ridge. I tilt the mirror to the left and right. I hold it up to my face, hoping I might sink into it, find Henry. But only my own pale eyes stare back at me. I flip it up, so I can see the night sky, longing for a glimpse of him up there, on his flight to the stars.

A different pair of eyes stare back at me.

Oh My God!

I swallow a shriek. My hand trembles. *Don't drop the mirror!* *Oswald.*

Oswald *is* there, just behind the cloud cover.

Oswald – right overhead. Just waiting for his moment to strike.

And then the Druids Way runs out.

It just comes to an open space bordered on three sides by sheer faces of piled-up slate.

George yells out, 'It's a quarry'. The ponies come to a stop. 'Let's back up a bit – see if there's a way round.' His voice echoes back oddly off the grey slag heaps in front of us.

But if we have to go round, that means we have to leave the path. (And that's obviously something Oswald would be very happy about.) Plus I'm too tired.

'We've come a long way,' I say. 'I need to rest. Keincaled needs a rest. So do we all. We can't leave the path now.'

Plus, apart from a tiny bit of moonshine, it's night and we can't see anything.

Rhiannon sways unsteadily on her ride. She's as white as a sheet.

'Just a short rest by that rock face over there,' I plead. I lean forward on Keincaled, until my head is lying on his mane. Just a little rest … a little snooze … a tiny nap for a good girl …

'No!' George says. 'Not a good idea. If we are still on the Druids Way we may be protected, but if the quarrying has removed the charms … '

George doesn't look like he's going to end that statement with a joke.

'OK. You look tired. Just a power nap. And don't move off the path.' He seems to relent. 'I'll stand guard.' He weighs his axe in his hand and nudges Graine to one side. 'I'll take the right. Davey, you up for the left? Keep Rhiannon in the centre with you, Elles. She looks half dead.'

'I agree,' says Davey. 'They could strike soon. When we are at our weakest, when they have gathered their numbers. If the Druids Way has run out, then we must prepare ourselves.'

'Maybe I could use the mirror?' I say. 'Maybe this is the right time? 'I have it here. I could breathe on it and see?'

'Now is not the time to experiment with the power of the mirror,' says Davey firmly. 'As I have said before, a witch's mirror is no plaything.'

OK. Now is the right time. Now isn't the right time. As ever, his jolly old self.

'Perhaps … what did Gran say? Look for unexpected help?' says George. He stares up at the slate face in front of us. 'I wonder … ' He jumps off Graine goes over and taps at a massive rock in its grey surface. 'We could try it,' he muses.

'Try what?' moans Rhiannon.

'Try to call out to the Coblynau.'[1]

---

1. The Knockers or Coblynau are gnome-like creatures. They are said to be half a yard (one and a half feet) tall, and very ugly. Apparently they dress in miniature mining outfits. They work constantly, but never finish their task, and are said to be able to cause rockslides.

'Who the *heck* are the Coblynau?' I say.

'The Bwca, the Knockers,' he replies by way of explanation.

'Knockers?' says Rhi.

I seriously hope she hasn't got the strength to make a crude joke.

'Call upon their hospitality,' explains George with a grin.

'Are they good? Bad? Or ugly?' I ask.

'They're the creatures that haunt the mines and quarries – the underground regions of Wales,' says George. 'They're like Welsh leprechauns – they sometimes trick miners to their death, knocking the tunnel walls.'

'They don't sound very good to me,' I say. 'And they definitely sound ugly.'

Davey laughs. 'There is nothing safe in Snowdonia, now the Fimbulvetr has begun. There'll be nowhere safe, until we restore the High Magick of Merlin.'

'Let's call them,' says George. 'If Gran's right and all the Olde Deepe Magicke is awake, they'll hear us. It's worth a try. Sometimes they're helpful. Sometimes their knocking leads miners to seams of gold.'

'And sometimes it doesn't,' says Davey, back in Eeyore mode.

'But why risk it?' I say. 'Maybe they won't be in a good mood.'

'Because if we try to move off this path, we're dead meat. Roast beef, shish kebab.' George picks up an imaginary knife and fork and slices at an imaginary piece of steak and chews it. Nobody laughs. Not even him.

'I'm hungry,' moans Rhiannon.

Davey strokes his chin and pulls at his wispy beard. 'OK,' he says, 'Perhaps the old code of hospitality will prevail.' He dismounts, turns to the rock face and knocks on it.

If I hadn't just survived a battle with the Cŵn Annwn, and seen the great hound, Gelert, in the flesh, I'd laugh. Like, what a *nutter*, knocking on a quarry face, like it was someone's front door, to beg a night's kip from mythical miniature miners.

He knocks again, his fist clenched, his mouth seemingly stretched ready to say: hello, sorry to disturb you, Mr Gnome-Leprechaun-Miner-thing, but could we come in?

It doesn't work anyway.

Nobody answers with, 'Bugger off, you annoying hippie'.

Rhiannon whimpers and says, 'I'm all achy too. I totally need to lie down'. She slides down from her grey mare and slumps on to a rock.

'Listen, Davey,' says George. 'I don't really think that's how you summon the Knockers.' He jumps forward. 'You don't tap on their walls, as if you're their next-door neighbour and their music is playing a bit too loud. I think we'll stand a much better chance of rousing them if we attack this quarry face – as if we're miners ourselves – and see if they'll knock back.'

George straightens up and draws out his axe.

'Sorry axe,' says George. 'You were my best, new, Husqvarna Forest, hickory, long-handled, steel, hand-forged axe; if this makes you blunt – just know it was all for a good cause.' And with that George raises his axe and strikes it hard against the slate face of the quarry.

'If it's blunt, you won't be able to defend me!' wails Rhiannon.

'There is little defence against those wolves,' says Davey cheerily, 'and even now they may have tricked us, for they are the hellhounds of Gwyn ap Nudd, and if they cannot rip us apart, or chase us into the Underworld, they will summon him: their fearsome leader.'[2]

Hi ho, very cheerful.

At that moment there's a sound, a bit like an earthquake. The rock face shivers, as if a huge landslide is about to start. I glance up at the towers of piled slate and hold my breath. I look goggle-eyed at George.

He shakes his head. No outline of a door appears on

2. Gwyn ap Nudd is a Welsh mythological figure, the ruler of the Welsh Otherworld – Annwn. He is described as a great warrior with a 'blackened face'.

the huge rock. 'Obviously: no vacancies. Not receiving visitors,' he says.

'Hang on,' I say. 'Look up there.' I point to a little scree of stones that has slid down the side of the quarry. Above them a dark crevice has opened up.

'And I'm tired too,' moans Rhiannon, not bothering to look up at anything.

I get down off Keincaled to get a better look. Even if it's not a 'please come on in', it is something. It looks wide enough to take the four of us, perhaps even the ponies. 'Maybe we could rest up there for the night?' I say.

'Not without mounting some defence,' says Davey.

'It might be possible for someone fit, lush and awesome to hold that entrance against a whole pack of wolves,' says George. 'Have I ever told you what a ... '

'*Geee-ooorge!*' wails Rhiannon.

I start to roll my eyes, but suddenly stop, as I see what Rhi is pointing at. There, glowering down at us from the corner of the quarry, is a tall figure, face dark, blackened with what looks like dried blood, and at his back slink the white wolves.

'*Gwyn ap Nudd*,' whispers Davey.

We race, tripping over slabs of slate, stubbing toes and shins, stiff legged, screaming.

Well, Rhi is screaming. OK, I might be screaming too.

The scree shifts beneath our tread. George stumbles. Davey hauls Rhi upwards. The ponies panic. My heart pounds. *That blackened face. Those hollow red-rimmed eyes.*

And the smell. Rotten. Putrid. George picks himself up, tears past me. '*RUN ELLIE!*' he shouts.

Oh my God. If George is scared, it's real. Nothing ever scares George. It must be bad. I race forward; throw myself at the slide of slate shingle. I gasp for breath. The icy cold hurts my chest.

The note of the wolves changes. The baying grows louder. They've cornered the prey, their victims are within reach.

Just run, Ellie, I tell myself. Get up there. Get above them. Run. Pray. Hope.

The ponies are up the little scree. All except Widow-maker. I can't see him. They've reached the crevice. Why the hell did we all dismount? It's just about wide enough for the fattest of them to get through.

Oh wait for meeeeeee.

I feel someone grab my arm, haul me forward, George is there. *Oh thank you thank you thank you.*

The wind stops.

I look back.

I see why we've escaped. I see why the wolves have not

yet ripped us to shreds. There stands Widow-maker.

He is slashing around him, twisting and kicking, rearing and smashing, teeth bared, ears flat back. Two wolves already lie twitching beneath his hooves. He flips and turns like a demon whirlwind. One hoof plunges straight through the skull of a wolf. One catches another wolf under its jugular. Widow-maker heaves and kicks. The dead wolf arcs in a great limp mess of bloodstained fur, away, back down the scree.

But this time there are just too many wolves.

And only one pony.

As I watch, Widow-maker is surrounded. More than ten attack his flank, his rump, three jump on to his back, two more go for his throat.

Oh my God. Oh my God.

He is dragged down under a sea of growling, biting, jerking, tearing creatures.

I shut my eyes.

Nooooooooo.

He can't survive, can he?

This can't be happening.

I feel George's hand on my shoulder. 'Get inside,' he says. 'Let me block the opening. There is nothing that can help him now.'

Oh Widow-maker. My little black pony from the Welsh mountains.

Oh no.

I turn into the cave. Tears well up. A lump the size of a tennis ball blocks my throat.

Those hideous foul things.

I can't swallow.

Poor, poor Widow-maker.

⁓

What happens now?

I can't think.

Just sniff and sniff.

If I come down from Cadair a poet, I'll write a ballad. Widow-maker should be as famous as the faithful Gelert.

He might still be alive?

We should go back.

I feel George's hand holding me.

I can't see properly.

Inside is much bigger than it first looked – a level floor – I think – I stumble forward.

George guides me.

'Well found.' Davey throws his arms around me. 'Well found! Thank God.'

'Help me, Davey.' George shouts and starts back for the cave mouth.

Davey lets go of me, jumps to help George. Together they shift a huge slab of slate across the entrance. Superhuman effort.

I drag my sleeve across my eyes.

Oh Widow-maker.

The cave turns dark. *Just breathe. Get control. Swallow tears. There is no way back.* The crunch of stone, the smash of slate fragments. The smell of dank cave. George and Davey pant, puff, lean their backs on the slate, 'til it settles into place.

'Thank God,' repeats Davey.

The ponies snort and blow. *Oh my God. They understand.* Tails swish. It's very dark.

'Are they gone?' whispers Rhi.

'Not really,' says George. 'We may have to make a stand here.'

George gets out his phone and shines the torch app on the floor. Dull slate – smooth, flat. 'This quarry might link into the northern tunnels of Llechwedd Slate Mine,' he says. He shines the torch over the cavern walls. 'If we can reach Llechwedd, then Cadair is only another thirty-five miles or so away. Tomorrow ... if all goes well,' his voice falters,

'I'll take watch.'

Thirty-five miles.

The torch beam bounces off great stepped sides of sheer slate. The quarried faces glint back in greys, deep greens, black almost.

'It's definitely been quarried,' I stammer.

Poor, poor, brave Widow-maker.

At the back of the cave there seems to be an entrance into some kind of gallery.

'We need to be careful,' says Davey. 'Knockers are not renowned for being helpful characters. They may have opened up, only to trap us.'

'Oh no!' cries Rhiannon.

'If we venture into the mine, we might come across a massive underground river that will carry us away. The Knockers may open up a chute beneath us. We won't even need to be chased into the Underworld by Gwyn ap Nudd, we'll get there anyway and that'll be the end of us and our quest.' Davey's voice drops mournfully.

Great. More cheerful by the hour.

From outside comes the growl of wolves. I look back towards the entrance. Widow-maker is out there, behind the slab, ears flat, teeth bared, throat ripped out. I squeeze my eyes tight, try to erase that image, try to remember him as that brave, rearing, vibrant pony.

Who gave his life for us.

George takes his axe from his belt, passes me his torch.

But before I have time to take it, or Rhiannon can get a fresh groan together, there's a ring of laughter. It echoes from all around. It ricochets off the walls. It resonates from further unknown caverns.

'You don't think much of us Knockers, then do ya?' says a voice, deep, gruff, earthy.

And into the torchlight steps a company of tiny men. And I mean *tiny*. They stand about half a metre tall and are all dressed in tiny mining outfits. Tiny picks are slung over tiny shoulders. Tiny hands are folded over tiny chests. Cloth wraps or mining helmets are jammed over tiny (ugly) faces (and oh my *dayz*, those ears!). Tiny cheeks are blackened with slate dust. Tiny belts and boots and waistcoats peek from beneath tiny overalls. Lamps hang on tiny lamp belts and safety hooks, hammers and chisels, cloths and drills and (rather worryingly) tiny sticks of dynamite with very long fuses are clutched in tiny hands. An army of tiny pipes droop from the corners of an army of tiny mouths; everything is in miniature.

The lead Knocker steps forward, removes his pipe and holds up a stick of dynamite.

'Perhaps you'd like to tell us why you're here, then?' he says with a mischievous grin. 'Before we decide to blow you up.'

Thirty-Two

However tiny a stick of dynamite is, it's still worrying, isn't it? Although blowing us up would mean blowing themselves up too. Which I'm guessing they might not want to do.

But then how would I know?

I've never met a Knocker before.

Three of them flick on the headlamps attached to the fronts of their tiny hard hats. They step up behind their leader. The glare of the lamps is directed straight up at Davey.

'Well, come on – spit it out! You don't think much of us Knockers, do ya?' repeats one of them.

Davey squares his shoulders, stops stooping, coughs. 'Erm, I do not have an opinion on the Coblynau,' he says. 'I have never sought their help before, and would not have done so now, had we not been in great need.'

Ouch. That was definitely a less-than-uber answer.

A shiver goes through the group of Knockers.

'Ha! We've got a sparker, have we?' says one of them.

'Not very polite, is he?' says another.

'What does he mean with his "do not have an opinion"?' says a third.

'Cheek, I call it,' adds a fourth.

Then all of them start.

'He's a cheeker.'

'He *should* have an opinion.'

'Ain't we big enough to have an opinion on?'

'I'll give him "an opinion" all right!'

The sound of a scuffle at the cave entrance interrupts them. A wild howling comes from the direction of the boulder. I flick the torch towards the slab. Shadows on the walls glide and spring. Maybe they've found a way through. Before Rhi can squeal, a company of Knockers quick-marches over to the closed-off entrance.

'What the black-damp's going on outside in the world of men, that they send out Gwynny Nudder himself?' says another one of them.

'Has the world gone nutters?' The murmuring starts again.

'Five goafers, blinkers enough to enter our kingdom!'

'With their carriers,' says another, 'don't forget them

hoofed carriers!'

The leader, a slightly taller Knocker – bigger than the rest, anyway – takes another step towards us. He's got a thick apron of weird coloured cloth held firm around his middle. He looks like the biggest little person in the world.

I step up and stand beside Davey. If they've got it in for him, they're going to have to deal with me too. The Knockers notice.

Outside, the howling changes key, becomes somehow fiercer, more menacing.

'She's a jumper for you, Boss!' laughs one of them. 'She'll be like your iron staff, jumping all over you!'

I'm not sure what a 'jumper' is, but if I have to jump on them, so be it.

'We come in peace,' says Davey trying to regain lost ground.

Rhiannon isn't so tactful. 'Are you *actually* a hobbit?' she asks.

Maybe a chute opening up under her might not be such a bad idea.

But the Knockers don't seem offended. They fall about laughing. One of them starts hammering on the wall. They all start hammering on the wall. The cavern booms with their hammering. I cover my ears.

When the din dies down a bit, the boss says, 'She's a fair charmer, a fair charmer indeed, and she's got an adder stone m'boys'.

Suddenly they all go quiet.

Not a laugh. Not a knock.

They flick off their headlamps. The cave goes dark.

'I have asked a question,' says the boss, all scary now, whispering through the dark. 'Though you've quite forgotten it. But it would be respectful and polite of you to answer me.'

Not a giggle, not a whisper.

I gulp; I stand up straight, and say, 'OK … '

'No not *you*, you jumper,' yell the Knockers. '*Her*, the charmer. She must answer the boss's question.'

Holy smoke, they mean Rhiannon!

We are doomed.

'Tell us about your mission,' says the taller boss Knocker. A score of lamps suddenly flick on, trained completely on Rhiannon.

'I don't know anything, they never tell me *anything*,' stammers Rhiannon.

Her answer seems to delight them.

'Lovely, lovely, lovely!' they chant.

'What a charmer! Lovely charmer!' yell the Knockers,

as if they've just heard the best answer ever.

'*Tell* them – you muppet,' I hiss.

The howling outside seems to reach a frenzied pitch.

'It's cos I did a witches' spell … I think,' she mumbles.

The Knockers seen even more delighted, and start tapping their hammers on the walls again. They set up a rhythm, and one of them breaks into a song:

'*She's the charmer who set the spell,*'

Another takes it up:

'*She's the one to make it well,*

She's the witch with the adder stone,

She's come to visit us – at home!

She's the charmer,

We can't be wrong,

She's the one to sing the song!'

'Oh Kaaay … ' I say hesitantly. I cast a hopeful look at George – extend it to Davey, but they are looking away from me. Cowards. Looks like I'm going to have to get Rhiannon out of this all on my own.

'It wasn't her fault … ' I say, lying. 'The spell released the Olde Deepe Magicke.'

The Knockers start drumming the floor. One of them even does a little tap dance.

'The White Dragon is loose, the whole of Snowdonia

is under the grip of the Fimbulvetr … ' I yell, trying to explain over all the noise. 'We are going to try and break the spell … '

Before any of them can respond, a squad of Knockers comes stumbling into the cave, dragging two white creatures behind them, one with its throat cut, fur stained red; the other still in its death throes.

'Howlers,' they announce, 'rushed our northern door … outside … howling their howls to the north wind … '

'Well done, well done m'boys,' says the boss.

The little squad throws down the two wolves and each of the Knockers doubles up, catching their breath.

One of them pants out: 'In the great white, a dragon in the sky … he's a mighty thrasher … whirling about like a great blower, pouring down snow … every peak … down the full range.'

'Yes, yes,' says the boss, 'our charmer told us all about the Fimbulvetr.'

I gulp. So unfair! Rhiannon didn't say a thing.

'Well, well,' says the boss, 'we'll have to decide what to do, and you boys better arrange for the singer to learn the song, but first of all – we cannot think on empty chompers.'

And with that he produces a whistle, which he blows sharply. Into the cave – right on cue – comes a procession of other Knockers carrying torches, then more carrying platters upon which are arranged piles of food.

Food!

Masses of it!

My eyes! George's face!

Haunches of deer, great knuckles of pork, shanks of lamb, legs of chicken, sides of beef, some dripping with sauce, some garnished with herbs, veggies, all kinds: fresh, roast, boiled, diced, sliced, cubed and mashed. Oh yum!

'Oh YESSSS!' says George.

'The taller says "YESSSS",' repeat the Knockers.

'Definitely,' says George, 'this here taller, whatever that is, is one hell of a hungry taller. What he needs is a good meal. Then he can sit down and make a good plan.'

The Knockers like that and haul George over to the table.

And without further hesitation, George sits himself down at the great stone table, where the platters are laid, and starts shovelling food on to a piece of slate.

God, he's such a greedy guts.

I'm starving too, but I'm wondering if it's all right to eat anything. I seem to remember Gran saying something about never eating food or accepting a drink from any magically inclined stranger – especially once you are in their kingdom …

I look at Davey, with his thin, pale, under-nourished look. No answers there. He's so scrawny he looks like he hardly eats anyway. As if he reads my thoughts, he says, 'I only eat that which is not cooked – raw food, and bread and salt'.

Yeah. I seem to remember.

The boss gives him a funny look and says, 'Well you're in the wrong movie then, aren't you?' Which is really random, but actually quite funny, coming from a hobbit/gnome/leprechaun-thing like him.

With that, the boss claps his hands. In comes more food: bunches of grapes, mountains of peaches, strawberries, raspberries and great slices of watermelon with rosy skins. The Knockers pile them up in front of Davey.

'Eat: you need to stay strong, you strange, bald goafer,' says the boss cheerfully.[1]

And with that, the boss sits down, fills up his goblet, drinks thirstily and piles food enough for about six full-grown men on to an assortment of bowls and plates around him.

And at that moment, when everyone's mouth and hands are full, a MASSIVE crash resounds through the cavern.

I jerk my head up.

---

1. I learnt afterwards that goafer is actually a mining term for waste material. Essentially, it means waste of space. Charming.

My heart rate shoots up, way above healthy.

And into the cave strides a HUGE female Knocker. Her red hair is braided down to her waist; her wide trousers are tucked into thigh-high mining boots. In her hand she carries a MASSIVE pickaxe and a HUMONGOUS hammer. Honestly, she's way bigger, even than George.

She steps up to the wolves – one is still twitching on the floor – and with a swing of her hammer, smashes through its skull. Blood and bone spray over the walls of the cavern. Then with one more stride, she reaches the table, kicks lesser Knockers out of the way and smashes the pick down into it. It penetrates deep into the stone tabletop, splinters fly, the table quivers, slates break.

George drops his fork.

I shrink behind a table leg.

The boss looks up, catches a bottle of something as it threatens to crash over.

'Oh, hiya Nan,' he says.

Nan grabs the bottle off him and drains it in one draught.

'Wh-wh-who is she?' whimpers Rhiannon.

The boss fills his goblet from a second bottle, and says, 'Meet Nan – my granny, Dad's side. She's your music teacher.' And with his mouth full, and his goblet held high, the boss shouts at a nearby group: 'Take. The. Pretty. One. Nan will teach her the SINGING.'

The Knockers move over to Rhiannon, catch her by the hand. Nan drains the next bottle of wine in one swig and does the same with three more.

She strides out again.

'Better do what he says, Rhi,' I suggest. 'Nan doesn't look like the kind to be kept waiting.'

Horror-stricken, Rhiannon is escorted out. I hear her whimpering. Her shadow dances into the distance, along the walls of a long gallery, until it dwindles and merges with the darkness. Even the flickering reflection of the torches fades, becoming mere pinpricks of light.

Her last sobs echo and die.

I gulp.

I think the Knockers have taken a great shine to her. ~~Tee hee.~~ Poor old Rhi.

I don't know what to do.

Should I race after her?

'Eat,' says the boss, deciding for me.

He pushes a huge pie at me. 'Ain't you goafers got any manners?'

Thirty-Three

I look at the food. My taste buds tingle. I don't know what to do. Tuck in? I really *am* hungry. Or heed Gran's warnings and hold back?

And Rhiannon. I ought to follow her – make sure she's OK. After all, she may be a hateful double-crossing ~~b~~witch, but she's still my friend. Plus how do I know what the Knockers will do to her? She might be having a great time. I'm not a mind reader like Davey, am I?

Slight problem. How *am* I going to follow her? I glance at the boss. I'll have to think up something.

Maybe George could go after her, or Davey?

I look at Davey. He's gazing at a bread roll.

I look at George. He's reaching for another knuckle of lamb.

I don't even know where they've taken her.

I look at the wolf with the hammered-in skull.

My heroic impulses shrink.

And I'm far too hungry to do anything without eating. And the smell of the food is intoxicating. I lean across the table and snatch up a chicken drumstick in one hand. With the other I take an apple from the pile, send up a silent prayer to the mountains and bite down.

Oooooh crisp apple juice.

Divine!

And, yum, succulent tender chicken …

I'm not sure I should have just eaten that chicken … or maybe that apple … things seem to go a bit jumbled after my first nibble … I'm sure I eat a lot more … maybe I even drink some of that winey stuff … not sure it was wine … I'm sure I hear music … something far away and beautiful … definitely a melody …

A pile of skins lies on the floor. A fire is lit. Smoke streams upward across the cave roof and out through some cracks. It stings my eyes. I rub them. It's very dark, I can scarcely see. And I feel soooo tired.

I'm lying down on the furs. George is next to me.

'Ah, at last I get to spend the night with the girl I love,' he whispers.

'Stop it!' I say and slap at a random hand that has landed on mine.

'What a pity,' says George. 'Just when a cuddle would make everything perfect.'

'Do not be too sure it's so perfect,' says Davey, from somewhere near, in the darkness.

Here we go again. Old Mr Cheerful.

'These are the Coblynau, gnomes of the earth, Knockers that mine the mountains in search of gold. For Welsh gold is very special and it is from Welsh gold that they wrought the Golden Throne of Arthur, which lies buried beneath the Pass of Arrows. From Welsh gold they manufactured the magical harps of the Old Ones. They are focused only upon gold under their mountains, and they have no dealings with us from above. I mistrust their friendliness.'

He definitely should have tried the food. It'd have helped him chill out a *lot*.

'Anything else, a little gloomier, you might want to add to that?' I mumble.

'They have only let us stay because the enchantment covering them is broken. If it stays broken, men will find their way into the mines and the Coblynau will have to retreat to the deeper caves, and in the deepest of all, there is the Afanc.'[1]

My head clears. 'Why not sneak back to the table and go for that bread roll you fancied?' I suggest.

'They help us, perhaps, because they want the enchantment cast over Snowdonia to be ended. They want to get back to their mining. They want to get back to holding their golden goblets and talking about their piles of gold.'

'Whichever way you look at it,' says George, still trying to snuggle up to me, 'they have helped us. All that food for starters – and let's not forget we were out on a mountainside with nothing but old Gwyn Ap Nudd and a load of wolves.'

Widow-maker.

'What about the ponies?' I say, suddenly worried.

'I made it my business while you were eating to check up on all of our faithful steeds,' says Davey. (Crikey, he *is* the little saint, isn't he?) 'They have been well stabled, and the grey mare has received the attentions of a Knocker who has the healing power of animals. Her wound has been bound over with a plaster of yellow Welsh gold, which has the power of curing all wounds. Tomorrow she will be strong enough to carry on.'

---

1. The Afanc is a lake monster from Welsh mythology that inhabits many lakes and all the subterranean caverns and rivers. Like most lake monsters, it is said to prey upon anyone foolish enough to stray too close to, fall in, or swim in its waters.

'Phew,' I say. 'We only have tomorrow, remember?'

'Yes, we must pass out from under these hills and reach Cadair Idris.'

'Rhiannon got back OK?' mumbles George into the darkness.

'*RHIANNON!!!*' I squeal.

'Yeah … ' George says sleepily. 'You know: fair hair, pretty, slim, in love with … '

'Oh no!' I shriek. I sit up and search the shadows.

NO RHIANNON!

~

Far away, deep underground, through a maze of tangled galleries, through huge passages; through solid slate, past open caverns where stalagmites grow like the obelisks of ancient Egypt over deep subterranean rivers, there is a chamber. And in the chamber sits a maiden.

She bends her pretty head and listens to a melody.

'Yes, listen,' says the Knocker Queen. 'For you are The One. You hold the adder stone.'

'But, I can't be,' says the maiden. 'And anyway it was given to me, by George's Gran.'

'But you are a witch,' says the Knocker Queen.

'Well, not really, it's not like I went to Hogwarts or anything, I was just doing love spell thingies,' says the maiden.

'But you released the Olde Deepe Magicke,' says the Knocker Queen.

'Yeah, but it was just an accident ... '

'And you have the voice of an angel,' says the Knocker Queen.

'Aw, d'you really think so?' says the maiden.

'And you are The One foretold of by The Song,' says the Knocker Queen.

'I am?' says the maiden. 'That's news to me.'

The Knocker Queen softly chants the Knockers' prophecy:

'She's the charmer who set the spell,

She's the one to make it well,

She's the witch with the adder stone,

Who'll vanquish the Afanc all-alone.'

'You see,' says the Knocker Queen, 'the Oracle of the Menhir of Mawr cannot be wrong.'

'Wow!' says the maiden.

'So hold the adder stone to your lips, and sing the song I will teach you to sing through the stone,' instructs the Knocker Queen.

The melody is lovely. It floats through the air and those that hear it are spellbound. It could tame a lion, it could gentle the north wind and Rhiannon has a good ear and a lovely sweet Welsh voice. She lifts up her chin and sings it as if she has known this song all her life.

'And now the instructions to defeat the sinker,' says the Knocker Queen.

'When the water boils,

And the ripples rip,

Place the adder stone to your lips.

When the monster roars,

And hope is gone,

Find the tune and sing the song.

When the Afanc on you does dote,

Take this blade and cut its throat.'

'CUT ITS THROAT!' squeals Rhiannon.

'Never fear,' says the Knocker Queen. 'You are The One, and in ridding this world of the Afanc, you will become the friend of the Knockers forever.'

The music rises and echoes from the chamber wall.

It is surreal, sublime, and it gives the maiden strength.

'Fulfil the prophecy and undo a great harm.'

'OK,' mumbles Rhiannon.

'I will return you to your friends now, but don't forget the things I have told you.'

'But how will I know when?' asks Rhiannon.

The Knocker Queen laughs. 'Oh, you'll know all right!'

'But how?' insists Rhiannon.

'Because if you don't act, the sinker will sink you all.'

Thirty-Four

In the morning, Rhi is back.

Thank heavens.

When we ask her what happened, she's curiously quiet.

We don't see the boss again. A small party – five or six of them – arrives to wake us up. They bring the ponies and have loaded on to each of them huge parcels, stuffed full with food.

'Brilliant,' says George. 'Wow! Breakfast too. If you promise I'll never have to chop wood again – I'll move in and eat everything you can think of giving me.'

'Not without me, you won't,' says Rhiannon.

I'm not at all sure we should eat any more Knocker food. Seems like it's much too rich. Knocks you out. Lol.

Get it?

Knocks you out. OK. Whatevs.

The Knockers look at each other rather sadly. They turn to Rhiannon. 'You mean you *actually* likes him?' says one of them. 'You likes a taller like that?'

One of the others starts slapping his thighs and stomping his feet and rolling his eyes and keeps on repeating; '*She* likes the taller! *She* likes the taller, when she could have any Knocker she fancied!' until Rhiannon blushes and we're all really fed up.

'Exactly where did you go last night, Rhi?' asks George for the umpteenth time.

Rhiannon shakes her head and looks worried.

The Knockers lead the way down a maze of galleries. The first passage we take is stunning. It meanders left and right through large, clean-washed beds of slate. The slabbed floors undulate in geometric waves. Here the passage is very large and a soft wind sighs through it.

From time to time, a high borehole tunnel disappears off from the main gallery, its grey walls, lit by the odd single flaming brand, and the rock face seems to glow yellow and rusty red.

As we pass each borehole, the flicker of torchlight suggests a depth and darkness that makes me shiver.

Even Keincaled swishes his tail nervously and seems anxious to reach the exit of the mines.

At one of the junctions the Knockers stop. 'We got to get back now m'boys,' says an older looking Knocker, who seems to be in charge. 'Wyrrik, you know what to do.'

His voice is hard, sinister almost. My eyes widen in alarm. Is this the bit where the Now-You-Know-Our-Secret-We-Have-To-Kill-You-Thing happens?

One of the Knockers steps forward. 'I'm Wyrrik. I'll accompany you as far as the South Gate. After that, we wish you well, and hope to the buddlers some other Childer of Llyr will help you too.'

Phew, big sigh of relief.

'We thank you,' says Davey. 'We are all deeply grateful.'

Lol. Davey's suddenly Mr Big Chief Spokesperson for everyone.

I narrow my eyes and fix them on him. I'm still working on my theory that he is an 'entity' too, some conjuration of the Olde Deepe Magicke. I mean that guru look, with that bald patch. That pale skin with the pimples. He's got to be. Nobody these days would let themselves look like that, would they?

But which 'entity'? I'm studying him closely, for clues.

Davey turns and looks at me. He smiles. A smile that says:

I know what you're thinking. I know that you don't know who I am, or why I appeared – right when you needed me.

I raise one shoulder and let it drop. It's true, I don't know, but as sure as hell, I'm going to try and find out.

'I'm not sure who I am myself,' he says, as if he can read my thoughts and as if that's still something that puzzles him too. 'But when I found myself up on the mountain, I knew I had a mission to fulfil. Some voice in my head told me to forget who I was, because Wales was in its hour of greatest need, and I was required to help. Then I met you and George and the fair Rhiannon. Now I see it much more clearly. I'm certain: part of my mission is to accompany you as far as I can, and to assist in breaking the witches' spell, because in that way, I can serve Wales best.'

I raise one side of my mouth. 'Let's hope we can do it.'

'Aw, glad you came along,' says George, slapping him on the back.

Davey smiles at George, murmurs, 'Just the little things. Makes all the difference.'

Rhiannon smiles super sweetly at George too.

Then she smiles at me.

I ~~frown~~ smile back.

We journey on.

We come upon a crystal-clear, turquoise-blue lake, below a rock bridge. We cross the bridge and plunge into deeper passages, darker and older than the Bronze Age. Probably. We wind down them through the mountains.

On and on, until at last we reach a huge timbered door.

'Ah, the South Gate.' Wyrrik hauls on a pulley mechanism on a nearby wall. He grunts a bit with the effort because he is very small and the doors are very large. George jumps off Graine and helps him. And the doors swing open.

Daylight, cold air and the blinding glare of snow greet us. The smell of frost.

The sound of branches creaking under their white load. This is it.

It's still here: the Fimbulvetr.

It's dawn on the third day of the Magicke.

Oh Henry, you believed in me. I'll try to do my best.

I wish I could see the future like you can.

I wish I could see what today holds.

What tomorrow will bring.

I wish I could be with you.

Just one more time.

Act Three

The Mabinogion

PEREDUR THE SON OF EVRAWC

And when Peredur came into the hall, there was a tall and stately lady sitting in a chair, and many handmaidens around her; and the lady rejoiced at his coming.

And when it was time, they went to meat. And after their repast was finished, 'It were well for thee, chieftain,' said she, 'to go elsewhere to sleep.'

'Wherefore can I not sleep here?' said Peredur.

'Nine sorceresses are here, my soul, of the sorceresses of Gloucester, and their father and their mother are with them; and unless we can make our escape before daybreak, we shall be slain; and already they have conquered and laid waste all the country, except this one dwelling.'

Until the Mountains are Washed to the Sea

Thirty-Five

The second we are out of the slate caverns, my phone starts pinging.

ELLIE'S PHONE Third Day of the Magic – 19 March 06.00
Status: Cold. Unhappy. Poor Widow-maker. Worried. Panicking. Only today left to do everything.

Missed Calls:

Mum (7)

Granny Jones (3)

Meryl (16)

07967843521 (2)

Recent updates:

<u>Sheila</u>

What is up with you? And where ARE you? ALL of you?

<u>Sheila</u>

You're up to something, aren't you?

<u>Meryl</u>

Hon, what's happening? You aren't picking up? Sheila's been over twice to quiz me on where you are? I'm worried. Text me.

<u>Sheila</u>

Is it anything to do with those cadets training over at Bangor?

<u>Mum</u>

Darling, I've been calling and calling you. And I know Gran says you and George and Rhiannon are OK, and I SHOULDN'T worry, and I do trust her, but I AM YOUR MUM and I do worry. It's just not like you to not ring or text or anything.

The school keeps ringing up as well, to say they hope you're feeling better?? Rhiannon's mum rang to say she hopes everything is going well with the geography field trip???!!!

Frankly, I didn't know what to say. Ellie, I don't really know what's going on. Please ring and explain. Granny Jones keeps telling me IT WILL ALL BE OK. So I'm trying to believe that. But when you don't pick up, I still worry. Xxx love u lots Mum. With all this snow I'm doubly worried.

Oh God! Poor Mum. I'm going to have to do something. Ring her? It'll be too hard to explain. Text then? Yes. Better text her right now.

Recent updates from Ellie:

Ellie to Mum

Mum, I'm OK. It's a long story. But I can't explain it right now. Check for a letter behind the clock on the mantelpiece – it'll put you in the picture a bit – then ask Gran – she knows everything. And just continue to trust me; however bizarre it all sounds. I love you so much XXX Ellie.

Ellie to Meryl

I'm fine. With Rhi and George – something came up. Fill you in later XXX E

Ellie to Sheila

Not over in Bangor, you nutter, but away with R & G with patchy coverage.

I wish I could tell Mum more. It really isn't fair on her. I mean not knowing *anything*. But she needs to read the letter I left her first, *then* talk to Gran about it, before I tell her the rest …

Plus if we don't make it, if the spell can't be broken, well then she'll understand: the winter won't end; ancient curses and monsters from the deep won't stay hidden for long.

Then everyone will believe everything.

I try not to think about that.

We can't afford to fail.

We must hurry and get to Cadair.

~⁓

The ponies are refreshed. They get a good pace going. The snow has stopped, settled into a thick crisp topping over everything. There's no wild wind, thankfully. People are on the move. The main road to Dolgellau has been sorted. They've got the snowploughs out and one lane of the A470 has been cleared down to the tarmac. As we trot along, a few cars pass. I imagine they're thinking: Ha ha – look at those stupid tourists, pony trekking in the snow! Lol.

Then George starts doing this pathetic thing. It starts like this: a car slows down, and as it passes, a window rolls down, some bright spark shouts out, 'On yer bike!'

So George shouts back: 'Knockers!'

I mean …

And from then on he manages to work the K word into every conversation. Starting with: 'It's all Knockers to me.' Even: 'I'm really Knockered.'

Please don't even snigger. It's not even funny. Particularly because Rhiannon *was* going to explain what happened to her last night. But when she starts with: 'They told me I was The One, a fulfilment of their ancient prophecy ... ' George shouts out: 'A Knocker prophecy!' and then gets the giggles. Honestly, he's so immature.

After that, Rhiannon wouldn't say a word. Now she just sends George dagger eyes and hums to herself.

I do try. I say, 'Don't mind him, Rhi. You know what George is like.'

But all she says is, 'I hate this mission. I hate horse riding. I hate everything.' Which isn't very uplifting and doesn't explain anything.

And then she hums even more furiously. I catch a few phrases of the tune. It sounds oddly familiar – sweet and sad.

We cross down the far side of Snowdonia, south of the Vale of Ffestiniog and reach Ganllwyd. The Druids Way merges with the old Roman road, Sarn Helen. Just ahead of us lies the prehistoric forest of Coed Ganllwyd.

Great, unbroken sheets of snow stretch across the countryside. A cold, clear, crisp breeze numbs my cheeks. Black dots wheel above us in the sky.

Ravens?

Crows?

That does not make me happy. Nor does it make Keincaled ecstatic either. I can see the way he rolls his eyes at them.

Ravens are OK though, aren't they? At least ravens might be on our side, or at worst leave us alone. Keincaled swishes his tail, as if he reads my mind. But what if they're carrion crows? An image of the inside of the lambing shed flashes before my eyes again. I bite my lip. *My poor poor babies.*

At least the birds can't sight us when we enter the forest. Snow-covered pine branches drop great loads of white on us as we ride under them. One lot goes right down the top of one of my hiking boots and soaks my sock.

'The large area of ancient oak and pine woodland here is called Coed Ganllwyd,' announces Davey. He's a tour guide now. ☺

'Do you think he's memorised all of the *Hikers' Guide to North Wales*?' I whisper at Rhi.

'It has two trees dating from the Dark Ages,' he continues.

That sounds spooky: the Dark Ages. A bit like the Ice Age. Which might come again if we can't break the spell.

'I think he's just trying to take our minds off all the worry,' says Rhiannon. Then adds charitably, 'He just isn't used to people'.

I blink. She's right. I look at her. She's actually put her finger right on it. I love Rhiannon sometimes.

She starts humming again, catches me looking. 'It's the song they taught me,' she says. 'I don't want to forget it.'

'Why did they want to teach you their song?' I ask.

'One of the trees stands alone in a meadow, it's the second largest in Wales, apparently,' continues Davey.

(I mean, did he just randomly know that?)

'Hang on,' says George. He rides over to a national park sign, reads it out:

Coed Ganllwyd ancient forest supports a variety of wildlife: deer, red squirrels, pine martens, polecats, otters, and birds from black grouse to merlins, buzzards, and red kites.

It doesn't mention Knockers, white wolves, dragons or the Coraniaid. I wonder whose side the polecats might be on, or the black grouse. It is not a comforting thought.

However, we see nothing. Just gnarled limbs decorated with icicles.

And snow.

The Roman road – Sarn Helen – isn't easy to trek along like the Druids Way. It's pocked with dips and hollows. Slabs of stone lie hidden underfoot, all seem placed to trip us up. Even our mountain-bred ponies stumble. The snow hides treacherous pitfalls. Bayard, who heads our straggling line, sinks flank deep in a hollow. Precious minutes are wasted digging him out, and by the time he's free, we're soaked and freezing.

'They want me to free them from the sinker,' whispers Rhiannon.

'The sinker?'

'It's a monster that attacks them when they go down to pan for gold in the underground rivers,' says Rhi.

'Sarn Helen was built by the Romans. I say, "built", but it was reinforced. Sarn Helen follows the Druids Way, a sacred route from long before the Roman invasion – here travellers could pass hidden from prying eyes. They say its banks were filled with wild flowers all the way.' Davey sighs, like he remembers walking the Druids Way himself – I swear, it sounds like he's getting all tearful.

'Before stones were laid and legionnaires tramped them

into the sod, from Neath in the south to Tomen y Mur and on to their stronghold at Segontium, Caernarfon, the Old Ones passed this way. Their footsteps echo on the road – as we pass into this ancient forest.'

Yes, in his own way, Davey is trying.

Very trying.

'There's something about travelling along a track that thousands have walked before – over thousands of years – that's spooky,' says George. He gets out his axe as if he's expecting an ambush.

I want to ask Rhi: but why *you*? But that'd be mean of me. After all, why *not* her?

'They think I'm *The One*,' says Rhi. 'You know like Neo in *The Matrix*.'

'They do?'

'But I don't think I am,' says Rhi quickly. 'I don't even like monsters, so why would they like me?'

I start to worry. Monsters. Girls. Bad memories. Oswald and why he needed girls …

'I'd stay out of their prophecy wotsit,' I whisper. 'Things might get nasty.'

'But I can't,' sighs Rhiannon. 'The Knocker Queen said if I don't fulfil the prophecy, the sinker will kill us all.'

Thirty-Six

The ponies struggle on. The temperature drops. An arctic wind springs up and rushes down the slopes of the mountains straight at us.

At least by afternoon we're well towards the southern reaches of Snowdonia. It feels like the Fimbulvetr is less fierce here, but that might be wishful thinking. The afternoon sun shines high above us. The snowfields glint brightly.

When we get down from the vale of Ffestiniog and across towards Dollgelau, it starts snowing again. I pull up my hood, and button my coat tight against my chin, as we push on towards Cadair. We *have* to reach there today.

But you can't hurry the ponies. They stick to a trail that I can hardly make out. Their hooves crunch softly into drifted banks of white. In our wake, the punch holes quickly fill again with fresh snowfall.

Beside sedge and stone wall, beside lake and hill, we plod on.

Until at last we see Cadair, rising up above us, through veils of pale cloud, beautiful, magical.

A few more miles and we'll be there.

But no sooner are we started on its slopes, than the breath of the great king descends. The Brenin Lywdd is on us like a fist. Cold mist smacks out all vision, stinging bare skin, bruising our chests as we struggle to breathe in icy air.

For some weird reason, I thought we'd left the Brenin Lywdd behind, clinging to the slopes of Snowdon, that it couldn't hold so much power down south.

I was wrong.

'Cadair is the stronghold of the Grey King,' explains Davey. Annoyingly.

A spectral breath and a grey mist descend around us. Strands of icy air slice into eyes and assault nostrils; snowflakes whirl, not in the same way that they had on Snowdon. This is a completely different kind of menace.

Instantly we are isolated. Total white-out.

Tbh, if not for the ponies we'd be dead. I mean it. I can't see further than one metre ahead. There just isn't a path. When I do catch a glimpse of it, there's a sheer drop: first on the left, then on the right.

I'm not joking.

One metre from the trail.

Sheer drops.

I actually close my eyes, squeeze them shut. My heart thuds. I feel dizzy. I hang on to Keincaled's mane, grip it, icicles and all, and whisper, 'Thank you, thank you! You're amazing Keincaled.' I kiss his rough neck. Oh my God.

Keincaled snorts, half turns his head and breathes lovely warm pony breath at me. It helps. He's bravely journeyed all the way, straight through the morning, through the afternoon, through the descending chill, though it has battled against him, and now that it seems to steal the air from his lungs he snorts to encourage me. O. Totally M. G. I think I am falling in love with him.

Sorry Henry.

Suddenly the mist rolls back a few metres. The shores of a wide llyn open up before us. Keincaled rears in abrupt alarm. I nearly fall, but Keincaled twists under me, sort of catches me, then snorts again. But this time it's not a warm, rushy breath of comforting air. His nostrils flare. Even Graine lets out a piercing squeal. At least I think its Graine. I can't see anything.

'What's up?' I call out to the others. They must be still there. My voice falls flat, swallowed up in the blanket of white.

'Can we go round the lake?' I shout.

'Not sure,' calls George. 'Can't see a thing.'

'There's no way round!' shouts Davey. Up ahead, his dim figure swims into view. 'Not from here. Landslide.'

Typical. This must be a trap.

'What're we gonna do?' shrieks Rhiannon.

'Wait?' I call. If it's a trap, we should be prepared.

'We need to get up the mountain soon,' hollers George. 'We can't climb Cadair in the dark.'

We can't climb it in a white-out either.

There is something about this place. I can hear the water of the llyn lapping innocently enough. But there's something …

The white haze seems to thin a bit. At last I can see the others. They are grouped together, dark outlines in the haze.

One of the ponies, I think it's Graine, rears, whinnies out in sudden terror. George (must be) tries to hang on. All the little hairs on the back of my neck prickle.

'We must get away,' says Davey, a note of alarm in his voice. 'This is Llyn Cau. It's bottomless. If you throw a stick into it, it'll sink. It'll be sucked down under Cadair and appear on the far side, and there are things down there – ' He stops, as if to name them would be to call them.

How the hell does he know this is Llyn Cau, though?

We could be anywhere.

Davey coughs. 'It's probably not as bad as I think,' he says, trying to reassure us. 'It's just that under Snowdonia is a vast labyrinth of rivers. They run through the slate caverns and link this lake up to all the other llyns in Snowdonia, and through these lakes swims the Afanc.'

'*Oh My God!*' shrieks Rhiannon.

Is it me, or is there something that Davey and Rhiannon know about that I don't?

'It's probably miles away, there's really no need to – '

The white haze clears. In the distance, I see the dim shape of the mountain.

'What's the Afanc?' I say. Haven't we had we enough with wolves and winter and weirdos? A shiver runs down my spine.

'You don't know?' squeals Rhiannon, a full octave higher than before.

'I think I can guess,' I say. 'Something ghastly with long tentacles that'll pull us down and drown us all – and definitely sides with Oswald?'

At the edge of the llyn a wave ripples out and hits the shore.

I stare at the swelling water. 'If it's worse than that, then I don't want to know.'

George dismounts, tries to calm Graine. 'Get off the ponies,' he says. 'I think Graine's trying to say this is where they quit.'

'Actually get *off* the ponies?' repeats Rhiannon.

Another ripple hits the shore, larger than the last. It breaks with a sharp slap on the pebbles. 'I think,' says Davey, 'we're about to meet the Afanc. You will be able to check out if you are right or not about the tentacles,' he says to me as he points at the lake.

That's it. The Afanc. The sinker!

Right in front of us, gargantuan waves seem to be radiating out from the centre of the llyn – as if the waters are being stirred by some giant hand.

'Quick!' yells George. 'Climb! *There!* Before we're washed away.' He points at a broad slate bridge that straddles an inlet.

From the centre of the llyn rises a gigantic breaker.

Davey and George sprint for the bridge. Rhi just stands there looking stunned. I grab her hand. 'Rhi!'

In the centre of the lake, the water boils up.

'What about the ponies?' she says.

'Bayard,' calls Davey. 'Save yourselves! *Run!*'

With alarming speed, the ponies turn on the spot and bolt back the way we've come.

'There goes all the grub,' groans George, as the dark shapes are swallowed up in the mist.

I shake Rhiannon. '*Move!*'

'I don't think I can do this,' she sobs.

'No choice Rhi.'

'That's the problem,' she whispers. 'They said there was no choice.'

~

We make it to the bridge.

The wave swells to an impossible height, as if some monstrous thing is forcing all the water out from the llyn. Where the water has frozen near the inlet, sheets of ice as thick as stone walls break with a screech. The bridge lurches. The massive slate slab we're balancing on shifts. A rush of air, I stagger, the shift catches me off balance. I stumble backwards. George flings out an arm, catches me.

'Ellie!' shrieks Rhiannon, her face white as death.

And then the wave breaks.

Carrying chunks of ice, it strikes the bridge with a terrible blow. The wooden rail splinters, the slate slab cracks, crumples underneath us. There is no time to grab at each other or defend ourselves – although George tries. He yanks his axe free and swings it wildly, but he misses everything and the thing, the Afanc, rises: one mass of crusted ice.

It strikes. The bridge splinters into shards. Pieces of slate skim out wide across the lake.

And I'm falling.

Cold.

Sub zero.

My bones!

The grip of freezing water. The touch of ice.

In a split second, I see the thing open its jaws and with one great swoop grab hold of the entire broken bridge.

And then I'm sinking.

George, Davey, Rhiannon!

Oh my God …

My mind numbs.

Relentlessly, the Afanc drags us down. Impossibly deep.

Down underneath the icy surface of Llyn Cau.

Thirty – Seven

There is a rushing in my ears. A deathly chill takes hold of me. My teeth rattle. My blood freezes …

I think, *so this is it then*. This is the end of all love, of all adventures.

Oh Mum.

It seems weird that here I am – dying – miles from home, on the shores of some place I've never visited. I could almost smile. I imagine trying to tell Mum how an Afanc, indescribable, bone-pale, appeared out of the lake and grabbed me and drowned me and that is the last thought I have.

Until I hear the singing.

'*She was in a subterranean ice cave, dressed in a cloth of gauze;*

*her voice was playing over the flowing walls. She wove the spell
around him thrice, intoning the hours of the earth, chanting the
way to paradise ... '*

Music.

Ethereal.

Beautiful.

Coming from the dark depths of the water. Coming in
waves of harmony.

Coming from Rhiannon.

Rhiannon?

I'm being pulled through the deep. I try to kick out, grab
at whatever is drowning me. But it breaks my hold.

I kick and I scratch. I want to scream.

But there's no air.

No throat.

No chest.

No light.

I try to open my eyes, blink out the dark.

A blow lands on my head.

This is it.

The black has turned deep green.

I feel dizzy.

I open my eyes and I can see. Everywhere is faintly green.

I am below the surface of the ancient llyn. And there is a lady with me.

And her face is white as bleached bones. And she says: welcome Ellie.

She tosses back her hair and it streams away from her pale face like dark seaweed.

And around her throat is a necklace. Each bead glistens, iridescent, as if deep inside each bead a rainbow flickers.

She bends her head. She says: 'use the mirror'.

And the lights around her fade.

I understand. If only I can get hold of the mirror … I tug and tug. I try and free it from its place inside my jacket pocket. If I could tell Henry …

At last!

I raise the mirror up, look into its depths.

And I see where we sat on the rock and looked out over a stretch of water and …

I remember Henry's words.

'*The adder stone!*'

That's what the mirror had been trying to show us!

The lake. The Afanc. Rhiannon and the adder stone.

I try and transmit the thought to Rhiannon.

I hear the words of the lady of the lake reminding me.

Use the mirror.

'Rhiannon,' I say into the mirror. *'USE THE ADDER STONE!'*

~~~~~⟩

I glance back at the lady. Her dark hair swirls around her face. 'Keep looking into the mirror,' she prompts.

And through the mirror I see a girl is rising up through the water. In her hand she holds an adder stone. She is singing. The song is beautiful. It sounds familiar. I think it is the song I heard last night echoing through the slate caverns. The girl is very lovely, golden hair held back by a band of shining pearls.

She looks like Rhiannon, as Rhiannon was intended to look, in the mind of the great creator.

She smiles and holds the adder stone to her lips. And she continues singing that song of such bewitching sadness through its airy centre. She rises out of the water and stands at the lake's edge. The song grows louder, the melody sweeter, the words more enchanting.

Out of the lake crawls the Afanc, huge, loathsome, a creature of ice and earth. The shore trembles as it heaves clear of the water. A rip tide swells, bellies out of the llyn, as it hauls itself on to the land.

And Rhiannon continues singing.

Her voice is pure, fluid, but even as I peer into the mirror, I see her hand shake.

Slowly, she steps along the edge of the lake and seats herself on a great rock. Slowly the Afanc crawls towards her.

Rhiannon!

I want to shout.

Warn her.

Call out.

Surely using the adder stone is meant to protect her?

'Rhiannon!' I shout into the mirror.

Her voice does not waver. Not once does she let the adder stone slip from her lips.

At last the Afanc towers over her.

Oh Rhiannon!

This is not what should happen.

But just when I think all is lost, and Rhiannon will be swallowed alive, the creature lowers itself, slides to her feet, lays its great icy head on her lap, and looks up at her through darkened eyes.

—

'He will sleep now,' says the lady. 'His final sleep. All will be well.'

'Are you sure?' I ask.

'I am always sure,' she replies.

'Where am I?' I say.

'In Ynys Afallon.'[1]

'Where's that?'

'Some call it Avalon,' she replies.

'And who are you?' I ask. 'And where are George and Davey?'

'I have already sent them to find Idris,' she says.

'But who *are* you?'

'I am the Lady of the Lake; my name is Viviane, but you can call me Nimue. It is for Merlin's sake that I have saved you. He cast his Magick over these mountains, so that they should stand forever and be a refuge for those creatures that hide from the eyes of men. It was not only the dragons that were enthralled to him. With his Magick undone, all are at risk, both fair and foul. Go quickly to the Stargazer and find a way to break this witches' spell.'

'Where is Rhiannon?' I say, casting a look back into the mirror.

'As for her,' sighs Nimue, 'she betrayed you, and her fate is out of my hands. When she allied herself with the Supreme One, she removed herself from any power I have.'

---

1. *Ynys Afallon* – or Avalon – is also called the Fortunate Isle. It is a legendary, enchanted lake island, situated underwater. The sword Caledfwlch was forged there and, after his battle at the Pass of Arrows, Arthur was taken to Avalon, a place of healing, to recover from his wounds.

'Who is the Supreme One?' I ask.

'She is the First One, the rawness of the Earth, the Goddess of Fecundity. She is terrible and she is great. She knows no law of any Magick, High or Deep. She finds willing followers wherever there are girls who seek her powers.'

'So she's ... '

'She is not mortal – she is a force, but she can be hosted by one who invites her in.'

'Sort of like an incubus?' I ask. 'A parasite that takes you over and makes you do horrible things?'

'Sort of,' replies Nimue, 'but much more powerful, for she is obscene and revolting – but if you meet her, you will love her and that love will be your destruction. For she boasts, "I am the womb *and* the tomb – the entire universe within the void." But, enough of Na Gig, for that is her true name. Instead make haste to the Bed of Idris and remember these lines, for it is said that:

"*On the feast day of St Cuthbert,*

When saints can play their part,

Where sleepers sleep, and mirrors crack,

By traitor's blood and hero's art,

It will take a sacrifice, to purify the heart."

'I will do what I can for your friend Rhiannon, for she has subdued the Afanc and helped you. She has one last act to perform. And I will guide her hand, and for that she will forever be a favourite among the Coblynau, those who mankind call the Knockers. Never fear. Now hurry. Look deep into my mirror and trust its magic. When you awake far from here, fear not.'

Everything fades to black.

Thirty-Eight

Before I even open my eyes, I know I am at the in-between place. I sigh in happiness.

I know he is here with me.

'Exquisite!' says the voice that I've been longing to hear.

I open my eyes. I look around. I am once again in Halfway House. Exactly where I've always wanted to be.

We're sitting on the old bench in front of a roaring fire. So familiar. Candles burning. The logs smell of pine. It's like we've never left – since that day we first met. A blanket is wrapped round both of us. Firelight sparkles off it in little dancing flickers. Together we cuddle under it.

Utterly magical.

There are tins heating up in the embers, we are warming ourselves and breathing in the pine-scented air. Beans sizzle, corned beef melts. The fire throws out golden shadows.

They glow from the old stone walls.

Henry tips beans and corned beef on to a solitary plate.

'Like old times, isn't it?' he says.

Oh. I. Am. So. Happy.

The food tastes of cinder and salt, baked beans and tinned meat. Delicious.

I look into his dark eyes and he smiles and says, 'More, my Lady?'

I smile back, not able to find words. My mouth is full anyway. I can hardly chew; can hardly swallow, so I just smile.

Smile and smile.

Two old cracked mugs are filled with fresh snow. We stand them by the fire until they melt. Snow tastes so funny. We toast each other with that melted snow as if it were the finest champagne.

'To you, Ellie,' he says.

'To you, Henry,' I reply.

'To us,' we laugh together.

'Look at that,' points out Henry. He raises his cracked mug at the words etched in stone over the fireplace.

Fight Fire With Fire

'What exactly do they mean?' I ask.

'Well Shakespeare first made the phrase popular when he put the words in a play. He wrote:

"*Be stirring as the time; be fire with fire;*
Threaten the threatener and outface the brow
Of bragging horror."'

'The brow of bragging horror?' I say. Sounds scary. Instantly I shiver. The lovely exquisite feeling disappears.

'But they come from a much older lore.'

'What lore?'

'The Way of Dragons,' says Henry.

'Why are you showing them to me?' I ask. I know now these visits to the in-between place have a purpose. I'm supposed to learn something.

'Just tell me.'

'I can't.'

'Please.'

'I'm doing my best.'

'But I don't understand.'

'FIGHT FIRE WITH FIRE.'

'But ... '

'Think Ellie ... '

Henry is fading ...

'Think: when you want to stop the path of fire, you have to burn out anything flammable ... '

The fire dies down. The candles snuff out.

'Henry?'

When I awake, I'm lying on a great bed of rock. I am as cold as stone. I am positioned as if I have been laid out to rest. High above me are stars. I blink. I try to figure out what's happened.

All I can remember is FIGHT FIRE WITH FIRE and the words that the Lady of the Lake told me:
'On the feast day of St Cuthbert,
When saints can play their part,
Where sleepers sleep, and mirrors crack,
By traitor's blood and hero's art,
It will take a sacrifice, to purify the heart.'

I try to understand what she meant. If only I could get a signal up here I could google St Cuthbert …

Everything's a muddle.

I stare upwards.

Standing over me is the tallest man imaginable. I swear he must be about twelve feet tall and more. He has straight golden hair down to his waist, a great beard and dark gentle eyes.

'Who are you?' I say.

'You have been calling for me,' he says, 'by name.'

'Huh?' I say.

'Yes, I'm quite sure. Unless there are two Idris Gawrs. Two giants of Cadair?'

The Stargazer? He must be!

I don't know what I was expecting, maybe some kind of mythical giant who's pretty dumb and carries a club? A bit like the trolls in *The Hobbit*. You know, stupid, cruel, lumpish.

Idris isn't dumb-looking; he isn't fat or troll-like either.

And he's definitely not cruel. In fact his eyes are the kindest ever. He's just a very nice sort of man, but built on a *much* bigger scale and crazily tall.

'Where am I?' I ask.

'You are on the summit of Cadair Idris, my mountain-top, and you are lying on my bed of stone,' says Idris, not unkindly.

'How did I get here?' I say. 'I thought I was under a lake.'

'The Lady Nimue sent you to me. You are lucky to have won her favour, and for her sake I will hear your cause.'

I try to take that in. I was under a lake, but I'm not wet. I'm on top of a mountain, but not out of breath.

Idris continues: 'Though I saw that you would come. The stars foretold this meeting, and I know you have a task for me, but first of all, before I hear your case, you must answer me this question: Why should I help you?

Why should I meddle at all in the affairs of men? Why should I take the part of the Red Dragon or act against the White?'

I look up at him. I don't have an answer – only that he should help us, because … he should. I mean, Henry is *good*. Henry is the best – and Oswald isn't. Henry wants to protect Snowdonia. Oswald wants the Fimbulvetr to destroy everything …

But instead of saying anything, I just stare blankly at him.

'Many many centuries – no – millennia ago, I foreswore all contact with mankind, and yet you seek me out, you shift me from my bed and from my dearest dreams. You wake me up, and want me to help you, and here I am asking you why.'

He looks at me with huge, sad, kind eyes.

I lie there staring at him. Actually, looking at it from his point of view, I don't know why he *should* help me, but equally, I don't see why he shouldn't. Like, I don't know what keeps him staring at the stars, and philosophising, and I don't know why he 'foreswore all contact with mankind', and until I know these things, I can't really answer his questions. Can I?

But, I've got a feeling that unless I answer his questions, I can't ask him to help us; so I simply look up at him and say, 'What is there – up there – in the stars? Why do you look at them? Why have you forsaken all things upon the earth?'

He turns his back on me and walks a few metres away.

I glance around and see the others laid out beside me – on some kind of stone ledge – though it's majorly dark. I see Davey on one side and George on the other. No Rhiannon, worryingly. George and Davey have their arms folded across their chests and lie as still as statues.

A chill creeps over me. Is this a bed of rest or a resting place for the dead?

I reach over and touch George's hand. Cold as ice. I suck in air. Try to get hold of myself. *Stay calm Ellie. Even if it's the worst, you can still break the spell. Everything will be restored to how it was. You can still save George.*

But I don't know if that's true.

Will everything be the same? Will George be saved if I break the spell? Perhaps nothing will *ever* be the same again.

And I can't break any spell, not without George. He's always been there.

Always.

Right from the first moment I saw Snowdon.

George running down the mountainside to greet me. *George promising to show me every stone, every blade, every stream. George and me exploring, rock climbing, scraping knees, climbing trees, catching slow-worms and watching the peregrines. George and me walking home from school in Llanberis. George and me on summer evenings, chatting about nothing, about football, food, mobile phones and Rhiannon and how she's always embarrassing herself by falling all over him.*

'Oh George,' I whisper.

Nothing. Not the flicker of an eyelid, not the shadow of a smile.

I remember the words of the old curse that lies over Cadair:

'In the land of Merioneth is a high hill that is called Cadair Idris. And on the highest crown is a bed-shaped form, great in length and width. And this is called The Bed of Idris. And it is said that whoever sleeps upon that bed, one of two things will happen to him: either he will wake a hero, or never wake again ...'

I woke up – does that mean I'm a hero?

But something isn't right about the way I'm remembering it. I'm sure there was some line about a poet? I struggle to remember the words correctly. They evaporate in my mind. I cannot shake off a conviction that if George does not wake up now, he never will.

I shake him. *'George!'* I cry.

Please, don't let anything happen to George.

And I realise how very much I care about him. How important he is to me. How he has always been soooo important. How I've never acknowledged it, and suddenly I can't imagine a future without him.

I shake his shoulder. *'George!'* I shout at him.

I yell into his face, '**GEORGE!**'

There's a long, deep silence. I can hear my heart beating. *His face is so deathly pale.* My blood feels as if it's clotting, clogging up in my veins ... the marrow of my bones is turning in on itself ... I'm confused ...

No George?

Thirty-Nine

Idris walks back towards me. I see that he's troubled, there's pain in his eyes. His face looks tired.

This can't be right.

My voice trembles. '*George?*' I say. 'Can you help him?'

There has to be George. In my past. In my present.

In my future.

'He sleeps.'

'Sleeps as in the *sleep of the dead*?'

Idris does not answer. My heart sinks so quickly I feel dizzy.

'I, on the other hand, do not sleep,' he says. 'You have woken me, and you must tell me why.'

I swallow air. I sway. I can't think. I'm trembling. 'Oh,' I say, 'I need your help.'

'But you have not answered my question,' says Idris.

'Why should I help a race of beings that has brought a thousand years of unhappiness to me?'

'Whoever created your unhappiness,' I say, 'it wasn't me, or Henry, or George. None of what is happening is our doing.' The snow glints in a bright, white blanket under the stars.

'It really isn't George's fault. He doesn't deserve this.' I pick up George's hand. *So cold.* 'Nor is it Davey's,' I add. I know Davey's annoying, but he is on our side and he definitely doesn't need to die.

'No,' he said, 'I also read that in the stars ... '

'Then why – ?'

'One thing at a time. You were saying ... '

I breathe in, steady myself. 'It's because of this spell over Snowdonia, that I've come,' I say. My voice trembles. 'It is the work of the White Dragon and as only dragons can fight dragons – we kind of need Henry back – here in Wales.' I gulp.

I need him back.

I stop. Far away I hear a rustling, as if someone is climbing up the far side of the peak.

'Yes?' Idris is looking steadily down at me, commanding me to continue.

'But because they tainted his heart, he's flying through

the skies towards Draco to take up his place as a star there and can nevermore be on earth,' I rush out.

Maybe it wasn't a rustling, more like a gliding, or a whispering.

'You love him, don't you?' says Idris.

I blink. How did he figure that out?

'That is why you are the chosen one,' asserts Idris.

'If we cannot purify his heart, then he can't return to fight the White Dragon – then this winter will never end, and then … '

My voice trails away. It is too hard to think about the 'and thens'. It was hard enough to think of him interred under Dinas Emrys, but at least he was nearby. If I listened sometimes, in the dead of night, I could almost feel his great heart beating inside the mountain.

'Only the true heart can purify the tainted one,' prompts Idris.

But now he will be as remote as the stars. Literally. And I won't even know which one of the stars he is. He will be lost forever.

And I don't think I can bear it.

'Be not afeared. I too know what it is to love.'

'You do?'

'And to bear a long parting; to even choose that parting.'

His voice breaks. Briefly he shuts his eyes.

When he opens them, I see something new in them, something as hard as steel.

'This night,' says Idris, 'will give dawn to 20 March. It is an auspicious date – for as you well know – tomorrow heralds in the vernal equinox, when all things will reach equilibrium. When one day will equal one night – when good will equal bad – when all will be balanced in perfection at exactly the same degree. At first light it will be decided whether or not the spell over Snowdonia can be broken, whether the heart can be purified and spring will start, or whether the dark will rise and swallow the light, and the Fimbulvetr never thaw.'

The whispering, gliding thing slips nearer. I can't see what it is, but I grow colder.

'There is only one place where the heart can be purified, and that is where the pure in heart dwell.' Idris straightens up, seems even taller. 'I am reluctant to help you get there, for to break the spell will be to **BREAK MY DREAMS FOREVER**.' His voice booms out.

I want to cover my ears, but I don't dare.

'I don't understand?' I say.

'The only place where that heart that you carry **CAN BE PURIFIED IS AT THE MENHIR OF MAWR IN THE**

VALLEY BENEATH THE CAVE OF THE SLEEPING KNIGHTS.'

His voice is loud enough to wake the dead. George, though, does not stir.

'In the Pass of Arrows?' I hardly dare ask, but I must. I have to save Henry.

'THE SAME.'

I must admit at this point, I think: we have just trekked all the way over here; we haven't *got* another day to trek all the way back … I don't know why my brain does that: goes all practical when I'm feeling scared and upset.

'But you must know that my beloved one, Angharad Golden-Hand, sleeps on the other side of my mountain. She is my true love and I am hers. For these last aeons we have been parted, for she died as a result of a witches' curse, The Nine Witches of Gloucester – evil women. May the Devil, Gwyn ap Nudd, take their souls and the Cŵn Annwn hunt them for eternity!'

Idris towers over me, and as he bellows, the rocks shiver.

'I HAVE NO LOVE FOR WITCHES.'

Suddenly I'm really glad ~~b~~witchy Rhiannon isn't here.

'And I laid my beloved to rest myself – under the capstone of her dolmen, and I alone raised a mound over her.'

And I know he's not bellowing at me, because I know

what it is to have your true love buried deep in cold earth.

'Yet,' a sad smile flickers across his face, 'for the last two nights, she has risen from her barrow and climbed up the mountain, and we sit together upon this bed of rock, and I put my arm around her and she lays her gentle head against my shoulder, and together we look up at the stars and search them to see our destiny.'

And Idris throws his arms wide. Suddenly he looks so happy, just as sunlight banishes shadow, all the pain in his eyes evaporates.

'I have sat here alone for hundreds of years, but now Angharad Golden-Hand has awoken and we sit here together.'

Angharad Golden-Hand – the name sounds familiar – wasn't she a girl in the *Mabinogion* who all men fell in love with? I stare at Idris. Is that how long he has waited to see her?

'If I help you to break the spell over Snowdonia, she will no longer come here. The Olde Deepe Magicke, which awoke her, will lose its dominion. She will remain forever shut up in her barrow again; and if I should die – for even giants cannot live forever – who will remember Angharad Golden-Hand, and worship her beauty? She that was so beloved in bygone times – by so many – but worst of all by Peredur.'

Idris suddenly yanks a HUMONGOUS rock off the top of the mountain and hurls it over the precipice edge of Craig Cau.

Whoa. Go easy.

I back away from him a bit. This Peredur character may have belonged to bygone days, but he's certainly ticked Idris off.

The whole mountaintop kind of shakes as Idris picks up another great boulder and throws it over the edge too. It crashes down the hillside joining the first with a rattle of stones.

I don't know what to say.

'**Cursed be Peredur! He sought to take her from me.**'

'Yes, curse him, the slimey git,' I say, joining in. 'I know how it feels. Sheila is always trying to get Henry off me too.'

'And because of him, the nine witches slew her and took her from me forever.' Idris's voice cracks, goes hoarse. Pain floods back in.

'I thought you said she comes to sit with you now?' I venture gently. Don't want him to get toooo upset. You know: avalanche, landslide …

'She does,' he says, 'because just three days ago, the High Magick was broken and now she can rise again and be with me. But if I help you break their spell, then her ghost will awake no more, and I will sit up here alone again.'

I think about ghosts, and the memory of the nun in Caernarfon police cells flashes across my mind. *Of course, with Merlin's Magick broken, ghosts can walk abroad too.*

Yikes.

'Oh,' I say.

I look at him. I understand, because to lose the one you love – even the ghostly shadow of them – even though you can't touch or hold them, is to face the loneliness of sitting all by yourself, year after year, knowing that you will never again see that beloved face, hear that beloved voice.

He turns to me. 'And you would have me forgo this last of all joys that I have waited an eternity for. To cradle her ghostly form, knowing that I do not have to lie upon my bed alone any more. And for what? So that you can save a love that you will never hold either?'

'What do you mean?' I say.

Never hold Henry again?

'If the Red Dragon can be recalled, he will not come back to *you*. Once he has subdued the White Dragon, he must descend under Dinas Emrys again, as myth dictates, and he must stay there until his time comes around again, when he can become a man – if such be his wish – by which time you may well be dead.'

Hmm, thanks for reminding me of that little gem, Idris.

'I have seen it all in the stars. And for this, you would have me forsake an eternity of being with the one I love?'

I think about it. I don't have an answer.

'But,' I say, 'it's not just about us any more; it's about the whole of Wales. The White Dragon *has* been released and if we don't try to stop him, the Fimbulvetr will spread – a new ice age will begin.'

I don't know quite what else to say, because somehow myth and magic and reality have all got mixed up inside my head, and I don't actually know what will happen any more.

Idris doesn't reply. He throws himself down on the stone bed beside me, and stares straight up at the night sky.

'OK,' I say at last. 'If it's too much for you, I get it. But I've got to try and stop Oswald anyway. Will you at least tell me the way down the mountain? I'm going to try and reach the Pass of Arrows.'

And then I get a sinking feeling, like everything in me has drained out, the energy in every cell flattened. *We have come all this way for nothing. Plus I'm not going to make it.* Even if the ponies have waited for us at the foot of the mountain and are willing to carry me: we're not going to get back to Snowdon by daybreak, are we?

I look up at the stars and blink back tears.

'I cannot help you to go or stay,' Idris says. 'And I cannot decide whether or not I should intercede with the stars for you. There is only one person who can decide that matter and she herself is near, for the hour of midnight has come, and my beloved has risen again. Angharad must decide her own destiny. She must be given that choice.'

Angharad – coming here?

'When the stars are at their brightest, she will come. When the Pole Star twinkles high above us, then you can ask her what her will is.'

Idris looks so sad.

'She alone will decide.'

'Oh, OK,' I say.

'And while we wait I will light a great fire to guide and welcome her.'

Idris lifts great slices of dried peat, piles them high, lights them, blows the embers until a fire roars.

I draw near to it and wait impatiently. If she's going to say no, then I'd be better off starting out right away. I mean, I'd say no if I was her.

I think about that. Whether I *could* actually choose never to be with Henry again, never to see him.

Or George.

Oh George.

I glance down at his cold, still form. 'You did not have permission to die,' I say, poking his icy shoulder. I take my coat off and cover him with it.

And then I burst into tears.

Forty

The sound of whispering is faint. I think it's only the wind stirring the snow, whispering up the mountainside.

Idris stops and listens. He smiles. 'She's here.'

I focus on the gentle swishing, the slight kiss of air on ice. I hear the smooth brush of something moving over the snow. There is no creak or crushing. I wait to hear anything definite. But there are no footsteps.

Idris beams. He jumps up from the fireside. 'Angharad!' His voice breaks with happiness.

A slight breeze whips up the snow on the top of the drifts, where it has frozen hard. The powdery snow spins. I watch, mesmerised.

When I was a little kid, I had a lava lamp. There's something about staring at shapes that form and morph that keeps your eyes glued. As I watch, the powder whirls and sways. I strain to hear the footsteps. More icy dust and the crust on the snow crumbles. It turns in an eddy of swirling. It begins to form into a pale, ghostly figure.

For some reason, I am not in the slightest bit afraid. The phantom is graceful, pure white like a swan, and as soft as spun candyfloss. Her step is light; a garland of fresh snowdrops adorns her long hair. On the cold hillside a lady stands, beautiful, unearthly, and she smiles, and sees nothing else but Idris.

Without a doubt, I know Angharad has the kindest heart.

But at her back, I catch the fleeting glimpse of pale princes, pale warriors, all deathly pale.

Shadows of the past …

I rub my eyes. They're doing that vision stuff again, like when I first saw Davey.

Angharad realises she and Idris are not alone. She looks from face to face – up at Idris's smiling one, across at me, over at George and Davey. She sighs. 'There has been some great sorrow here, I can feel it,' she says.

'Great sorrow, my beloved,' he says, 'and great joy now that you have come.'

He reaches across and holds out his hand. She lays her ghostly one in his.

'Then let me share your heart's pain,' she says.

'I would share everything with you, but this sorrow is so heavy to bear. I am loath to lay it on your slim shoulders – come, before the heartbreak – come, let us be merry! Won't you sing for us my beloved?'

She smiles a sweet sad smile. 'It will not do,' she says. 'There cannot be joy until we lay the sorrow down, and until I feel its weight, I cannot do so.'

'Come, it will keep,' says Idris.

'No,' she says, 'it will not keep.'

I'm afraid Idris will grow crazy and tear another huge boulder from the pile on the summit and hurl it somewhere, maybe at the stars – maybe at me.

'Is it something you have seen in the heavens?' asks Angharad.

'No, it *is* something in the heavens,' I say. I send Idris my best pleading look.

Angharad turns to me. 'We have not met,' she says, 'but already I want to know you. Your directness is refreshing. You remind me of myself, once long ago, when I was a girl … ' She looks at me, kindly, and immediately I like her.

'Come,' says Idris, 'then if the sorrow must be felt, come then and sit beside me, and I will tell you of the heaviness of my heart, and once I have shared it with you, then there will be no more songs and no more kisses and no more gladness in the world.'

'Is it so serious then?' she says, her face searching ours.

'I would have rather smashed this mountain of mine to the ground than tell you, for I know your heart and I know which way you will choose; and I know that even though you will do so with a smile, inside your heart will break.'

And Idris cannot continue. He strides quickly to the end of the long saddleback, his form tall and grey in the mist.

'You must not judge him,' Angharad says to me. 'He is the kindest and bravest of beings, and he has waited for me – though princes have claimed me and kingdoms have fallen and witches have conspired. He is as true as his stars, as fixed, as constant as bright Polaris, the Pole Star, itself.'

I think of the Pole Star and constancy and waiting for too many years and find I cannot say a thing.

'There,' she says, 'now he is searching the skies for a sign, you shall tell me. To carry the bad news is enough, let us spare him the pain on my face and the anguish in my eyes when I learn of what this is.'

And I look into her eyes, and realise that I have never seen such a beautiful expression anywhere before, and I can see why Idris loves her, and why he would wait through eternity to be with her.

Tears well up in my eyes. I know before I even tell her

my story what she will decide. I glance across at Idris. I understand. Because to be alone and sit on the mountain where your beloved is buried and to have little hope of ever seeing them again is a tortuous thing.

I wouldn't wish it on anyone.

Forty-One

But I tell her anyway, because it is not just about my longing to save Henry, or to be with him again. It is because, if somebody does not try to stop Oswald, the spring will never come; more lambs will die, their throats ripped out. Sheep will freeze in their snow holes. People will despair and the things that Merlin with his Magick hid, deep below the hills, will tunnel their way out to terrify and destroy.

And the winter will never end and the next ice age will begin.

But as I tell Angharad what has happened and what must be done and our only chance of saving Wales, her eyes darken with sorrow.

'Ah,' she says, 'let me not be ungrateful for the two days and nights that I have already been given. It is indeed an evil curse that brings no one any joy. For the spell that your friend, the witch, cast has had one joyous unintended and beautiful effect. For I have risen from my barrow and again I can see the hills and smell the air and be near my beloved Idris. And for two nights we have stayed awake holding hands, entwining our arms, looking out over the mountains. And for this bliss it has been worth waiting in my deep barrow, under dark earth.

Tears start rolling down my cheeks. I sniff; drag my hand across my nose.

'And if this must come to an end at daybreak, then I do not want to be ungrateful. For it was unlooked for, and gives me great hope. For now I believe that somehow in the future I will see my beloved Idris again – another chance will surely come. I must believe this.'

'I'm so sorry,' I whisper.

'It is not your fault,' she says.

She reaches out a ghostly hand and lays it upon mine. 'Do not be troubled,' she says. 'Do not grieve for us. Where there is love there is always great joy and great sadness. I would not have lived my life in any other way.'

The tears keep coming and, even though I swallow hard, I can't speak.

'I cannot sacrifice the future of our beloved Wales in order to sit here and hold hands upon the summit of

Cadair Idris. And if I did,' she sighs, 'the sweetness would be gone from it. There would be a bitter taste in my mouth; my heart would despair, knowing the cost of being with the one I love.'

The powdery snow whirls as she stands.

'So, think only of your mission. Try to stop Oswald, and if you fail, know it will have freed me and Idris, and some other good may yet come of it – even if only for the shortest of times.'

For a moment she turns and looks at me. She is more beautiful than sunrise.

'Now, you wait here and I will go and tell Idris my decision.'

More beautiful than the full moon sailing against the night sky.

She floats over the snow to Idris. Not one footstep does she leave in the crusted snow, only a trail, a dusting of white stars.

Angharad entwines her arm around his waist. She lays her lovely ghostly head against him. She, so small and slender; he, towering like an obelisk. They stand there and I know that she has told him, because I see his broad shoulders droop, his grip around her spectral waist tighten.

Now the decision is made, I want them to hurry.

I know that sounds cruel. In a perfect world, they should have as much time as they need to be together, to think about the choice they've made.

But hey, this isn't a perfect world. In fact it's so imperfect there is no time to lose.

Their help will be of no use if we cannot persuade Draco to release Henry, if we cannot get to the Pass Of Arrows and the Menhir of Mawr at Cwm Dyli by daybreak.[1]

It's all a bit mad. I suppose I'm hoping Draco will free Henry and zap! Kapow! Somehow he'll fly here and pick us all up, and whoosh us over to Snowdon in time for the first day of spring. And *Raaaarrr!* He'll just breathe one breath; a flame will ignite everything, and it'll all be solved.

I say 'us'. I look at George and Davey.

Whoosh *me* then.

There is so little time left.

Henry won't arrive. I don't know how I'll get there.

---

1. After the mortal wounding of Arthur in the Pass of Arrows his men ascended to a ridge called Y Lliwedd and then down into a vast cave called Ogof Llanciau Eryri, 'the young men of Snowdonia's cave', inside the cliff beside Llyn Llydaw. This place is called Cwm Dyli. A standing stone, the Menhir of Mawr, once marked the spot.

It's a rubbish idea. It can't happen like that. George is so cold beside me, I can't leave him anyway. I stare out over the mountain. Only the ghostly glow of the moon gazes back.

Idris and Angharad return. Instead of a bitter glance from Idris, he actually smiles. I can see the pain in his eyes, and I can see why Angharad loves him so much.

He bears it very bravely.

'Come,' he says, 'let us sit upon my lumpy old bed together and talk to the Great Dragon himself. His voice is even cheerful. I wonder how you can hold in so much sorrow, and still be so kind, so caring.

'I'm sorry,' I say.

'We are all sorry,' says Idris.

'What will happen to George?' I ask. 'Is there any hope for him and Davey?'

At this, Angharad laughs, a beautiful melodious peal of laughter, it chimes like a mountain stream.

'You must not worry about your two companions,' she says. 'When I am gone, they will wake.'

'Now,' says Idris, 'let me lie upon my bed and see my stars.'

I don't understand.

Angharad bends her head slightly and her silvery hair falls around her fragile face.

'When I was alive,' she says, 'the Nine Witches of Gloucester put a curse upon me. The curse said: whichever man looketh upon me, will fall in love with me.'[2]

I'm not entirely sure that is a curse. In fact I'm totally positive that if Sheila had such a 'curse' put upon her, she would see it as a blessing. Who knows, even Rhiannon might enjoy a little bit of spellbound admiration.

Idris shifts George and Davey gently over and stretches out beside them.

Angharad shakes her head slowly: 'It is not a blessing,' she says, as if she reads my mind. 'For when men fall in love with you under enchantment, it is to their ruin. They fight over you, as those possessed. They become jealous and vengeful, wild and enraged, and because their love is forced of them and not given freely and truly, no good comes of it.'

I'm pretty certain Sheila wouldn't mind the downside.

'And I only had love for one being.' She glances up at Idris. 'And he was not a man,' she says, 'and perhaps that is one of the reasons that I loved him the more, because not being a man, he did not fall in love with me through any magical means. He saw the real me and still loved, despite

---

2. In the *Mabinogion*, Peredur accompanies the Nine Witches of Caerloyw to the Witches' Court where he learns the manner of their fighting. Peredur learns that the Witches of Caerloyw have slain a cousin of his. Peredur slays the witches, but not before they put a love curse upon Angharad to break his heart with her beauty and ensure that she dies when they do.

the curse upon me.'

Idris stops looking upwards, turns to her. 'And I still do, and I still will – 'til the stones of this mountain crumble and all the seas run over its heights.' He reaches out, softly touches her hand.

'If your two friends were to wake,' Angharad continues, 'they would fall so deeply in love with me, it would ruin the rest of their lives. It is always like this when you employ magic against the natural will of a human soul.'

She shakes her head.

'Their glimpse of me would haunt them. They would scour the earth to find me; nothing would satisfy them again. A terrible affliction and a terrible craving would start eating away at their hearts. It is for this reason I have cast a sleeping spell upon all men to whom I draw near. They will remain asleep while I am here.'

I can't believe it! My blood races. *George is OK.* 'Not forever?' I need to hear her say it again.

'When I am gone,' she glances again at Idris.

'Do not go,' he whispers. 'Stay with me through this last night?'

'Then when I am out of range,' she says, 'your two companions can be easily awoken.'

Yay! I am soooo happy!

Suddenly, I see that the spell cast over George and Davey is for their own benefit. How horrible it would be to be forced to be in love with someone you could never have. I catch my breath. *Am I in love with someone I can never have?*

'Then I will return to you, my beloved,' she looks up at Idris, 'and we will be alone until daybreak.'

Idris sits up, pulls her close, nods, strokes her hair. It shimmers like stardust.

'No,' she glides away. 'Speak to your stars first.'

Idris thumps back down on the stone bed. Gazes upwards at the skies. Suddenly he cries out in a loud voice, '**Do you hear me, Dragon?**' I'm surprised at the way he addresses the Great Draco – so directly. I don't know quite what I was expecting, maybe some bowing and scraping and: 'Oh Great, Wonderful Lord' type thing.

Maybe he doesn't want Draco to agree …

I bite my lip.

I wouldn't blame him.

Idris looks directly up into the sky and shouts: '**Draco! The will of Merlin has been broken on earth, and you are to blame for it. Aeons ago you took the part of the White Dragon against Merlin. That was wrong and now the venom brewed by the two of you that day has poisoned Wales.**'

Wow! That was one sucker punch of an opening.

Idris continues. 'Your most beloved, true and faithful fellow, the Red Dragon of Wales, has been forced to leave his homeland and fly back to join you in your constellation of stars,' he bellows out with a righteous tone.

Even Angharad looks shocked.

'YES, while you continue to weave your snake dance around the Pole Star, we endure the evil you have sown!'

Crikey, he isn't mincing his words is he?

'Your deeds have done this. I hold you to account. The Red Dragon is blameless and innocent, yet HIS heart has become tainted, when yours should have been.'

Angharad looks wide-eyed at Idris, as if she never realised how loud a giant could get when he was angry.

'I will not appeal to you to meddle in the affairs of mankind; I know that the stars are eternal, and mankind just a short blink in the passage of time, and if the Fimbulvetr stays and mankind dies out, it is not your concern. So instead I conjure you by the powers of the Olde Deepe Magicke to put right this wrong.'

I blink.

'By the Olde Deepe Magicke on this night to either undo your evil or stay forever fixed, unable to turn further in the precession of the equinoxes, when tomorrow the vernal equinox arrives.'

I gulp. He's not giving Draco any wriggle room, is he?

'**Dragon, have a care! You may live forever, but if you do not release the Red Dragon of Wales to resume his watch upon these mountains, you will be forever held by your own wickedness. Therefore I invoke the lore of the Olde Deepe Magicke, I command you to choose: his freedom or your imprisonment. For so it is that the Olde Deepe Magicke works. An eye for an eye. A tooth for a tooth.**'

Now I really am taken aback. I'm not entirely sure that you can command stars to do anything. But Idris does not seem unduly worried. And he is the Stargazer. He is the one who watches and understands their orbits around the sky, so have a little faith, Ellie, I tell myself.

Idris lowers his face and turns to me. 'It is done,' he says.

'*Already?*' I ask.

'He does not need to answer,' says Idris, 'and even if he did, you would not hear his voice, for the language of the spheres is a symphony so beautiful, it would break your heart – even if you heard the slightest refrain. But I know all its melodies, and I know that for the stars to spin in their orbits, they must be true and all in tune. And especially this is so for Draco. For he is the one who guards the point upon which all else take their true compass. If he should make a false decision, then the Harmony of the Spheres will be in discord. There will be dissonance and a great shattering. Planets will explode, suns will burn out. He cannot allow that to happen.'

And now I understand how Idris could address Draco so boldly.

'As you have heard, I have put to him the case of the Red Dragon, his banishment from earth was not wise or timely nor in the spirit of true Dragon Lore.'

'So he'll release Henry?' I realise I'm not really breathing, just sucking in tiny sips of air as my heart does some kind of wild tango inside my chest.

'Have no fear, he is already released.'

Already released.

A trembling begins in my shins. Then I feel it in my fingers. I can't seem to hold on to the stones I'm sitting on.

Henry is released.

And my heart is singing louder than any crummy old Harmony of the Spheres.

I throw out my arms.

I want to put them around Angharad, around Idris. But she's too wispy, so that's impossible, and he is too large and I've never considered kneecap-hugging before.

But I do now.

And I throw my arms around his leg and squeal out 'THANK YOU! OH THANK YOU!'

And for one tiny moment, I think I almost hear it: the music of the heavens.

I think I hear just one note.

And that note is singing:

'HENRY IS FREE! HENRY IS COMING! HENRY WILL RETURN!'

Forty-Two

Status: UNBELIEVABLY HAPPEEE ☺

Recent updates:

Rhiannon

Hon, where are you? Please don't say you drowned. I've tried George's phone, but it's dead. I'm having a horrible time. You don't know how sorry I am that I ever did that spell. I don't want to be a witch any more. I had to do something that was very yucky. I don't feel good about it. But the Knockers are happy. They came and got me and they are taking me home via their underground links (Lol – you could say I'm on the tube!). Just gonna eat some supper now. See you back home??

You didn't drown did you?

I'm dizzy and excited and scared and happy and terrified, and in the process, I miss seeing Angharad leaving.

There are no footsteps, just a gentle swishing. At the back of all my muddle of thoughts, I hear the brush of something moving away over the snow. There's no creak or crush, just the slight kiss of air on ice.

'*Angharad!*' Idris's voice breaks, grows hoarse.

I snap back to now.

Angharad has gone, before I even had time to say goodbye.

A slight breeze whips up the snow on the top of the drifts. The powder spins. Shapes form and morph, I watch the particles whirl and sway, hoping to catch one last glimpse of her.

More icy dust. The crust on the snow by the cliffs crumbles. It turns into an eddy, spinning in small circular twists.

Just for one second on the cold hillside, beautiful, unearthly Lady Angharad swirls and is gone.

The last of the powdery snow settles.

I catch my breath. I will never see her again. A dull ache starts. Something of the enchantment over her has burrowed its way into my heart too.

'Now,' reminds Idris, 'your companions may awake with no harm done.'

I'd like to ask Idris one more thing, because now I'm starting to panic. *Has all this been for nothing?* Henry is coming back, but *to where* and *to whom* and *how long will it take*? And we need to get his heart to the Menhir of Mawr, the Oracle stone, in the Pass of Arrows, by daybreak.

And we only have a few hours …

And …

I say as much. 'Everything may be lost,' I say, 'all sacrifices in vain, if I cannot get the heart to the Pass of Arrows.'

Idris raises himself up. '**You would tempt me, would you?**'

I don't understand. I look at him, confused.

'**Yes,**' he says. '**It would be very tempting to leave you stranded here upon my mountain and glory in the fact that *still* your errand may fail.**' His voice grows loud, his face suddenly terrifying.

Then he passes a hand before his eyes, as if he is brushing away some evil spell that nearly trapped him. He sits down again, and smiles.

'But,' his voice gentles, 'Angharad Golden-Hand has chosen, and I love and trust her. I respect and honour her. I believe in her, and so I will help you.'

'You will?' I gulp.

'You will be by the Menhir of Mawr near the Cave of the Sleeping Knights when the first light of the first day of true spring breaks.'

'I will?'

'With the heart.'

'But how?'

'We giants have some cleverness that is our own. It is not only dragons who have special gifts.'

I look at him.

George rolls over, throws out an arm. *He throws out an arm!*

Thank God.

'Yes,' says Idris, 'every self-respecting giant has a pair of seven-league boots, a golden harp, and of course a hen that lays golden eggs.'

He's grinning now. I'm not sure if he's pulling my leg.

'Is that true?' I ask, warily.

'Fi fi fo fum,' he teases.

I roll my eyes.

'Well, everything except the hen,' says Idris, 'and actually the harp belongs to Angharad.'

George sits up and shakes his head.

GEE-ORGE!!!!

I forget everything and throw my arms around George's neck. One MASSIVE bear-hug.

'WOW!' says George. 'Whatever did I do to deserve that?' Hastily, lest I change my mind, he hugs me back. Very tightly. Very, *very* tightly in fact.

'Oh SHUT UP!' I say.

And I'm so relieved, I kiss him.

Yep, a real smacker straight on the lips.

'Bloody hell!' says George.

I promptly burst into tears.

'Crikey!' he says. 'I'm not that crap a kisser, am I?'

'I thought you were DEAD!' I scream in his ear. (We are still hugging V V tightly.)

'Oh I see,' says George. 'Well, for you I can do dead any time.'

'No you can't. You've got to stay alive. Totally and completely and forever from now on.' I unwind myself from his arms. Though they *are* very nice and muscly and manly.

'Only if you'll snog me – just every now and then – you know – just to remind me to stay alive,' says George.

'It's a deal,' I say. *I'm so happy.*

I even give pimply Davey a ~~little~~ minuscule hug cos I see he's waking up too.

'Good,' says Idris. 'So, if we're ready to go … I've got a certain lady to get back to for one last hour before you stop the Olde Deepe Magicke.'

'Right. The boots,' I say. 'Are they for real?'

'You know this deal? The life-saving snogs?' asks George. 'Can I have an advance payment?'

'I do believe you must be the giant, Idris Gawr?' says Davey very formally.

'Just a *quick* peck on the cheek?' George persists. 'Nothing major to begin with – just a little lip-lingering that might inspire confidence.'

'Yes, I am Idris the Stargazer.' Idris does a little bow to Davey.

'Something that might encourage you to cross the Channel?' George goes a bit dreamy-eyed.

'Whaaat?'

'I am … ' Davey frowns. 'Call me Davey.' He sticks out his hand at Idris, in that oddly formal way of his.

'I have heard much of you,' says Idris to Davey.

'To France,' continues George, blowing me a stream of air kisses.

'The boots?' I remind Idris. 'Are they for real?'

'Yes, I do have a pair of seven-league boots,' says Idris.

'France,' repeats George, pointedly.

'Huh?' What is George on about?

'You know, to sample the French kiss?'

'Oh stop it,' I say.

'Oh dear. OH DEAR!' George squeals, 'In that case, I think I'm dying.'

I lean over and kiss his forehead. 'That's to keep you going,' I say. 'Now we've got to go. Henry is free and the dawn is coming. We've only got the Cŵn Annwn to defeat, the White Dragon of Wessex to confront, various other mythical wotnot to subdue and a heart to purify in the first light of spring.'

George jumps up. 'Have axe. Have true love. Have promised snog. Cannot die!'

'We'll never make it,' says Davey entirely in character.

'I'll put my boots on then,' says Idris. 'Yes, I don't have much else, but these are mine.' From beneath a rock beside the bed Idris drags out a pair of mega-sized boots.

I really like the idea of seven-league boots.

'And they are giant boots too,' says the giant.

But even though I like the idea of the boots, and I can see it might only take a few strides to get us back to Snowdon, I can't see how that will help all of us.

Davey brushes one skinny forearm over his eyes. 'I had such a weird dream,' he murmurs.

Perhaps I could beg Idris to carry me and leave the others here?

Bad plan. You know, me alone against the entire Olde Deepe Magicke.

Luckily Idris has thought of this too. 'My plan,' says Idris, 'is to carry all of you.' He smiles down at me from his great height. 'I think I'm strong enough, don't you?'

And I see, despite the heartbreak behind his smile, Idris is actually quite excited about wearing his seven-league boots again.

'When was the last time you wore them?' I ask.

'It was quite a long time ago, says Idris. 'Probably over 50,000 years, when I took a trip up to Scotland with Finn MacCool to get involved in a little giants' business.'

I laugh. 'You look like you're pleased to see them again,' I say.

'Ah!' he says. 'With the wind in my beard and the stars rushing by – who wouldn't be?' Idris sighs and goes as dreamy-eyed as George. Then that old haunting shadow flicks down like a visor. 'But to get you to Snowdon will only be two steps. Actually not even two steps – one and a halfish. Each boot can cover twenty-one miles, you know.

But it's just as well; then I can get back quickly to my beloved, and spend what little time remains before dawn with her.'

He pulls on the boots. They are large and dark green with huge laces. Once he has them on, he shuffles a little. Sparks fly and mini-lightning bolts shoot out from the rocks under the soles of his boots. His feet seem to move at blinding speed and a great rush of warm air hits me.

'Now,' he says, 'this is going to be a bit tricky. I think you, young man,' he points at George, 'had better get on my back. You look like the heftiest of the three.'

George stands up and looks around, a bit confused: 'Where the heck are we?' he asks.

Idris casts an eye over Davey. 'You're pretty scrawny,' he says. 'I should be able to hook one arm around you and hoist you up on to my shoulders.' Sure enough, with one hand he picks Davey up. It's pretty funny actually. Davey dangles there while Idris weighs him up like a sack of potatoes.

Idris puts Davey back down again. 'As for you Ellie,' Idris says, 'you will have to be held in my arms.'

I try to imagine George on his back, Davey on his shoulders and me in his arms. Hmmm, interesting.

'Now,' Idris says, 'if I sit down on my bed, can you all please get into position.'

And with that he sits down.

George climbs on to his back and hangs there for all the world, like a backpack. Idris chuckles, puts one arm back around Davey and hoists him shoulder high. Davey clings on, already looking giddy.

Then with both arms free, like King Kong, Idris sweeps me up. He cradles me gently, as if I were as light as a cobweb and just as fragile. Then he stands up.

Immediately I get a head rush, an overpowering sense of vertigo. The air whizzes past with such speed I am dizzy and hot.

'Hey!' I yell, really scared.

'What?' says Idris. 'I haven't even moved yet.'

'Oh!' I say.

'If you're going to get dizzy when I just stand up, it will be quite disorientating when I move,' Idris warns. 'The seven-league strides, may upset you.'

'I'll be fine,' I say nervously. (Henry, the things I do for you!)

'Hang on then. Maybe shut your eyes.'

They're already shut.

'I want to see what it's like,' says George.

He would.

Getting back to his normal self, Davey says, 'I put my faith in God'.

And then, before we can say any more, there's a rushing that feels like a tearing, feels like a whirlwind, a hurricane. Blowing. Straight. In. My. Face.

But as quickly as it comes, it stops. Only now I feel like I'm in two places. My stomach is thirty-odd miles behind. My lungs are thirty-some miles ahead and my nostrils feel stretched between the two places. Which they probably are.

It's a bit like going up in a lift but A. Lot. Worse.

A huge hollow has opened up in my body and my innards, stomach and heart feel like they have dropped out the bottom. Then, with a woosh, everything seems to catch up and I feel totally sick.

And we are on the side of Snowdon, in the Pass of Arrows and Idris puts us all down with a rather unceremonious thump.

'Won't you stay?' I ask.

I know it's a big ask. And I know the answer it deserves. But we could do with a giant on our team. I don't know what forces will come to fight us.

Well, I know of course that Oswald is not going to be flapping about harmlessly like a kite while we purify Henry's heart. And what about the Coraniaid? Have they been listening to everything they can? Goodness knows what happened to the copper piping. I can't even remember the last time we used it. And if they have been listening, what are they going to do? Will they actually show their faces – or do they only eavesdrop and whisper secrets to one another? And if they do appear, will they attack us? Note to self: read the *Mabinogion*.

And what about the witches? Surely they will come waving their wands too, trying to stop us from breaking their spell.

And now I come to think of it, how do I actually break the spell?

Eek!

There must be some formula or a counter-curse or *something*.

Hold firm, I tell myself. Henry is released. He will come. He will save the day. All is not lost, even though you haven't got a clue how you are going to sort it.

Idris shakes his head. 'Do not ask me to stay,' he sighs. 'It is enough that I have spoken to Draco. It is enough that I have carried you here. It is enough that I have sacrificed my own happiness for the sake of Wales. I cannot do more. Let me return and spend some last few moments with my beloved, before I begin my eternity of loneliness. For my heart is there, not here on this ancient battlefield.

And in truth, this battle must be won by the pure in heart only. Those tainted by despair will not help you.'

He is right. I don't want to ask more of him. I throw out my arms and hug his leg. (It's a bit like hugging a tree trunk.) 'Thank you so much,' I say. 'Kiss Angharad from me.'

Idris runs a hand over the top of my head. 'It is nice to do selfless things,' he says, 'but sometimes, think of me alone at night, sitting on my bed on Cadair Idris's summit.

'I'll climb up there and sit with you,' says George. 'You can tell me about her. I know it's not the same, but it might be some comfort.'

'You'll find me there,' says Idris. 'But once the magic spell has been broken, you will not be able to see me.'

'Will you be able to see us though?' asks George.

'Yes, I will see you,' Idris replies.

'It's a deal then,' says George. 'I'll come. I'll talk to you. Will you be able to hear me?'

'Yes,' says Idris. 'I will hear you.'

'Cool,' says George. 'Then I will come and sit with you, and even though I can't hear you, you will hear me; it might ease your loneliness a little bit.'

'But you know the saying, don't you?' I say to George. 'If you sleep on the bed of Idris, you will either return a great poet or a total nutjob.'

'Yes,' says Idris with a twinkle in his eye, 'and I am the one who decides. So have a care if you say something stupid, I will not let you off lightly.'

'No worries,' says Geoge. 'I'm a bit mental anyway – so hopefully no one will notice.'

In the east, the sky is lighting up a little. Davey shivers. George draws near.

And the shadows shrink, and the light grows, and in the eastern sky a rosy dawn starts to blossom.

Idris tightens the laces on his boots and strokes their toecaps. 'Might pay old Finn MacCool a visit after all this,' he muses. 'Challenge him to a race on that old causeway of his. Stir up a bit of bother with those Scottish lads … be like old times … '

I smile up at him. I'd rather think of him doing that than sitting alone on his bed.

'Well, I'm away,' says Idris.

One whoosh, the swell of warm air and he's gone.

And in the red light that spills over the jagged silhouette of Yr Wyddfa, I see them.

Thousands of them.

Swarming towards us.

Forty-Three

There they come, flooding over the hill, down the mountainside, hordes of white wailing creatures. And above me I hear the ghastly flapping of skeletal wings.

I look into the dawn: rosy clouds above grey green light; a certain bilious shade of yellow, creeping like molten sulphur along the skyline, until the whole summit of Snowdon is silhouetted against the dawn. A light mist lies along the bed of the pass. Long shadows suddenly strike out from the mountain; fingers of darkness, reaching towards us.

Yep, this is it.

Dawn is breaking on the first day of spring.

My heart pounds. A cold sweat trickles down my back. *Henry, where are you?*

At our back towers the great standing stone: the Menhir

of Mawr, that some call the Oracle. Above it in the pass, hidden somewhere on its high slopes, lies the entrance to the Cave of the Sleeping Knights. If we fail them today, the dark forces will rout them. Their resting place will no longer stay hidden. Their watch will end. They cannot hold out against the forces of the Olde Deepe Magicke, Oswald will seize the Golden Throne. And after that?

Henry, we need you.

The air trembles with the howling of wolves. They've come in their numbers. *God, I feel sick.* The whole flank of the Pass of Arrows is filling up with their jostling, thin, wiry bodies. Snouts lift up to sniff the coming dawn … but the *wailing! My ears!* Wailing that could wake the dead.

I wish it could wake Widow-maker.

And at the front of the pack come the witches. I think I can make out twelve of them, hooded faces, black cloaks swirling in the mist. A dark energy hangs over them. They move all together flapping and shuffling like one loathsome creature. I shiver.

At their head, the thirteenth witch struts: she they call the Supreme One. I gulp: they've made up their number again then – a full coven is marching against us.

Closer they come and still closer.

Somebody must help us.

The being they call Na Gig, Goddess, the Supreme One raises her arm and throws off her hood …

WHAAAT??

She pulls her mask aside …

You've got to be joking!

I don't believe it …

She steps closer.

And I recognise her.

OMG.

I was not expecting this.

I ACTUALLY RECOGNISE HER.

I can't believe it.

I really can't.

My eyes!

MY EYES!

She's right in front of me and it's her!

SHEILA?

IT'S SHEILA!

I don't understand: *Sheila's my friend.*

How can she be the Supreme One?

Not. Even. Funny.

'Yes, I am Sheela Na Gig,' she says, right up close in my face.

I should have gone with my instinct right from the start.

Note to self: always go with your instinct.

This is so not funny.

'I AM SHEELA NA GIG, GODDESS AND DEMON, THE GIVER AND TAKER OF LIFE. **AND I CLAIM THE HEART OF HENRY PENDRAGON.** ALL HEARTS OF ALL MEN BELONG TO ME! I am the womb. I am the mouth that swallows. I am the tomb of all. None can stand against me!'

And I see.

At last, I understand.

When she challenged me over Henry, *she meant it*. She wanted him for herself. She used every means possible to get him. When all her natural charms failed, she turned to magic: the Olde Deepe Magicke of the mountains, because she knew that he too was a creature of magic. She was *totally prepared to have him or die trying* – and if she couldn't have him, nobody else was going to either.

I just can't believe it.

'Don't look at me like that, Ellie,' she says, her face horrible, yet beautiful somehow. 'It was your fault. You refused to hand him over. You drove me to seek a solution more powerful than you, more powerful than dragons, more powerful than love. It's all your fault.'

All *my* fault?

I'm so flabbergasted, I have to blink and gasp to take

it all in. But whether she's a goddess or not, she's wrong about one thing:

'Nothing is more powerful than love,' I say.

'You wish, you fool,' she says.

'But Sheila,' I say, 'there are so many boys. You could've had *any* of them. Henry is the only one for me.'

With one wave of her hand, she brushes my argument aside. 'Just hand over his heart,' she says, 'and we can save a lot of bother and bloodshed.'

I look at Davey's pale face (he's twiddling with his straggly beard). I look at George standing straight, narrow-eyed, axe in hand. There's no way the three of us can stand against the Hordes of Sheela Na Gig.

George looks at me, shakes his head. 'If you love him,' he says, 'don't give his heart to her. I'd never give yours away. I'd die defending it. I am ready to die here, for you, right now.'

Oh George.

I clutch the heart to me. 'No,' I say. 'Henry's heart is not to be given away. When the first ray of sunlight comes over the mountaintop and strikes it, his heart will be purified, and he will have it back. Then you'd better watch out.'

Sheila throws her head back and laughs. Something evil and creepy in her cackling makes my legs feel like they're dissolving. Really. A bit like overcooked instant noodles.

'If you do not give me the heart, I will call upon these wolves to rip you apart. I will open my book of spells and I will chant until the Coraniaid come out of the ground beneath you – and beware for they are hideous goblins who will come in their thousands. And they'll bang you up and mash you senseless – you and both your little girly-boys.' She waves a dismissive hand at George and Davey. 'I will destroy *everyone* you love. Yep, girlfriend, suck *that* up! You saw what I did to your lambs. Your home will be smashed to the ground, your mother torn limb from limb.' Sheila raises her head and screams at the dark sky: 'Everyone who has taken your part will be slaughtered like sheep!'

George steps forward, holds my arm. 'Stand firm,' he says. 'I'm here beside you.'

'Moron,' scoffs Sheila.

'Don't waver,' says George. 'Remember, the pure in heart can accomplish anything.'

'The Great White Dragon will strike from above,' shrieks Sheila. 'The Coraniaid will strike from below. My witches will strike you from in front, on either side you will be surrounded by the Cŵn Annwn, and Gwyn ap Nudd will strike you from behind. YOU CANNOT HOLD AGAINST

THE MIGHT OF SHEELA NA GIG. GET IT?'

Stones rattle. Her voice echoes off the mountain. I instinctively look up and there he is, Oswald, a great white sinister shape beating the air with bony wings. One of her companions steps forward. 'You can summon no help against us,' the witch hisses. 'For amongst our coven now are the two witches of Betws-y-Coed; shapeshifters, who have robbed unwary travellers – and, more powerful than they, are the Nine Witches of Gloucester who have slain the brave and murdered Angharad Golden-Hand.'

Dawn is breaking. The light over the horizon is creeping upwards. Soon the sun will reach over the top of the mountain.

'Ellie doesn't stand alone,' George says, axe in hand. 'When you unleash all your evil against us, you should know that there's one boy standing here whose heart you do not have. You Will. Never. Have.'

'Oh pul-eese. You're pathetic,' sneers Sheila. 'You're sooo nothing, you waster!'

'OK, Sheil,' says George, 'Maybe I am a waster, but can't you see what you've become? Just stop it. Look around you. You're no goddess. You can't borrow Na Gig's power here. Not on Snowdon. I'm George. I live on this mountain. This is Wales, remember? And I'm not afraid of you, let alone in love with you. Ellie is my best girl. I'll die with my axe in my hand, right here where my family have lived for generations, to defend her right to love who she likes. Get real, Sheil. Think about what you're doing. And go home.'

Oh George.

Sheila's face grows dark. She splutters, can't seem to form words.

Davey puts his hands together, appears to be praying. As if that will do any good.

'And Ellie is your *friend*,' continues George. 'Yet you set her up. That was mean and not worthy of you. I can't imagine you really want to be that kind of person? Horrible, like them?' George waves his arm at the witches, smiles his most winsome smile to date, speaks in his most rational tone.

Davey intones another low hymn, mumbles a bit of prayer.

My heart thumps. *I'm so scared. I'm so proud of George.* I realise I'm gripping my hands so tightly around the heart that my nails have gone right through the skin of my palms.

'It's simple – just stop it,' says George. 'And let's *all* go home. What do you say?'

I look out over the sea of wolves, at the tall, blackened figure among them. I look up. Even Oswald has paused. He's flapping his great grizzly wings, waiting for the outcome.

Everyone's waiting for Sheila to command. She must be getting such a total buzz off this. It's what she's always wanted: to be the centre of everything; to be in absolute control.

I glance nervously up at the horizon. What chance have we got if she attacks? Seriously? *If only Idris could have stayed, chucked a few rocks perhaps, then that might have helped. A little bit, anyway.*

Everything is poised, waiting.

Sheila sees me looking. 'Last chance,' she says, holding out her hand.

Oh Henry, Where Are You? You are supposed to be here by now!

The first tip of light reaches the crest of the hillside. Very soon, dawn will break. *Just try to survive until it breaks.* The standing stone at our back will be lit up by a beam of gold. *Just hang on. Get ready to catch that first ray.*

If only I knew exactly where the Cave of the Sleeping Knights was, maybe I could jump inside and ring the bell – wake them all up?

Surely this is why they sleep, isn't it? To be woken and to defend Wales in its darkest hour?

But I don't know where the entrance to the cave is. Stupid. No one knows where it is. That's the whole point.

Sheila is impatient. 'Time's up, you minger,' she says.

I freeze.

She turns.

She waves her hand: 'AS ABOVE, SO BELOW, SO MOTE IT BE!' she yells.

Out of the sky, the White Dragon swoops. In one ghastly breath, he sends a ton of ice racing towards us.

In one wave, the wolves bound forward. The witches start chanting.

'Fair is foul — foul is fair —
By water, fire, earth and air,
Fair is foul — foul is fair —
Let those who challenge us, beware —
Fair is foul — foul is fair —
Claws that bite, teeth that tear,
Wolves and goblins everywhere,
Destroy through earth and ice and air ... '

Brilliant tints of ice glint on the grass. We duck down behind the standing stone. I can see it'll be hard for Oswald to blast us properly while the wolves and Sheila block the way. The wave of ice crashes by. *So near. So near.* My chest's thudding. I hold on to Henry's heart. *Just wait for that first splinter of light, Ellie. Get ready to jump out – even under the club of Gwyn ap Nudd – hold it up.*

Oh please, let the first beam of light strike now.

In the distance, I hear a terrible knocking. *Oh my God.* It's bound to be the Coraniaid, the goblins digging under our feet. *The ground we stand on is going to collapse.*

Sheila laughs. The chanting continues.

'*Fair is foul – foul is fair –*

Let those who challenge us, beware – '

The knocking continues.

The wolves close in.

Davey drops to his knees.

'*In nomine Patris, et Filii, et Spiritus Sancti …* '

Suddenly the side of the hill quivers. A bit breaks off. A lump of turf falls away. Some pebbles slide. A chunk of rock falls out and a hole opens up. *The side of the mountain caves in.* Right beside us.

My heartbeat is so way above healthy, I'm probably dead already.

And out of a newly hewn cavern a shape appears.

Tall. Mighty.

Terrifying.

A HUGE female Knocker. Out she strides, her red hair braided down to her waist, her wide trousers tucked into thigh-high boots. In her hand she carries her MASSIVE pickaxe and one HUMONGOUS hammer. She steps in front of us, raises her pickaxe.

The wolves back away. Gwyn ap Nudd, his face darker than ever, steps forward. 'You are no match for me,' he booms.

'Well, if it ain't our old underworld enemy number one, ol' Gwynny Nudders!' Nan, the Knocker Queen shouts.

'Out of my way! I can crush you with one blow,' he hisses.

'If you wanna prove that true, me hearty,' yells Nan, 'come an' get it!'

Forty-Four

A wolf rushes at Nan, the Knocker Queen.

With one swing of the hammer, she smashes through its skull. Blood and bone spray over the icy ground. She strides forward, reaches Gwyn ap Nudd. She raises her pick. 'Taste iron, creature of the dark!' she yells.

Gwyn ap Nudd jumps sideways. The pick thunders down. It penetrates deep into the stone he was standing on, splinters fly, rocks quiver.

George cheers.

I watch from behind the standing stone. I dodge and circle round it, always keeping its majestic height between Sheila and Henry's heart.

Please let the first beam of light come soon.

Gwyn and the Cŵn Annwn regroup.

The wolves split off to one side. I see their plan: cut the

Knocker Queen off – isolate us. Then close in for the kill.

But then a battalion of Knockers comes marching out of the mountainside. They surround us, surround the stone.

And at their back, comes a stumbling figure.

A very pale-looking Rhiannon.

'*ELLL-IEEEEE!*' she wails.

Out of the mountain pour more and more Knockers. They form a moat of little men, ten metres wide around us.

Rhiannon rushes at me sobbing, '*ELL-IEEEE!!!*'

But as she catches sight of Sheila in full witch's garb, she hesitates, grows even paler. 'SHEIL?' she gasps,

'Well, well, what do we have here my smashers?' says the Knocker boss, who heads up the tiny army. He shoots a worried look at Rhiannon and shouts across at Sheila. 'Sheela Na Giggers, try picking on our princess,' he says, jerking his head at Rhi, 'and we'll have to get very personal.'

'Sheila Na Giggers?' repeats Rhi.

But at that moment, Oswald swoops. He sends an ice blast at the newly opened cavern. Four of the last Knockers to come marching out are frozen solid. *Oh God, those poor Knocker-men. Little white statues. The wolves creep forward.* Gwyn ap Nudd moves into position.

'Get back!' Sheila screams. 'Get back to where you belong, under the hills, inside the mines. You are not wanted here

– this is *our* hillside. None can stand against me! For I am the most desirable of them all. It is I who will hold the hearts of all men!'

'Well, I'll tell you one thing,' says the boss, 'and I won't mincer up my words with it neither. You do not have *our* hearts, young lady. There's only one gal for us and she's our princess and if she's crying, we'll knocker you flat.'

And all of them, in unison, pull their mining picks and their hammers free, and they line up around Rhiannon, hammering on the frozen rocks at our feet.

I watch the skyline. *Please. Please.* The clouds swirl close around the summit. The hump of Snowdon grows dark against the coming dawn. *This is it.* The sun *must* soon come. I'm ready. I'm standing at the Menhir of Mawr, the standing stone, the Oracle, in the Pass of Arrows, guarding the heart. *Let it break sooooon. We can't hold out much longer.* I look at the Hordes of Sheela gathering again for another assault. I stand with my back against the stone. The clouds break.

The witches start a fresh chant.

'*Fair is foul – foul is fair –*

Let those who challenge us, beware – '

And there is the dazzling face of the sun! Just rising over the edge of the mountain. One ray of sunshine breaks free. One long shaft of light shoots out from the clouds, shoots straight from the crest of Snowdon.

It glances down the mountainside, over the scree, past the front of the lake, and hits the standing stone with incredible brilliance.

The Hordes of Sheela draw back. It's as if the light burns them. Just for a second, there is a quivering in the air. The blade of sunlight is too intense.

This is it.

ACT.

I jump into the beam of sunlight. I hold Henry's heart tight. Right by the standing stone I raise my arm. *This must be the right place. Has to be.* I open my fist, hold the heart on high. The full light of the first ray of the vernal equinox hits home.

I feel the heat on my hand.

Work. Please work.

It must work …

The sunbeam lights up the heart. It starts to pulse. There's a roaring heat. So hot. I can't hold it any longer. *Don't let go.* It's blisteringly hot. *Hold on.* For a moment it seems it hovers there, all by itself. No longer the hard black object it was. *Beating. Growing. Shining.* As if a star has broken from the heavens and entered it, filling the entire world with its radiance. Light swirls and …

Henry, where are you?

Sheila leaps forward. She twists my wrist forwards. She yanks my fingers backwards. She wrestles the heart from me. *Hold on. Hold on.* My fingers loosen their grip.

'MINE AT LAST, YOU DUMBO!' she shouts. 'SO MOTE IT BE!' She capers in a wild dance in front of the stone.

I've been tricked! She let me re-animate the heart – use my love – in the pure light of the vernal equinox – *so that she could possess it.*

'NOOOOO!'

George wheels his head around. He leaves himself undefended. Oswald sees his chance. Zooms in. *George!* A dreadful swipe from the White Dragon catches George side-on. The power of the blow lifts him off his feet, flings him back several metres. George crashes against the face of the mountain. He crumples, lies there. Red blood seeps into the snow under him. The White Dragon circles on high, waits for Sheila's sign.

GEORGE!

And then the wolves burst forward. Snarling and snapping, they rush toward the limp form of George.

And still no Henry.

But no sooner have the wolves covered the flank of the slope, than there is the hammering of hooves. And –

incredibly – *amazingly* – a stampede of fleet-footed Welsh ponies charges over the edge of the hillside and stands guard around George's fallen body.

Thank God. Thank God.

The wolves, powerless to stop their attack, crash head-long into the army of ponies.

And still no Henry.

I see Graine rear up, toss his mane, snort and stamp down on the lead wolf.

How did the ponies get here so quickly? They must have galloped all night …

Oh my God!

And there at their rear, ears laid flat back, rearing and snorting, teeth bared, slashing wild razor hooves … the ghost of a black pony …

Widow-maker.

Davey leaps up from his knees. 'Now is my hour,' he declares. 'God has shown me what I must do. *I have remembered my mission!*'

The wolves close ranks, go for the smallest of the ponies, a tiny piebald mare. George dizzily sits up.

He's alive! George is alive!

Davey jumps at Sheila, as if his body weight alone will crush her. He catches hold of her hand, catches hold of the heart, as she dances in triumph.

She halts. She snarls. She spits in his face. 'Nobody can stop me now,' she says. '*Henry is mine.* Oswald will claim Wales. His winter will destroy any that oppose him. He will destroy the sleepers in their cave. He will take the Golden Throne of Arthur. And all the wild Olde Deepe Magicke will be free!'

She cackles and capers and looks truly mental.

'Not if I can help it,' says Davey. 'For in the name of the Father and the Son and our Lord the Holy Ghost, I defy all evil.'

But before he can take back the heart, Sheila and the other witches surround him and strike him down.

Down with their daggers.

'*DAVEY!*' I cry out in horror.

His blood flows over Sheila's arm, over Henry's heart. Then he staggers, falls and is trodden into the packed snow around the standing stone.

I scream. My screaming dies on the air.

As he falls, he calls out: '*I put my faith in the Lord ... I have completed my mission ... my sacrifice will purify the heart ...* '

The Olde Deepe Magicke? What had Idris said? An eye for an eye. A sacrifice for a sacrifice. Fight fire with fire.

'*Dominus noster Jesus Christus te absolvat; et ego auctoritate*

437

ipsius te absolvo ab omni vinculo excommunicationis (sus-pensionis) et interdicti in quantum possum et tu indiges. Deinde, ego te absolvo a peccatis tuis in nomine Patris, et Filii, et Spiritus Sancti. Amen.'

Sheila cackles on: 'Die foolish saint. Is this all the Olde Magicke can conjure from its favourites? The pathetic Patron Saint of Wales! Sent to save the world. What a joke. Die, and as your lifeblood ebbs away, know that Sheela Na Gig IS the Olde Deepe Magicke – it is from *her* power it flows and to her it will return.'

Saint? My mind turns cartwheels.

Davey – a saint?

From the Olde Deepe Magicke?

I've been travelling around with Saint David – the Patron Saint of Wales?

Breathe.

He can't die.

I shake my head. I knew there was something strange about Davey. *But a saint? Surely not?*

He can't die. Can he? Isn't he already dead?

But Gran knew. She knelt before him …

Can you die twice?

Don't let Davey die.

But he *is* dying.

As if he hears my thoughts, Davey feebly lifts his head and smiles. '*Arglwydi, vrodyr, a chwioryd, Bydwch lawen a chedwch ych ffyd a'ch cret, a gwnewch y petheu bychein a gly-wyssawch ac a welsawch gennyf i. A mynheu a gerdaf y fford yd aeth an tadeu idi*,' he whispers.

Oh my God.

Those were his last words to his followers.

We learnt them in school.

We said them in chapel …

'*Lords, brothers and sisters, be joyful, and keep your faith and your creed, and do the little things that you have seen me do and heard about. And as for me, I will walk the path that our fathers have trod before us …*'

Walk the path …

The little things he used to go on about

His mission. Does he know he's fulfilled it?

Has he realised who he is?

He smiles at me again.

He seems to know.

'*May the Lord bless you, St David!*' I cry.

Forty-Five

The sky brightens. Davey smiles one last time. I can almost hear Idris's Harmony of the Spheres; almost hear angels. A small white bird flutters from the sky. It falls beside Davey.

My heart beats wildly. I want to run to George. But all I can see is a mass of flailing hooves and bloodstained fur.

I don't understand why Henry hasn't come. A hollow carves itself out under my rib cage. My legs go all weak. The Knockers back away, shielding Rhiannon, trying to get her back under the mountain. But even as they try to retreat, the ground around them seems to give way.

Out of cracks and pits and holes and ditches come streaming the Coraniaid.

Goblin creatures.

Misshapen and dwarfish.

Orc-like.

Not much bigger than the Knockers. But not at all like them. Large-limbed and distorted. There's an evil impish look about them. Out they swarm like insects.

Like insects …

In biting, slicing movements they hack at the Knockers. It might have been a fair fight if the Knockers hadn't been trying to defend Rhiannon. But she makes them vulnerable. The Coraniaid cut off their retreat; force them back towards the standing stone, until once again we are all huddled around it.

And still no Henry.

My mind is blank. I can't think what to do. I don't know why Henry hasn't come. *Idris had been so sure that he was released.* The Coraniaid drive forward, the ponies neigh wildly. There's something in their whinnying; so desperate, so pitiful. It rings in my ears. It bruises the air.

Oh no. Please no. Graine is down …

I try to remember anything that can help.

I hear George calling from the side of the pass. For a minute I think he's calling to his pony, his trusty Graine, the cob that carried him so faithfully to Cadair. But then I hear him more clearly: '*Gran!*' he calls. And my heart breaks. *He's calling for Gran.* He's in pain. Maybe dying.

Rhiannon turns to me, her face pale, terrified. 'George

is going to be OK, isn't he?' she says.

I catch sight of the adder stone swinging around her neck.

Gran?

Of course!

George isn't calling for Gran because he's scared and wounded – though he probably is. He's trying to tell me that Gran gave me something for my 'darkest hour'.

The insect powder.

The flipping insect powder!

I dive deep into my jacket pocket. I find the small sealed yogurt pot. As the Knockers fall under the blows of the Coraniaid, I pour the contents of the plastic carton in to the palm of one hand. Instantly my skin starts to itch. I'm glad to take a deep breath and blow hard, as I throw it at them.

The dust flies up into the air, swirls and is carried on the wind. The tiny particles spread and scatter and rush straight into the faces of the Coraniaid and Knockers alike.

The Knockers shake and sneeze a bit, but among the ranks of the Coraniaid a terrible screaming breaks out. Quickly it escalates into murderous shrieking, as if hot coals have rained down upon them. Their goblin features twist in pain. There is a chorus of unholy screeching, and before my eyes, flesh seems to dissolve, disappear, like candlewax melting. What is left of them slips and slithers away into the cracks

442

and pits and ditches that they came from.

And suddenly I realise how stupid I've been. I haven't listened to any of the advice I've been offered – I mean *really* listened: it wasn't only Gran who told me things. The Lady of the Lake told me everything – that song, that riddle. I remember the words:

'*On the feast day of St Cuthbert,*
When saints can play their part,
Where sleepers sleep, and mirrors crack,
By traitor's blood and hero's art,
It will take a sacrifice, to purify the heart.'

I run the words on a loop through my head. *Think, Ellie. Think.* What does it mean? Today must surely be the feast day of St Cuthbert. And sure, one saint at least has 'played their part'.

'Where sleepers sleep' seems obvious. I guess that must refer to the sleeping knights, those knights of the pure in heart asleep in the cave of King Arthur somewhere close by. But where 'mirrors crack'? I touch the mirror still inside my pocket. I don't want my mirror to crack. It's the only way that I can speak to Henry and speaking to him is the one thing I want to do more than anything now. I pull the mirror out. I look into it. 'Henry?' I call, 'Henry, where are you?'

I am so busy looking into the mirror trying to summon

Henry, for a moment I forget the battle. Rhiannon starts shrieking. She's pointing and screaming. I look up to see that Gwyn ap Nudd is raising his arm up; Nan, the Knocker Queen, has fallen, her last defenders dead around her. In Gwyn ap Nudd's hand is a great black club.

I watch, horrified, as he brings it down. Her skull splits open. Blood and bone spray over the mountainside.

My scream hangs on the air, is drowned under other screams. Screams that have filled this mountain pass before. Blood that has stained this landscape red, when Arthur was defeated here.

Oh my God!

Then I breathe. My chest expands. The Knocker Queen lies where she has fallen, somehow smaller. Limp.

Oh my God!

Poor Nan.

I look away. *Breathe. Think.*

I force myself. Think of the Lady of the Lake. *Is there anything that can help us?*

Traitor's blood?

There is only one traitor among us. She is right beside me, screaming her head off.

Hero's art?

I'm surrounded by bravery but there's only ever been one

truly selfless hero in my life. He has his back pinned against a rock face and is defending himself against a pack of wolves with a few wild ponies. While above waits the mighty White Dragon. Looking down, biding his time, saving his energy. God, how he must be enjoying this little scene.

Oswald swoops nearer, draws back his monstrous head, set to freeze George to the rock face.

Henry, where are you? We need you now!

The sacrifice?

I look at the fallen body of Davey. *There have been too many sacrifices already.*

Not George too.

Perhaps this pass is cursed.

I step forward. Raise my hands. Scream. And even as I am rushing towards Oswald, hoping, praying that I can distract him, the penny drops.

There has been a sacrifice …

The hero is playing his part …

This is St Cuthbert's Day …

What we we need is the blood of a traitor.

Rhiannon hasn't got one tiny cut on her …

And even as I realise this, the hammering of the Knockers on every stone of the mountain resounds in my ears, fills the air. The air quivers. A reverberation starts. The mountain seems to shake. The hammering grows louder. *They are hammering up an avalanche!* I look up.

'GEORGE!' I scream.

George looks up. Just as Oswald swoops in.

Tonnes of ice. A white fearful mass. A cracking and tearing. The sky darkens. Snow swirls.

Over and over.

Thick and fast.

The avalanche speeds towards him.

'NO! NO! NO!'

Forty-Six

I watch.

The avalanche hits.

Covers George.

Bowls the ponies over.

Even knocks Oswald flying.

Buries one flank of the wolves.

The mass of snow heaves to the left, misses us and rumbles away past the fallen body of the Knocker Queen. Past Davey, lying stretched out on the ground, past the stone I'm pressed against. Rumbles on and away. The hammering stops.

'Rhiannon!' shout the Knockers.

'RHIANNON! RHIANNON! RHIANNON!'

They pound the ground. I'm terrified they'll start hammering again. Start another avalanche.

Sheila turns towards the Knockers.

'Fair is foul – foul is fair –

Let those who challenge us, beware –'

Rhiannon shouts, 'No!' She steps forward, confronts Sheila.

George. He may still be alive. Must get to him.

'Leave them alone!' Rhi yells. 'They're only little. It's mean to keep hurting them. They've lost their queen. I won't let you hurt the Knockers.'

Sheila laughs. 'You stupid, spoiled little rich twit. What makes you think I'd take any notice of you? The only reason I let you join my witches' coven was so that you could lure Ellie out. Ha! You wanted to make George fall in love with you!' Sheila scoffs. 'You're pathetic! What a joke.'

'I HATE YOU!' cries Rhiannon.

'And you fell for it! I think I would have enjoyed it more, if *you'd* been the sacrifice.'

'You're horrible,' weeps Rhiannon.

For answer, Sheila laughs louder, a maniacal look in her eye, unlike anything I've ever seen before.

Something snaps.

Rhiannon's face goes beetroot red. Her eyes light up. She seems to be almost growling. For your information, Rhiannon does not get furious. She is much more of a moaner, much more of a wanting-other-people-to-do-it, rather than a getting-up-and-doing-it-yourself person.

448

But right in front of my nose, she leaps forward, snatches a dagger off one of the witches and jumps towards Sheila.

'*You ... you ... you!*' yells Rhiannon.

With one easy motion, Sheila twists the knife, rips it from Rhiannon's grasp, slashing it across Rhiannon's hand as she drags it free.

For a moment I'm unsure whether to rush and try to help Rhi, or throw myself into the snow and dig and dig and dig for George.

Rhiannon goes to grab the heart. The blood from Rhi's hand drips down.

Her blood baptises the heart.

I leap to help George.

The heart grows huge. It pulses with a sudden energy. Sheila screams, can't hold it any more.

She lets go.

Then suddenly it happens. The heart seems to shoot straight up, like a comet, leaving a trail of silver behind. The sun rises above the horizon. DAZZLING. But it's not the sun. It's so bright, I can't look. VIBRANT. I close my eyes. BRILLIANT. The image on my closed eyelids burns, incandescent.

Dragon shaped.

Fiery.

Resplendent.

A wave of heat. And such radiance.

The heart and the sun meet in an explosion – so intense the whole mountain seems to be on fire.

And there, refulgent in the air, is the dragon: the Red Dragon of Wales.

Like a new star.

So bright.

I cover my eyes. My heart explodes.

Henry is back.

It's done.

The mission is complete! If anything else happens, here on this mountainside, I know that *Henry is back.*

'Yes!' Henry roars. '*I'm back!*' And as he roars, he sends a tunnel of flame out across the mountainside. The snow sizzles, steams, melts.

And there is George, gasping and flailing. The snowmelt drips off him.

George! I breathe.

Tears well up in my eyes.

For one glorious second Henry hovers, immense, an inferno in the sky. For one instant there is a sunrise across the valley, more glorious than a midsummer afternoon. And then Oswald strikes.

The mountain falls into shadow. Beams of light suddenly

snap out, a dark icy cloud shoots across the pass.

The side of Snowdon glitters in ice crystals. But at the same instant Henry roars again. Flames singe turf and grass. Solid rocks literally crumble into embers.

Henry seizes the advantage. He strikes. His blow would have killed a thousand men. The mountain shakes, the earth actually buckles under my feet. If I hadn't been within arm's reach of the Menhir of Mawr, I'd have fallen over.

'*Oh no!*' screams George. 'The hillside's gonna split open!'

And he's right. Huge chunks of rock crack loose and crash down with a screeching that deafens. My heart races. I watch spellbound, horrified …

George is on his feet. Unsteady but strong. He ducks and races, steps over fallen bodies of fur and tail, bounds over tumbling rocks. He shoves Sheila, grabs Rhiannon, drags her from under Sheila's wielded knife and throws her to the ground, shielding her with his body.

Oh my God.

The full blast of the Red Dragon hits Oswald in the face and chest. But the White Dragon doesn't fall. His skin doesn't even smoulder or tear. It wrinkles and clinks like chain mail, but it does not give. He twists in the air. His bony carcass ripples beneath him, and his huge wingspan shudders. He sways, rights himself, realigns his whole body, and draws his head up ready to strike back.

And this time Henry receives the blow head on.

George stays low, hauling Rhi with him, makes it back to the stone beside me.

Henry doesn't speak, and yet I hear him in the depths of me, crying: '*NO! You will not have her, nor George, nor will you have the better of me!*'

But I can see he is dazed. And though he shakes his spiny head and sends back a blow in retaliation, The White Dragon of Wessex shakes it off, like a dog shaking off raindrops.

'*No,*' sounds out Henry, '*you will not defeat me.*'

But the White Dragon is unstoppable, even the blows Henry delivers – across face, shoulders, flank and back – make little impact. Oswald dips one wing, wheels, dodges in the air and shakes Henry off.

Ice particles blast everywhere. Moss and lichen, turf and grass freeze, the whole place glitters and crackles.

The wolves and Gwyn gather closer to the stone.

And the witches set up their wailing chant again.

'*Fair is foul – foul is fair –*

Let those who challenge us, beware – '

Rhi and I huddle against the stone unable to defend ourselves.

George lifts his axe.

Forty-Seven

'Isn't there anything we can do?' yells Rhiannon. She clutches George. She does not want to let him go, although her grip is hampering his axe hand.

'Prepare yourselves,' says George.

Desperately I search my mind for help. *What about the mirror? Can't we use it?*

Davey said the mirror was powerful. Once again I hear his voice: *you must get to know its powers. Work out how to use it.*

But I didn't.

And now there's no time.

The witches chant. The wolves howl and circle around the stone. I can see they are only waiting for Gwyn to step through their ranks and smash our brains out with his club.

Something is still nagging in my mind: the Lady of the Lake. What was it she said?

'*Where sleepers sleep, and mirrors crack.*'

The mirror is holding the magic in place.

That's it.

I know what to do.

'*George!*' I yell. '*Help me!*'

George peels Rhiannon's arms off him. I turn to face him. 'When I say so, use your axe to strike the mirror,' I holler at George.

'OK,' he says.

It's the only thing I can think of.

Oh Henry. There will be no more glorious afternoons lying on the springy turf of the mountainside, with the warm sun on our faces. No more holding hands on summits, no more gentle kisses, no more summer breezes stirring the heather around us …

I raise the mirror way above my head. *No more magical moments in that in-between place …* And as if I'm taking a gigantic selfie, I turn my back on Gwyn and the wolves, turn my back on the witches. I catch them all in the reflection of the mirror. Sheila with her evil chanting, the Nine Witches of Gloucester, the two of Betws-y-Coed, Gwyn ap Nudd. They're so near, all of them.

I wait until they are framed perfectly in the mirror's glass. I wait until Gwyn is one step away, his club raised.

'NOW!' I shout.

George swings his axe across.

Shards of glass fly wild.

The mirror smashes.

This is for you Angharad, as I watch the witches splinter.

This is for you Widow-maker, as I watch the wolves scatter.

This is for you, Nan, Knocker Queen, as Gwyn ap Nudd shatters into tiny pieces.

I bite my lip. *This is for you Davey. I see Sheela Na Gig shrink and twist in a distorted image, become a sudden rush of something leaving the body of Sheila.*

The magic is undone.

Like smoke, the energy of Sheela Na Gig vanishes into the morning.

All gone.

The Hordes of Sheela diminish, shadows fly across the heath, back through the Pass of Arrows, over the slopes of Snowdon, shadows that thin and fade.

Sheila, now just plain old Sheila Griffiths, seems to shake herself, as if she has come out of a trance. She looks wildly about her. Her fellow witches – those ghostly apparitions – shiver and blink into oblivion. Only one witch from her coven remains. Sheila grabs the other girl's arm. The two turn and take to their heels like the Devil himself is after them.

A wave of clean air seems to sweep through the pass and the bloody body of Davey, the broken form of the Knocker Queen, the dead and the fallen, all are swept away.

The magic is undone.

Only the limp bodies of Graine and Keincaled remain.

Oswald howls a terrible, gristly sound. He twists in the sky.

The magic is undone.

The Olde Deepe Magicke that he was sucking his power from is smashed, broken, gone.

With one baleful look, Oswald hisses. '**BEWARE THE WRATH OF DRAGONS**.' He beats his pale wings, roars out the timeless words of the dragon's curse:

> *'If ye treat a dragon,*
> *By foul means or force,*
> *On thy own head will fall,*
> *The full dragon's curse.'*

And he too disappears over the horizon.

Henry sweeps down.

The liquid glow of the sunrise pools around him.

'**Well met my faithful friends**,' he booms. '**Well met my one true love**.'

He's so bright, I cover my eyes.

My heart soars.

Henry is back.

'Today we have rid Wales of a terrible threat, AND DRAGONS NEVER FORGET.'

'OMG!' squeals Rhiannon.

'Take courage and do not be afraid,' he thunders.

'I'm BACK!'

Forty-Eight

ELLIE'S PHONE 20 March 08.30

Status: IN LOVE Unavailable Foreva

Recent updates:

Rhiannon

Guess you guys need some space. LOL (dragons are like SOOOO BIG). G an me gonna stroll.

George

Elles, don't forget I love you.

Rhiannon

We'll just hang out in a nice little cave ☺ until you've caught up with H.

George

And you promised to snog me, if I was dying.

Rhiannon

George is going to have a look at my poorly hand, and take care of me because I. Am. In. Shock. Obvs.

George

I WAS dying.

Rhiannon

Take as long as you like. I think G needs some healing-the-shock therapy toooooo (u get me!!!!!!!!!!!).

George

I AM dying.

Rhiannon

George is soooooo lush.

George

So you owe me a snog.

I mean a KISS.

A BIG one.

Rhiannon

Take as long as you like.

George

And you've got a court hearing this afternoon.

Rhiannon

I'm gonna get G to help me plan that Easter party – more chance for games of FIND and EEK. !!!!!!!!! (U know what I'm thinking!)

I turn my phone off.

'So what happens now?' I say, as I look into Henry's eyes.

'Let us only glory in today,' he says, 'because today you have saved my heart; you have stopped my journey towards the constellation of Draco, you have vanquished the Hordes of Sheela and put a stop to the Olde Deepe Magicke. And I am, once again, home in my beautiful Snowdonia.'

'Yes,' I say. I stop myself from thinking of all the tomorrows that might be filled with emptiness – of all the yesterdays, when I was lonely. I am here now with Henry.

I am here now with Henry!

'But you must know one thing,' he says, his voice breaking. He pauses, draws in a great breath. 'I can never become human again.'

A freezing wind blows off the mountain. I shiver. Suddenly I can't control it. I'm so cold.

I can't stop shivering.

Henry lifts up his head, seems to focus on the horizon far, far away.

I want to say something. To shout. To raise up my fists and smash them down. To break the rocks of the mountain.

To scream. *NOOOOO!*

'I tried to tell you, when we were in the in-between place ... ' His voice trails off.

He's right. He did. I remember his words: 'We also need to talk about us ... sooner rather than later ... ' I didn't want to listen. This is what he meant.

Henry sighs. Little sparks of fire surround us. His voice is strained. He makes the point very clearly. 'The enchantment of Merlin has been broken, my crystal has been shattered, there is no magick, high or old, that can transform me into a human again. The days of magicians like Merlin have passed. My heart is restored to me as a dragon. I am now the Red Dragon of Wales, forever and forever.'

'*Forever?*' I repeat

He laughs sadly. 'Maybe, forever is too long a time – perhaps someone will work a different spell.'

Never become my Henry again?

I just sit there.

I can't take it in.

'But for now, with the Olde Deepe Magicke banished and Merlin's stronghold over Snowdonia damaged, I will remain a dragon. But thanks to you and all your courage and bravery and the loyalty of your friends, I have my heart back.'

He is making the point extremely apparent.

He is determined that I must understand.

I must understand.

Must!

'But,' I say.

'I know.' he says. 'I release you, Ellie. I release you from any promise that you made to me. I can never be yours. For as a dragon, we cannot meet as equals, and neither can I give you what it is that you need in your life. You already have the love of the most loyal and trustworthy person I have ever met, and for his sake too, I release you.'

I think of George and his steadfast love, and how he's always been there. How I felt when I thought he was dying …

'No,' I say, 'I won't accept that. I'll find a way.'

'Here,' he says, 'we should treasure this meeting. Climb on my back, and let us sit and watch the first morning of spring together from the summit of the mountain.'

I look at his flank and spiny back, how the heck am I going to climb up there?

'Step on my foot,' he says.

Heart pounding, I step up on to his outstretched leg. I balance there, he curls a huge wing down towards me and I am scooped up, rushed through the air and set down in the hollow of his back.

'Hold on,' he says.

'To what?'

He laughs, a deep roaring laugh.

I clutch at the spiny horns that stick out of his neck.

He beats the air with his huge wings and there's a rushing. I hang on for dear life. Heart pounding, I grip his back with my knees. I squeal. Icy air rips my voice from me. I'm hurtling upwards.

Up and up. I feel the dizzying rush of blood. My knees tremble with the effort of hanging on, my stomach feels weak; my arms ache with holding him so tight.

And there we are, chasing our own shadows on the mountain below, and diving amongst the clouds.

Heat rushes up from Henry's body, warms me. I cling to him as he glides and swoops, the land below a blur; the skies above pale swift shadows.

Way down below is the Pass of Arrows. We circle over Snowdonia. Far away to the south, I think I see the shadow of a tall man, his head buried in his hands, looking out across a wide saddleback ridge towards a barrow and a stone and a pool of golden sun …

I think of him, of Idris, and how he will sit on his mountain and how his love is buried in her cold tomb.

I think of Angharad and how she was so cursed and so beloved, and died because of it. And I think: *if Angharad can bear it, so can I.*

We alight on the summit of Snowdon. I climb down from Henry's back and we sit there, as the morning seems to go on forever and ever.

Together we look out across the range. Henry puts one wing around me. I lean my head on the scales of his crimson shoulder. There are clouds: pink and green and blue slowly turning in bright air.

There, below us, is the cafe. Beside us the circular stone pinnacle at Snowdon's very peak. I settle against him. The wind is blowing up at me, driving sunlight into my eyes. I squint through the pure light; below us, the valleys tumble away.

Hearts beating, we cling together, the clouds at our feet, the mist swirling up, until I can hardly even see the cafe.

With one taloned limb, he pulls me even closer against him. He holds me. He presses himself to me. Gently. Kindly.

He says, his voice tight and hard, 'Be brave, beautiful Ellie. I should never have involved you in the way of dragons … may the stars forgive me.'

I won't think about tomorrow.

A part of me will always be here.

Always.

'Be brave, my love,' he repeats. 'When nightfall comes, Oswald will seek me out; for as you know, it is our destiny always to do battle. By then he will be stronger, for he draws strength from the darkness. I will wait over by Dinas Emrys. I will go there very soon to prepare everything: the pit, the stones, the landslide, the burial.'

'*No!*' I say. '*Please not that.*'

'It must be so,' says Henry, 'and so I choose it. But I will not be buried there under any spell again, but by my own choice – for Merlin was right to constrict us – it is only like this that I can protect you and mankind from Oswald, for I will drag him down and bury him with me forever.'

'There must be some other way,' I say, jerking to my feet.

'None that I know of, or can bring about so quickly. For every day he is free, you are in mortal danger. You heard him curse you. You know how devious he is. You know how his ambition drives him. Granny Jones can weave strong charms, but the hour will come when he will break through all protective enchantments and strike you down, and … ' Henry's deep dragon voice breaks.

A cloud sails across the face of the risen sun.

Henry inhales. Small eddies of mist spiral around us.

'I can't bear that to happen,' he says quietly.

I sit back down again; wearily I lay my head against his.

'But in your hour of great pain,' he says, 'I have brought you this.'

Henry pulls out a small phial, tucked behind a flashing crimson scale. Inside it, something swirls and glitters.

'What is it?' I ask, as I take it.

'Stardust,' says Henry. 'I collected it as I winged my way through the cosmos. All you need to do is dust it over your eyes – it will bring the gift of forgetfulness.'

'*I don't want to forget*,' I say breaking into tears.

'One day,' he says, 'one day you might.'

Forty-Nine

ELLIE'S PHONE 20 March 11.50

Status: So SAD.

On the slopes of Yr Wyddfa the sun is risen, George waits for me just above the upper pasture on our side of the mountain. He gives me his coat, wraps his arm around me. Far away, hidden by the turn of a mountain spur, is the ancient fort of Dinas Emrys. I know by now Henry is there, digging out the pit, preparing the trap – the burial chamber for himself and Oswald.

'Don't take it too hard,' says George. 'We did our best. Nobody can change the way it has to be.'

I say nothing.

'Elles?' says George.

I put my head on his shoulder.

'You owe me a snog, you know.'

I sigh.

'Two actually. And if it's not pushing my luck, another new axe would be handy – the Husqvarna's a bit blunted.'

I barely hear him.

'I'll come with you to Caernarfon.'

My mind is far away, on the other side of the mountain.

'Elles?'

I will see you again Henry. I won't rest until I do.

'I called your mum. She says they've dropped the case, but you still have to show up – something about procedure. Your statement about calling the police from Pen-y-Pass about the landslide checked out. Watertight alibi apparently. Plus all the witnesseses seem to have disappeared – or given false addresses – or weren't contactable – or something. Anyway, she's going to pick us up at my place.'

I bring up my chin and straighten up my shoulders, though my mind is far away …

'Elles?'

In my imagination, I see what will happen. Dusk will fall on the first day of spring. Henry will wait in the deep cavern under Dinas Emrys; the White Dragon of Wessex will find him, furious, filled with venom.

Icy sheets of white will bloom on the rocks. The Red Dragon of Wales will roar, instantly the ice will melt. The rocks will glow red.

'I wish you'd say something,' says George.

And eventually Oswald will pounce on Henry, blasting his polar breath straight into Henry's face. There, trapped in the confines of the pit, the clash of their two huge wills will shake the mountain as they dodge and weave and strike and dive.

'Rhi's OK to come to court too. She's down at mine, waiting for us. She says she'll speak up in person and admit she made a false statement. She is trying hard to put things right, you know.'

Henry will take Oswald's blows, wearing himself out, trying to lure Oswald in deeper. Huge exhalations of flame. Stalactites blossoming in white-hot silhouette. Oswald's breath of death, freezing rock and lichen, crystal and crevasse.

Until …

'Oh and I sent Sheila a text earlier. You're gonna love this!' George holds up his phone and shows me.

GEORGE'S PHONE 20 March 09.03

Updates beween George and Sheila

Get back OK? Did you have to walk? Or did you use your broomstick?

'Not funny? I was just trying to make you smile.'

The whole side of the mountain will give way.

It will all be over.

And it will be too late.

Down will topple the hillside, down over the Worms of Dinas Emrys.

Fin

So Mote It Be

Later that spring – 30 April
The Eve of Calan Mai[1]

> **ELLIE'S PHONE 30 April 11.30**
>
> **Status:** In a committed relationship

This morning the sun is shining. I've biked all the way up to the top of Pen-y-Pass.

I rest briefly. I check the straw man I've made is safe inside my pocket.

Then carry on with my plan.

I'm going to Dinas Emrys for the first time since March.

My heart pounds. I bite my lip. But I'm ready.

---

1. *Calan Mai* (or *Calan Haf*), the first day of May, is a holy day in Wales. Celebration bonfires start on the evening before, known as May Eve. This night is considered an *Ysbrydnos* or 'spirit night' when spirits are out and about, and divination is possible.

'I'm coming Henry,' I whisper.

Going downhill from Pen-y-Pass is scary. The road falls away in front of me, there's a hairpin bend just ahead, so I cling on. The road drops and drops away, and I have that feeling, as if I'm flying off into nothingness.

I hold my breath. I tear through the sunshine, all the way down to the junction, on to the Beddgelert road. Then I race through the morning like the wind. The bike flies beneath me. I want to reach Dinas Emrys quickly. I want to lay my charm on Henry's lair, before Sheila or anyone else tries their magick there again.

I hit the Beddgelert road at speed. Air whips my hair back, stings my eyes. The sky is as blue as blue. Sunlight slants off everything. The sides of the mountain lie covered in thick purple heather. The air is charged with such sweetness.

I shoot downhill, all the way to Llyn Gwynant.

The water on the lake stretches out shining black. Sundrenched slopes rise from its shores. The road lies totally deserted; the mountain is all mine. Sometimes I like it best that way – just Snowdon and me.

I race past Llyn Gwynant crouched low. Just the grey road, winding on down alongside the Afon Glaslyn, down to Llyn Dinas.

I squint into the distance. My heartbeat jumps about. The fortress of Dinas Emrys lies smack ahead.

472

I think of Henry lying curled under the earth, so near, so far.
He'll be there.

I need to keep it that way.

What did George say?

'Be careful Elles. Tonight – May Eve – is auspicious. Gran says you must lay a charm to protect Henry.'

No more witchy stuff with covens. No more trying to wake up my Henry.

An image of Sir Oswald flashes across my mind. Pale eyes. Hooded eyelids. He'll be under the mountain too.

I slow down.

I swing off the road and cycle up towards a lush green pasture.

I take my shortcut, through a turning to a farm, behind a row of mobile holiday homes, where I can scramble up a steep slope between trees, and get to the fortress from the back. The bracken is tight and scratchy, but it's really not too far and saves a good three-mile hike.

I go through the farm gates; it's private property, but there's no need to worry about the holiday homes now. They'll be full of tourists at this time of year. They won't give me a second glance.

I chain the bike to a handy sapling behind the first chalet.

In front of me rises a steep bank, covered by spindly trees. Thick green moss coats every patch of bark. Their roots are tangled knots of black. In parts, the rocky hillside is almost sheer.

High above, a skylark trills out short, rapturous notes. I hoist myself up from trunk to trunk. I try to stay strong.

Since the spring equinox, I've stayed away from here, too many memories, too much sadness, but I guess I'm needed today.

I climb up to the top of Dinas Emrys. Pause. Pant. Just breathe in warm air.

Since the second landslide, the hill is not much changed. That is the way Henry planned it.

I turn to look up towards Snowdon. Everywhere is thick with brilliance, but through the blinding sunshine, blurred by the shimmer of late spring warmth, I think – no – I'm certain, I see a figure.

There he is: the figure of a young man poised on the edge of the mountain.

I smile.

I rub my eyes. Is it really a figure? Or just a trick of the light? A memory perhaps? Or George checking I made it safely? Rays of sunlight dazzle me. By the time I look again, he's gone.

My heart starts pounding.

I squint just to be sure.

I wish so much it were Henry.

Nothing.

But then this is Snowdon.

Yr Wyddfa.

The great burial den of the dragons.

Here anything can happen.

Especially on May Eve.

*Yes, May Eve and I have come here for crogi gwr gwellt:
'hanging a straw man'.*

*It's a tradition on May Eve that when a lover has lost their
sweetheart, they make a man out of straw and put it somewhere
in the vicinity of where the lover sleeps.*

*The straw man represents the enemy, the one that seeks to
take the heart of the beloved away.*

I find the right spot.

Just where I stood with Rhi.

Just where half of the north face of Dinas Emrys split open.

*A vision flashes before me ... trees uprooted, boulders
cracked; great half-broken tree trunks sticking up in the air.
That overpowering smell of crushed foliage, that sickly scent
of damp earth, that great scar, huge open depths ...*

The vision passes.

I pin a note to my straw man.

Gran helped me craft the words:

'By water and fire, earth and air,

Let Henry's enemies beware.

Let the words of my charm,

Protect his heart from any harm.

Let the power of my love,
Strengthened by the stars above,
Keep him safe, keep him secure,
Keep his heart forever pure.
By the flowers of Blodeuwedd
Let none attempt to breach his bed.'

———⌒

I place the adder stone on the note.

I sprinkle the place with a potion Gran brewed for me.

I look up to the mountains.

'I will find a way to be with you again, Henry,' I whisper.

Then I pray to Snowdon to keep him safe, out of the reach of any evil.

Until I can keep my promise.

Acknowledgements

My thanks and appreciation goes to:

Jon Barton
Jane Beagley
John Coefield
Anna Coombes
Joy Coombes
Ruth Eastham
Lorna Hargreaves
Sophie Hicks
Caroline Johnson
Christine M'Baye
Nathan Ryder
Susie Ryder
The staff of Llechwedd Slate Caverns
All of my readers who have encouraged me
And all of the very helpful and informative residents
of Llanberis, Beddgelert and Blaenau Ffestiniog.

Diolch

© Roger Bool

Author Biography

Sarah Mussi is an award-winning author of children's and young adults' fiction. Her first novel, *The Door of No Return*, won the Glen Dimplex Children's Book Award and was shortlisted for the Branford Boase Award. Her second novel, *The Last of the Warrior Kings*, was shortlisted for the

Lewisham Book Award, inspired a London Walk, and is used as a textbook in Lewisham schools. Her thriller, *Siege*, was nominated for the CILIP Carnegie Medal (2014) and won the BBUKYA award for contemporary YA fiction. Her thriller, *Riot*, was longlisted for The Amazing Book Award amongst many others and won The Lancashire Schools Award. In 2015, Hodder Children's Books published her novel, *Bomb*, followed shortly after by *Here Be Dragons*, the first book in the Snowdonia Chronicles trilogy, published by Vertebrate Publishing. *Here Be Witches* is the second title in the trilogy.

Sarah was born and raised in the Cotswolds, attended Pate's Grammar School for Girls, and graduated with a BA in Fine Art from Winchester School of Art and an MA from the Royal College of Art. She spent over fifteen years in West Africa as a teacher and now lives in London where she is the current Co-Chair of CWISL (Children's Writers and Illustrators in South London). Sarah splits her time between writing, visiting schools as an author and promoting creative writing for children. Sarah also teaches English in a Lewisham School.